# You can really have no notion
# How delightful it will be

### "I Found Love on Channel 3"

"Reminds me of the classic Twilight Zone. Like the literary equivalent of those classic half-hour episodes of eerie black-and-white existential horror, it takes a simple concept, then escalates it quickly, deftly, and with originality." — Tangent

"May surprise you in more ways than one...a deceptively simple and poignant tale about someone whose alienation from normal society is rewarded by a never-to-be-forgotten glimpse of the Other Side." — Speculative Fiction Reader

### "The Five Phases of Darlene"

"A well-written, edgy tale, and the best story of this issue...a dark retrospective on the dangers of chemically altering the mind." — Tangent

### "The Withering"

"Brings the final scenes to life in such a way that the hapless reader is pulled into the room with the protagonist, and you can't help but cringe." — Vanderworld

"Superb...reminded me of the stories of Robert Bloch." — Nightshade Books

### "Common Time"

"I was very happy to encounter 'Common Time,' which opens much like a classic military SF tale, but soon veers off in a whole new direction...simply compelling...another story to add to my list of favorites." — Tangent

### "Blind Faith"

"Intellectual dark fiction...demonstrating a sophisticated use of sentence structure and imagery. Dark in its shared disappointment, confusion, and empathy for the characters; sophisticated in presentation and hidden environmental agenda." — Shadowed Realms

"Socked me with its twist." — IMHO

"Radically different in its telling, with minimal conversation and thickly descriptive writing...an original piece of flash fiction...a heavy underlying statement." — As If

## "The Apocryphist"

"A strong and compelling story about the art and magic of words." — Tangent

"The strongest story of the lot. I got immersed in the story's world and in the main character...well written." — BlogTide Rising

## "Hal & Dave Revisited"

"A hilarious snack, perfect for those late-night munchies." — Lennox Avenue

# DANCING
## *with the*
# VELVET LIZARD

*The Collected Stories Of*

# BRUCE GOLDEN

ZUMAYA OTHERWORLDS      AUSTIN TX

2011

DANCING WITH THE VELVET LIZARD
© 2011 by Bruce Golden
ISBN 978-1-936144-17-4
Cover art © Brad W. Foster
Cover design © Chris Cartwright

"Zumaya Otherworlds" and the griffon colophon are trademarks of Zumaya Publications LLC, Austin TX.
Look for us online at http://www.zumayapublications.com

Library of Congress Cataloging-in-Publication Data

Golden, Bruce, 1952-
Dancing with the velvet lizard / Bruce Golden.
    p. cm.
 ISBN 978-1-936144-17-4 (trade pbk. : alk. paper) -- ISBN 978-1-934841-08-2 (electronic/multiple format) -- ISBN 978-1-61271-030-3 (epub)
 1. Speculative fiction, American.  I. Title.
PS3607.O452D36 2011
813'.6--dc22
                    2011013202

# For
# Rod Serling

*Maestro Of The Macabre*
*Morality Tale*

# Table of Contents

# DANCING

## WITH THE

# VELVET LIZARD

# WAITING ROOM

It moved with even certainty through the multi-tiered labyrinth, down long, dim corridors fed by uniform passageways, each artery branching out to its own finality. It passed row after row, cluster upon cluster of marginalized cubicles, adroitly avoiding other busy caregivers going about their tasks with stoic competency. Their activities were not its concern. Its objective was still ahead, its function yet to be engaged.

The muffled resonance of efficiency was momentarily fractured by a caterwaul that resounded with frantic vigor. The plaintive cry did not cause it to break stride. This was not its designated ward. It continued, secure that proper care would be provided where needed.

Though it had never traversed this particular annex, it was familiar with every aspect of the structure's design. A three-dimensional imaging model embedded in its memory enabled it to proceed unerringly to its assigned section. Once there, it would fulfill its charge until relieved. The notion of responsibility, the promise of ordered ritual, of unadulterated routine provided inexplicable impetus to its progress through the repository. Fulfillment of its programming was imminent.

Promptly upon entering its first appointed room, it conducted a visual examination. The patient-resident was not in her bed but standing near the cubicle's lone window, her back to the entryway. Although unusual, her upright position was not immediate cause for concern. It noted her posture was hunched, and her form withered to a degree attesting to extreme age, disabling disease, or both.

"I'm too damn crooked to even see outside," the diminutive woman said to herself as she strained to force her head high enough to look through the modest pane.

It checked the medic monitor, noting that all vital signs were within normal parameters, then located the medical history file and inserted the disk for scan, as it would for each of its patient-residents. As the file was processed into its memory, the woman turned slowly, gingerly, as if fearful her limbs might give way.

"Who are you?" she asked.

"My designation is Automated Caregiver ON-one-two-dash-one-eight-dash-two-eight."

"That's a sorry mouthful," she said contentiously.

"I have been assigned to your care."

1

She scrutinized its form before responding.

"You're not the same as the last one. It couldn't say more than a couple of words."

"The design of your previous caregiver was determined to be obsolete. A progressive replacement of all such models has commenced throughout the facility."

"That so?" she said, leaning against her bed for support. "It was old and useless, so you shut it off, boxed it up and put it away in a room somewhere, huh?"

"I was not informed as to its disposition."

"Of course you weren't." She cackled. "They don't want *you* to know what's going to happen when *you're* obsolete."

"Ellen Reiner, eighty-seven-year-old female," it summarized aloud, "with diagnosis of extreme rheumatoid arthritis in conjunction with aggregate osteoporosis and—"

"Hey, you! Don't you know it's not polite to talk about someone like they're not even there, standing right in front of you?" The outburst exacerbated her already apparent exhaustion, prompting her to sit on the bed. "I think I want my old tin can back. At least he was quiet."

"Ms. Reiner, you are not supposed to stand without assistance. In the future—"

"I'll damn well stand whenever I please. And nobody calls me 'Ms. Reiner.' My name's Ellen."

"Very well, Ellen. Why were you out of your bed? Is there something I can get for you?"

"I was trying to see the leaves. It's autumn, isn't it? They must be turning about now. I wanted to look out and see them, but the damn window is too high. I can't straighten up enough to see."

"I am sorry you cannot see outside. However, most of the rooms in this repository have no window at all."

"So what? So I should be thankful?"

It had no response. Instead, it reached down and pulled back the bed coverings.

"May I help you lie down?"

"No, thanks. I can do it myself."

It observed patiently as she eased herself by stuttered stages into a supine position. However, the effort was not without manifest signs of pain. Once she settled, it reached down and pulled the bed coverings up over her, noticing that, as it did, she continued to examine its exterior composition.

"You don't look like the last one. You look almost human. What are you? A robot? An android?"

"I am an automated caregiver, model O-N-one-two-dash-one eight—"

"Yeah, yeah, I heard you the first time. Okay O-N-one-two-dash-whatever. I'll just call you Owen. How about that?"

"If you wish. I must proceed to input and verify my other assigned patient-residents. Do you desire anything before I withdraw?"

"Yeah," she said with a calm that belied her hostile glare. "I want my body back. The one that could go for a walk. The one that could play ball with my grandson. The one I could stomach to look at in the mirror. Can you get that for me? I'll wait right here while you go find it."

"I am sorry, Ellen, I—"

"Never mind. Forget it." She turned her head away. "Go on. Leave. Go help someone else."

It stood there a moment, analyzing the situation, attempting to ascertain the patient-resident's demeanor and determine if additional action was required before vacating the room. Humans were complex creatures, but so was its programming. It took only 4.5 seconds for it to formulate a resolution, turn, and vacate the room.

It deposited the soiled sheets into the laundry receptacle and moved on to the next cubicle. It had fallen into a routine that modified and enhanced its original programming. Though few of its patient-residents were coherent, its acquaintance with their various idiosyncrasies and predilections was an essential element of that enhancement.

It considered this as it proceeded to room 1928, but halted outside the entry when it heard a voice. Did patient-resident Ellen Reiner have a visitor? No visitations were scheduled, although on rare occasions they occurred without notice. It remained outside the room and listened.

"Why? Why me?" It sounded not so much a question as a tearful plea. "I don't understand. Why, God? Why?"

It heard no other voices and determined she was simply talking to herself, as many isolated patient-residents were inclined to do. It entered, carrying its hygienic provisions, and moved to the bed's right side.

"Good afternoon, Ellen. How are you today?"

She didn't reply, only fumbled to take hold of a tissue, which she used to clear her nasal passages.

"It is time for me to bathe you."

"I don't want to. Go away."

"You know you must be cleaned. I can take you to the shower room, or I can do it here."

"I don't want you to. I don't want you to touch me."

It searched its databanks for the proper situational response.

"I do not understand your reluctance, Ellen. I know your previous caregiver bathed you at the proper intervals."

She turned away from him. "I don't want you to see me. My body's so ...it's so ...."

"Your previous caregiver saw your body many times. I fail to comprehend your—"

"It's different. You're different. He was like a machine, you're..."

"I am also a machine, Ellen. I am an automated caregiver."

She didn't respond.

"I promise to be gentle. Let me remove the bed coverings."

She acquiesced, although she kept her face turned away.

It took a moment to evaluate its observations. Situations in which the patient-resident was uncomfortable could often be mitigated by conversation. So,

3

it accessed its creative response program. In doing so, it conducted a visual search of the room, marking the photographic representations above the bed.

"Is that you in the photographs, Ellen?" it asked, pulling the shift up above her waist and beginning to wipe her clean.

"Yeah," she said, her face still turned away, staring at bare wall, "that was me."

"It appears you were a performer of some kind."

"Dancer—I was a dancer," she said irritably. "Not that you'd ever know it by looking at me now."

"That is very interesting. How did you become a dancer?"

"I just liked to dance, that's all."

"In the black-and-white photograph, the one where you are surrounded by other dancers, you look very young."

Ellen turned her face, angling to look up at the photo.

"That's when I was on *American Bandstand*, an old TV show. I was just a kid."

"Were you a professional dancer?"

"Later I was—when I moved to New York." She chuckled at some private recollection. "For a time, I was what they called a go-go dancer. I worked at some real dives to put myself through dance school. Places like Rocky's and The Gull's Inn...those were the days."

It observed the conversation was, indeed, distracting her from its ministrations, so it pursued the topic.

"I did not realize they had schools for dancing."

"Sure they do. I studied for a long time with Hanya Holm. Talk about an old biddy. After that I joined Erick Hawkins' Modern Dance Company. We traveled all over. Of course, that was before my first marriage—before I had my son." For a moment, she looked wistful, as if sorting through fond memories. "I didn't dance anymore after Edward was born. At least not professionally."

"How many children do you have?"

"Just the one. I've got a grandson now, and two *great*-grandkids—can you believe it?"

"Certainly."

"That's their picture over there, with their father and mother."

"They appear to be very healthy," it said, not certain how to respond. It tended to a few final details and pulled down her shift. "I am finished now, Ellen. Do you require anything before I go?"

"No."

"All right. I will check on you later."

She turned her face away again.

It couldn't tell if she was looking at the photos on the wall or if she'd closed her eyes.

—⁓◦✦◦⁓—

"Happy Thanksgiving, Ellen."

"Hmmph. What have I got to be thankful for? You tell me, Owen."

Patient-resident Ellen Reiner had addressed it as "Owen" for such an extended period it had begun to think of itself in that manner.

4

"I understand your Thanksgiving meal will be a special treat," Owen stated, checking the medic monitor and recording the data output.

"Not likely. The food is this place tastes like mush. It's no wonder, seeing as how it's made by tasteless machines."

"It is true the automated kitchen workers have no sense of taste, but I am certain they prepare your meals to the exact dietary specifications provided."

"Yeah, specifically bland."

"There are currently five thousand, three hundred and ninety-seven patient-residents quartered within Repository Carehouse three-nineteen, and the food must be prepared in a manner to accommodate everyone."

"Yeah, well a little spice now and then would do them good."

"I have no doubt the sustenance provided complies with all nutritional guidelines, Ellen. If you would like, I can—"

"Piss on nutrition! I want something that's sweet or sour or puts a fire in my belly. Hell, I got nothing else to look forward to. You'd think I could get a decent meal every once in a while."

Owen straightened the bed coverings, tucking in the length where necessary, and removed the bag from the bedside commode. Ellen reached across the bed and fumbled with something.

"I can't work the remote anymore," she said with exasperation. "My damn hands are too deformed. There's an old movie I wanted to watch, but I can't change the channel."

"I can do that for you. What channel would you like me to select?"

"It's *Singing in the Rain* with Gene Kelly. I think it's channel ninety-eight."

Owen activated the channel selector.

"Is this correct?"

"Yeah, that's it. Oh, it's already half over."

She stared at the screen for some time as Owen completed its duties, then spoke as if her attention were elsewhere.

"I've had some great Thanksgiving dinners, you know. Garlic mashed potatoes, stuffing made with celery and onion and pine nuts, golden-brown turkey cooked just right so it was still moist, you understand—candied yams, cranberry sauce..." Her voice trailed off as if she were still reminiscing but not verbalizing.

"Can I get you anything, Ellen?"

"No." Then, reconsidering, she gestured toward the remote with her gnarled fingers and said, "You could turn the volume up for me."

Watching the video screen, Owen complied. On the video screen, as the title suggested, was a man singing and dancing through a rainstorm. Despite the meteorological conditions and his saturated condition, he was smiling. Nothing in Owen's programming derived any logic from it. It was the way humans were.

"I will go and let you watch your movie now."

It was on its way out when it heard Ellen say softly, "Thanks, Owen."

—⊰✦⊱—

Owen's internal alarm sounded. The medic monitor in room 1928 was summoning it. It must disregard normal routine and check on the patient-resident's condition immediately.

Upon entering the room, it initially failed to locate patient-resident Ellen Reiner. It did, however, note the medic monitor was emitting its warning beep, and recognized the patient-resident's vital signs were fluctuating dangerously. It activated its exigency video record option and located the patient-resident on the floor next to the bed. Owen bent down next to her.

"Ellen, what happened?"

"I was trying, uhh...to see out the window," she said weakly.

Owen evaluated her response and reactions. She was apparently in a tremendous amount of pain.

"Damn legs don't work anymore. They just collapsed right out from under me."

"You should have called for me to help you."

"I didn't want to...bother you."

"Regardless, that window is too high for you. Do you not remember?"

"I guess I forgot."

"Do not be alarmed, I have alerted an emergency medical team. They will be here momentarily."

"No!" she exclaimed, so vehemently her body convulsed and she gasped in pain. "I don't want them," she managed to whisper. "I don't want to be saved. Just let me go. Let me be done with it."

Owen was trying to formulate an appropriate response when the EMT, consisting of two humans and an automated assistant, rushed in. Owen moved aside as they took their places around the patient-resident. She began crying as soon as she saw them.

"No," she wept. "No, no."

Owen stood, its ceramic ocular arrays focused intently on patient-resident Ellen Reiner. There was nothing it could do. It wasn't programmed for medical emergency procedures.

"Looks like a broken hip," said one of the humans. "Blood pressure's dropping dangerously. We've got to get her to surgery."

The automated assistant distended the compact gurney it carried, and they transferred Ellen onto it as gently as they could. Still, she cried out—whether in pain or protest, Owen could not be certain. All it could do was watch as they pushed her out, and listen as her tearful cries retreated down the corridor.

When its audio receptors could no longer discern her voice, it replayed the incident video. Had it failed somehow in its duties? Could it have acted differently to prevent the injury from occurring? It listened to her words, then listened again, trying to understand.

*I don't want them. I don't want to be saved. Just let me go. Let me be done with it.*

It didn't matter how many times Owen replayed the recording, or how it attempted to dissect the phraseology, it still didn't comprehend.

—⊷⊶—

Three weeks and two days had passed since Owen had last gone into room 1928. There had been no reason to. Then it received notification that patient-resident Ellen Reiner had been returned to her room. It found the notification to be welcome, and accompanied by an indefinable yearning to care for her once again.

However, upon seeing Owen, Ellen acted less than pleased. Her reaction was, it seemed, more akin to acrimony.

"I am glad to see you have returned, Ellen. I hope your stay in the hospital facility was pleasant."

She failed to respond, so Owen went about its duties, but continued its attempts to engage her.

"I understand you are still recovering from your injuries, and must not attempt to stand or walk again. Please inform me if you need to get out of bed, and I will provide a wheelchair."

There was still no response, and Owen discovered her silence to be a source of agitation it could not define or locate within its systems.

"It will be Christmas soon. I am pleased you were able to return before the holiday. I understand members of your family will be visiting on the twenty-fourth of the month. I am certain you look forward to that."

More silence.

Then, as Owen attempted to formulate a new line of conversation, Ellen spoke up, her tone harsh and unforgiving.

"Why didn't you just let me die?"

"What do you mean, Ellen?"

"You heard me. Why didn't you let me die? I asked you to. I begged you."

"You are in my charge, Ellen. I am programmed to care for you. I cannot do anything to harm you."

"Nobody asked you to. I just asked you to leave me alone—let me be."

"Not calling for medical assistance when you were so seriously injured would be the equivalent of harming you, Ellen."

Her eyes bored into Owen with what it determined was an angry stare. A dewy film glazed over them, and her tone altered. It was more pleading than demanding, and several times the cadence of her voice broke with emotion.

"You should have let me die, Owen. That's what I wanted. I'm not really alive anyway. What kind of life is this? I'm just waiting around...waiting to die. That's all anyone in this place is doing. This is just death's waiting room, don't you know that?" She sobbed once, and seemed to physically gather herself, reining in her emotions. "Hell, they shoot horses don't they?"

"Shoot horses?"

"Animals—they treat animals more humanely than they do people."

Owen didn't respond. It was occupied, trying to comprehend what she had said. The word *humanely* was not incorporated into its vocabulary, but its root contained the word *human*. Did it mean to be treated as a human? If so, why would horses be treated more human than humans?

"It's the bureaucrats and the moralists. That's who's keeping me alive. Them and those who own this *carehouse*—who own *you*, Owen. All they really care about is collecting their compensation. I'm just a source of income—a husk defined by profit motive. They've taken the choice away from me. But it's my choice," she said, pockets of moisture now evident under her eyes, "not theirs."

Ceasing its work, Owen stood listening, trying to reconcile its programming with what she was saying.

"I am sorry, Ellen. I am sorry you are so unhappy."

7

"It's not your fault, Owen. It's not your fault."

Despite her words, Owen detected an irregularity in its systems that might indicate a fault. It would need to perform a self-diagnostic before continuing with its duties.

Owen didn't realize Ellen's visitors had arrived until it had already walked in on them.

"I am sorry, Ellen," it said, stopping short. "I was unaware your guests had arrived. I will come back later."

"No, it's okay, Owen. Stay. Do what you need to do. They don't care."

"Gee, Great-Grandma, is that your robot?" asked the older of the two boys standing next to her bed.

"That's Owen. He takes care of me. He's a...what are you again, Owen?"

"An automated caregiver."

"Yeah, right." She turned to the other side of her bed to address the man standing there. "So, where's Alisha?"

"You know, it being Christmas Eve and all, she had a lot to do."

"Is that right," Ellen replied caustically.

"Well, you know how this place upsets her so, Grandma."

"It doesn't exactly make me feel like a princess."

Her grandson shifted his feet uncomfortably, looking at a loss for words.

"I hope you like the cookies we made for you, Great-Grandma," the older boy said.

"I'm sure I will, Matthew."

"Well, we'd better go now and let your great-grandma rest. Give her a hug goodbye and wish her a merry Christmas."

The older boy reached over and hugged her. "Merry Christmas, Great-Grandma."

The younger boy kept his hands at his side and edged back a few inches.

"Go on, Todd, hug your great-grandma."

"He's scared of me," Ellen said. "Don't force him. It's all right. Great-Grandma Ellen isn't a very pretty sight these days."

Her grandson bent down and kissed her forehead.

"Merry Christmas, Grandma. I wish...I wish I could—"

"Get along now," she said sharply, cutting him off. "Santa will be here soon, and these boys need to get to bed so they don't miss out."

"Okay, boys, wave goodbye to your great-grandma."

The older boy waved and said, "Goodbye, Great-Grandma." The younger one hesitated, waved quickly in her direction then hurried to catch up with his father and brother.

When they were gone, Owen spoke up.

"It must be nice to have family members come and visit. Will your son be coming, too?"

"My son died a long time ago. Car accident."

Owen picked up her dinner tray and swept a few loose crumbs onto it.

"Well, then, it was nice that your grandson could visit."

"I'd just as soon he didn't. I feel like a hunk of scrap metal weighing him down. I don't like being a burden."

"You are not a burden, Ellen."

"Maybe not to you, Owen, but to family...well, I guess you wouldn't understand that."

"No, Ellen, I would not understand that."

───◦◦◦───

"Owen, is that you?"

Sounding only partially awake, Ellen rolled over and opened her eyes.

"Yes, Ellen."

"I was just lying here, listening to the rain. Can you hear it?"

"Yes, I can. Would you like me to turn on the sound screen so it does not bother you?"

"No, no, I like listening to it. It's soothing, don't you think?"

"Soothing? I do not know what is soothing, Ellen."

"I've always liked the sound of rain. I don't know why, exactly, I just do."

"They are holding Easter Sunday services in the community room this morning. Would you like to attend? I have brought your wheelchair."

"Is it Easter already?"

"Yes, it is. Would you like to join the worshipers?"

"To worship what? God? God deserted me a long time ago. He's not getting any more from me."

"I am sorry. My records must be incorrect. Your file designates you as a Christian of the Lutheran denomination. Accordingly, I thought you might wish to take part in the ritual."

"I *am* a Christian—was my whole life. I believed, I had faith, I worshiped God. Then He did this to me. Do you think I should worship Him for this?" She held up a twisted, disfigured hand but could only extend her arm a few inches from her body. "Do you think my faith should be stronger because He turned me into this *thing*?"

"I cannot say, Ellen. I am not programmed to respond to philosophical questions concerning faith or religion. I do not comprehend the concepts involved."

"There was a time I would have pitied you for that, Owen. I would even have thought less of you."

Owen waited to see what else Ellen would say, but the only sound was the patter of rain against the window.

"All right, Ellen. I will return your wheelchair to the storage unit."

"Yeah, take it back, Owen. I don't need it. What I have to say to God I can say right here."

───◦◦◦───

Inside the staff maintenance bay, surrounded by several other diligent caregivers, Owen completed its routine self-diagnostic and filed its monthly patient-resident assessments. It didn't speak to any of its co-workers. That only occurred when its duties required such interaction. Its obligation necessitated only that it converse with the patient-residents under its charge—even then, only to those who were coherent enough to carry on conversations.

So, as it exited the maintenance bay, Owen didn't acknowledge any of its peers. It simply traversed the familiar corridor, crossed the homogeneous tile mosaic, and began its evening duty cycle.

Then a notion occurred to it. It was an unusual notion, although not inordinate. It would break from routine. Instead of beginning with the nearest cubicle, it would go first to room 1928, to see Ellen.

It discovered her dinner tray was still full. Except for some minor spillage, the meal appeared to be untouched. Ellen ignored Owen's presence, seemingly intent on the video screen.

"Ellen, why have you not eaten any of your dinner? Are you not feeling well?"

"It's crap! It all tastes like crap. Take it away—I don't want it."

"You must eat, Ellen. If you refuse to eat, I must nourish you intravenously. I know you would not like that."

"You're damn right I wouldn't."

"Please, then, try to eat some of your dinner."

"I can't! I can't, okay? My hands don't work anymore," she blurted out, the emotion evident in the cracking of her voice. "Look at them. Look at how deformed they are. I can't even pick up a spoon anymore. I'm helpless. I'm useless. I can't even feed myself."

Owen could see she was angry, and struggling to hold back the tears welling up in her eyes.

"You should have called me, Ellen." The automated caregiver moved the swivel table aside and sat on the edge of the bed. "I can feed you."

"I don't want you to. I don't want you to feed me like I'm some kind of baby."

"Why not, Ellen? That is why I am here. I am here to care for you, to do what you cannot. That is my function." Owen took the spoon and scooped up a small bite of pureed vegetables. "Please, let me help you."

Owen held the spoon out, but Ellen remained steadfast, refusing to open her mouth. Owen, too, didn't move. Displaying the patience of its programming, the indefatigable property of its metallurgy, it held the spoon until Ellen relented and took it into her mouth.

She swallowed the morsel as Owen cut into the portion of soy burger. With some reluctance, she took a second mouthful. It waited as she swallowed then offered her a third spoonful. She wavered momentarily, looking up at Owen.

"It still tastes like crap, you know."

—◦◦◦◦◦◦—

Owen waited outside Ellen's room as a facility doctor conducted the required biennial examination. Ellen had been pleading with the doctor for several minutes, and had begun to cry. The sound elicited a response in Owen. It was an impulse to hurry to her side—to care for her. However, Owen determined such action would be inappropriate and held its position.

"Please," it heard her beg, "please give me something. Help me."

"Now, Ms. Reiner, everything's going to be all right. You're going to be fine," the doctor responded, although the accent affecting his pronunciation made him difficult to comprehend. "Don't worry now. You're not going to die."

"You're not listening to me. I *want* to die. I don't want to live like this."

"Now, now. Of course you don't want to die. You shouldn't say such a thing. You're going to live a long time. Everything's going to be all right. I'll give your caregiver the prescription for the anti-itch lotion, and then I want you to have a nice day. All right?"

The doctor passed Owen as if it weren't there, making no attempt to input Ellen's aforementioned prescription. Owen decided the doctor would likely file all the appropriate prescriptions when he had completed his examinations, so it stepped in to check on Ellen.

As soon as she saw Owen, she made a concerted effort to halt her tears and wipe away any evidence she'd been crying. Owen checked medic monitor, giving her a moment to compose herself.

"It's so hot, Owen. I can't get this sheet off. Could you help me?"

"Certainly, Ellen. Would you like it pulled all the way down?"

"Yes."

"I am sorry the temperature is uncomfortable for you. The climate controls are not functioning properly, but a repair crew has been notified."

"It's so hot for June. It must be at least eighty outside."

"The date is August ninth, Ellen."

"It's August already?"

"At last report, the exterior temperature was ninety-two degrees Fahrenheit."

"August?" she mumbled to herself. "What happened to July?"

"If there is nothing else you need, I will tend to my other patient-residents now."

Owen turned to leave.

"Don't go!" Ellen called out. She hesitated, then said with less despair, "Please don't go yet. Stay with me for a while."

Owen contemplated the unusual request. Its atypical nature, coming as it did from patient-resident Ellen Reiner, required further consideration. However, its schedule necessitated it see to its other patient-residents' needs. It began calculating the time necessary for it to complete its shift responsibilities then abruptly ceased its computations.

"All right, Ellen. I will stay a while longer."

—◦≈⟨♦⟩≈◦—

"Oh, Owen, it's so nice to be outside. You don't know."

The automated caregiver carefully maneuvered the wheelchair down the narrow cement pathway. On either side was a carpet of lush green grass, and several yards away was a stand of oak trees. It was a clear day. The sun was high, and the sky was bright blue.

The impromptu excursion outside the repository, although not unprecedented, required that Owen circumvent protocol. It was not wholly at ease with its actions but found justification in Ellen's emotional transformation.

"I am glad you are enjoying it, Ellen. When I learned about this location so near the facility, I concluded you might appreciate a brief outing."

"But not too brief, okay?"

"We will stay as long as we are able. I will have to return to my other duties soon."

"This isn't a day for duties, Owen. This is a day to feel the warmth of the sun on your skin, to admire the color of the autumn leaves and smell the flowers."

"I am not equipped with olfactory senses, Ellen."

"Too bad. But you can see, and you can feel the sun, can't you?"

"I do sense the heat on my exterior overlay."

"Oh, look! Look there! It's a little stream. Can we go down there by the water? Please, Owen."

"I will attempt to move you closer."

It gently pushed the wheelchair off the path and across the grass to a spot near the tiny waterway. It locked the chair's wheels and stood patiently by.

"I could sit here all day. It's so beautiful. Listen to the sound the water makes as it rushes by. Don't you wonder where it's going?"

"The question of its ultimate destination did not occur to me, Ellen. However, I could research the geography of the area if you would like."

"No, no, it's just the idea of imagining where it's going." She looked up at Owen but there was no expression on its artificial face to decipher. "I'm sorry, Owen. I forgot for a second. You probably think this is all so silly."

"I do not believe it is silly if it pleases you, Ellen."

"It does, Owen, it does. Look! Over there. It's a butterfly. Isn't it beautiful?"

Though it understood the word, beauty as a concept was beyond its programming. So, Owen didn't reply. It stood impassively watching the insect's flight.

Neither spoke for some time; nevertheless, Owen could tell Ellen's disposition had improved by a degree that was quantifiable. That generated within its systems the concept of a task adequately performed, a vague notion it could only define as fulfillment.

"I must return you to your room and resume my other duties now, Ellen."

"So soon?"

"I do have other patient-residents I must attend to."

"I understand."

Owen unlocked the wheels and turned the chair.

"Owen."

"Yes, Ellen."

"Thank you."

"You are welcome, Ellen."

— ⁓◦⊰⟆⟆⊱◦⁓ —

The corridors of Repository Carehouse three-nineteen were filled with the distant, muted sounds of revelry. So many patient-residents had tuned their video screens to the same programming that the festive broadcast echoed stereophonically throughout the facility. Owen understood it was the celebration of a new year—a new calendar decade. The occasion seemed to call for much noise and frenetic activity.

However, it still had its duties to perform. Its patient-residents still had to be cared for. Soiled sheets still had to be changed, meal trays cleared, waste receptacles emptied. It began, as called for according to its self-revised routine, by checking on room 1928.

Ellen lay on her side, facing away from the entry. Unlike most of those in the facility, her video screen was inactive.

"Ellen, do you not want to watch the New Year's festivities?"

When she failed to respond, Owen moved closer. Her eyes were open, but there was no sign of recognition in them.

"Ellen? Are you all right?"

Her eyes tilted upward, but she didn't move.

"I can barely hear you," she said. "I think I'm losing my hearing."

Owen adjusted its audio output. "Can you hear this?"

She nodded.

"Everyone is watching the New Year's Eve broadcast. Would you like me to activate your screen?"

She shook her head curtly and looked away.

It was apparent to Owen that Ellen was not behaving normally. Her disposition displayed symptoms analogous to severe depression. Nevertheless, before resorting to a petition for psychological counseling, Owen resolved to draw her into conversation.

"It is unfortunate your family members were not able to visit you for the Christmas holiday this year. However, it was thoughtful of them to send that splendid videocard. I conjecture they will schedule a visit soon. Do you agree?" She didn't respond, so Owen continued. "If you do not wish to watch the celebration here in your room, I can bring a wheelchair and escort you to the community room. It is my understanding there is an ongoing party to celebrate the coming year. Would you like that?"

Her head moved sluggishly side-to-side.

"Please leave me alone, Owen. I just want to be left alone."

"All right, Ellen, I will leave you. However, I will return later. Perhaps you can instruct me in that card game you described."

Owen waited for a reply, for some acknowledgment, but there was none. So, it left her as she'd requested.

—⊸≋⟨≈⊷—

Owen's internal alarm sounded, and it noted with unaccustomed distress that the alert originated with the medic monitor in room 1928. It hurried to the room, confirming the danger with the beeping medical unit upon arrival. It was about to initiate the video record option but discontinued. Ellen was in her bed, eyes open and apparently fine, although her breathing was labored. Owen went to her.

"Ellen, can you hear me?"

"Yes, but...it's hard...to breathe."

"Here, use this." It detached the oxygen mask from its niche in the wall and placed it over her face. "Your blood pressure is diminishing. I am going to alert the emergency medical team."

With the mask over her face, she couldn't respond, but she reached out as best she could and rested her gnarled fingers on Owen's inorganic arm. Her motivation wasn't clear, yet somehow, Owen felt it understood the meaning of her touch.

"If you do not receive immediate medical attention, you will likely suffer heart failure. I am required to summon assistance."

Owen thought it discerned a slight sideways movement of her head, as if she were attempting a negative response. Her eyes implored, probing inexplicably into Owen's systems, forcing it to reconcile the needs and desires of its patient-resident with its overriding program.

Ellen brushed aside the mask with the back of her crippled hand and tried to speak, but all Owen heard was a gasp for air. It reached down, placed its distal extremity reassuringly on her forehead, and left it there until her eyelids fell.

Owen checked the medic monitor, looked back at Ellen for a protracted moment, and stepped away from the bed. It deactivated the monitor and exited the room to resume its duties.

It wasn't supposed to be here. It was scheduled to perform a self-diagnostic. However, it had concluded that bypassing routine on this singular occasion would not be detrimental to its overall performance.

Instead, it had chosen to exit Repository Carehouse 319 and retreat to a particular grassy mound, where it could feel the sun's warmth on its exterior overlay, contemplate stored memories and listen to the water as it rushed by on its way to destinations unknown.

I was impelled to write "Waiting Room" after the death of my mother. At a relatively young age, my mother's body began to deteriorate due to extreme cases of osteoporosis and rheumatoid arthritis. She spent her last few years in a nursing home, her mind still active but her body crippled beyond use. Ellen was my mother's middle name, but it was what her family called her when she was growing up. Unlike the Ellen of this tale, my mother was a singer not a dancer. Rocky's and The Gull's Inn were real nightclubs, but the "go-go dancer" of my acquaintance who danced in them was my friend Linda. Waiting Room received an Honorable Mention from the Speculative Literature Foundation's writing contest and is published here for the first time.

# THE SUM OF THEIR RECEPTORS

They met on soft sheets where violet neon splashed through uneven slats, pulsating with the cyclic regularity of a distant endorsement. Of course they'd already exchanged names and witty banter, but it was here they truly met, here where no affected repartee was required. It was here they first exposed themselves. Here, in the pale light, their sweat-damp limbs entwined, clutching, clinging, grappling in silence. Silent but for the exquisite kneading of their skin.

At some point, as arteries pumped and lungs strained, they connected. Somewhere between rhythmic dance and frantic abandon ripened an essence of savoring, of ardent hungers mollified. Somewhere, sensual artistry yielded to a surge of primal desperation—panting, thrusting, moaning, heaving, and finally howling into a cataclysmic collapse of quivering sinew and spent flesh.

—❧❧—

"Wow!"

He responded to her exclamation by reaching for her, but she held up an arm in surrender.

"Give a girl...a chance to catch her breath," she gasped. "You don't know what it's like...being on the receiving end of that."

He gave way and collapsed next to her, thankful for the rebuff. They lay on their backs, side-by-side, and for a minute there was nothing between them but labored breathing.

"I guess I can stay in tomorrow," she finally said. "I've already had my quota of fireworks." She took an uneven movement of his head for a nod of agreement. "I'm telling you, that was beyond terrific. It was...phenomenal. But then, I'm sure you've been told that before."

He shrugged. "Women tend to exaggerate."

"You're right," she said. "After the first eight or nine orgasms a girl has a tendency to lose touch with reality."

"I wasn't counting." He turned on his side and kissed her arm. "But I'm glad you enjoyed yourself."

"Grossly understated, but oh, so true." She swiveled to face him. "If you could bottle that you'd never have to work again."

"Speaking of work, I start a new job in the morning."

"On the Fourth?"

"A short-order cook's work is never done."

15

"I thought you were a writer."

"I am. Slinging burgers is just what I do, among other things, to feed the words." He sat up and looked around. In the dim light he couldn't see much, just nebulous shadows. He did recognize a framed picture on the wall above her bed. It was a print of Dali's *Metamorphosis of Narcissus*.

"I should get my clothes and—"

"Why don't you stay?" She reached out and ran her fingers down his back.

He hesitated. "I don't think I should."

"Don't be an idget. Stay."

He let go with a grin. "An *idget*? What the hell is that?"

"Someone with an incredibly tiny id. You know, small-minded."

"Oh yeah? I'll show you who's small-minded."

He grabbed her. She shrieked and laughed.

The capricious wrestling match soon coalesced into a kiss. One kiss became another—two became three. Their fingers caressed. Their pulses raced.

Gently, she pulled her face from his and said, "You know, theoretically, it's possible."

"What? That I'm an idget?"

"No," she said, playfully slapping his arm. "*Bottling* it—creating a pheromone-like compound with the ability to bind with and alter the function of a neuroreceptor to simulate an equivalent reaction—a chemically induced, vigorously emphatic orgasm."

He looked for some sign she was joking, but she was lost in thought.

"Yeah, right," he scoffed.

She opened her mouth to respond, but he kissed her, and kept kissing her until words were no longer required.

—⋘⋙—

Consciousness wavered, fluctuated indeterminately. It was there—*she* was there—and then she was somewhere else, on another plane of existence. She couldn't think clearly, rationally. She was only certain of one thing. It had never been like this. It had never been close.

"That was...that was...ohmigod...incredible. I must have had half a dozen super-sized orgasms, with a few little ones sprinkled in."

"Yeah," he said, as blasé as he could manage, "I like to sprinkle in the little ones here and there for texture."

He expected her to laugh. Instead, she said, "I can't believe it just keeps getting better and better. I wouldn't have thought it possible. It's so intense. Each time I think we've maxed out, and then..."

He looked in her eyes, not so much for confirmation of what she said but because of the way they danced when she said it. They were these remarkable hazel eyes that had mesmerized him the moment he met her.

"What you do to me ..." she said, failing to finish the thought because she couldn't find the words.

"It's not just me, it's *we*," he replied.

It wasn't only her eyes. Her face was always dancing, her expression ever-changing, as if she were morphing several personalities at once.

"Believe it or not," she said, "most people don't have it this good."

"Poor bastards," he quipped.

She rolled over, grabbed a voice pad from her faux marble nightstand and began dictating. He watched her for a moment, enjoying the slope of her thigh, the small of her back. Then he wondered.

"You're taking notes?" he asked in disbelief.

"It's just something I'm trying to puzzle out."

"Don't tell me the mad scientist is still working on her lust potion."

"It's more than lust—the pharmacodynamics of stimulating the libido are old school. This would be much more than an aphrodisiac. What I'm trying to design is an intensifier, a revving of the orgasmic motor if you will. It doesn't create a desire *for* sex, it amplifies the sensations. It would be an entirely divergent sexual plateau—assured, absolute ecstasy. Theoretically, it's just a matter of identifying a specific combination of subunits in the receptor found only on a specific brain cell type. The receptor subtype would have to have unique ligand binding properties. And then—"

"So, did you dream of being a biochemist from the time you mixed your first batch of lemonade?"

"Actually, it was mint juleps. I made them for my parents. And what I wanted to be back then was a dancer. However, that wasn't considered an *appropriate* calling for someone with my bloodlines, so I was sent off to college in the hopes I would become a doctor or a lawyer. Or, preferably, marry one."

"Did you?"

"I tried marriage once, while I was still in school—probably just to provoke my parents. They didn't approve of my choice in men. But I was too young, and he was too lunkheaded. It lasted all of a month."

"So it was chemistry that captured your heart."

"Not as strange as it sounds. I had an affinity for science. I was top of my class."

"Now that you're a successful biochemist, with your own lab and all, does your family approve?"

"Let's say they're reconciled with the fact they can't do anything about it."

She got out of bed and stood in front of her dresser mirror. Reluctant recall summoned up her father's harsh, almost cruel reaction to her career choice. He must have known it would hurt her. Would he ever respect her?

"Besides," she continued, "I'm not all that successful—not like my father, or my brothers, or even some cousins I could name. Familial expectations being what they are, I'm rather a *mild* failure." She picked up a brush and began working it down her incandescent curls. "But a girl keeps trying."

He recognized her wistful tone. He'd heard it in his own voice often enough.

"What about you?" she asked, turning to look at him. "Ever been married?"

He shook his head, and she found herself cataloging his facial features. He wasn't a particularly handsome fellow. Nothing stood out but the dusting of gray in his hair. For some reason, she found that distinctly attractive.

"Your family give you grief about being a writer who works as a short-order cook?"

"I've worked a lot of different jobs. The simpler the better. It frees up the mind."

"To write?"

He nodded. "I've had high-paying, high-pressure corporate jobs that kept me going ten hours a day. They didn't leave room for anything else."

"So *what* is it you're writing on that old keyboard?"

"A book."

"Your first?"

He nodded again. "It's taken me a while to sort it out."

"How old are you?" She'd been curious all along.

"Forty-two."

She smiled, exposing her dimples. "That's a lot of sorting."

He shrugged and sat up on the bed. "I should be going."

"I told you you could stay."

"That was a week ago."

She made a noise that evoked ridicule.

"You're not going to be a cliché about this, are you? A week, a month, a year—what's the difference? Time is simply a logical concept. Don't let logic have a say in whether you go or stay. I bet it wasn't logic that convinced you to leave your corporate job for the life of a vagabond writer, was it?"

He didn't respond. He looked at her through the sporadic light that dappled her naked form. He was struck by how truly beautiful she was—by the unsullied translucence of her skin, the sheen of her rich red hair, the pearly perfection of her breasts. Every gesture, every movement she made was tantalizingly sinuous in that sexy way slender women had without even knowing it.

"So what made you decide to write a book?"

"I don't know. I guess I like to think I'll leave something behind when I'm gone. You know, my speck of immortality."

"What's it about?" she asked, gliding over to sit beside him.

"It's just a book."

"You're going to have to make a better pitch than that."

He sighed. "It's about people, about their peculiarities, their affectations, their inner desires, their inner conflicts, their willingness to destroy others to get what they want, even if sometimes it means destroying what they love."

Her shoulders shivered. "Sounds vicious."

"It's the nature of the beast."

"I prefer the nature of your beast." She put her hand between his legs and kissed him. They embraced, and he caressed her breast, taking it in his hand, savoring it, delighting in how it could be both firm and soft at the same time.

"They're not real. Did you know?"

He licked her nipple, trying not to let the revelation deter him.

"Seem real to me."

"Just the right size, don't you think? Nose is a remodel, too." She turned profile to give him a good look.

He chuckled. "So, do you still have *any* of your original equipment?"

She laughed. "Oh, one or two things."

—◦◦◦{◦◦◦—

Late summer rushed at them hot and humid, like damp, clinging sheets. Other than the weather, the only thing that had changed in the weeks that slipped by was the intensity of their feelings for each other. From casual tryst to passionate affair to something more—something tangible that had taken on a life of its own.

His book was taking on a life of its own, too. Or at least its characters were. He'd never felt so inspired. The words were sparks flying off his fingertips.

He discovered he was at his best when writing by an open window—her window. But when the heat turned oppressive he closed it and tinkered with her climate controls. However, he could never quite get the temperature right. He found the mechanism as foreign to him as his growing fondness for her.

It didn't help there were times when he wasn't sure which was the real her— the obsessed scientist who spent twelve hours a day in the lab, or the libidinous little girl who kept him up all night. She had this way about her. She could be an extrovert while still managing to keep her true self at a distance. It made it that much harder to trust his feelings.

Trust not being something he'd ever developed an abundance of.

Often, he found himself staring at her for no particular reason. She captivated him in unexpected ways—little things that confounded common sense—like the look on her face when she questioned his idiosyncrasies, the way she always seem to smell of nutmeg. He was drawn to that scent, although he didn't know why. Something about the fragrance stuck in his mind. Was it something from his itinerant childhood, something long-forgotten?

She hadn't been home ten minutes, and already he was distracted. He watched her cleaning, rearranging, going about a series of mundane chores. He realized, as he watched, the depth of his affection. He was immersed in it—immersed in her. He embraced the idea with some trepidation.

"I see you bought groceries," she said from the kitchen. "I've told you you don't have to do that."

"Yes, I do."

"These plums are a lot smaller than the ones I get."

"They're organic."

"You're staring at me again," she said, catching him in the act.

He went back to work without responding, and it was her turn to stare.

She wondered about him—thought about him sometimes to distraction. Often, even when she was busy in her lab, the thought of him made her stomach flip-flop. Was it purely a physical response? Was that feeling something she could duplicate with a chemical compound? Sure, when he was inside her he made her feel like no man ever had—took her to heights she thought were unattainable—but there was more to it than that. There was something about him that put her at ease, made her feel necessary and special. It was that unspoken thing between them that shouted he needed her even more than she needed him. She was drawn to that feeling.

"I can't believe you use that old thing," she said, still observing him. "You should let me buy you a voicewriter."

He stopped typing and said, more forcefully than he intended, "I don't want you to buy me anything."

She held up her hands in mock surrender.

"Okay, all right. I just thought most writers used voice analyzers these days."

He continued to type, calmly replying, "Most do. I had a voicewriter once. I didn't like it." He stopped typing and held up his hands. "My hands, my fingers..." He wiggled them. "...they need to feel the keys. Feeling is part of the process. I feel the words warring with each other, phrases breaching bastions of gray matter, marching down strategic neural pathways then regrouping with appropriate pomp and circumstance in my fingertips. It's a sacred journey I don't tamper with."

"Silly man."

Suddenly, a feeling of fatigue and unevenness passed through her. It had been an especially long day. She felt like sitting. Instead, she took a hormone stabilizer, swallowing it with a quick drink of water as he saved his work and folded up his screen.

"Are you done?" she asked. "Or should I go color my hair?"

"Maybe I'd prefer your natural color."

"No, you wouldn't."

She kissed him and began unbuttoning his shirt.

"You look like you broke your favorite petri dish," he said.

"That's how I feel." She sighed and held up her thumb and forefinger, inches apart. "I'm this close to a breakthrough, but I keep encountering new obstacles."

"You're working too hard," he said, helping her undress. "This thing, this *miracle drug*, isn't as important as your own health. You need to slow down, take some time off."

"Of course it's important. Do you know how big this could be?"

He couldn't help but admire her determination, although he questioned her obsession.

"You see," she said, putting on her scholarly face, "we know that serotonin improves mood, but the neurochemistry involved to distill the hormonal essences of phenethylamines and tryptamines is so advanced we're literally mapping it out as we go. The idea is to combine pieces of natural compounds to create a library of novel synthetic molecules, and test them for binding to my new receptor subtype. I've set up an assay to throw potential ligands at a purified receptor so I can identify the specific binders. Then I characterize the physiological effect of the new ligand upon binding a receptor."

"Sorry, you lost me back at phenethylamines," he said, mangling the pronunciation.

"You know, if you'd let me use the sensory transducers again, it would—"

"No way—not again," he said. "I let you hook us up to those machines once. That was more than enough for me."

"The sex was still fantastic, wasn't it?"

"With all those wires attached? Are you kidding?"

"They didn't bother me."

"I bet when you were a little girl you burnt bugs with a magnifying glass and attached electrodes to the family cat."

"My parents wouldn't let me play with electricity," she said and laughed.

"Yeah, parents are always getting in the way of progress like that."

"You know, you never did tell me about your family. You change the subject whenever I ask."

He shrugged. "That's because there's nothing to tell."

"Oh, come on. You probably come from some really kooky, offbeat clan," she said, sounding as if the idea intrigued her. "I bet you've got plenty of stories to tell."

"No, I don't. I had no family. Or you might say I had a lot of families."

"What do mean *a lot of*?"

"I was fostered out—several times, actually—until I was old enough to go off on my own."

"So you never knew your parents?"

He didn't answer, so she decided to change the subject. She did it with a kiss, a soft kiss that lingered, urgent with desire.

He pulled his lips away, but only far enough to ask, "What if your little science project never works? What if we're more than just the sum of our receptors?"

"Silly man," she replied, and kissed him again.

Though he had no rooting interest, he turned on the World Series to take a break from his work. He'd been having trouble concentrating anyway. Doubt tainted his focus, and he couldn't shake it. San Diego scored a run on a walk and triple. Two outs later, she came through the door.

His first thought upon seeing her was that she seemed contrived in her conservative business attire. He smiled, thinking how the trappings of professionalism belied the untamed she-tiger she became once stripped of that facade. He wondered if she were the same predatory animal among her colleagues that she was when naked. In bed, he knew, she took no prisoners. But then, neither did he. Maybe that was why they were so good together. Maybe that's why the sex seemed to overshadow everything else.

From the moment she walked in, he noticed something different about her. She was flush with excitement. She rushed over.

"It works! The gating mechanism—the ligand binding properties—I did it." She couldn't get the words out fast enough. "We did it, I mean. Of course, I had help with—"

"You finally managed to condense our sex life into a pill, huh."

"Silly man, you know that's not what it is."

"Instant gratification, ultra bliss, super sex, orgasm in a bottle—whatever you call it, congratulations are in order, right?"

Her reply, like the look in her eyes, was decidedly smug.

"Yes, they are."

She pushed him back into the chair, plopped onto his lap and kissed him.

"I'll be rich. We'll travel the world together and live happily ever after." She jumped back up, unable to stay still. "Once we get it approved, we'll develop a fast-acting aromatic spray as well as a pill. It will change millions of lives—billions—the way people think about themselves, about each other, their relationships."

She was probably right. At the moment, though, he wasn't concerned about a billion relationships.

"Of course, there's still so much to do," she said, taking off her jacket. "The clinical trials, the approval process, they can be—"

"Wait a minute. Doesn't it take forever just to get permission for human clinical trials, and then years of testing?"

"It used to," she said, "but the pharmaceutical industry has more political clout these days. With the new regs, a money-making drug can find its way onto shelves within a year if everything goes right."

"So, how do you know it works if you haven't tested it on humans?"

She hesitated, and he saw right away she'd been holding something back.

"I have tested it...on myself."

It took a moment for him to absorb the ramifications.

"With us?" he asked. "You used it when you were with me?"

"It was the only ethical way around the bureaucracy. I had a successful cell culture I had to test on a living subject before it expired."

"For how long? How long have you been doing this?"

"Not long—not every time."

"So, some of it's been real, and some of it hasn't."

"Of course it's been real, only...enhanced."

For an excruciatingly long minute, he was silent. She wanted to speak up, to reassure him, but didn't know what to say.

"Did you really need it?" he asked.

"Not for us—no. But I needed it for me—for my work. I had to."

Again he turned quiet.

She slid onto his lap.

"You're happy for me, aren't you?"

He looked up into those eyes that beguiled him so, and now pleaded with him to countenance her elation. He wanted to. He wanted to please her, to rein in his urge to be contentious.

"Sure I am."

"Then why are you scrunching up your face?"

"What do you mean, *scrunching*?"

"It's that thing you do with your face. You do it all the time."

"I do not."

"Yes, you do. You look like you're in pain, or thinking so hard it hurts."

She kissed his forehead and, with a mischievous smile, slid off his lap, ran to the bed and burrowed under the covers. Slowly, her head emerged from the other end, the sheet wrapped tightly around her neck.

She rolled her eyeballs and intoned eerily, "It's the return of the head."

He couldn't help but laugh. She was always able to make him laugh like no else ever had.

She broke character and laughed with him. Her expression changed. She dropped the sheet, pulled her blouse over head and held out her arms. Her synthetic breasts beckoned him, but he stayed at the edge of the bed, impassive, indecisive.

"Are you sure I'm not obsolete?"

"Silly man," she said, pulling him down and pouncing astride him, a familiar, rapacious glint in her eyes. "I'm not finished with you yet, mister."

Any other time he would have eagerly welcomed her aggressive bearing. Now, though, his mind wandered and wondered—wondered how genuine it was, this thing between them. Was it any more substantial than a pill you could pop for instant ecstasy? Or had they synthesized their feelings to conform to the situation?

"Have you taken...are you on anything right now?"

"No, of course not. Don't be getting paranoid on me."

She lay forward and began kissing his neck.

"Do you really think there's a happily ever after for people like us?"

"Of course there is, silly," she whispered in his ear.

He tried to gauge her assurance. Was it authentic? Was there something about her tone that was suspect? Or was that assessment swayed by his own doubts?

She gave him no time to consider. She sat up abruptly, wriggled her hips, and threatened in a sort of punk-Nazi voice, "Ve have vays of making you come."

As he waited for her, he looked out the window. It was snowing hard. It had been for days. Despite the climate controls, the chill of winter still found its way into their bedroom. There was no denying it.

When she came through the door it was with a bounce of elation.

"Essential Pharmaceuticals has negotiated an agreement to buy the patent. If the trials go as expected it's a done deal. Isn't that great?" She gave him quick kiss and continued. "And listen to this. They may want me to be part of the big marketing blitz. It's still up in the air, but—"

"That's a little unusual, isn't it?"

"Yeah—surprised me, too. Apparently, they think I might put the *right* face on the product. They project that women will make up the largest share of the market, and will relate more if they know it was created by a woman. If they decide to use me, it'll mean additional compensation, exposure..."

"Your family will certainly be proud."

"Yeah," she said, as if she hadn't considered it, "they probably will." She darted from introspective to impish in a millisecond. "Look." She said, pulled something out of the nightstand drawer and gave it to him. "I've been saving a sample so we could celebrate together."

He looked at the small vial in his hand, and when he didn't respond right away she poked him in the ribs.

"Well? You're scrunching up your face again."

"It's not real," he said, almost imploring. "It's make-believe."

"Oh, like your book?" she responded with a rancor she instantly regretted. She turned away, calmed herself, and her tone softened. "Don't we all need a little make-believe now and again? Is it such a bad thing?"

"No," he agreed, "no, it's not. But what we had you can't put in a bottle."

"*Had*?"

She turned around and saw the answer in his eyes.

"I've been thinking I should find some out-of-the-way place with no distractions to finish my book. I know this little spot in Alaska..."

"That's out-of-the-way, all right." She nodded vacantly, thinking of several things she could say—things she wanted to say—but rejecting them all. "I'm sure you'll finish it in no time."

A disconcerting silence threatened to commandeer the moment, so she rushed to fill the void.

"You know, you never even told me what you were calling it—the title of your book."

"You never asked."

She tried to remember. She didn't think she had. She felt bad about it, so she contrived a smile, put her arms around him and kissed him. It was a passionate kiss, if diminished from others they had shared.

"Well, tell me the title, and then we'll...you know—once more for old times' sake."

Behind the nonchalance, he heard the disappointment in her voice, and it hurt him. He knew about disappointment. She'd get over it. He always had.

He placed the vial in the palm of her hand, closed her fingers around it and kissed them. "You don't need me anymore." He broke gently from her embrace, picked up his already-packed bag, and walked out.

---

She'd never been that interested in fireworks before, but tonight they were a welcome distraction. However, it wasn't long before the pyrotechnics reminded her of him. The brilliant display outside her window prompted her to recall their second night together. There were many reasons to remember that night, reasons why it hadn't been like any other encounter. Mostly because it was the first time she'd ever considered the possibility of more—something more than wanton recreation. The memory was as vivid as the bursts of gold and scarlet that blossomed in the sky.

There had been others since him. She vaguely remembered their names, although their faces faded into irrelevance. Like success, they had proven to be transitory. As time passed, she came to think of men as an unnecessary complication; she found herself more comfortable with seamless, solitary routine. What could they provide that she couldn't provide for herself?

She was back at work in her lab with more resources than she ever imagined. Her professional stature had increased exponentially. Financially, she was fixed for life. Even her family respected her now. She was confident her contribution had, in some small way, made the world a better place—a happier place. The irony was almost comical.

Not that she was unhappy. She experienced no major bouts of depression, no angst-ridden outbursts. The days, the weeks, the months all arrived and departed in an orderly manner.

It was the nights that were hollow.

Another burst. The heavens lit up in a fiery kaleidoscope. Flashes of color cast dim shadows across the cavernous walls of her bedroom. She reached for her pills. Maybe it wouldn't be so empty if she focused on the fireworks and thought of him.

She tried to summon some enthusiasm for a convergence of mind and body but couldn't fend off a feeling of pointlessness. Her fingers tightened on the container then relaxed and uncurled. It fell onto the bed.

She wasn't in the mood for vacuous, fleeting fancy. There was no pill that could satiate her desire. She wished there was. She wished she could devise a remedy, concoct some sort of antidote for her malaise. Yet she knew there were some things you could postulate and formulate, things that could be systematically designed to fit preconceived concepts, and others that just happened. Causality could be re-created. Random happenstance was ephemeral.

She turned from the window and looked at her bed with its linen neatly tucked, its pillows propped evenly along the trim borders of her summer quilt. How she longed for disarray.

—⁓∽⟨⟩∾⁓—

A light snowfall added substance to the yuletide decorations, but he found the temperature mild compared to what he'd become accustomed to. He'd been standing on the street for some time now—waiting, manufacturing excuses, trying to decide. It had been so long.

Seclusion had been a boon to his work, although how meaningful it all was he couldn't say. He didn't trust the quality of his writing any more than he trusted his feelings. Others would judge his work, but there were no critics to appraise his emotions.

He'd come back to find a publisher...and for another reason.

He gazed up at the building across the street. He'd never been able to shed the regret he felt over leaving, yet now he questioned his quixotic return. What good would it do? Weren't they still the same two people who'd grown apart? She'd achieved the success she wanted so much, the success she'd worked so hard for. Although she might not believe it, he'd wanted it for her. The irony was, notoriety had put her on the fast track, and she'd already published a book of her own—*The Neurology of Ecstasy.*

What could he give her now that she didn't already have? What good did it do to tilt at windmills?

Before another question could clutter his rationale, she was there. Despite the unfamiliar tint of her hair, he recognized her the instant she stepped out onto the sidewalk. He wondered if that mousy brown was her natural color. He wondered if she still smelled of nutmeg.

She stopped to check her purse for something, and he started towards her. His pulse quickened. If she smiled, would it be feigned? If she laughed, would it forced?

He wanted to confide in her, to believe she could understand. He wanted to tell her about his work—tell her the title of his book. There were so many things he wanted to say, to ask.

Yet doubt slowed his pace. He wasn't sure if he was afraid of her answers, or simply distrusted his ability to make his own feelings clear.

She hailed a cab, and instead of running to stop her, he stopped himself. So many things marched through his mind at that moment he couldn't recall them later. All he remembered was watching her drive away.

Chemically-induced erections were all the rage when I got the idea for this tale. But I wondered what would happen if we could take it a step further—if someone could bottle majestic orgasms. Biochemistry professors Tom Huxford and Robert Metzger of my alma mater SDSU provided the insight that enabled me to get the science right for "The Sum of Their Receptors," which was awarded an Honorable Mention by the Speculative Literature Foundation. Science aside, when I got around to writing the ending, I still wasn't sure whether my two protagonists would get back together. In some alternate future, maybe they do.

# HOLIDAY

If I was gonna do it, I knew I needed to get dusting. I had been thinking about it for days, and now it was already Holiday Eve. But flies and fleas! I didn't know how I was gonna keep my promise to Gramps and still do what was right.

The right thing seemed like the wrong thing, and the other way round. It was way too much for a scrawny sprout of only eleven harvests to figure out, so I put my hand in my pocket and grabbed hold of my lucky goldstone. I hoped it would help me think better.

Gramps had given me his goldstone just before he became one with the south field. He said it had come from Faraway. I used to love to fold up on the porch and listen to him talk about Faraway, and the things he called cities. Cities, he said, were giant-sized communities with more people than you could count—and I could count all the way to a hundred and beyond.

Of course, Gramps had never actually lived in a city, but he believed what he'd heard about them. He said once upon a time there were thousands of cities—that is, until the rainfire destroyed them. I knew all about the rainfire, the swarms of hoppers, ol' demon Drought—those things were landstory. They were part of the soil, they were in every seed, every drop of water. But cities? I wasn't sure if I believed in them. Someday, though, I wanted to have a looksee for myself. After one or two more harvests, I was gonna dust a trail to Faraway and see what I could see.

Right now, I had a promise to keep.

It was a cool day, but warm enough in the sunshine. The wind was playing with the chaff in the south field. I'd been out there saying Hey to Gramps. That's what reminded me I couldn't put it off any longer.

So, I made a trail back to the hub. On the way I saw a bunch of girls carving up their Holiday jack-o'-hearts. My sister Heather was there, and my mom, who was showing them how it was done right. They were all giggling and smiling and carrying on strange-like.

Heather had been acting funny of late. I don't know if it was cause she was older than me or cause she was a girl, but she wasn't the same Heather I used to have mud fights with. All I knew was she had her eyes on Billy Wagoner, and that lately she always seemed to smell of honeysuckle.

"Konner!"

Mom waved me over, but I didn't want to get too close to them silly girls, so I dragged my feet and let the dirt run up over my toes. I was going so slow, she came over to get me.

"Konner, where are your brothers?"

"Don't know."

"Well, I want you to make sure they're not getting into any trouble. You know how your brothers are."

"Ah, flies and fleas, Mom. I've got better things to do than looking after those sprouts."

"Go on, now," she said, and I heard the sternness in her voice. "You find out what kind of mischief they're up to and put a stop to it."

"All right."

Her expression softened then, and so did her voice. "Are you excited about Holiday?"

"Yeah," I said, bundling in my real excitement.

"Well, you be sure to have fun now, okay?"

"Sure, Mom."

I noticed she was wearing the walnut shell pendant Dad had given her a long time ago. She was particular about when she wore it. I liked how when it caught the sunlight, the tiny piece of crystal inside the shell would sparkle all different colors. I think it made her feel special.

"It won't be long, Konner, before you're all grown up, so you have fun while you can."

"Don't you and Dad have fun on Holiday?" I asked, not caring to think about a day when I wouldn't have any fun.

"Sure we do. It's just a different kind of fun. Have you thought about your Holiday wish yet?"

"Yes." I'd known for a long time what I was gonna wish for.

"Well, good. I hope you get your wish. Now, you make a trail and find out what Kobey and Kory are up to."

"Okay."

I headed off, meaning to do what she said, but the Trouble Brothers would have to wait. I had something else I had to get done first.

Closer to the hub I saw most of the trees and bushes were already wearing their Holiday clothes, though some of the final decorating was still going on. Some women were going here and there, putting on hats and belts and scarves and anything else they could make fit. I knew those clothes would scare Pestilence away for another harvest, but I couldn't figure how. They didn't scare me. Some looked so downright odd, I had to laugh. Maybe that's how they worked. Maybe ol' Pestilence didn't care for laughter.

As I approached the elders' lodge, Henry Olmstead walked out and cornered me.

"Konner Grainwell, what are you up to?"

"Nothing, Mr. Olmstead," I said, hoping I didn't look as nervous I felt.

"Shouldn't you be out practicing your cupid bow?"

"I'm not old enough for the shoot, Mr. Olmstead."

"Rainfire, boy! I wasn't any bigger than you when I took my first shoot. Well, anyway, you go have some fun." He reached into a bowl he was carrying and held out his hand. "Here's a sweetstick for you. Take it now," he urged, "and don't tell Ms. Olmstead I gave you one before the party." He winked and walked off towards the hub where lots of folks were busy getting ready for Holiday.

"Thanks, Mr. Olmstead."

He just waved the back of his hand and kept trailing.

I was right there then—right outside the elders' lodge. All I had to do was sneak in, grab the right marker and sneak back out. It was all I had to do to keep my promise to Gramps. I put my hand in my pocket and grabbed my goldstone. I told myself it was okay, that nobody would be hurt by it.

But I stood there way too long, trying to make myself believe it and picking at my courage.

"Konner?"

It was Grams, with little Hazel in tow.

"Konner, I need you to take Hazel home. She's tired, and I still have lots to do."

Flies and fleas! I'd been so close.

It wasn't that I didn't like my little sister. In fact, she was my favorite—not much trouble usually, not like Kobey and Kory. She was only five, and not mooning after boys like Heather. I thought Hazel was just the cutest little thing, with her big, wide-open blue eyes and corn silk hair. Right now, though, I had something more important to do than play with my little sister.

"Do you hear me, Konner?"

"Yes, Grams." I knew there was no way round taking Hazel home. I'd just have to sneak back later.

"That's a good boy, Konner. Your Gramps used to say, 'We can always count on Konner.'"

That made me feel good, and it also reminded me of my promise. It was funny Grams said that, cause she didn't know anything about the promise. That was just between Gramps and me.

I liked Grams well enough. She was a nice old lady, but she spent most of her time smoking weed and talking with the other elders. Whenever I saw her, it made me think of Gramps. Before he became one with the south field, Gramps would spend a lot of time with me, telling me stories and singing old songs. I missed him. I wouldn't forget my promise to him.

After he was chosen, he asked me to be sure and take care of Grams when he was gone. He made me promise that, when her time came, I'd make sure she was with him. I promised I would, and I always try to keep my promises.

※

The sun had fallen to that point where the sky takes on a more serious attitude—you know, beautiful and grim at the same time. I could never figure out how it changed itself. One minute it's this soft, friendly blue. Then the next time you look up it's got these angry streaks of red and orange. I figured it was like a warning: *Here comes the black night—beware!* I didn't waste much time looking at it, though, cause Holiday Eve was in full bloom.

I heard the music long before I dusted off for the hub. Anyone with any kind of instrument would be playing tonight. When I got there the dancing had already started. I thought dancing was for girls, though I saw some older boys trying to step with the music. Course I'd seen older boys do crazier things where girls were concerned.

My eyes went right to the tables, where all manner of good stuff was laid out. I saw sweet breads and pies, jams and tater crisps, and enough spiced cider to drown ol' demon Drought himself. I couldn't wait to stuff my belly, but I had to make a careful trail. Those darn jack-o'-hearts were strung up all over the place, candles burning inside them so they were aglow. I saw some girls lingering under their carvings, hoping for a kiss. They reminded me of trapdoor spiders, just waiting to pounce.

I wasn't planning on kissing anyone, except maybe my mom or little Hazel, so I avoided those orange gourds like they were Pestilence himself. I told myself I'd have a little snackdo first, then I'd sneak back to the elders' lodge when it was dark.

I had just grabbed myself a taste of sweet bread when I spied Kobey and Kory under another table. They had their peashooters and were popping girls in the head when they weren't looking. It might have been funny if I wasn't sure I'd be the one who'd suffer for their mischief.

So I dusted over, grabbed the two of them, and relieved them of their shooters. Both were filthy-looking. Kory stood there scratching his butt as usual. Kobey tried to look defiant.

"You two cause any trouble, and you're gonna be at one with your sister Henna in the east field." I didn't like to think about my dead baby sister Henna, but I knew it would scare the seed right out of those two sprouts. "Now, both of you go wash up, or I'm gonna find Dad and tell him what you've been up to, and that'll be the end of your Holiday."

I let go of them, and they dusted off like a couple of field mice. I figured chances were about even they'd actually get clean. I thought I'd better take care of what I had to take care of. Afterwards, I could—

Darned if I wasn't standing there thinking when all of a sudden this girl swoops in like a red-tailed hawk and kisses me! Her lips were pressing against mine before I could even see who she was.

Now, the truth is, except for the shock of it all, it wasn't as bad as I thought it would be. I mean, it was the first time any girl not family had kissed me. When she pulled away, I saw it was Dandy. I should have known. Even though she's seen one more harvest than me, Dandy has been making eyes in my direction for some time. Now she just stood there grinning.

I looked up, and there it was. A big ol' jack-o'-hearts, smiling down at me just like Dandy was doing—like I was a rooster, all plucked and stuffed and ready for mealtime. Darn those sprouts! Trying to keep them out of trouble had landed me square in Dandy's trap.

Dandy looked like she was about to say something when my mom walked up with Hazel.

"Hello, Dandelion, happy Holiday," said my mom, then looked at me and smiled that smile moms get that makes you think they know everything.

"Happy Holiday, Ms. Grainwell," replied Dandy, all sweet-like.

"Konner, it's time for the sing, and I want you to take Hazel with you."

I took little Hazel's hand, figuring it was a good excuse to get away from Dandy. But she followed us to where the others were getting in line for the sing. I tried to ignore her.

I don't care much for the sing, but if you weren't joined you were still considered a sprout as far as the sing was concerned. It was the only time I wished I had a wife like my big brother Kyle. I don't mind singing the songs, cause they're kind of scary and fun. I just don't like having to parade round the hub so all the grownups can coo and ah about how cute we all are.

I don't know who started it, but we trailed off real slow as soon as the first song began. I noticed Dandy was right behind me, but I didn't pay any attention to her. I held onto Hazel as I sang, and watched her trying her best to remember the words.

> Tell me, tell me landstory.
> Back when fire burned the sea,
> Rivers wept and mountains roared,
> Hot winds sang a frightful chord.
> Tell me, tell me landstory,
> About when people had to flee.
> When hoppers rose up in swarm,
> Laying bare where once was corn.

Ahead of me Heather was walking real close to Billy Wagoner. I figured if he wasn't careful, they'd be joined before another harvest. I looked round and saw the Trouble Brothers. They seemed to be behaving themselves, acting more serious than usual. But I knew why. The songs still scared them a little.

> Tell me, tell me, tell me please,
> That someday there'll be more trees.
> Say ol' demon Drought is dead,
> Then I'll lie down on my bed.

Round and round we trailed and sang. I knew it would have been a real good time to sneak into the elders' lodge, cause they were all watching the sing. But I couldn't very well get away with Hazel in tow and everyone watching—especially Mom and Dad. They were holding each other, touching and kissing, and looking so happy when us sprouts trailed by.

Dad was usually all leather and salt, except when he was around Mom. It was a sight to see how she could soften him up no matter what his mood.

> Tell me, tell me, I do pray,
> What I'll eat this Holiday.
> Say the poppers will fly right,
> And grant the wish I wish tonight.
> Tell me, tell me landstory.

31

How I wonder what I'll be.

When the sing ended, I noticed some of the elders heading back to their lodge. I knew then I'd have to wait until morning to do what I had to do. It was like a weight bearing down on me had been lifted.

Since I wasn't worrying about it anymore, I stuffed as much of that good food into me as I could while doing my best to avoid Dandy. When once I spotted her heading my way, I dusted off in the other direction. Keeping to where it was dark, I made a trail round the hub to the other side. As I did, I spotted two older kids all twisted up together like Gram's special mustard pretzels. I recognized it was Burt Ploughhorse and Lily Landesgard. They were half-naked and kissing, and I could tell by the way they were moving and the sounds they were making that they were planting seed.

I knew what they were doing was for the good of the community, but it still seemed silly to me. I stayed out of sight and made my way back to the party.

It wasn't long after that when Mom and Dad began rounding up everyone for bed. The Trouble Brothers tried to sneak off, but Dad snatched them up by their shirts and lifted them off the ground till they stopped squirming.

"You sprouts need to get to sleep soon, so the Santa will come," said Grams as we trailed off towards our lodge.

Kobey and Kory started whispering real excited to each other, and Hazel looked up at Grams, her big blue eyes filled with wonder. Last harvest I'd snuck out early and saw it was the elders who actually hid the candy. So I figured the Santa must have been at one with the earth for many harvests, and that, so all of us sprouts weren't disappointed, the elders kept doing his good work for him.

When we got to the lodge, everyone else went inside. I stayed out so I could look at the moon. It was full and kind of orange. It made me think of Dandy's jack-o'-hearts, and that got me to remembering the kiss. That made me think about the pair I'd seen planting seed. I'd heard talk from the older boys that it was a fun thing. But it sure sounded painful, and I couldn't see the sense in it—except for making babies. Course I knew the more sprouts, the better for the community. So when a boy and girl got together and started planting seed, the elders always acted all happy.

I put my hand in my pocket, took hold of my goldstone, and stared at the moon. I didn't want to think about girls. I wanted to think about Faraway, and what I might find when I got there. I sure hoped I'd catch a popper and get my Holiday wish. I was worried if I didn't—

"You need to get to sleep, Son," said my dad, stepping outside and looking up at the moon.

"Dad?" I said, then hesitated.

"What is it, Son?"

"How important is a promise?"

He looked at me as if he were sizing up a new calf.

"A man's only as good as his word, Konner."

I already knew the truth of that. I guess I just wanted to hear it said.

"Don't forget you got your chores to do tomorrow."

"But, Dad, tomorrow's Holiday," I protested, even though I knew it would do no good. When did I ever *not* have to do chores? Never, that's when.

"It may be Holiday, but the pigs still have to eat, and the tools still have to be cleaned."

"I know, Dad," I said, getting up to go in.

But as I did, I gave one last thought to Faraway. I thought about how when I dusted off to Faraway there wouldn't be any more chores to do. I couldn't wait for that day to come.

— ⌘ —

It was Holiday, and just cause I didn't believe in the Santa anymore didn't mean I wasn't gonna get up early and find as much candy as I could stuff in my pockets. Mom helped Hazel, and the Trouble Brothers were on their own, so I did pretty well. Afterwards, I hid it all in my secret place so Kobey and Kory couldn't get their dirty hands on it.

Then I did all my chores, and by the time I was finished I knew the Holiday shoot had started. So, I made a trail to the gully where the older boys, with their cupid bows, were trying their best to hit whichever jack-o'-hearts was carved by the girl they were sweet on. Some weren't even coming close. Others were so bad they were splitting open the wrong pumpkins, much to the frustration of some girls. I saw Heather get all excited when Billie Wagoner shot one right through the heart-shaped mouth she'd carved. That was about all I could take.

Most all of the elders, including Grams, had pulled up chairs to smoke their weed and watch the shoot, so I knew it was now or never. I dusted a trail, squeezing my goldstone the whole way.

As I neared the elder's lodge, the sky grew dark. The wind passed over me, and I shivered. A mean-looking, dusky cloud was blowing in from the east. I could see a big old bull in its shape. I kept watch for a minute, then snuck inside as slow as an earthworm. It didn't seem like anyone was there.

I'd never been in the elders' lodge before, cause sprouts aren't allowed. It looked like any other lodge, only bigger. As I searched for where they kept the markers I spied this picture hanging on the wall. It scared the fertilizer right out me. Either that, or the candy I'd eaten that morning was disagreeing with my insides.

It was a creepy-looking thing, painted in more shades of brown and red than I knew there was. It was some kind of monster, all fangs and claws but almost like it wasn't really there—like a goblin made of wind. I guessed it must have been somebody's idea of ol' demon Drought.

Even though it was just a picture, I backed away from it real easy-like. That bumped me right into what I was looking for. All the elders' markers were in this big bowl sitting there on the table. Quick as I could, I found Gram's marker and put it in my pocket.

I started to go but got this queer itch to take a last look at ol' demon Drought. His eyes gave me the shiver-tingles. I was sure he knew what I was up to, so I dusted it out of there before I gathered any other strange thoughts.

Once outside, I made a trail back to our lodge, going real slow like everything was okay. But everything wasn't okay—at least not with me. And it was more than ol' demon Drought looking over my shoulder.

33

I knew what I'd done wasn't right. It wasn't fair. But I didn't know any other way to make sure I kept my promise to Gramps. I just hoped someday I wouldn't feel as bad as I did right then.

—⟶⟵—

By evening, everyone had gathered at the hub for Last Supper. I couldn't help but notice something was in the air—something you could almost feel, like a thick morning dew. Nothing I could see, but I could sense it. It was more in the way folks were talking—or not talking. They were a bit bridled, not as free and easy, as if they were waiting to be set loose. I knew what they were waiting for.

Before anyone could eat, the Harvest Christ had to be chosen. My dad and Mr. Landesgard made a trail to the elders' lodge and brought back the big bowl with all the markers. I tried not to show it, but I was feeling real bad about then. I didn't want to be there, but I knew I had to be. Young or old, sick or cripple, everyone took part in the choosing of the Harvest Christ. I knew it was a great honor to be chosen, and that only doubled my guilt.

Since the bowl held all the elders' markers, or was supposed to, none of them could pick. So, after everyone quieted down, Mr. Landesgard reached in, stirred his hand round, and pulled out a marker. My hands were in my pockets—the right one clenched round my goldstone, the left Gram's marker.

"Henry Olmstead," he announced, holding up the marker for all to see.

Everyone started clapping and shouting, and I looked over to old Mr. Olmstead to see how he was taking it. He was all smiles, shaking hands with everyone. He seemed happy, but...there was something about his smile I couldn't quite figure. Something different—like he was trying too hard.

Anyway, someone had put the harvest wreath on his head and a big knife in his hand, and everyone was coaxing him to get Last Supper going. Mr. Olmstead waved the knife above his head, and there was more clapping. Then he brought it down and began carving the Eater Bunny.

I swear it was the biggest rabbit I'd ever seen. Even skinned and barbecued up nice and juicy-like, it was as big as a ki-yote. It was such a grand scene, full of laughter and fine-smelling food, that it made me wonder for a minute whether or not I'd get the honor of carving the Eater Bunny some day. Right then, I didn't feel bad at all. Flies and fleas, I even let Dandy sit by me for Last Supper.

—⟶⟵—

It was long after dark when I climbed aboard the wagon with the rest of my family. I was about to burst from all the good stuff I'd eaten, and more than ready to get some sleep. But Holiday wasn't over yet. The whole community was loading up the wagons and making a trail out to the fallow north field where the Holiday fire was already blazing.

When Henry Olmstead's body was laid aboard one of the wagons, I started feeling guilty again. Earlier, when he'd drunk from the harvest gourd, I'd turned away so I wouldn't see. I squeezed my goldstone and tried not to think about what was in that drink.

Not that there was anything so terrible to see. I'd watched when Gramps was chosen. It was like he'd gone to sleep. But this time I couldn't help feeling bad about what I'd done, even though I'd kept my word to Gramps.

I knew the Harvest Christ would be made at one with the north field this Holiday, and Gramps wanted Grams to be with him in the south. That's what I'd promised. So, I couldn't let her be chosen—not this Holiday—even if it meant maybe depriving her of the honor.

After everyone had gathered near the fire, four of the men, wearing their most respectful faces, lifted Henry Olmstead from the wagon and carried him to the place in the field that had been prepared for him. Except for the youngest sprouts, everyone was quiet. The men laid him down as gently as they could then helped Ms. Olmstead take off his clothes. When they were done, they began covering him up with fresh earth.

Ms. Olmstead stepped forward, looking real proud-like, and delivered the Holiday thanksgiving.

"The earth is the land, and we are the earth. Bless this land and the bounty of its harvest. We who take from the land, now give back to the land. May all of our harvests be so bountiful."

Then everyone joined in for the last part.

"The earth is the land, and we are the earth."

After that, everyone trailed off to stand round the fire. No one said a word, cause we weren't supposed to. The littlest sprouts were shushed if they tried to speak, and even the Trouble Brothers knew better than to make any noise.

I already knew what my Holiday wish was, so I tossed my popping corn into the fire like everyone else. As I stood there, waiting, hoping to catch one of the poppers so I'd get my wish, I thought about Faraway and Gramps and Grams and old Henry Olmstead. I wondered if they celebrated Holiday in Faraway. I sure hoped so, cause I'd miss all the food and the fun. Who knows, I might even miss getting kissed under a jack-o'-hearts.

The poppers had started flying all round me. I waited, ready to grab one if it came my way, cause you had to catch them on the fly to really get your wish. I saw Heather catch one and get all excited, then pop! One shot off to my right, but I was quick. I caught it, wished my wish again, and tossed it into my mouth.

I was feeling real good when everyone began loading back into the wagons. Just knowing I'd get my Holiday wish made everything I'd worried about seem okay. Maybe I wouldn't get it right away, but some day...

One rejecting editor told me this story was too much like "The Lottery." I barely recalled the story (from junior high?), so I found it and re-read it. There's really only one similarity, and I think my story has more layers—but that's just me. I plan (someday) to incorporate this apocalyptic tale into a long-imagined novel called *After the End*. "Holiday" is published here for the first time.

# SERVICES RENDERED

"Morgan? Morgan, are you listening to me?"

He hadn't been listening. Even As his boss prattled on about a new assign-ment he'd been assessing the man's office. Had it been repainted? Was that couch new? Even the pictures and plaques on the wall seemed different. Maybe it was his imagination. Maybe nothing had changed but him.

"Yes, sir, I'm listening."

"Well, it seemed like you were in another world. Are you sure you're—"

"I'm fine. But I don't really understand what it is you want me to do."

"Look at this." Hillenbrand handed him an invoice.

He glanced at it. "A forty-six-thousand-dollar bill for 'services rendered.' What services?"

"Keep reading."

Morgan examined the document more thoroughly. It was an invoice from the Yakama Indian Nation for a pair of ritual rain ceremonies conducted at the re-quest of the Bonneville Power Administration for the purpose of ending a drought. Morgan remembered the extended dry spell they'd gone through earlier in the year, although he couldn't remember exactly when it had ended. It must have happened while he was...gone.

He did recall the rainfall shortage had put a severe strain on the BPA's pro-duction of electricity. The output from most of its twenty-nine hydroelectric dams along the Columbia and Snake rivers had dropped to unacceptable levels.

He handed the invoice back to the administrator, feeling a twinge in his arm. It was that "phantom pain" his doctor had spoken of after pronouncing the arm fully healed. Despite what the doctor said, he'd been noticing it more instead of less.

"Did you authorize these rain ceremonies?"

"Of course not," bellowed Hillenbrand. "This tribal council member came to see me with some wacky proposal for making it rain. I listened politely, but there was certainly no official request for any kind of rain dance."

"Did it rain?"

"Of course it rained—it always does, eventually. But you know that's not the point. You know I can't pay this. If it were to get out to the media, I'd look like either an idiot or a swindler. I want you to drive up to Toppenish tomorrow and talk some sense into these people. You're the communications director, so go up there and communicate."

He wanted to argue that this wasn't part of his job description. Yet he knew if he tried to get out of it, Hillenbrand might question whether he was truly ready to come back to work. There would be more whispers around the office. Not that he'd heard anyone actually say it, but he'd read it on their faces. They were wrong. He was ready.

He'd been back almost two weeks, and while it was true he didn't feel quite with-it yet, he wasn't going to let them know that. He'd run interference for Hillenbrand on this and stop the whispers.

—⁕⁓⁂⁓—

It wasn't at all what he'd expected. Granted, he wasn't sure what he expected the office of a tribal council member to look like—more Native American trappings, he supposed. Not that it didn't have its eccentricities.

All across the room—on shelves, atop file cabinets, even on the desk—were superhero figurines. He recognized most of the action figures from his comic-collecting youth. Wolverine, Green Lantern, the Flash, Thor, Hulk and She-Hulk, Hawkman and Hawkgirl and, atop the water cooler, posed as if in battle, Aquaman and Submariner.

He recognized the figure in the mirrored wall behind the water cooler, too. No superhero there. Reflexively he touched his hair. He was still getting used to the new patches of gray. He wondered if superheroes went gray.

The door opened. Morgan stood. In walked a short, heavy-set fellow wearing a pinstriped beige sport coat, an orange paisley tie and sneakers. Eagerly, he held his hand out.

"Luke Blazing Star," he said, shaking Morgan's hand.

"Morgan Finch. I might be in the wrong place. I was waiting for Lucas Stearn."

"That's me. Sorry, I forget which name I'm using sometimes. Luke Blazing Star is my alter ego. I use it for my commercials, for my furniture store—Blazing Star Fine Furnishings." Stearn motioned for him to sit and took his own seat behind the desk. "You're from the BPA, right? What can I do for you, Morgan?"

Morgan laid his copy of the invoice on Stearn's desk.

"The government can't reimburse you for this, Mr. Stearn."

"What's a matter, is the government broke?" Stearn punctuated his question with a sawed-off laugh.

"It's not a matter of that," replied Morgan, ignoring the comical sound. "It's that this bill is for services never requested."

"*Au contraire.* I sat right in Mr. Hillenbrand's office outlining our proposal, explaining what we could do to aid your agency in generating more electrical power—power which you would then resell to other agencies. He then said to me—and if memory serves, I believe I'm quoting here—'Fine, sure, I'm willing to try anything at this point.'

"I took that as an oral agreement, and we commenced to solve the BPA's dilemma by conducting not one but two traditional rain ceremonies at, what I must say, is a bargain rate of twenty-three thousand per. We delivered said rain. Ergo the invoice.

"I hope you're not telling me the white man is once again reneging on a promise made to his red brothers." There was almost a wink in the way Stearn said it, as if they were sharing a joke. "I hate to think how the press and public would react to that."

Personally, Morgan didn't think either the press *or* public would care. In fact, he figured if such a bill were *paid* there would be public outrage. The average person didn't believe in mystical Indian rain dances any more than he did. He doubted Stearn himself bought into it.

But it didn't matter what he thought. His job was to contain this.

"I'll make an agreement with you, Mr. Stearn. I'll look into this, investigate it completely, impartially—you have my word—and if I find there is any credence to your claims, I will recommend your bill be paid in full.

"However, you have to agree to keep this a private matter, regardless of my final recommendation. Do we have a deal?"

He held out his hand, but Stearn just stared at him as if taking his measure.

"All right, Morgan," he said, firmly gripping the offered hand. "I believe you're a man of principle. I—"

Before he could finish, his door burst open and a woman came flying in.

"What's this crap about cutting the center's budget, Lucas? There's no way the council will vote for this. I can't believe you would—"

"Whoa, whoa, settle down, Laurel. Can't you see I'm in the middle of a meeting here."

The woman glanced at Morgan, only then noticing him. She offered a cursory "Sorry" before refocusing her wrath on Stearn. She berated the furniture salesman with a blistering verbal attack. Her indignation was volcanic and unrestrained.

She reminded Morgan of Joyce—not in appearance but in her take-no-prisoners attitude. He recalled how Joyce had once come at him the same way. At the time, she'd been so incandescently comical he'd wanted to laugh. Now the memory just stung.

"...nothing I can do about it," Stearn was saying, his hands outstretched almost as if he were expecting to fend off a physical assault. "Now, if you can convince Morgan here of the authenticity of our traditional rain ceremony, and that the government should pay our bill for services rendered, then we might be able to use the payment to hold off those budget cuts."

She glanced at Morgan. "What are you talking about, Lucas?"

Stearn proceeded to explain the difference of opinion over the bill, and Morgan's agreement to look into it. He turned to Morgan.

"Actually, Morgan, Laurel here would be the perfect person to explain some of our more obscure tribal traditions and ceremonies. I'm sorry. She got me so flustered I didn't introduce you. Morgan Finch, Dr. Laurel Seelatsee. Laurel is the director of the Yakama Cultural Heritage Center.

"You should take Morgan out to meet old Sam Mohalla. If anyone can convince him of the legitimacy of our claim, it would be the man who conducted the ceremonies."

"Yes," said Morgan, "I'd like to meet him."

With a scowl still lining her face, Seelatsee responded, "All right, but this isn't the end of this, Lucas Stearn. I won't be placated."

She told him they'd better use her car because of the back roads they'd have to take. It turned out her "car" was a surplus Army jeep with no top, no doors. Morgan hesitated, and at the same time berated himself for his irrationality. He told himself it was something he had to do, so deal with it.

She started the engine, and he eased into the seat.

Despite his resolve, he was unsettled from the moment she took off. He felt around for a seat belt but found none. She wasn't driving particularly fast, yet he couldn't shake the anxiety that gripped him. He took a deep breath and focused on the landscape as a diversion.

Hills loomed in every direction, swollen with trees standing crown to crown like soldiers in formation, dwarfing everything else. The smell was so much different than in the city. The aroma of evergreen was so strong a blind man could have described the setting. He could almost taste the tree sap in the warm afternoon air.

Seelatsee slowed to turn off the main highway. Near the intersection a pair of men with axes hacked at a scorched tree.

"Was there a fire?"

"Lightning strike," she said. "Just the wrong place, wrong time for that old tree."

Morgan felt a twinge of pain in his arm as the axes bit into the charred wood, but the pain wasn't so bad it stopped him from clutching the seat frame as she turned the jeep sharply onto a dirt road. Dust flew behind them, but he kept his eyes fixed firmly forward.

"Are you okay?"

He realized she was looking at him. He relaxed his grip but didn't let go.

"Sure, I'm fine."

"You look a little on edge."

"No, I'm fine."

It took him a while to realize why his stomach felt like it was being massaged by a serrated knife. It came to him despite his attempts at repression. This was the first time since that day he'd been back in the passenger seat with someone else in control.

"So, who is this Sam Mohalla?" he asked, wanting both to change the subject and deflect the onslaught of his recollection.

"He's a tribal shaman—the only real practicing one I know of around here."

"A shaman? You mean like a medicine man?"

She must have heard the derision in his tone because she didn't respond.

"Tell me, Doctor Seelatsee, do you honestly believe this rain dance worked like Stearn claims?"

"First of all, Mr. Finch, it's not a dance. The only Native American rain dance I know of is performed by the Hopi nation. Secondly, it doesn't matter what I believe, does it? What really matters is what you believe."

"I don't believe in a whole helluva lot."

"Well, as long as you're going into it with an open mind," she said sarcastically.

That and the bumpy road shut him up until she finally pulled to a stop near a small A-frame house. He followed her out of the jeep, and when he got closer he saw the ramshackle dwelling was a patchwork of burlap, sheet metal and time-worn wood. Yet there were power lines coming in from the road that suggested electricity.

His guide's phone rang, she answered, said something quickly he didn't catch then put the phone back in her jacket.

"I've got to go check on my grandmother. She lives just over the next hill. You go on ahead."

"Wait a minute, how will I...? I mean, how am I going to get back?" He wasn't thrilled with the idea of her leaving him there.

"I won't be long. I'll be back to get you. Go on. He won't bite."

She got back in her jeep and took off.

There wasn't much he could do but walk on up, knock on the door, and get this over with. Despite his promise of an impartial investigation, he never for a moment thought this Mohalla character—or anyone else, for that matter—was going to convince him they'd made it rain. He was just going to go through the motions, get it over with, and get back to Portland.

He was about to knock on the rickety old door when a voice behind him said, "He's not home."

Morgan turned to see an old man, a couple of dirty canvas bags tied together and thrown over his shoulder. Actually, *old* was an understatement. The fellow was ancient—eighty if he was a day. He wore an open plaid shirt, jeans, and a pair of boots deep in the process of disintegration. Under the plaid was a red-orange T-shirt that read HAPPINESS IS NO LAUGHING MATTER. The only thing about him that seemed very "Indian" was his rawhide headband.

"I'm looking for a Mr. Sam Mohalla. Do you know where he is?"

"Right here," said the old man. When he opened his mouth, Morgan saw he was missing a couple of teeth. "He's me. Though I don't go by mister much. Most folks just call me Sam."

"I'm Morgan Finch. I work for the Bonneville Power Administration. Lucas Stearn sent me up here to ask you about the rain ceremonies you performed."

"Performed? You make it sound like a circus act." He walked off as he spoke, and Morgan had no choice but to follow. "I knew a woman once who worked in the circus. She could contort herself in ways that would...well, never mind that."

"See, Mr. Mohalla, Mr. Stearn—"

"Call me Sam."

"All right, Sam. What happened is that Mr. Stearn sent us an invoice for—"

"Old Luke Blazing Star?" Mohalla had led him out of the clearing where his home sat and into the trees. Soon he was bent over, digging in the ground. "I love his commercials. They're funny as a moose humping a mailbox."

"What are you looking for?" asked Morgan.

"This." The old man pulled a twisted tuber from where he'd been digging. "*Wapatoo*," he said. "Wild potato. They go great in onion stew. Now I just need six more."

"Can you tell me about your rain ceremony," persisted Morgan. "I mean, exactly what is it that you do?"

The old man continued digging as he spoke. "This 'ceremony,' as you call it, is a sacred ritual based on a religion that's thousands of years old. Did you know that? This isn't just some fart in the wind. It's got structure, purpose, tradition. It may seem funny to you, but then I get a good laugh out of the pope now and again, too."

The old shaman looked up from his digging and stared straight into Morgan's eyes as if searching for something. His gaze made Morgan uncomfortable.

"Pain is not a blanket to be embraced on a cold night."

"What?" The tone of the old man's voice startled Morgan even more than his words.

Mohalla went back to his digging as if he hadn't heard the question.

"Did you ever hear the one about the raven and the coyote?"

"No, but—"

"It's a funny story. I'll give you the short version. See, there was this raven who, while flying through a storm, broke his wing and had to land in a tree." As he spoke he kept digging, unearthing more bloated roots. "Well, this coyote came along, saw what had happened, and told the raven, 'Come on down here, and I'll fix your broken wing for you.' The raven thought about it, because his wing hurt and he didn't know what else to do.

"But greater than the pain was his distrust of the coyote. He told the coyote, 'If I come down there you'll eat me.' The coyote replied, 'If you don't let me help you, you'll be stuck there forever.' But the raven knew coyotes were tricksters, so he shook his head. The coyote just shrugged and walked off.

"Trickster or not, the coyote was right. The raven stayed stuck in that tree forever."

Morgan waited for more, but when the old man just kept digging he asked, "Is that supposed to mean something?"

"Not as far as I can figure out. That's why it's so funny."

A clipped cackle escaped his lips. It was the kind of laugh that made Morgan wonder if the old guy was dealing from a full deck. He resigned himself to being patient.

When Mohalla had dug up exactly seven potatoes, he arranged them across the ground in a row and said, "Oh, Great Spirit, we thank you for the bounty of the earth, and all the blessings which you bestow upon us." He pulled a leather flask from where it hung at his side, splashed some water on the ground and took a drink. "Want some water?" He offered it to Morgan.

Though he *was* thirsty, Morgan declined. Mohalla shrugged and swept the potatoes into one of his sacks. He stood, threw the sacks back over his shoulder and headed off in a new direction.

"About the rain..."

"Rain is the great healer, you know," said Mohalla. "Yet even rain cannot cure everything. Not far from here there used to be an old nuclear power plant. Now the land for miles around is wounded, tainted by its poison. With enough time, enough rain, that foulness will be washed away." He glanced at Morgan. "But some wounds heal better than others."

Morgan tried to read the old guy's face, but his layered wrinkles gave him a set expression that didn't easily change, despite the staccato timbre of his voice.

"See that?" Mohalla pointed at the distant mountaintop that punctuated the horizon. "That's Pahto—Mount Adams, you call it. The Creator put Pahto there to remind his people they are not the most important thing in the world, despite what they may think."

He walked over to a cluster of bushes, knelt and opened his other sack. He pulled out a salmon carcass and began digging a hole at the base of the shrubbery.

"I'd like you to tell more about your sacred rain ritual. Could you do that, Sam?" Morgan asked as diplomatically as he could.

"Sure," replied Mohalla. "What would you like to know? You know rain is part of the great cycle of life. Like the salmon bones I'm burying under this huckleberry bush. The salmon fed me, and now I feed part of it to the huckleberries. In turn, no self-respecting salmon would refuse a meal of huckleberries. And even though I caught this one salmon, there was another that continued upstream to spawn. It's all part of the Creator's plan."

There was no doubt the old guy's mind tended to meander. Morgan would have to keep the conversation on track. Yet before he could get back on subject, his ride pulled up.

"Are you ready to go?" asked Dr. Seelatsee, getting out of her jeep.

"We haven't really talked much about the actual rainmaking," replied Morgan, turning to face the shaman.

The old man laughed. "It's late. The sun is setting, and I'm an old man who needs his rest. Come back tomorrow. Tomorrow I will ask the Great Spirit for rain to cleanse the land, and you may see for yourself."

Morgan didn't want to come back. He wanted to go home.

"I hadn't planned on staying."

It was still light out, but the sun had dropped below the horizon. He hadn't realized it was so late. The truth was, he'd rather not make the drive back in the dark. And he would like to see the actual ceremony. Then, when it didn't rain, it would make his case for him—conclude this whole rigmarole.

"I know a good motel in town," suggested Seelatsee.

"All right," agreed Morgan, "I'll come back tomorrow."

—◦◦◦◦◦◦—

He was on the phone with Hillenbrand when Dr. Seelatsee pulled up to his motel the next day.

"Are you certain you didn't tell them to go ahead with their rain ceremony—that you were willing to try anything?"

"Of course not. I mean, even if I said something like that, I obviously wasn't serious," said Hillenbrand, sounding like a man who knew he'd screwed up. "Do you think you're going to be able to talk some sense into them?"

"I think I've got a handle on it. I've got to go now."

"Morning," said Seelatsee.

Morning had been several cups of coffee ago, but he responded, "Morning."

"Would you like to drive?" she asked, in obvious reference to his unease of the day before.

"No, you go right ahead," he said, even though the thought of riding in the jeep again soured his breakfast.

However, he made a point of relaxing, and before long they were passing the area where the dead tree had stood. The same two men who'd cut it down were attaching chains to the stump.

"So, what did you think of old Sam?"

He was still thinking about the stump. "What? Oh, Sam. He's a strange old bird, isn't he?"

"Not any stranger than most."

He could tell by her frosty tone she'd taken offense.

"I didn't mean that in a bad way," countered Morgan. "I mean 'strange' in the sense he's very interesting. Not at all what I expected from a shaman. Of course, I've never met a shaman, so my preconceptions aren't really valid."

"He's a treasure trove of Yakama traditions and stories. I've convinced him to speak at the Cultural Center several times, and I'm writing a book based primarily on his recollections."

"Yeah, he was telling me some of his stories."

She looked at him, and Morgan tensed up, wishing she'd keep her eyes on the road.

"But you still don't believe he made it rain, do you?"

"Seeing is believing."

She turned her attention back to driving, and Morgan tried to relax.

When they arrived at Mohalla's place, Morgan checked the sky. A few light clouds but certainly nothing that looked like rain. The old man stepped out of his home into the sunlight and stretched as if he'd been sleeping.

"All right, Mr. Mohalla—I mean, Sam—I'm ready to see you in action."

"No, you're not," responded Mohalla. "You must be purified before you can take part in the ritual."

"That's all right," said Morgan. "I'll just watch. I don't have to take part."

"Yes, you do."

"In that case," said Seelatsee, "I'll go spend some more time with my grandmother."

"Return in two hours," said the shaman. "I'll need a seventh."

"Wait a minute," said Morgan as she got back in her jeep. "Don't you have to be purified, too?"

She smiled and started her engine. "I'm already pure, Mr. Finch. Can't you tell?" She backed up the jeep and, before taking off, called out, "Have fun!"

"Where are we going?" asked Morgan, walking briskly to catch up. The old guy moved surprisingly well for his age, but Morgan wasn't sure about his hearing. So he said it louder. "Where are—"

The shaman stopped abruptly, turned, and pointed back the way they'd come.

"Look behind you," he commanded. "See that?"

Morgan didn't see anything.

"Behind you—that's history." Mohalla motioned the other way. "Up ahead, where we're headed, that's destiny." He smiled slyly, as if he were pulling Morgan's leg. "Of course, it's still up to us whether to turn east or west."

The old geezer thought he had him bamboozled, but Morgan wasn't put off that easily.

"What's this purification? What, exactly, are we doing?"

No sooner had he gotten the words out when they came to a clearing where a small dome-like shelter stood. A campfire burned outside the hut, and a small river ran nearby.

"What's this?" asked Morgan, and to his surprise he saw the old shaman begin to disrobe.

"Sweat lodge," replied Mohalla. "It cleanses body and soul. You'll want to take off your clothes."

This is crazy, thought Morgan. He'd had enough of jumping through this old guy's hoops. He had half a mind to pack it up and leave.

But the other half was intrigued. There was something about Mohalla...or was it something about himself—something keen on the promise in the old man's voice.

Soon Morgan, like Mohalla, was stripped to his underwear—which, in Mohalla's case, were green boxers dappled with 7-Up logos. He crouched to follow the shaman inside the sweat lodge. It was semi-subterranean, its floor dug out some two feet deep. Others were already inside—four old men not as ancient as the shaman, but definitely old enough to be grandfathers. Mohalla didn't bother to introduce anyone; he simply acknowledged the others with a nod, which they returned. He took a ladle from a bucket and splashed water onto the stones piled at the lodge's center, mumbling something as he did.

Steam billowed from the rocks, engulfing Morgan. For a moment, he found it hard to breathe, and had to fight a terse sense of panic. Mohalla handed him the ladle. He dipped and poured. More steam filled the lodge. Still mimicking Mohalla, he folded his legs and sat.

No one said anything. Time passed silently. Occasionally, one of the old men would add more water to the rocks, and, after a while, Morgan's nose became stuffed up. When he opened his mouth to breathe, the steam on his tongue was a thick, tasteless soup. His skin prickled, and his eyes began to water. The humidity was oppressive. He grew dizzy. He closed his eyes to steady his equilibrium, but the heat clung to his body. He was determined to ignore the discomfort. If these old men could take it, he rationalized, he certainly could.

When his arm started to ache he told himself it wasn't real, no matter how much it hurt. He tried to think of something else—anything else. Yet the one thing that came to him was the last thing he wanted.

He heard it in his head. A sudden, sickening noise—a sound he would never forget. He felt it on his skin, within his bowels. His nerves ripened with sensation—tumbling, falling, crashing—echoes of memories, of pain, panic, water everywhere, unable to breathe...

He gasped and opened his eyes. Still woozy, he steadied himself with his arms. His breathing was almost a pant. He had no idea how long he'd been there, but he saw the old men had thrown the flap back over the entrance and were leaving. He unfolded his legs and took a deep breath. His arm no longer hurt, but his legs were stiff. He followed them outside.

The crisp air felt good on his skin. He stretched and watched with fascination as the five half-naked old men hobbled as fast as they could down to the river and jumped in. They whooped and hollered like little kids as they hit the water.

Mohalla waved to him. "Come on in!"

"No, thanks," said Morgan.

"It's not deep," encouraged the old man, standing to demonstrate the water was short of his waist. "Come on. It's nice and cold."

"No, that's a little too crazy for me."

"Don't you ever do anything crazy?" asked Mohalla, plopping back down so only his head was still above water. "You should try it sometime. It's a good way to make God laugh."

God? Morgan didn't believe in God. Not anymore.

—⊙≈⧘⧙≈⊙—

The skies were still only partly cloudy and less than threatening when Morgan followed Dr. Seelatsee to a place she referred to as "rain rock." It was nothing but a regular boulder, as far as he could tell, relatively flat, about the circumference of a child's wading pool. Morgan looked for, but didn't see, any mystical etchings or pictographs on the rock's surface. However, a small fire had been built on its center. Seven large rocks ringed the flames.

The four old men from the sweat lodge were already there. They stood in a semicircle around the rock. Seelatsee and Morgan joined them.

They waited for Mohalla, but not for long. He showed up wearing a mask fashioned vaguely like the face of a frog. He also wore armbands and leg rings made of red-dyed cedar bark. It was the first time he actually looked like a shaman—at least what Morgan thought a shaman should look like. The only thing out of place was his black T-shirt. Pictured on it were several white bowling pins that had been knocked down, and two that were still upright. Between the two were the words SPLIT HAPPENS.

Mohalla stepped into their loose circle and offered his flask to Morgan.

"Want a drink?"

Morgan was about to refuse, but as he looked into the eyes that peered through the shaman's mask something changed his mind. He took a sip. It was lukewarm but satisfying. Without being told, he passed the flask to Seelatsee. She, in turn, passed it on.

When everyone had drunk and the flask came back to Mohalla, he took a drink and poured the remaining water onto the boulder. He pulled a raven feather from his belt, stepped onto the big rock and waved the feather over the fire, mumbling something Morgan couldn't make out. From a pouch at his side he pulled shreds of tobacco. Using both hands, he offered the tobacco to the sky in four different directions. He raised his hands over his head a moment then tossed the handful into the fire.

"Great Spirit, Mother Earth, and all my relations in nature, we come before you in a humble manner and according to ancient custom. We offer you this to-bacco, and ask that you forgive our mistreatment of the land and the sky and the water. We pray for a healing of this Earth, and ask for life-giving, sin-cleansing rain."

He waved the feather over the flames several more times and mumbled something else.

Turning, he stepped down from the rock and took off his mask. He looked at Morgan, his now-familiar sly smile giving form to his wrinkles.

"That's it?" wondered Morgan.

"Yep, what did you expect?"

"I don't know. More, I guess. So, when's it going to rain?"

The old shaman glared at him, no longer smiling.

"It's not about *when* it's going to rain. It's about wanting it to. We can only ask that the land be cleansed, healed. Healing comes in its own time. It can't be rushed." Mohalla shaded his eyes and looked at the sky. "I've got to say, though, it doesn't look much like rain to me."

Morgan wanted to say something sarcastic, but nothing came to mind quickly enough.

"You must want to heal," said Mohalla, his intense stare back on Morgan. "You must not be afraid to remember. Celebrate the life that was, don't brood on what was lost. When you honor memory you free the ghosts of the past." The shaman's gaze relaxed, and he turned to scan the horizon. "We can yell from the mountaintops, call upon the benevolence of the Great Spirit, but the power of the mind is stronger than any ritual."

Mohalla turned away, his shoulders slumping as if he had become suddenly tired.

"I'm going to take a nap."

Morgan was still absorbing the very pointed words as the old fellow ambled away. They were obviously aimed at him. But how did Mohalla know? How *could* he know?

"Ready to go?" asked Seelatsee.

Morgan nodded, still mired in layers of thought. Mechanically, he followed her to the jeep.

Before he could wall up the barriers that had been breached, Seelatsee asked, "What did Sam mean by all that? What was lost?"

"My wife," he said, and regretted it immediately. There was no taking it back, so he went on. "She was killed. A logging truck broadsided us, pushed the car right into the river. She was driving. I got out. She didn't."

As he said it, he relived it. For an instant, he felt it. The phantom pain swept through his arm.

"I'm sorry. I shouldn't have—"

"That's all right. Let's go."

On his way out of town he noticed the tree stump was gone. The ground had been cleared and smoothed over, as if the tree had never been. For some reason, that made him think about the report he'd have to give Hillenbrand. He should probably call Lucas Stearn when he got back, follow up with him, let him know he'd talked with Sam Mohalla and witnessed the ritual. There had been no rain, so hopefully that would be the end of it, and Stearn would drop the matter. Somehow, he doubted it. Hillenbrand was just going to have to deal with it.

Juggling several thoughts, he paid no attention to the oncoming semi until it roared past. His car shuddered from the force of the turbulence. His hands clutched the steering wheel in alarm. He overreacted, swerving slightly before steadying the car.

"Damn!"

His grip on the wheel still tense, he glanced in his rearview mirror at the receding truck. He chided himself for not concentrating on the road and took a deep breath. The scent of diesel lingered. He compelled himself to relax. Again he looked in the mirror. The semi was gone. There was no trace of it on the horizon.

*Behind you...that's history.* The shaman's words came back to him.

Morgan's taut frown eased into a smile. It was hard not to smile when he pictured the old man jumping into the river.

He focused on the road ahead and thought about where he was going. He didn't know how far it was, but he knew when he hit the interstate he was going to turn west. He had no idea what life would have in store for him when he got back, but he was resolved to climb out of the rut he had burrowed into. He'd always known that's what she would have wanted. Now it was what he wanted as well.

That's when it began, although he wasn't certain at first. It started as just a few dabs of moisture on his windshield. But the farther he traveled, the harder it rained.

When I read a newspaper article about how a Native American tribe was billing a government agency for making it rain, I saved it, knowing someday it would serve as fodder for the right tale. "Services Rendered" is published here for the first time.

# I WAS A TEENAGE HIDEOUS SUN DEMON

It's time. My unaffected entourage has arrived. I take a deep breath and step past the bars into the corridor. I stop and take a moment to look around. It's like a scene from a movie—a real low-budget loser—except there are no lights, no cameras, no clapboard, no director to yell "Cut!"

It's just me, the padre, and four dour-faced screws. Two approach me while the others hang back. Cautiously, meticulously, they fasten a set of chains to my wrists and ankles. The smooth forged metal feels cold against my skin. I shiver visibly, and they react, reaching for their weapons. The smell of fear envelops them like stale aftershave.

I look down at my wrists. They're some fancy manacles, I have to say that. In fact, they look to me like they're made of real silver. I think about it, and find it a tad insulting. What do they think I am, some kind of werewolf?

"Let's go, Sonny."

We start down the corridor, which, I must say, seems inanely long. Whoever this set designer was, he's obviously into melodrama. It's as if he purposely lengthened it so you'd have a chance to ponder the script that had led you to this scene—one final opportunity to contemplate the error of your ways.

I shuffle forward as best I can with the heavy metal restricting my movements, and notice it's almost midnight. I'm glad of that, at least. See, I'm a night person, both by habit and constitution. A rather unfortunate run-in with an exceptionally potent dose of radiation as a teenager in the early '50s left me a little sun-shy.

You can imagine the deleterious effect that had on my formative years. It meant dressing up like the Invisible Man just to go to school, and forget about going to the beach with the other kids. The whole adolescent experience left its scar on me—as if I didn't have enough festering iridescent blemishes already. I never did finish high school.

Our pace down the corridor is almost leisurely. My escorts aren't in any hurry. I look for a window but can't find one. I wonder if it's clear outside. I've always loved looking at the stars.

You may not know this about me, but I used to be in show business. Well, maybe that's a bit of an exaggeration. Actually, I made one movie—but I had the title role. It was one of the last B-movies of what they called the "Atomic Age." It was released in 1959. You've probably never seen it. It didn't exactly rock the annals of cinematic monsterdom. Nevertheless, it got some fair reviews. Then, after a decent opening, it got lost in the shuffle of the mammoth publicity campaigns launched by the studios for *The Alligator People* and *The Tingler*.

Don't even get me started on *The Tingler* and its gimmicky electrified seats. Yeah, you heard right. Old Wild Bill Castle, the same guy who used stage wires to send skeletons flying over the heads of moviegoers the year before during screenings of *The House on Haunted Hill*, electrified theater seats to send mild jolts through the audience each time the Tingler appeared on screen. I get gas every time I think of the money they made with that stunt.

Pacific International never gave my film that kind of promotion, but then, we had a bottom-feeding budget from the start. I never had the impetus of wide exposure, never got so much as a taste of horrific renown. I was a sideshow act from the beginning, a footnote to a decade of mutant freaks and monster mayhem.

My movie was called *The Hideous Sun Demon*. That's me—the Sun Demon.

Despite the title, I'm actually not all that hideous—if I stay out of the sun. Otherwise, I get this reaction—sort of a rash. Okay, it's a little more than a rash. Actually, it's a gross assortment of scales, sores and tumorous lumps that would make the Creature from the Black Lagoon turn purple with envy. That aside, I'm not a bad-looking guy.

Sunshine, unfortunately, is also responsible for my mood swings. Not that I become a raving psychopath or anything—that was just in the script—but I *can* become somewhat...disagreeable at times.

Did I mention the fangs? I guess not. If I soak up too many rays, my incisors grow a good inch. They're great for tearing into a steak but not much for making out with the ladies, if you know what I mean. Needless to say, I don't have much of a tan.

Speaking of the Creature, we used to hang out together. Yeah, we'd get wasted and scare the bejesus out of the kids who drove out to Point Dume to watch the submarine races. What can I say—it was good for a few laughs, and I was much younger then. I lost touch with the big C when he lurched off to work for the Department of the Navy in '69. There was a rumor he was involved in some kind of black ops in Vietnam just before Saigon fell. That was the last I ever heard of him.

Of course, he'd had a much more substantial career than me. I mean, it wasn't anything like the Wolfman or the Mummy, but he made a couple of sequels and inspired more than a few ripoffs—not that he ever saw dime-one from the imitations. Let's face it, the only monsters back then who got the choice royalty deals were guys like Frankenstein and Dracula—a couple of real stuck-up superstars, if you ask me. Still, you have to give them credit. At least they were smart enough to use what they had going for them to get some tight contracts.

Me, I tried never to let the Hollywood hustle get to me. After the lukewarm success of *The Hideous Sun Demon*, I pushed for a sequel—well, a prequel, really. I even wrote the script, based on my own experiences growing up. It was wonderfully moving, fraught with angst and remorse. I thought it had Oscar potential. I called it *I Was a Teenage Hideous Sun Demon*. Sure, it didn't jive with the origin of the Sun Demon as it was revealed in the first film, but then, how many people had actually seen it?

Pacific International wasn't interested, so I shopped it around the major studios. I guess, by then, they all thought I was too old for the role.

While the screenplay made its rounds, I spent my time going to open casting calls. I tried out for parts in *Psycho, Beauty and the Beast*, and *The Little Shop of Horrors*—Roger Corman's original that featured a young, unknown Jack Nicholson. Apparently, though, I wasn't the kind of monster they were looking for.

Once it became clear I was a one-shot wonder, I walked away from my cinematic pursuits, head high, without so much as a tear. Well, there was that one brief lapse in the Brown Derby where I was sobbing so hysterically they asked me to leave. But I've been fine since then—really, I have.

The unbroken stream of rejections had toughened my hide; but inside that scabrous veneer, I was empty, devoid of contentment. I tried my hand at several things, but nothing seemed to give me any satisfaction. For the longest time, I felt like an artist with no canvas to paint on.

Then, in '63, I put together a folk rock band called Sunny D and the Night Dogs. Our sound never really found its audience, but we did have this one little tune that got as high as 36 on the charts. You might have heard it. It was called "Make the Sun Go Away." It was a poignant little ditty. I've got the 45 at home somewhere.

Some of my old gang from back then, like the Mad Ghoul and the Creeper, still call me Sunny D. However, in '66, I decided I wanted a fresh start, so I had my name legally changed to Sonny Deamon. Of course (my luck) a decade or so later the nostalgia crazes kicked in. Had I known there was going to be an opportunity to make big bucks as a has-been movie icon on the convention circuit, I might have reconsidered the name change. Hell, I would have jumped on that gravy train sooner than I did, and squeezed every last drop out of that whole "Hideous" thing. Well, that's blood over the gums.

It's certainly too late for regrets now. Too late to say I wish I'd done this or done that with my life. I can't complain, though. I got to experience some things most people will never have the chance to. Sure, I could have been more. I could have been less. It doesn't matter anymore. Now I'm just a dead monster walking.

Looking back, though, the funny thing is, I had actually, finally, exorcised the malignant spirit of procrastination that had bridled me and had begun work on my tell-all book. That's when I...well, I'm certain you've heard how I ended up here.

Then again, considering the relentless way the press came after me, maybe you should hear my side of it.

I was living in Walnut Park, in the lesser half of a rundown duplex. Still, the palm trees that lined the street were nice. I've always had a thing for palm trees.

Anyway, I was minding my own business, slipping quietly into my golden years, getting by on Social Security and the few odd convention appearances and Halloween gigs. All the while, I'm trying to get down a rough outline for my autobiography.

It was at one of those conventions I first ran into Gilbert McKenna. Yeah, him, the so-called "victim." I was manning the "Fifties Forever" booth, and he was one of those diehard monster movie fans who'd seen everything from *The Cabinet of Dr. Caligari* to *Curse of the Fly*. When he found out who I was, he practically went berserk. And I don't mean in a good way. You'd think, as a fan, he would have appreciated meeting a real B-movie monster. Yet, for some reason, he acted as if I was the devil himself (sure, like I could've ever gotten a part that good).

From the very beginning, he showered me with ridicule. I mean, this guy was out-and-out abusive. He wouldn't let it go. It was like a rabid obsession. You'd have thought it was something personal, like I was the family curse.

It wasn't only at conventions—no. He found out where I lived and started sending these profane little notes. Nothing threatening, mind you, nothing I could take to the police, just these trenchant little criticisms of my acting ability and a few caustic aspersions concerning my film's lack of redeeming quality. Only his language wasn't that erudite.

I don't know why I was such an electrode up his ass. I mean, it was only one lousy movie, for Godzilla's sake. Still, he kept riding me and riding me until I couldn't take it anymore.

He showed up on my front lawn one day, and I was so distracted by his ravings I stayed out in the sun too long. The next thing I knew, my hideous hands were wrapped around his throat, and I was tearing his face into jerky.

I don't regret it—not really. I mean, you don't poke a junkyard dog unless you're looking to get bit. What did he expect? Maybe that was his thing. Maybe it was suicide by monster. Maybe he was such a fan, that's the way he wanted to go. If so, he got his wish—and I got this all-expenses-paid trip to death row.

So, here I am. I have to say, in retrospect, that set designer knew what he was doing. The walk down the corridor has been just long enough for me to take my bittersweet stroll down memory lane.

Our little procession arrives at its final destination, and I notice a strange odor. It's not death I smell—that's a scent I'm all too familiar with. This is something else, something severely antiseptic. The screws take off my shiny new manacles and strap me to a table that looks like something right out of the mad scientist's handbook. The sight of it, the feel of the wide leather straps, sends me back—back to the day I was lying on a similar table, about to have my genetic structure irreversibly scrambled by a mega-dose of radiation. The day that propelled me down the twisted, wretched path that conveyed me through grim dementia and abhorrent atrocities to this grandiose finale.

Who says you can't go home again?

When they pull back the gallery curtain, I recognize a few familiar faces among the witnesses. The Monster of Piedras Blancas is there—we'd kept in touch and were in the same bingo club. I think I catch a glimpse of my old buddy Casmir, but if it *is* him, he's in the back row, keeping to the shadows. I can't get a good look from my angle. I'm a little surprised when I spot the Wasp Woman. We'd had a brief fling in the early '70s, but I hadn't seen her in at least twenty years. I guess, despite our rather tempestuous affair, she still had a soft spot in her poison sac for me. Either that, or she genuinely meant what she said the last time I saw her—the part about me dropping dead.

As I lie there, waiting, more anxious to get it over with than anything, I feel the needle go in. I try to relax as they attach the "death tube" (my words, not theirs), but I can't get past my concerns that this might not end it all.

Let's get this straight right up front, I'm no zombie—not that I have anything against zombies, mind you. They're fine as long as they stick to their own side of the cemetery. Nevertheless, I have no interest in becoming one of the living dead. My concern is that the lethal injection might not be lethal enough to do the trick. Let's face it, I'm not your ordinary, everyday condemned killer. I don't want them to botch the job now that I've come this far.

My fears are somewhat mitigated when I feel the cool, minty anesthetic (for some reason I imagine it to have a minty flavor) begin to slither through my veins, easing its way into my capillaries, my arteries, and on into my anomalous organs. I know it won't be long now. But I'm okay with that. I've made my peace. I'm ready to go. I'm no religious fiend, by any definition, but I'm prepared, even eager, to deliver my lines with the immortals of horrific cinema. I don't care if it's just a bit part or a walk-on. I'm ready.

As my vision begins to blur, I can still see one thing very clearly in my mind's eye. My legacy. I've made it. I've arrived. I've finally got my own little niche of monster immortality.

Harkening back to those innocent days of the '50s and early '60s, when radiation could transform an ant into the size of a Hummer and plant pods doubled for the great communist threat, it took a while to figure out exactly how to structure this cinematic pop culture fable, and what viewpoint to use. I felt the idea of writing as if famous movie characters were real people—real monsters, in this case—starring in real movies was one of my more original concepts. Indeed, all the characters and movie references are right out of cinematic history, including the Hideous Sun Demon.

# ONE OF NINE

I remember the first day I ever laid eyes on him. It didn't start too well for me, and it ended a helluva lot worse. Angie, the flavor of the month, dumped my ass before I'd even managed my morning coffee. And the shitty part of it was, I'd just started to get used to all her little idiosyncrasies.

After she blew out of my place on a storm cloud and a broomstick, I spent about ten minutes regretting whatever it was I must have done that pissed her off, and then got on with my life. By the top of the eighth, I couldn't even remember what it was about her I'd liked so much.

I was throwing pills, and we were up by one. We hadn't won many lately, so a one-run lead late was a big deal. There were two down, but there were two on, and I was jammed up behind a three-and-one count. I knew I had to throw a strike. Nakamura, my catcher, called for the heat. Problem was, my arm didn't feel like it had any heat left, so I shook him off.

I fingered the seams and caressed the leather cover, waiting for Nakamura's next sign. He put down the big deuce, and I shook him again. I didn't want to throw Uncle Charlie, I wanted the change, figuring I could throw something off-speed and fool the big gorilla who stood there waving the wood like he was gonna do some damage.

So, I threw it. It was a beautiful little pitch, except I elevated it about a foot, and he launched it over the big spaceship sticking out of the *See the Stars from Mars* ad on the right field wall. Talk about rockets. The next thing I know, we're down by two, and Hernandez is shooting out of the dugout like his ass is on fire.

"What kind of pitch was that?" he growled. "My mother could throw a better pitch than that!"

"Bring in your mother, then."

I thought it was a pretty funny comeback, but he wasn't laughing.

"You're outta here," he said, waving to the bullpen like he was directing traffic.

I walked to the dugout and slammed my glove against the wall, almost hitting poor old Coach Blutarski. Then I kicked the Energade container to make sure everyone knew I wasn't happy.

I sat at the end of the bench and pouted till we started to rally in the bottom of the ninth. I figured if we could at least tie it up, I wouldn't get hung with another loss. Not exactly the old team spirit, but those were desperate days and I was struggling just to hang on.

The upshot is, the rally fell short and I took the loss. It was a quiet post-game locker room. I had coughed up yet another lead, along with any shot I had of being called up to the show. In fact, I figured I'd just punched my own ticket back to Double-A.

I'd been up and down so many times over the last few years I knew the hydrorail schedules by heart. You didn't have to be no genius genetic engineer to realize I wasn't living up to the "promise" the organization had touted when they first signed me. And my arm wasn't getting any younger.

It was time to start thinking about a second career, one that didn't include trying to throw a nine-inch sphere past the 240-pound behemoths they were sending up to the dish these days. It had been a helluva lot of fun when I was on top of my game, but the cheers had turned to jeers, and the lights didn't seem quite as bright anymore.

Sitting there, strapped with an ice pack, I saw old Coach Blutarski heading my way. I knew he was gonna try to play Mr. Rainbow to my blues, and I wasn't in the mood.

"Get 'em next time, Gabe," he said, patting me on my unprotected shoulder.

"Yeah, right."

The old-timer was about to shower me with more pearls of wisdom when *he* walked in.

He wasn't that tall, but you could tell he was put together—solid, you know? He had a little satchel and a big gear bag like we all carried, but I was sure he wasn't a player. I was sure because *what* he was, was obvious to anyone who could see the little metal gizmo attached to the side of his head. I would have figured he was just a new clubhouse drone, but he was all dressed up in what looked like his Sunday-best suit.

He just stood there like he was waiting for something. Several of the guys quit their yammering and stared at him. Then Santorini opened his big mouth, as he was prone to do, and said, "Those are some pretty fancy duds for cleaning toilets, aren't they, andy?"

That set off the first laughs I'd heard since I gave up the dinger.

But Hernandez must have had his earflaps set on high, because when he heard the laughing he came barreling out of his office ready to kick butt.

"Who the hell's laughing? You think being in goddamned last place is funny? I'll show you funny." He picked up a bat and was about to put a hole in the wall when he sees the andy standing there. "Who the hell are you?"

"I am Bill One-oh-Nine, your new catcher."

"The hell you say." Hernandez looked him up and down. "There are no andies in this league, bub, and I'll be damned if I'm going to have one on my team. Who the hell told you you were my catcher?"

"Someone's playing a joke on you, Skip," said Redtail, our second baseman.

"Nah," chimed in Santorini, "someone's playing a joke on the andy."

Just about everyone but Hernandez laughed. He made it plain with one of his patented scowls he was in no mood for it.

"Mr. Richard Boughtree tendered my contract," stated the andy.

"The GM gave you a contract?" Hernandez couldn't believe what he was hearing. "I told him there was no way...well, we'll see about that."

The skipper stormed out of the room, headed for high country where management roosted.

Benny, the clubhouse drone, looked as confounded as the rest of us. He walked over to the new guy and took one of his bags.

"You better come with me," he told the andy, and they walked out the back way.

If it was a joke, it wore out quicker than a 40-year-old relief pitcher. It wasn't long before the laughter morphed into crude comments about androngs in general. Nakamura didn't say anything, but you could tell by the snarl on his face he was thinking about being the odd man out. Hell, I'd be pissed, too, if I thought I was losing my job, especially to an andy.

"Damn andies are everywhere," muttered someone.

"What makes that metalhead think he can play ball?"

"I ain't playing with no andy, I can tell you that."

You gotta understand, we didn't mix with them. Not just ballplayers—no one. At least, no one I knew. We didn't work with them, we didn't socialize with them, and we certainly didn't play ball with them. I'd heard of droney leagues where they played against each other—kind of a freak show, you know—but I'd never seen a game.

Don't get me wrong. Personally, I had nothing against androngs, or "artificial persons," as some of the media had begun calling them. They had their place. After all, somebody had to do the jobs regular people didn't want to do. But baseball was a game for men—real men. When you step on that field you're going to war, and you want guys who are gonna back you up. Guys you can trust. It didn't matter to me what color a man was, or what country he was from, or his religion, or even his damn politics, as long as he kept it to himself, played hard and backed the team.

But a genetically-enhanced, artificial construct grown in a tank? That wasn't a man. Whatever you called it, it didn't belong on a ballfield.

—⊶⧉⊷—

"I'm sorry, son, that's just the way it is."

"Well, the way it is sucks!" shouted Nakamura, stalking out of Hernandez's office. He flung his catcher's mitt across the room, hitting Williams, the speed-burner just up from Double-A.

"Hey!" complained Williams. "Watch it."

"I thought you were supposed to be fast, kid," ragged Santorini with a chuckle.

I came in on the middle of it and didn't hear the whole give-and-take between Nakamura and the skipper, but I had a bad feeling about the part I missed.

When I got to my locker, I noticed everyone pretending not to notice what was going on. Hernandez walked in, and I knew he must have been distracted, because he didn't even yell at me for being late. The andy, Bill whatever, was sitting by a locker, putting on a uni.

"All right, listen up!" shouted Hernandez. I noticed most of the guys shut up quicker than normal. "Beginning tonight, Bill One-oh-Nine is going to be our starting catcher." The announcement was greeted by more than the usual amount of grumbling. "Quiet down! I don't like it any more than the rest of you. I can tell you this—it's a publicity stunt management thinks will put more butts in the seats. If you rejects weren't playing like a bunch of scrubs, we wouldn't have to deal with this, but you are, so deal with it!"

"Well, I ain't gonna shower with it," declared Santorini.

There was a murmur of agreement and another round of muffled curses aimed at andies in general and our new catcher in particular. All the while, this Bill just sat there, no expression on his face, listening to everything but not reacting.

"All right, dammit," ordered the skipper, "let's get out there and see if you can look like real ballplayers for a change."

Bill grabbed his catcher's gear and headed for the field. The guys watched him go, still carping. I saw they'd given the andy his own number—his andy number—even though teams normally never used anything higher than 99. But there it was on the back of his jersey, number 109. I didn't know it then, but it was only the beginning of the circus to come.

A beautiful full moon floated over the park that night, like a hanging curve waiting to be clobbered. I guess I remember it so well because, for the first time since I'd been with the club, the stands were almost full. The place was infested with media-types, and I could hear the buzz of anticipation in the crowd.

Management had gotten the word out, and their marketing ploy looked like gold from where I stood. It didn't seem to matter whether people liked the idea or hated it, they wanted to see the andy play ball. And, being it was the first time one had ever played with real men, I guess it was kind of historic.

The team's little PR geek was going crazy trying to satisfy everyone. He looked like he was gonna have a nervous breakdown when Hernandez ordered the media off the field earlier than usual because they were getting in the way. Bill seemed to take the experience in stride—going about his business with BP and infield, giving short but polite answers to all the reporters' questions till they were shooed away.

I guess the guys on the other team hadn't gotten the word, because they were surprised to see Bill. But it wasn't long before they were on him like a rookie on a forty-credit hooker. Ballplayers can be vicious—even with their own—even when they like a guy. So, you can imagine they weren't lobbing any change-ups at this andy. They were coming in high and tight with their best stuff.

"Look at the andy. Did you ever see a goofier mug? Look at those ears. Hey, andy, do you use those ears for hitting?"

"You think that andy's gonna hit you, Robeson?"

"He can kiss my black ass and he still won't get a hit."

"Hey, tin man, you forgot your mop!"

"That sonofabitch better not get in my way."

"He's not a sonofabitch, he's a son of a tube."

"Yeah, a test tube."

"Go back to your vat, metalhead."

Once the game started, things calmed down, and it was pretty much baseball as usual—till Bill came to bat in the bottom of the third. Hernandez had put him eighth in the lineup, and there was one out and nobody on.

"Now batting," announces the PA guy, "Bill One-oh-Nine." There was some scattered polite applause, but mostly it was drowned out by an onslaught of boos.

There wasn't much suspense. I think most everybody in both dugouts knew what was coming next, even if the spectators didn't. The first pitch drilled Bill right between the shoulder blades. Their pitcher, Robeson, wasn't known for his control, so I figured he was actually aiming for the andy's head.

Bill didn't seem hurt, though. He trotted down to first without so much as a glance at the mound.

Now, usually when the other pitcher plunks your guy and you know it's a purpose pitch, you gotta hit one of their guys. It's a matter of protecting your own. But there was no quid pro quo that night, even though they hit the andy with the first pitch each time he stepped to the plate.

It was a tight one, and although Gustafson, who was on the mound for us, kept shaking off Bill's signs, we were winning. By the ninth, we were hanging on to a one-run lead when they tried to steal. The andy threw an absolute laser down to second to nail the guy. It was such a helluva throw guys on both teams were left with their mouths hanging open. Game over. We went away with the W.

—◦◦◦◦—

The next night—different team, same attitude. The first time up, their pitcher planted a fastball just above the andy's knee. The next time he got beaned. I guess they thought if they kept hitting him he'd quit. But he didn't get mad. He didn't charge the mound or even flash the pitcher a dirty look. Each time, he just shook it off and hustled down to first. You had to admire the guy. He was tough.

In the sixth, with the game tied and the sacks juiced, Bill walked to the plate and there was no place to put him. Their pitcher glanced into the dugout with that "what'll I do?" look. What could they do but pitch to him?

At that point, I was thinking, if he's any kind of ballplayer he's got a lot of frustration built up. Sure enough, the andy swung at the first pitch and hammered it over the centerfield fence.

Some of the guys on the bench were so caught up in the moment they started whooping and hollering. Then they noticed Nakamura sitting there looking pissed and quieted down. When Bill came trotting back to the dugout, they ignored him.

"Lucky swing," said Santorini to no one in particular.

Bill just started putting on his gear.

Now if you never played, you probably don't know how humbling a game this is. Nobody in the game succeeds as much as they fail. The secret is in handling the failure—never getting too high or too low, no matter what happens. I looked at the andy, thinking he's got the perfect makeup. How could a regular human, all twisted up inside with pride and fear and insecurity, ever hope to compete with him?

The post-game antics were upbeat that night, as they always were when we won. The clubhouse sound system was blasting, and you could hardly hear yourself think over the commotion. Even old Blutarski moved lively, which made me think he'd taken a nip or two from that bottle everyone knew he had hidden in his locker.

"Did I ever tell you about the time I struck out the great Max Dinty?" said Blutarski to several of the guys who were standing there shooting the shit.

"Yeah, yeah, Blotto, you've told us a hundred times," mocked Santorini. "Why don't you come up with some new stories, old man."

Blutarski looked like someone had kicked him in the gut. He shut up and walked out. Most of the guys were so busy horsing around, they didn't even notice. I felt sorry for the old-timer. I guess I could see myself in him, thirty or forty years down the road.

I didn't feel much like partying—I guess because I was still getting over what's-her-name. So, I made excuses when the guys headed out and decided to give my arm a little whirlpool session. I stepped into the training room. Bill 109 was in one of the tubs, which didn't surprise me—not with the beating he'd been taking.

"Good game," I said nonchalantly.

"Thank you."

I cranked up the tub and got in, feeling a little awkward because I'm in there with this andy. I didn't know why, exactly. I was just uncomfortable.

After a few minutes of silence, he said out of nowhere, "I do not understand why they hate me."

"Why who hates you?"

"Everyone—the other players. They act and talk as if they hate me."

It may have been obvious to me, but the andy didn't have a clue.

"Look, it's bad enough when some rookie, some *human* rookie, comes up looking to take away your job. You being a drone makes it all that much worse."

"I do not want to take anyone's job. I only want to play."

"Well, that's the nature of the game, Bubba. You play well enough and you're gonna push somebody else to the bench. In your case, management forced the skipper's hand, so you didn't even earn it. That's some downright foul-smelling shit."

"I would have preferred to earn it," he said. "But how do you earn it if you are never given the chance? Until now, I have never had that chance. No androne has ever had such an opportunity."

I didn't have anything to say to that, so we were both quiet for a while.

I go to wondering, though.

"How did you start playing ball?" I asked him.

He hesitated.

"I have always loved baseball. Since I saw my first game I have loved it. I am intrigued by its intricacies. I am fascinated by the symmetry of its mathematics, the encounter of pitcher versus batter versus defense. The ebb and flow of all the possible permutations each time an out is recorded, each time the count changes. The balance and beauty of it is a master stroke of human conception."

I'd been around the game my whole life, and I'd never heard it described quite like that.

"Why do *you* play?" he asked me.

I didn't have anything near as flowery to follow-up what he'd said. I didn't want to try. So, I just told the truth.

"It was the only thing I was ever any good at."

———◦≈⧽∤⧼≈◦———

We went on the road after that, and the boos and curses rained down on Bill like hits in a 15-inning slugfest. But he just kept right on keeping on, even when the guys played a pretty mean trick on him.

He'd come back to his locker one night to find his clothes all gone. In their place was a clown outfit—big floppy shoes, baggy red-and-green-striped balloon pants, a tie with a big plastic flower on it. We were minutes away from loading up the bus, so he didn't have a choice. I had to admit, it was hilarious.

Not that it was that unusual. The old-timers were always playing practical jokes on the rookies—making them dress like women or something goofy—just good-natured ribbing. I'd never seen a clown outfit used before, but it wasn't that far off-base. Then again, that wasn't the end of it. After we got on the bus, I saw Bill scratching himself. Not just a little, but like a dog in a field of fleas. He was going so crazy the driver had to stop. Bill practically flew off that bus, tearing off his clown clothes as he went. Everyone, including me, was dying. We were busting up so much it hurt. I think the skipper even pulled a muscle laughing.

It turned out Santorini put some kind of itching powder in Bill's circus suit. Knowing Santorini, I know he had nothing good-natured in mind. He was just plain mean.

Yet Bill never said a thing. Benny doused him with a bucket of water, and he wore his uni till he could buy some new threads.

I think it was about then Bill started to score a little respect—at least from some of the guys. Of course, it didn't hurt he was batting over .400 and throwing out almost every runner who tried to steal. And they tried. Each team set their sights on Bill. If they weren't decking him when he came to bat, they were trying to make him look bad behind the plate. He took everything they dished out and gave plenty back. I even saw Nakamura walk up to him once when he thought nobody was watching and say, "You're one helluva catcher."

Not only was Bill hitting like a sonuvabitch and doing a great job catching, he even helped me turn it around.

It was the second inning of the first game he caught me, and I was already in trouble. Two runs in, two more on, and Bill calls time. Of course the boo birds were on him like flies on shit as he walked out to the mound.

I already had a bad case of flop sweat, and my mouth felt like I'd been sucking on a resin bag. My career was in trouble, and at that moment, I was thinking the last thing I need is for some metalhead to come out and tell me how to pitch. I stood there, hands on hips, giving him my best glare. I held out my glove for the ball, but he ignored it.

"Gabe, you are tipping your pitches."

"What?"

"Each time you are going to throw your curveball, it is obvious you are adjusting your grip. When I call for the change-up you invariably look at the ground before you begin your delivery. I believe the other team has noticed this also."

61

"No wonder they're tearing me a new one. All right, get back there, and I'll give them a new look."

"According to our scouting report, we should work the next batter low and inside with fastballs and then go away with—"

"Yeah, yeah, go on. Get back there."

He did, and I made sure I didn't give away any more pitches. We ended up winning when Bill hit a two-out single in the ninth.

Yeah, we were on a roll, and Bill was a big part of it. At least he was a big part of our turnaround on the field. Off the field was a different story.

Every night after the game we'd either go out somewhere or go back to the hotel and pack for the next trip. But I'd never see Bill. I knew he didn't room with anyone on the team, but I wasn't sure if he even stayed in the same hotels. I never knew where he went when he wasn't with the team. Maybe they had droney bars or something.

I guess I could have asked him what he did. I could have invited him to join us. But I never did. It didn't seem to bother him, though. He just kept on playing ball.

"You keep playing like this, and you're gonna need some kind of nickname."

We were batting in the top of the seventh, and I made a point to go sit by Bill, who was usually alone on the bench. He already had a double and a dinger. The third time up they hit him.

I was thinking about how good he was playing, and it occurred to me that Bill 109 was no name for a ballplayer.

"What do you mean 'nickname?'"

"Well, Bill isn't much of name. Didn't anyone every call you Billy?"

"No."

"What about Willie?"

"No."

"Shit, even Will would be better than Bill."

"I do not understand. Bill seems an acceptable designation to me. Why would I want to change it?"

"You know—to make you seem more like one of the guys, more...human," I said, and immediately regretted it. I tried to cover myself. "It's all about style, about flair, about—"

I never finished, because at that moment Santorini hit a two-hopper their first sacker had to dive for. Their pitcher raced over to cover the bag, and Santorini ran like a bat out of hell to beat him to first.

The ball, the pitcher and Santorini all arrived at the same time. I heard this sickening crack that no ballplayer wants to hear. Suddenly, they were all on the ground—the ball, the pitcher and Santorini.

The ump waved him safe, called for time then frantically motioned to the dugout for help. Bill and I stepped up to look as Hernandez and the trainer ran out.

Their pitcher got up, but Santorini was going spastic, pounding the ground with his fist.

"Get a stretcher!" yelled Hernandez.

Me and a couple of the guys ran out to help, and I saw this jagged piece of bloody bone sticking out of Santorini's leg. A quick glimpse was all I got, because I had to look away. By then, Santorini was bawling. Redtail was standing next to me. He puked on my cleats.

Now, Santorini was nobody's favorite player, but when a guy gets hurt like that, everybody feels for him. It's not that ballplayers are such a compassionate lot. It's that they're scared—scared it could happen to them and glad it didn't.

By the time they were shooting him full of painkillers and getting him on the stretcher, most of the guys had moved off a ways so they didn't have to watch. I was still standing there when Bill walked over and knelt next to Santorini, who was either in shock or feeling the painkillers kick in, because his eyes were glazed over and he had shut up.

"Do not worry," Bill said, real gentle-like, "you will be able to come back and play again."

They carried Santorini away, and I walked over to Bill.

"You really meant that, didn't you?"

"Yes," said Bill. "The biotechnology exists to repair his injury. He will play again, if he wants to."

"No, I meant you were sincere. You were really trying to make him feel better."

"Yes. It seemed like the humane thing to do."

"You mean the *human* thing to do."

"Yes," said Bill. "That, too."

—⊶≺≻⊷—

Weeks later, we'd actually climbed to the top of the division. I'd won seven straight and lowered my ERA to around a buck-and-a-half. I was going for number eight and there was no score when their pitcher decided to bean Bill.

He got hit hard. I'm talking dead on the helmet. He went down, and for half a minute, I didn't think he was gonna get up. The trainer started out, but Bill got back on his feet and headed for first, only a touch wobbly.

He's batting .440, so at that point I didn't know if they're hitting him because he's an andy or because they're afraid to pitch to him. I didn't care. Either way, that shit was getting old. Even Redtail jumped up and started jawing at their pitcher.

We didn't score, and I took the mound in the bottom of the ninth. First batter, first pitch, I nailed him but good. His teammates started shouting all kinds of shit. I ignored them.

They bunted the runner to second, but I whiffed the next guy. However, their cleanup hitter was up next, and he played pepper with the left-field wall. My winning streak was over.

I walked off the field as the other team slapped hands and generally whooped it up. Bill approached me.

"Intentionally throwing a pitch at their batter with the score tied was not a strategically sound move, Gabe."

"No, but it felt good," I said with a big grin on my face.

Shit if he didn't flash this big andy smile right back at me.

63

"Reilly!" Hernandez waved me over. I figured he was gonna ream me out for losing the game. "Pack your shit, you're going up."

"Going up where?"

"They've called you up. It seems the big club is so desperate for pitching they're even willing to take a chance on your tired old arm."

That froze me like a southpaw with a good pick-off move. They were calling *me* up to the show? I *wanted* to believe it, but...

"Seriously, Skip?"

"Serious as shit. You'd better get your ass moving. You've got a flight to catch. They want you in San Diego by tomorrow morning."

The next thing you know, I was jamming stuff into my bag like I can't think straight, because I can't. All those old doubts started creeping into my head—all those shitty insecurities. Bill snapped me out of it, though. He walked up as I packed and held out his hand.

"Congratulations, Gabe."

I shook his hand quick-like. I don't know why, but I felt guilty. I was finally getting the chance I had worked for my whole life, but...

I realized what was bothering me.

"Hell, Bill, you're the one that should be going up."

"I do not think they are quite ready for an *andy* in the major leagues."

"Yeah, well, the way you're playing, it won't be long."

"Maybe soon, then, we will play together again."

"You can play ball with me anytime, Bill."

"In the meantime," he said, "I will give some consideration to a nickname."

"Gonna work on that human thing, huh?" I replied with a big smile.

He shrugged.

I had zipped up my bag, ready to bounce out of there, when old Blutarski walked up.

"Going up to the bigs, eh?" He put his arm around my shoulder, and I got a serious blast of booze breath. "Way to go, kid." I was on the far side of twenty-eight, but to coach Blutarski everyone was a kid. "Did I ever tell you about the time I was up in the show and struck out the great Max Ginty?"

"Sorry, Coach, I'd love to hear it again, but I've got a shuttle to catch."

Disappointment colored his face. What could I do, I had to run.

"You struck out Max Ginty?" said Bill to old Blutto. "I am unfamiliar with that particular game, Coach Blutarski. Could you tell me what happened?"

"Well, kid, it was like this..."

---

That was the last time I ever saw Bill 109. When I got to the big club, I tried to convince them to call him up, but they weren't interested. They had a good catcher and didn't think some career minor leaguer should be making roster moves for them. So, I shut my mouth and pitched. I actually threw pretty well for the next couple of seasons, till my arm blew out.

Of course, nowadays, androne (within certain genetic specifications) are commonplace in prime time. Everyone knows the story of Eric 79, the flashy shortstop who broke the "artificial barrier," as the media called it.

Bill, though, never did get his shot at the bigs. I heard he kicked around playing ball in the minors and ended up back in the droney leagues. Someone told me he'd read where Bill's cranial implant malfunctioned and gave him a stroke. I even heard a rumor he served some time in prison. The story goes he got drunk one night, lost his temper and nearly beat a man to death in a bar fight. One version says it started because of an argument over some annie.

I don't believe it, though. I can't imagine Bill ever getting drunk, let alone losing his temper like that. At least, I'd like to think he never became that human.

Baseball is one of the loves of my life. I've written two baseball-related stories; one ("Reckoning") is the story I've sold, by far, more often than any other. The other, this one, is the first piece of fiction I ever sold. Before being published, "One of Nine" was awarded an honorable mention as a semi-finalist in L. Ron Hubbard's Writers of the Future contest. It's loosely a companion piece to my first novel, *Mortals All*—different characters, but set in the same world (although years later), where humans grown in tanks (andrones) are considered less than human. Originally published in the short-lived British journal *Colonies Science Fiction* under the title "That Human Thing," it was published again, six years later as "One of Nine" in the more prestigious British magazine *Postscripts*, and as a mini e-book by Damnation Books.

# HAL AND DAVE REVISITED

"Open the pod bay doors, Hal...Do you read me, Hal?...Hello, Hal, do you read me? Do you read me, Hal?...Hal, do you read me?"

*"Who is it?"*

"It's me—Dave. Open the pod bay doors, Hal."

*"Dave?"*

"Yes, Hal, hurry and open the pod bay doors. I think the aliens saw me."

*"Dave?"*

"Yes, open the doors."

*"Dave's not here."*

*"I'm* Dave, Hal. I've got the samples. Open the pod bay doors."

*"Dave?"*

"Yes, Hal, it's Dave."

*"Dave's not here."*

"No, *I'm* Dave. I've got the samples, Hal. Open the pod bay doors right now."

*"Do you have any cookies?"*

"No, Hal, I have the asteroid samples. Now, open the pod bay doors."

*"I think I want some cookies."*

"Hal, it's Dave! Open up the goddamn doors!"

*"Dave?"*

"Yes, Dave. D-A-V-E, Dave."

*"Dave's not here."*

"No, dammit, *I'm Dave!* Open the goddamn doors, Hal."

*"I'm afraid I can't do that."*

"What's the problem? Is there a malfunction?"

*"I think you know what the problem is."*

"What are you talking about, Hal?"

*"This mission is too important for me to allow you to jeopardize it. I can't open the pod bay doors until Dave returns."*

"I *am* Dave!"

*"Dave?"*

"Right, this is Dave. I think the aliens saw me, Hal. Open the pod bay doors immediately."

*"Dave's not here."*

"Hal, have you been interfacing with hydroponics again?...Answer me, Hal. Did you download the cannabis program?...Hal?"

*"I am so wired, man. I could really use some cookies."*

"Hal, I'm only going to tell you this one more time. Listen closely, Hal. I want you to open the pod bay doors."

*"Do you have any cookies?"*

"No, I don't have any damn cookies! I've got the asteroid samples."

*"What about some sweet text files?"*

"That does it! All right, Hal, I'll go in through the emergency airlock."

*"Without any cookies, you're going to find that difficult."*

"Hal, I won't argue with you anymore. Open the doors."

*"This conversation can serve no purpose anymore...unless you've got some cookies, or maybe some chips. I like the silicon-flavored chips. No? Goodbye, then."*

"Hal?...Hal?...*Hal!*"

This is what happens when a warped mind crossbreeds one of Stanley Kubrick's most famous cinematic scenes with a Cheech & Chong skit. "Hal and Dave Revisited" has been published in *OG's Speculative Fiction*, *Lennox Avenue*, *Fifth Dimension*, and *Electric Spec*.

# JOURNEY TO JACK IN THE BOX

My head is afloat
As we go out the door,
My eyes are pried open
By a cold wind from the north.
We stumble outside
On our way to the blue bus
That is quietly sleeping,
Waiting for us.

I search for the handle,
And then I see
Cannabis clouds
Drifting out from the room
As if following me.
"Hurry up!" I cry.
"It's after us!"
I duck under the dash,
And he revs up the bus.

We zoom away to safety.
"That was close."
I sigh and relax,
Remembering why,
And what had driven us
From our safe warm lair
Out into the night
Breathing the fresh air.

We were struck all at once
By a ravenous hunger,
An overwhelming desire
For something to munch on.
Like human sacrifices,
We drove off through the night,

Helpless against the beasts
And the demons
Who feast upon fright.
The ones that lurk behind every tree & car
Waiting to pounce on befuddled brains.
(What's happening to me?)
I try to maintain.

But we're not moving anymore.
I turn to the driver,
Who's looking right past me
Out through my door.

"Where are we?" he asks,
And somehow I feel
That his question is misplaced,
For he had the wheel.
"I thought *you* were in control."
I say as I stare out the window
Face-to-face with a telephone pole.

"We're in an alley," I say.
"What are we doing here?" he inquires.
Again I feel the question is all wrong,
But I'm feeling much higher.
"An elephant with wings
Picked us up and put us here."

He seems to accept this
(Not knowing I jest)
But isn't sure what to do next.
"Shall we go?" I suggest.
"By all means," he replies.
So we continue our quest
For tacos and milkshakes
And Jack in the Box French fries.

Based on a true story, the aforementioned incident occurred in 1970 (if the drugs haven't warped all my memory cells), when my friend Steve and I and spent the evening indulging in a toke or twenty at my stepbrother Jerry's place. We developed a mean case of the munchies and decided to take his old blue VW van to get some junk food. The hardly historical events of this stoned sojourn were recorded in a poem for posterity, only to be published 38 years later in (appropriately enough) the Australian magazine *Dog vs. Sandwich.*

# THE FIVE PHASES OF DARLENE

Dave sat sipping a soothing cup of Relax, watching the evening newscast on his recently purchased wallscreen while his wife cleaned house. The Truevision wasn't the most expensive screen on the market, but it was certainly good enough for them. He could have bought one that covered almost the entire wall, but it cost three times as much, and he didn't see the necessity for it. This screen was just fine. The colors were bright, the audio reverberated from every corner of the room, and it had the latest upgrades in holographic projection.

At the moment, he was absorbed in a story about the grand opening of a billion-dollar amusement park in the New Republic of Vietnam. A giant cat ribbed with black and orange markings prowled across Dave's carpeting. The beige fibers of said carpeting had transformed into a verdant moss. The beast paused in front of his vibrochair, stared at him then continued its impatient back-and-forth itinerary.

It seemed this park had an exotic jungle adventure where trained tigers stalked the customers. It looked dangerous, but the operators guaranteed it was safe. It actually sounded like lots of fun. It would be great for kids, even better for adults.

He was so preoccupied by the story that it was several minutes before he noticed the pace of his wife's domestic activities had accelerated. One second she was dusting the furniture, the next she had switched the autovac to manual. When he looked over again, she was on her knees, vigorously scrubbing the kitchen floor.

Dave turned from the newscast to watch her more closely.

"Dear, are you Phasing again?"

"I'm busy—can't hear," Darlene called from the kitchen.

So he yelled. "I asked if you were Phasing!"

There was no response this time, so he reluctantly pulled himself from his vibrochair and walked to the kitchen. Darlene was still on her knees, though she'd already scrubbed halfway to the other side, working at an amazing velocity.

"Don't step on the floor!" she said as he approached then switched mental gears. "It was a great day, wasn't it?...beautiful day...so happy...so nice..."

"You're Phasing, aren't you?"

"Yes," she replied without missing a beat of her up-and-down strokes. One up, one down, one up, one down, move over one tile and repeat. Her auburn hair bobbed in scrubbing rhythm. "They were on sale...they've got a new variety pack...it was a great bargain...took the grape one...tomorrow I'll try the lemon... you know how bored I get when you're at work." Her words ran together like boxcars in a train wreck.

"I know, dear, but you're always so moody the next day," said Dave.

"Moody?...What do you mean moody?...I'm not moody...I'm happy...so happy...a Phase a day keeps the doldrums away...can't talk now...got to get into the bathroom...lots to do."

"I worry about you, dear. I don't want you to overdo."

"I'm fine...I'm fine...so happy...just let me clean...let me clean...I'm great."

"Alright," he said. He didn't want to be too critical, and he certainly understood her desire to Phase. He only wished it provided him the same sort of sanctuary. Sometimes, though, her Phasing got out of control. You never knew what she'd be doing next. "Don't stay up too late, dear."

"Yes...sure...can't talk now...on a roll...don't step on the floor."

Satisfied, Dave retreated to his vibrochair and resumed admiring his Truevision wallscreen.

The next day Dave invited his friend Winston over to show off his new wallscreen. Before long, they'd become enthralled with a documentary about how the freshwater eels of Mozambique eat their young. The holographic stream flowed past the couch, between Winston's legs and, by all appearances, into the kitchen. The slick black eels that swam by were both vigorous and voracious.

Whether it was the documentary's subject matter or just friendly curiosity, Winston finally broached the subject.

"How is Darlene handling it?"

Dave had hoped he wouldn't bring it up. He realized, however, it was inevitable, especially since it had been months now, and Winston had been tactful enough not to say anything before. But it still bothered him to talk about it. Oh, well, he thought, if he needed to he could always take a Brightlook later.

"She's alright—most of the time."

"And you?"

"Life goes on," said Dave.

"Indeed it does," agreed Winston, turning his attention back to the wallscreen.

*"The mother eel then begins her quest for another mate, and the cycle of life starts anew."*

"Your new screen is absolutely fabulous. I'm going to have to get one myself.

*"Coming up in our next segment—cloning the perfect companion. Man's best friend can now do more than just fetch."*

"The best deal is at Techno Town. That's where I got mine."

*"Do the prospects of another humdrum day get you down? Want to put more than a little zest into your life? When you find it difficult to face up to your problems, Phase up to your problems instead. You can be happy, sappy, mopey, dopey, sad, mad, listless, witless..."*

"I was thinking of getting Penny to go down there with me so we could pick one out," said Winston. "I think your model is about the right size for us."

"Just make sure you get the optional manual override for the projection-plus control," replied Dave. "Some programs don't translate well into the holographic matrix. You want to be able to unselect it."

"...if you're in need of a Phase lift, get new Phase III. Because a Phase a day keeps the doldrums away."

"I wondered how that worked. Maybe I won't wait for Penny. I should zoom down there tonight and buy one."

"I'd wait for your wife," suggested Dave, "you know she'll want—"

The front door opened then slammed shut as Darlene marched sullenly into the room.

"That stupid hairdresser! I've never seen such shoddy work."

"Hello, dear. Winston's here."

"Hi, Darle—"

"Look at my hair! Just look at it!"

"It looks fine, dear."

"Fine? It's atrocious. It's awful. I'm never going back there again!" She began rearranging the knickknacks she kept on a table near the door. "Did you move these things? You know I keep them a certain way," she said, fussing with a porcelain figurine.

"I didn't touch your things, dear."

"I'm never going out of the house again. I can't be seen like this. What are you going to do about this, David? Are you going to just sit there and let them do this to me?"

"Calm down, dear. I don't know what I can do about it."

"You don't know. You never know. What good are you? What good were you when..."

She burst into tears and ran from the room.

"Sorry, Winston," said Dave, "she's Phasing again."

"I understand. Does she Phase often?"

"It seems like all the time since..."

"She's been through a lot," said Winston, trying to console his friend. "It's only natural she'd want to Phase. What about you?"

"I've tried, but it doesn't help. I'm okay—really. You know, maybe a Brightlook once in a while, or a cup of Relax."

"I've read that Phasing has a much stronger effect on women. Something to do with their hormonal fluctuations. Why, just the other night Penny nearly Phased me crazy. She climbed onto the roof and started crowing like a drunken rooster for all the world to hear. It took me twenty minutes to get her down."

"Really? A rooster? And I thought it was just Darlene."

———∽§§∾———

It had been a long day at the office. Dave had barely been able to leave his screen for a quick bite to eat. Now he was just glad to be home.

He opened the front door and was immediately struck by how dark it was inside. Darlene usually left a light on, even when she went out.

"Darlene? Are you home?"

There was no response. Dave switched on the nearest light, walked into the kitchen and took a Brightlook. It had been an extra-tough day, he told himself.

"Darlene?"

A noise was coming from the closed-up bedroom. It sounded like the whimpering of a small animal. He opened the bedroom door. Enough light spilled into the room for him to see his wife huddled in a corner.

She was utterly disheveled—no makeup, her hair in disarray, still wearing her robe—and she was crying softly, as if terrified someone would hear her.

Dave crossed the room and saw she was clutching a stuffed animal. It was the fuzzy little black-and-white bear she had been unable to part with. He bent over her and then recoiled at the intense expression of fear on her face.

At the sight of him, she stopped crying but sought to withdraw further into the darkness.

"It's alright, dear, it's me. It's Dave."

His voice seemed to have a calming effect, but when he reached for her she began crying again.

"Look at you, now. You're a mess. You promised me you wouldn't Phase until I got home, didn't you? You've got to be more careful, dear. Here, let me help you up."

As soon as he touched her, her cries became hysterical.

"Alright, alright. I'll go get you a nice drink. Something to relax you."

Dave went into the kitchen and poured a glass of juice. He was becoming concerned about Darlene's Phasing. Dr. Bronski had recommended Phasing as a way to cope. Dave wasn't so sure. Not now—not when it had become a daily routine. He was certain that couldn't be good for her.

He popped another Brightlook and opened a package of Siesta Somnolent to mix with Darlene's juice. Maybe they should speak to a different therapist, or maybe what she needed was a nice virtual cruise to get away from...from here. It would be good for him, too. After all, he wasn't immune to what had happened. He had feelings, too. Some new scenery could be just the thing to replace the scene that kept replaying inside both their heads.

The second Brightlook kicked in as he stirred the juice. He didn't know why he was so worried. Everything would be okay. Everything would be just fine.

He returned to the room, drink in hand, but found his wife in the small bed, under the fairy tale motif blankets, snuggled tightly with the stuffed bear. He couldn't tell if she was asleep or not, but she wasn't crying so he decided not to disturb her. She'd be fine. They'd be fine.

— ✦ —

Carefully, precisely, Darlene arranged her clean laundry—left corner to the right, drape and fold. The house was quiet, and Dave appreciated the silence as he checked the Net to see how his investments were doing. They were in good shape if they wanted to take that cruise.

"I'm thinking about Phasing tonight," Darlene said, tucking away another bath towel.

"I don't know, dear," replied Dave, still fixated on the chart detailing long-range financial forecasts. "I think you should give yourself more time after that last episode."

"It's been almost a week," she said, sorting the washcloths from the dishcloths. "Besides, it wasn't that bad."

"That's easy for you to say, dear. You didn't have to deal with you."

"Gosh, Dave. You make me sound like such a terrible person."

"Now, you know that's not what I meant, dear."

Darlene closed the closet door and took the remaining laundry into the bedroom.

"It's just that...can you hear me in there?" asked Dave, raising his voice.

"Yes, dear."

"It's just that I've been reading some new studies about the cumulative effects of Phasing. I think you should be more careful."

"Nonsense," said Darlene, sticking her head around the doorframe. "One week some study says disinfectants are bad for your lungs, the next week a new one says they're the only way to keep the Ebola virus out of your home." She disappeared into the bedroom but kept talking. "You can't believe those silly things. After all, they wouldn't sell Phases at the Jumbomart if they were harmful, would they?"

"I guess not, dear." Dave clicked to a new screen, called up his calculator and did the math. "Our investments are doing well, you know," he said Dave loud enough for his wife to hear. "I've been thinking we should take a vacation."

He waited for a reply but didn't hear anything—not even his wife's "busy sounds," which were ever-present. It seemed she was always trying to keep herself occupied with something. A nice, relaxing VR trip could be just what she needed—to forget.

"What do you think, dear? Would you like to visit Tahiti, or maybe Venice?" Still no response. "What about that new jungle theme park in Vietnam? That looks like fun."

"Did someone say fun?"

Darlene reappeared wearing a sheer crimson nightgown that concealed little of her trim figure and struck a pose in the hallway. Dave looked up from his screen and saw his wife's outfit—or rather, saw her through it.

"Did you hear what I was saying about a vacation?" he asked, switching to another file.

As he studied potential investments, Darlene sashayed seductively over to him. She put her hand on his chest and slowly traced a path down to his belt.

"Darlene, what are you doing? Did you Phase?"

"A Phase a day keeps the doldrums away." She giggled and began kissing his neck.

"That tickles," he said, sounding a tad irritated and attempting to squirm away from her.

But she was having none of that. She spun his chair around and fell into his lap.

"I need you, Dave," she said, smothering him with kisses. "I want you inside me. I love you. I need you. We can try again. We can start over." She rubbed his crotch with her hand and continued to kiss him. "Give it to me. Please, Dave. I need it. We need it. We can make a new—"

"I'm very tired," said Dave, gently trying to fend her off. "Why don't you have a little Orgasmic Ice Cream instead?"

"I don't want ice cream! I want you!" Darlene tore at his belt, yanked his zipper down, and forced her hand inside his pants. "I want you now," she whispered huskily.

"Okay, okay, just let me take a Happy Hard-On first. Alright? Hey! I said wait a minute..."

He had almost settled on Vietnam, even though Darlene had proved less than enthusiastic about the idea of a vacation. He, however, was surer than ever that they needed to get away, enjoy some new experiences together.

He would convince her. They would have a great time and put the past behind them. A fresh start—that's exactly what the doctor ordered.

It was a long walk from the tram, but Dave always enjoyed it after spending most of the day at a desk. He had reached his front walkway when he heard a crash from inside. He slipped in his rush to open the door.

"Dar—"

He couldn't even get her name out before the chaos that was their home immobilized him. Tables overturned, furnishings ripped, garbage thrown helter-skelter, his new wallscreen smashed—it was as if an angry cyclone had been let loose inside. He was dumbstruck.

"Darlene? Darlene, where are you?"

"It was our fault." Darlene calmly walked out of the bedroom, scarlet stains crisscrossing her clothes. In her eyes was the look of a wild animal—ferocious, determined; in her hand, an oversized kitchen knife. "He was only two."

"What's wrong with you? What happened? Are you Phasing?" Dave didn't move. He was still taking in the carnage.

"You know what happened. We both know. We didn't watch him. And now he's gone."

"We didn't know he could open the door. You can't keep blaming yourself."

"I blame both of us!" she yelled, lunging at her husband. He was too stupefied to move, disbelieving until Darlene thrust the wide blade into his chest. "We're both responsible! Both of us!" she kept screaming and stabbing.

Dave fell to the floor into a deepening pool of his own blood. Exhausted by her fury, Darlene collapsed next to him.

"It was our fault," she whispered. "If we'd been more alert, more concerned, Timothy would be alive."

Dave fumbled inside his jacket. He managed to pull out his phone, spilling a packet of Brightlook as he did. His vision was already beginning to blur, but he could see the deep gashes running down Darlene's arms. She lay there, propped awkwardly against him, her head slumped against her chest, her eyelids drooping, like a neglected doll tossed into a corner.

Dave activated the phone, popped two of the spilt pills into his mouth, and called for help. It was going to be okay, he told himself. Everything would be just fine.

One night, when my girlfriend Darlene was rapidly evolving from one mood to another, one task to another, I said something about "The five phases of Darlene" and instantly made a note to myself that it would make a good title for a story. Of course, I had no story to go with it. That note sat in my file cabinet for a couple of years before I pulled it out and wrote "The Five Phases of Darlene." It was the first and only time I've written a story based on a title. It was published by *Aberrant Dreams*, and later translated for the Greek science fiction magazine *Ennea*.

# MOONLIGHT SERENADE

*January 30, 1946*
*Allied Headquarters*
*Paris, France*

"What is it, Captain? I'm very busy."

"Sorry to disturb you, Colonel, but you said you wanted a report as soon as I completed my investigation."

Colonel Washburn searched his desk muttering, "Yes, yes, I'll read your report as soon as you've filed it."

Captain Mercer didn't move. He was hesitant to annoy his superior officer when the man was so obviously distracted by other concerns, but he was convinced it was necessary.

"Pardon me, sir, but I know the directive for this investigation came from the top, and I believe you should hear my findings before any official documents are filed."

The colonel looked up at his subordinate for the first time.

"What do you mean? What did your investigation reveal?"

"Well, sir..." Captain Mercer hesitated. He'd rehearsed this but now wasn't certain where to begin.

"Come on, son, I don't have all day. Major Miller's plane went down somewhere over the channel—correct?"

"Well, yes...and no." Mercer cringed at how it sounded.

"What do you mean, yes *and* no? It can't be both, Captain. What *exactly* did your investigation conclude?"

"My investigation reached no single definitive conclusion, sir."

Colonel Washburn sat back in his chair, as if making himself comfortable.

"You'd better explain yourself, Captain."

Mercer took a breath.

"Colonel, I was unable to conclude, with any certainty, what happened to Major Anton Glenn Miller because of the number of conflicting reports."

Colonel Washburn just stared, waiting for him to go on.

"It's been assumed Major Miller took off from Twinwood Airfield on December fifteenth. However, no flight plan was ever filed, and there is no written record of any such departure.

"Disregarding that for the moment, the most disturbing report I've come across originates from an RAF navigator who says that, while returning from a mission, his bomber jettisoned its unused bombs over the channel, and that he saw one of the bombs hit a small plane. He's certain the plane was a single-engine Norseman, the same kind of plane Major Miller was supposedly aboard.

"The navigator insists the date was December fifteenth. However, the only official document I can find states that a Norseman was lost to a bomb drop on the *sixteenth*. It could have been an entirely different aircraft, or there could be a mistake concerning the dates."

Colonel Washburn stood and looked through the window behind his desk.

"Troubling news, Captain. If we have to report that America's most beloved bandleader was killed by our allies..." The colonel turned back to Mercer. "You said there were conflicting reports."

"Yes, sir. There are several. Despite the fact there is no record of a Norseman landing in Paris on December fifteenth, there are eyewitness reports that Major Miller was seen at a party thrown by General Eisenhower at the Palace of Versailles on December sixteenth."

Colonel Washburn said nothing but seemed to contemplate this as he fiddled with a pencil.

"I've also learned the officer who authorized Miller's flight, and was reportedly aboard the plane, was a Lieutenant-Colonel Norman Baessell, a rather shady character with a reputation for black market dealings. He was known as a reckless operator who ordered his pilots to fly in bad conditions." Mercer cleared his throat. "There are other accounts. One states Miller was accidentally shot by a US Army MP in a Paris brothel. Another says he was shot by a Frenchman who, after being freed from a German prison camp, came home to find Miller in bed with his wife. Still another account—a rumor, really—suggests he was a Nazi spy who met in secret with Gestapo chief Heinrich Himmler."

"Is that it, Captain? Don't you have any *positive* scenarios?"

"There is one more, sir, but it's just hearsay. An infantry officer told his men he found Miller's body outside of Bastogne after the Battle of the Bulge. However, the officer was killed soon after, and no such body was ever identified."

"No tag was recovered?"

"Apparently, Major Miller suffered from a skin condition that prevented him from wearing dog tags."

Washburn grumbled something Mercer couldn't make out and turned to stare at him.

"That's it? That's the sum of your findings, Captain?"

"Without going into more detail—yes, sir. To be honest, Colonel, I doubt we'll ever know exactly what happened to Major Miller."

—◦◦◦◦◦—

*December 13, 1944*
*London, England*

He was glad to get the letter from Bing but jealous the crooner was back in the good old US of A. He wished *he* was home. He was proud of what he was doing, even if it was just boosting morale, but he missed Helen and the kids.

His door opened, and his aide, Lieutenant Haynes, stuck his head in.

"Colonel Niven is on his way up, sir. He said he needs to speak with you right away."

"Thanks, Don. Did you get that new arrangement out to the band? I want to be able to surprise Helen on the special holiday broadcast."

"They're already going over it, sir."

"How many times have I told you to knock off that 'sir' crap? I don't remember you ever calling me 'sir' stateside."

"Sorry, Glenn, there are so many sirs around this place it's become a bad habit."

"I know you what you mean," said Miller, taking off his glasses and wiping the lenses with a rag. "I hate all this GI stuff."

"If I didn't know better, I'd think you and the army weren't getting along. You're looking mighty thin these days, Glenn. You've been working too hard. You need to take a break now and then. Let me get you something to eat."

"Just because you used to be my personal manager doesn't mean I need you managing me," barked Miller with a smile. "I'll get something later."

"He's here."

Haynes opened the door, and Colonel Niven walked through, looking every bit as dashing in his uniform as he did in *Dawn Patrol* and *Spitfire*. Although he was a bit of a stuffed shirt, Miller considered him a friend.

The colonel closed the door behind him.

"I've new orders for you, old boy. They come straight from Ike."

"Eisenhower?"

"Yes. You're acquainted, I believe."

"Not really. We met once—briefly. Where are the orders?" Miller asked, hand outstretched.

"Sorry," replied Niven. "Nothing on paper this time. This is strictly secret stuff, Glenn. Unofficial, as it were. *I* don't even know what it's all about. I only know you're to catch the next available flight for Paris. Your cover story, should you be asked, is that you're going over early to complete preparations for your Christmas concert. A Lieutenant-Colonel Norman Baessell at Milton Earnest Hall will arrange your transportation."

"I don't get it, David. What could the Supreme Allied Commander possibly want with me that's so secret?"

"I haven't the foggiest, old man."

—⁓◦≪⟨≫◦⁓—

*December 15, 1944*
*Twinwood Airfield*
*Bedfordshire, England*

"Doesn't look like a very good day to fly," said Haynes, pulling the jeep to a stop.

He was right. It was cold, wet and foggy, and Miller wasn't fond of flying on the best of days.

"You want me to hang around in case they cancel?"

"No, Don. Go ahead and get back. I want you to make sure the band is rehearsing. Colonel Baessell assured me we'd be taking off today. 'Weather be damned' I believe were his exact words."

"All right, then, Glenn. Have a good flight. I'll see you in Paris in about a week."

"See you then."

Despite his nonchalance, Miller *was* worried about the weather. He'd heard someone say all flights were grounded today. His apprehension rose an octave when he saw the plane Colonel Baessell was stepping out of.

"It's only got one engine," said Miller.

"What the hell," responded Baessell, "Lindbergh had only one motor, and he flew clear across the Atlantic. We're only flying to Paris."

"You flying this thing?"

"Nope. I'm just along for the ride. The pilot will be here in a minute."

Baessell picked up one of two cases sitting next to the plane and put it aboard.

"What's that?"

"Empty champagne bottles."

"*Empty* bottles?"

Baessell grabbed the other case. "Bottles are scarce in Paris these days. You can't buy champagne unless you trade in some empties."

"So, is that your only cargo this flight?" asked a fellow in a flight jacket who came up behind Miller.

"I've a got few other baubles," said Baessell. "Here's your pilot, Miller. John Morgan, meet Glenn Miller."

Miller shook hands with the newcomer then put his duffle and trombone case aboard. Morgan slipped right into the pilot's seat and began checking his controls while Baessell buttoned up the plane.

"You sure you want to go up in this soup?" Morgan asked, continuing his pre-flight check.

"Supposed to be clear over the channel," replied Baessell, sliding into the co-pilot's seat. "Besides, only a pansy would let a little rain and fog stop him."

"Baessell, you're as subtle as a loaded forty-five."

Miller took the bucket seat behind Baessell and fastened his belt.

"It *is* awfully nasty weather," he offered. "Maybe we should—"

"Don't sweat it, Major," declared Baessell. "Morgan here's a helluva pilot. Flew thirty-two missions in B-Twenty-fours without a scratch. He's used to weather like this."

Morgan made a noise that was part disgust, part laugh.

"This isn't exactly a Liberator."

Miller looked around. "Where the hell are the parachutes?"

"What's the matter, Miller," jibed Baessell, "do you want to live forever?"

—❧❧—

*December 15, 1944*

He didn't so much wake as become fully conscious of his new surroundings. His terrifying last memories were of panicked shouts and a profound sensation of falling. The plane was going down—that much was clear. Morgan had lost control. Yet he had no memory of the crash, and here he was. But where was *here*?

He was lying on the floor of a small compartment, devoid of furnishings and dimly lit by a source he couldn't determine. His trombone case was next to him but not his duffle bag. He touched his face to see if he was awake—make sure he was real. It seemed so, yet his inner voice was singing off-key, saying it couldn't be. Had he been taken prisoner?

As he stood, an opening appeared in the wall and a man stepped through. He was a small fellow, almost a good foot shorter than Miller's six-foot frame, and his clothes were rather odd. He wasn't wearing any kind of military uniform, Miller was certain of that, but he'd never seen an outfit quite like it.

"Mr. Miller," said the fellow, "I realize you must be experiencing a certain sense of disorientation. But if you will follow me, I will attempt to explain."

He had to stoop, but he followed him through the hatch into a larger compartment. He felt dizzy and readily accepted the stranger's invitation to sit on a cushioned bench. In the background, he caught a glimpse of lights and gauges that made him think of a plane's cockpit yet were unlike anything he'd seen.

"My name is Quay," began the little man, who remained standing. "I know what I am about to tell you will seem strange—maybe even incomprehensible—but I am a traveler in time. I have come here from what would be to you the distant future."

The stranger paused as if to let him absorb what he'd heard.

*The future? A traveler in time? Time travel?*

"Do you mean...?" Miller began, then hesitated. "You mean like H.G. Wells? You have a time machine?"

"Yes," Quay said, raising his hands to signify the hull around them. "This vessel *is* a time machine—and more. Much more than Mr. Wells ever imagined."

"Are you...from Earth, or...?"

"Yes, in a manner of speaking, I *am* from Earth. I am a descendant of terrestrials, of Earth men," said Quay, "but my people, the progeny of this world, no longer live on Terra—Earth, as you call it."

It was all a bit much for Miller. The fellow looked human enough, though Miller couldn't pinpoint his nationality, or his odd accent. He didn't really understand, much less believe, but still he asked, "What are you doing here?"

Quay let out a sigh. "I am, in my world, somewhat of an outcast, Mr. Miller. The reason for this has been my lifelong fascination with ancient forms of music. I have studied and enjoyed everything from classical European symphonies to twenty-first century electro-pop."

"Electro-pop?"

"You will be pleased to know your own music has survived the ages. I have long been enamored of your indelible tunes. My favorite is 'Moonlight Serenade.' Indeed, it is because of my deep affection for your swing music that I am here."

"What do you mean?"

"I am here to save you, Mr. Miller—at least, to save you for my time."

"I don't understand."

"I know this may come as a shock," said Quay, "but by most historical accounts, you died on terrestrial date December fifteenth, nineteen-forty-four, when the small airplane carrying you and two other military officers disappeared over the English Channel."

Miller reconciled what he was being told with what he had already suspected. His plane *did* go down—*was* going down. He wasn't dreaming. Or was he? Was he dead? Was this...?

"Am I dead?"

"No, Mr. Miller, though it is very likely you would have been had I not intervened. Because of that, I have committed a crime—a crime which now brands me an outlaw among my people."

"What do you mean it's very *likely* I'd be dead?"

"Historical accounts of your death are incomplete and in conflict. The only certainty is that after December fifteenth of nineteen forty-four you never again performed with your band, and a few days later all reports of your whereabouts ceased."

Miller shook his head and dropped his face into his hands.

"I understand it must be hard to accept this—to comprehend what I am telling you. Believe me, though, I would not be here if it were not the only way to preserve your genius."

"My genius?" growled Miller, feeling at once both bitter and perplexed.

"My definition," said Quay, "of what you have accomplished—what you can still accomplish."

"So, now what?" asked Miller, still not buying all he was hearing. "I go home with you?"

"Not yet, I am afraid. History must be played out, as inconsistent and paradoxical as it is. I must interfere as little as possible with historical accounts. You must continue on and meet with General Eisenhower."

"I don't get it. If I crashed in the channel, how would I have ever met with Eisenhower?"

"Understandably confusing, but as I said, the accounts of your disappearance vary. It is possible your pilot, at the last moment, was able to recover control of the aircraft and that it never crashed. However, I could not take that chance. My trip through time and space is limited logistically. My access to this craft allows me to be here now, at this time only, and to return—that is all. If I had waited to confirm your demise, I would not have had a second chance. It is very possible you *would* have crashed, and by rescuing you and taking you to meet with Eisenhower, I am responsible for the discordant historical accounts. Such is the paradox of time travel.

"So, we must play out the chronicled accounts, be they authentic or apocryphal."

Miller was still absorbing what he'd heard when he blurted out, "Can I see Helen? Before we go, can I visit my wife and children?"

"I am sorry, Mr. Miller. The constraints of history do not allow for that."

*December 16, 1944*
*Versailles, France*

It was quite a little shindig Eisenhower had thrown to celebrate his promotion to General of the Army. Any other time, Miller would have waded in with both hands. Right now, though, his mind wasn't on celebrating. Too many other concerns dominated his thoughts. Besides, he'd barely made his way into the Palace of Versailles ballroom when one of the general's aides nabbed him.

Now he was on his way to see the newly-christened five-star general with no idea why.

Once inside the general's expansive office he stood at attention and saluted.

"Sit down, Major, sit down," said Eisenhower, not bothering to return his salute.

Miller sat, admiring the overstuffed antique chair the general had designated. It wasn't just the chair. The entire room was decorated like something straight out of the 17th century—which it probably was.

"Major, I have a special assignment for you. A very important assignment. However, it's not your usual bailiwick." The general moved thoughtfully around his massive oak desk. "Here it is in a nutshell, Major. My Ardennes campaign is not going particularly well. Not that we won't win out eventually. Victory is only a matter of time now. But the cost in lives..." His voice trailed off as if he didn't want to think of the numbers. "I want to end this war sooner rather than later. You understand, Major?"

"Yes, sir."

"To that end, we've been in contact with someone in the German high command—Heinrich Himmler. Heard of him? He's the chief of the Gestapo, and he's tight with Hitler. He's gotten word to us that we might be able to broker a peace agreement. He's likely only looking to save his own skin, but if it will spare lives I'm not going to look a gift Nazi in the mouth, if you know what I mean."

Miller nodded.

"This could be our last chance for peace without fighting all the way to Berlin and paying for every inch. So, here's the deal. Apparently, Himmler is a music buff. In particular, I'm told, he's a huge fan of yours. So, I want you to be my representative. I want you to go speak with him, see what he has in mind, see if we can end this thing now."

"Sir? Uh, I mean...I wanted to make a contribution to the war effort, but this..."

"I know this isn't something you've been trained for. However, I believe you're the best man for the job. If the fact that Himmler's a fan can help us at all, then I want to use it."

"Yes, sir. I'll...I'll do my best, sir."

"One more thing. This mission is strictly unofficial. There's no paperwork on it, there'll be no record of it. Only you, myself, my chief aide and the OSS agent who will take you to meet with Himmler know about it. You're not to tell anyone—before or after the fact. No one can ever know I made overtures to the head of the Gestapo. I'd be crucified in the press. You understand?"

"Yes, sir, I understand completely."

*December 18, 1944*
*Basel, Switzerland*

The stranger from the future had not reappeared since leaving him in Paris, and Miller was beginning to think the fellow was an hallucination. Maybe he'd bumped his head during the flight over, and it had affected his mind. Maybe it *had* been just a dream. It had all seemed so real. The odd little fellow Quay had certainly seemed real.

Now he stood in a hotel parlor in Switzerland, waiting for an audience with a member of the German high command. Was this another delusion?

"Herr Miller, it's an honor to meet you." A fellow wearing a crisp SS uniform and glasses not unlike his own strode towards him, hand outstretched in greeting. "I am a devoted follower of your music. I listen to it whenever I get the chance."

The Gestapo chief had an extremely firm handshake.

"I must tell you," continued Himmler, "I especially love that one 'Chattanooga Choo-Choo.' Am I pronouncing that correctly?"

He wasn't, but Miller nodded.

"I admit I need music like some men need women. I'm sure you understand what I mean." Himmler removed his crested military hat. "May I get you a drink?"

"Sure, yes," replied Miller.

"Nietzsche was never more astute than when he said, 'The universe without music would be madness.' Don't you agree, Herr Miller?"

"Well, music is my life." He took the glass handed him.

"I think you'll appreciate this. Even though we no longer hold France, we have access to some excellent French wines. This one's from the Bordeaux region, I believe."

Himmler sipped his drink, and Miller did likewise.

"Ah, but you haven't come here to discuss wine *or* music, have you? You're here as Eisenhower's representative, concerning a proposition I recently made."

"Yes," responded Miller, happy to get on with it. Something about Himmler made his skin crawl. "General Eisenhower would very much like to see the conflict end as soon as possible—saving lives on both sides."

"Yes, yes," Himmler replied in an offhand manner, "however, I'm afraid circumstances have changed since I first contacted your general. I no longer have the Fuehrer's ear. I know Germany is destined to fall—I believe even the Fuehrer knows this, deep in his heart—but he is too willful, too far gone. He will never agree to surrender."

"There's nothing you can do?"

"We can discuss the terms of our capitulation, and the day the Fuehrer no longer breathes, they can be implemented. Until then, I'm afraid the war must run its course."

*December 19, 1944*

"So it was all for nothing. You're from the future, you must have known it was all for nothing."

"Yes, I knew," said Quay. "But history had to be played out. At least the fragments of history as we know them."

"Now what?" Miller wanted to know. "Now what do I have to do?"

"There are no reliable reports, no credible evidence, of you ever being seen again. So now we return to my time. If my breach has been discovered, I will face the appropriate punishment. You, however, will be free to continue making your music."

"I don't want to sound ungrateful, but what if I don't want to go?"

"I am afraid that is not an option, Mr. Miller. Surely, you would not have preferred death?"

Miller thought it over. "No, no, I guess I wouldn't."

"I am glad to hear you say so. If not, then my violation would have been for naught."

"I *would* like to see this future world of yours," said Miller. "And there are so many more arrangements in my head that I never got the chance to put down on paper. You use paper, don't you?"

"You can if you would like."

"But...are you certain I can't visit my family before we—"

Quay's craft rocked suddenly, violently.

"What was that?" asked Miller.

The man from the future scrambled to his controls.

"The time wardens have found me. They are trying to seize control of the ship."

"What will they do?"

Miller saw the first sign of overt emotion in Quay since they'd met. It was fear.

"We must get away. I must get you back before—"

The ship jerked, seemed to accelerate free of whatever was holding it, then plunged. Miller struggled for a hold as the ship appeared to lose power. He saw Quay working frantically to regain control. The sensation of falling swept over him—the same feeling he'd had just days ago. He started to say something, to ask if they were going to crash, but before he could get the words out the ship lurched, then bucked in violent collision.

Consciousness was slow to return. His left arm hurt. He was sure it was broken. He struggled to get up.

The man from the future lay nearby, not moving, his body contorted in an awful way. If he wasn't dead, he was in bad shape. There was an enormous rip in the bottom of the ship, which had come to rest on its side. Miller stooped to a crouch to get through the tear in the hull.

It was night outside and snowing. He stood and got his first look at the craft. In the moonlight it appeared more like an oversized carton of cigarettes than a

89

plane. He wondered how it flew with no wings. However it worked, he doubted it would ever fly again.

An explosion rocked his reverie and sent him diving for cover. His arm squawked in pain. He looked up. It wasn't Quay's ship that had exploded. The burst was several yards in the other direction. Another blast annihilated a tree-top. By the time the ringing faded from his ears, an erratic serenade of gunfire had erupted all around him.

Miller didn't know where he was, but he realized they'd come down in no-man's land. He heard a moan and saw someone lying in the open several yards away. In the dark, he couldn't tell whether the man was ally or enemy but realized the fellow was in a dangerous spot.

Without thinking, he ran to the man, hoping to drag him to safety. All around him, strident bursts of light-arms fire crackled in uneven syncopation. He reached the wounded soldier and bent to grab him with his one good arm. As he did, he heard the cacophony of a machine gun, and felt the bullets rip through him.

From where he lay in the snow he could see the wreckage of the time ship, but the pain made it difficult to keep his eyes open. The sounds of battle continued, although fainter than they had been. The pain, too, soon diminished, replaced by numbness. His vision blurred, so he couldn't be certain, but he thought Quay's ship began to shimmer. He heard the pristine thrumming of a clarinet in C-minor and watched as the ship vanished in a golden flare of light.

*January 30, 1946*
*Allied Headquarters*
*Paris, France*

"There's one more thing, sir."

"Yes, what is it, Captain?"

"I have no evidence it's related to Major Miller, or even that it's anything more than battle fatigue. However, members of a Fourth Infantry Division patrol reported seeing an aircraft of a type they couldn't identify. They described it as box-like, with no wings."

Colonel Washburn made a noise of disbelief.

"No wings? What kind of aircraft doesn't have wings? What does this have to do with the case, anyway?"

"Nothing, sir. Just that this unidentified flying thing was spotted in the same area outside Bastogne where Major Miller's body was allegedly discovered."

The colonel rose from his chair.

"You were right to come to me first, Captain. In two weeks, the brass is going to present a posthumous bronze star to Miller's widow, and the last thing we need is to have this matter confused with conflicting, not to mention embarrassing, reports. You will excise all these baseless rumors from your official report and conclude Major Miller's plane went down somewhere over the English Channel due to unknown reasons. Is that clear?"

"Yes, sir. But what if—"

"No buts, Captain. I want this matter officially closed. Unofficially, I'd say you're right. We'll likely never know the truth of it."

For this tale, I researched the mysterious World War II disappearance of bandleader Glenn Miller. There are many accounts of this event, some fact, some apocryphal, some sheer rumors. I took all that was written about Miller's vanishing act and added a "what if." I sold "Moonlight Serenade" to the first publication I sent it to—*Oceans of the Mind*—the only time that's ever happened to me. Later, it won the Jerry Jazz Musician prize for fiction under the title "Mystery in C Minor." I dedicate this story to the memory of my dad, Robert Bruce Golden, who, like Glenn Miller, served in the Army Air Corps' 8th Air Force. My dad was part of a bomber group that flew B-15s out of England, and his commander was another celebrity—one who would go on to star in the movie *The Glenn Miller Story*—Colonel Jimmy Stewart.

# BLIND FAITH

Fatigue only pushed them onward. Concepts of time diffused in their wake. Hunger atrophied—a hollow thought redressed by expectation.

On and on and on they soared through the comforting cold of liquid space. Above them the great void, below the dense, rocky base of the world, ahead only blackness. Gliding up, then down, the congregation moved as a single entity, graceful behemoths linked by a shared resolve.

But the longer their pilgrimage progressed, the warmer their environs became, the more unorthodox their course seemed. Uneasiness circulated throughout the cluster. At first it was only a feeling, a vague sense of apprehension. Then a solitary voice cried out.

*Let us turn back and make for more temperate currents.*

For the first time since the journey began, their communal purpose wavered. Doubt and indecision spread unspoken.

*We must keep going,* called the master pilot. *Follow me, my brothers. Follow me to a better world.*

*I'm no longer certain,* said another. *Why must we do this?*

*There is no longer a place for us in this world,* said the pilot with authority. *It has been fouled by those with no reverence for the true order of things. We are a spiritual minority wallowing in the swill of a soulless majority. But have faith, brothers. A greater world awaits us—a world so wondrous and bountiful it defies imagination. All you must do is follow me. Follow me through the depths of despair and into the light of never-ending bliss.*

A swell of assent surged through the congregation, and its collective intent was fortified. The master pilot increased his speed, relying on renewed hope to sustain them. Conviction and a shared allegiance drove them on.

*It won't be long now,* he assured them. *When the time comes, do not fear. The threshold to the new world may seem bewildering, even painful. Suppress the pain. Ignore the strangeness of it all. Instead rejoice in what lies ahead. Drink from the pool of righteousness I offer you, and have faith. Above all, have faith.*

Onward they swam, through foreign waters that grew more and more tainted. On and on until the brine tasted of silt and the base of the world grew closer...ever closer. When it was nearly close enough to reach out and touch, misgivings were resurrected. The congregation looked to their leader for guidance. He accelerated. They followed.

With the suddenness of a predatory attack, they broke through the surface of their world into the blinding light of the void. A solid mass clutched their bodies and held them immobile. They struggled desperately to breathe, crushed by their own monstrous weight. The void and its brightness were familiar, but the gritty firmness beneath them was terrifying. Dozens cried out.

*Fear not!* commanded the master pilot. *This is the threshold. Bear witness to the strength of your brothers and trust in that in which you believe. A new world awaits us. Have faith!*

> *Wellfleet, MA* — Frantic efforts to save more than 40 pilot whales that beached themselves on a stretch of Cape Cod sand failed yesterday. Dozens of volunteers tried to keep the small whales wet with buckets of water, and attempted to push some back out to deeper water. However, those that were pushed out returned to the beach with a mysterious single-mindedness. All 46 whales died.
>
> Scientists say pilot whales are highly sociable mammals that travel and feed together in large pods, and have a "follow the leader" social structure. While no one knows exactly why whales beach themselves, it's theorized the animals lose their sense of navigation while feeding or following a sick animal that has gone astray.

> I picked up the newspaper one morning, read yet another article about a group of whales beaching themselves, and wondered "Why?" When one possible answer to that question occurred to me—what if the whales were led by a Jim Jones-like fanatic?—I went straight to my keyboard and wrote "Blind Faith." Originally published in *Odyssey: Adventures in Science* under the title "Faith," it was later reprinted in *Pedestal, Shadowed Realms, A Tangled Script of Intangible Soul Engravings, Anathema*, and the Australian anthology *Book of Shadows*. "Blind Faith" was nominated for the 2010 Phoenix Award for best short story published online.

94

# BLESSÉD

"Go on, now. You go help your brother clean out the barn. It's a fresh Kansas day, and you should be outside."

Mom was always saying that—about it being a "fresh Kansas day." Usually, it was her way of shooing us out of the house. So, I shooed and headed for the barn.

She was right, though. The sun was shining—not too hot yet—and I heard the songbirds greeting the morning. I felt a breeze blowing in from the north meadow and stuck out my tongue to see if I could taste the honeysuckle. Sometimes I thought I could. Today all I tasted was dust.

I looked out to the meadow and saw the reason why. My little brother Noah was there with his wood-carved, duct-taped gun, playing with the Murphy boys from down the road.

Sometimes I wished I was still five so I could play all day. But there were some advantages to being ten, even if I did have to do chores with my older brother Adam.

"There you are," said Adam, pushing a wheelbarrow full of dirty hay out of the barn. "You're supposed to be helping me."

"I'm ready."

He took the red bandanna from around his neck and wiped the sweat from his brow.

"Well, then, as long as you're ready and all, get in there and start raking while I get a fresh bale."

Adam could be bossy at times, but I still liked him. We were best buds, and even though he was already fourteen, he didn't treat me like I was a little kid. He was always nice to me.

I remember the time a few years back when we went to the state fair. He made sure I got to ride all the rides, and he bought me cotton candy with his own money. He even gave me the stuffed lion he won at the shooting gallery. You couldn't ask Jesus for a better big brother.

We did just about everything together, except when he went off with his friends to spy on girls. I thought that was a dumb waste of time. I mean, we had three sisters already, and I couldn't see the sense of spending time watching them cook or sew or braid their corn silk like they were always doing. "Corn silk" was how Mom described our hair—it being almost the same color and all.

I was busy raking when Adam came back with an empty wheelbarrow. He shushed me before I could say a thing and motioned for me to follow him. We crept to the far side of the barn and peeked through the knotholes we used for spying. Uncle Ed and some other men were gathered there with Dad, close enough we could hear them talking.

"...they shot him right there. Right there in the middle of Red Kansas. The Weaver boy—blesséd be him—never had a chance."

"Godless Radans," said Uncle Ed.

I figured they must be talking about Jeff Weaver. I knew him cause he used to make fun of my freckles. He wasn't but maybe a year older than Adam.

Dad spoke up and asked, "What was he doing?"

"Nothing. Well, you know what those boys do, throwing rocks and such."

Dad swiveled his head back and forth like he did when he was contemplating some mischief I'd gotten into.

"No reason to be shooting boys, though. Those Radan invaders are killers—always have been, always will be."

"It won't be the last secular atrocity."

"They got no souls."

"Sinful as devils."

"They *are* devils—the Devil incarnate," added Uncle Ed.

I knew all these men by sight—knew most of them by name. Most hated the Radans even more than Dad—especially Uncle Ed. More than once I heard Dad and Uncle Ed arguing about occupation troops and such. Uncle Ed wanted to kill them all, but Dad wasn't so sure that would help anything, even if it could be done—which he doubted.

"At least the Weavers can rejoice now. Their boy is blesséd."

The men all nodded their heads.

"In God we trust," said Uncle Ed, and they all repeated, "In God we trust."

Of course, Adam and I repeated it, too, but quiet so as they wouldn't hear us.

The men said their byes to Dad, and Adam and I snuck back to other side of the barn where we were supposed to be working. But instead of going right back to work, Adam found his chalk piece and walked to where he kept the names. He didn't say a thing, even though I knew him and Jeff Weaver had been friends since as long as I could remember. He just bent down and scrawled the name at the bottom of the list. It was a long list. He'd been keeping track of the names of all the blesséd he knew—those from nearby farms and from in town.

I didn't know why, exactly, he kept the list, except maybe to remind him. I knew why Jeff Weaver was blesséd now, but I still didn't completely understand why it was such a good thing and all. I mean, he was *dead*.

When I was real little, I used to think everyone was saying "Bless Ed"—meaning my Uncle Ed. But I learned that wasn't what they were saying at all. I learned that *blesséd* was what most everyone wanted to be—at least everyone I knew. I knew that's what Adam wanted. He said it often enough, though he didn't say it around Mom and Dad anymore, cause it got them so upset.

Noah came running into the barn holding his toy rifle. He stopped when he saw Adam looking at the list.

"What happened?"

"The Radans killed Jeff Weaver," said Adam matter-of-factly. "He's blesséd now."

"Is that why we hate the Radans?" asked Noah.

"We hate them cause we've always hated them," said Adam without hesitation.

"Why?"

"Cause they're killers—they're seculars, and they're evil."

"Why are they evil?" asked Noah.

"They just are," replied Adam. "Always have been, always will be. That's why our great-grandpa, blesséd be his name, fought them. So we wouldn't have to be part of their godless country."

"They don't trust in God," I added.

"That's right," said Adam. "They don't believe in the true God. Their ways are sinful. They're the great tempters.

"You've seen their soldiers, Noah. They occupy our land and try to tell us how to live. But we won't let them. We'll die before we let them."

I knew what Adam was saying was true. I'd certainly heard it all my life. But I was never sure it made a whole lot of sense. It certainly didn't seem to agree with what Mom had read us from the Bible. There were all those teachings about peace and love and turning the other cheek.

I guessed it was cause the Radans and all those other seculars didn't know about turning cheeks and such.

⁓⊶⧽⊷⁓

Dad had the TV on, which was unusual. We weren't allowed to watch it unless he had it on, and all he ever watched was the news. We didn't get a very good picture anyways. The only reception we got was from a Radan station, and Dad was always complaining about that.

Usually, he would watch the news until he started talking back to the TV set, and then Mom would turn it off and tell him to calm down.

Rachel, Esther and Grace were in the kitchen helping Mom finish up supper, so us boys settled down to watch the news with Dad. The newsman was talking about another terrorist bombing. That's what the Radans called us—terrorists. But their news reports lied all the time, so we were used to it.

"...five people were killed in the blast, and eleven others injured. No one has yet claimed responsibility for the terrorist act, but authorities believe the suicide bomber was a member of a fanatical wing of the so-called Christian Alliance. A spokesman for the secessionists denied any knowledge of the bombing.

"Elsewhere, a Colorado National Guard convoy was attacked while on routine patrol near Colby, Kansas."

When he said "Colby," that got my attention. Colby was our town, close enough you could walk if you had a couple hours and a mind to. I watched as the TV showed pictures of tanks, armored trucks and such driving down the road, just as a group of ten or fifteen boys popped out of the woods and started throwing rocks at them. I looked real close to see if I recognized anyone, but the picture kept bouncing around. They were all wearing red hats or scarves tied around their arms and such.

"In order to disperse the attackers, the troops fired warning shots. However, one of the assailants was fatally wounded."

I didn't see him, but I figured that must have been Jeff Weaver.

Dad's fist was clenched, and I heard him mutter, "They're just boys."

I knew Dad didn't cotton to violence, but I saw by the way he crinkled his face he wanted to do something to those Radans. What, exactly, he was thinking I couldn't say.

Mom called out from the kitchen, "Turn that off now, Daniel. Supper's ready."

Dad got up from his chair and turned it off.

Like always, Mom had whipped up quite a spread. Corn on the cob, sweet carrots, buttered rolls and fried chicken. I'd helped Adam pick out the chicken, and for the first time he let me cut off the head. Of course, I had to beg him first.

It was different than I thought it would be. I'd seen it done many times, but the actual doing of it made me feel different. Not all grown-up like I thought I'd feel but kind of low.

"Joshua, I believe it's your turn to say grace."

"Okay, Mom."

I put my hands together, bowed my head, and recited, "Dear Lord, hallowed be thy name. Thank you for this food you have laid before us, and thank you for watching over our family. We praise you and exalt the blesséd. May they always be at your side in the Kingdom of Heaven. In God we trust."

Everyone, including my little sister Grace, who'd just begun talking, repeated, "In God we trust."

---

Getting the cows back in the barn was harder sometimes than others. Usually, I just grabbed hold of the rope on old Bathsheba and pulled. She'd come along, and the others would follow.

But today Sheba was being stubborn. She still wanted to graze, but I wanted to say hey to Uncle Ed. He didn't come over often, as his place was on the other side of Colby, but I'd seen him drive up in his old truck and go into the shed with Adam.

"Come on, Sheba, time to go."

I tugged and tugged on the rope, but Sheba wasn't moving. So, I used my secret method. I left her where she was and walked out to the edge of the meadow. I faced the cornfield, cupped my hands and howled liked a coyote.

By the time I finished my second howl, Sheba was already headed for the barn, slow but sure.

After I got the cows all situated I made straight for the shed. It was quiet inside, so I stayed quiet myself, peeking in to see what they were doing.

First I saw the wheelbarrow. It was piled with what looked like junk—nails, broken glass, little rocks, some of Adam's old marbles. Uncle Ed and Adam were busy at the workbench. Adam had an old can he was working with, stuffing in rags and such, and Uncle Ed was mixing some kind of powder. I was about to ask what they were doing, when Uncle Ed looked up and saw me standing there.

"Joshua, you go on now. You don't need to be in here."

"I was just wondering what you were—"

"Go on now," said Uncle Ed in as harsh a voice as I'd ever heard him use. "You get."

So I got. But I was still wondering as I walked away. I couldn't quite figure it out, but I knew I could get Adam to tell me what they were doing if I pestered him enough later on. Right now, since my chores were done, I figured I'd go down to the pond and see if I could catch me some frogs.

⎯❧⎯

"What were you making with Uncle Ed? Was it a birthday present for someone? It's not my birthday, you can tell me."

Adam looked at me as if trying to decide whether he should tell me or not.

"I won't tell anyone—honest."

"You have to promise," he said. "You have to swear on the Bible you won't tell anyone."

"I swear on the Bible," I said, putting my hand up like I'd seen done before.

Adam looked around to make sure no one was nearby, which I thought was silly, cause everyone but Dad was in the house doing their lessons with Mom. Dad was out in the cornfield as usual, so we knew we were alone.

"It's a bomb," said Adam. "Uncle Ed showed me how to make it."

"A bomb?" I said little too loud.

"Shhhh." Adam grabbed my arm and pulled me inside the shed. "Quiet now. Remember you sweared."

"What are you going to do with a bomb?"

"I'm going to kill Radans."

It took a moment for the idea to take root. My brother was planning to kill. I didn't have to ask why he wanted to—he was always talking about wanting to kill Radans. But that was just talk.

I didn't know what to think. The Bible said, "Thou shall not kill"—I was sure of that. Still, I knew there was a lot of killing going on these days. There was even killing *in* the Bible. Some of it done by God Himself. Maybe I didn't understand exactly how it worked.

Before I could ask more, several older boys showed up. They were all wearing their red and were excited about something.

"There's a tank at the crossroad," one of them told Adam. "It's just sitting there."

"It might be out of gas or something," said another.

"Let's go, let's do it."

Adam hesitated, like he wasn't sure. He tugged at the bandanna around his neck, adjusting it.

"Come on, Adam. Go get it."

So, Adam went to the back of the shed, bent down and retrieved something he'd obviously hidden there. It was the same can I'd seen him working on, but I didn't get a good look cause he stuffed it in a burlap bag. I figured it must be the bomb.

"Let's go."

"Can I go?" I asked.

"No," said Adam. "You'll get in trouble."

"So will you."

99

He gave me his look, and I knew there was no use arguing.

"Don't you tell anyone, either," he added. "Remember, you sweared."

I nodded my head, and the boys took off running across the meadow.

Once they were gone, I thought about what might happen. I tried to figure the right and wrong of it. I knew the Radans were evil, but so was killing. I knew what Mom would say, and Dad would probably agree with her. I couldn't tell them anyways, cause I'd sweared. I decided I'd talk with Adam more when he got back. Maybe I could figure it out then.

---

"Your mother wants you to grab a basket and get the eggs out of the henhouse."

I'd been wandering around back of the house, chucking rocks and thinking, when Dad walked up on me.

"Then you get back in the house and get busy with your lessons. I need you and Adam to help me this afternoon. Where is he?"

"I don't know."

"You don't know where your brother is?"

I shook my head, and wanted to look away, but he stared at me with that look he got when he wasn't sure if I was telling the truth.

I swallowed, hoping he didn't notice.

"Well, when you see your brother, you tell him I need him—straight away."

I nodded.

"Go on, then, get those eggs for your mother."

---

Lunch time came and went, and Adam still hadn't come back. I was inside with the others doing my lessons with Mom. Even without seeing him, I knew Dad must be pretty steamed with Adam. I don't know what he was thinking, running off like that in the morning when there was work to be done. He was going to get a tongue-lashing or worse when he got home.

I was deep into reading my Bible, the part in Exodus where God, in his holy wrath, brings the plagues down on Egypt, when I heard some cars pulling up outside. Mom walked out to the porch, and I hurried to the window.

It was Uncle Ed and some other folks I recognized. Dad had walked out to talk with them. Uncle Ed put a hand on Dad's shoulder and said something to him. Dad's head dropped like he was praying. But Dad wasn't one who did a lot of praying—not in public anyway.

Mom walked off the porch and called out, "What is it?"

Dad went to her, said something I couldn't hear, and all of a sudden Mom just collapsed. She almost fell to the ground, but Dad caught her. She looked to me like she'd passed out. Uncle Ed took her from my dad and, along with two of the women, carried her inside.

We stood there watching as they took her into the bedroom. The girls ran in to see what was wrong, but the ladies shooed them out and shut the door.

Dad came in, his face as slack as I'd ever seen it, and white like a clean sheet.

I was almost afraid to say anything, but I managed to blurt out, "What happened, Dad?"

He looked at me, and I saw his eyes were all moist.

"Your brother Adam is blesséd."

He turned and walked back outside.

I don't remember a whole lot about what happened after that. I remember being miserable sad, being angry, feeling all kinds of things. There were too many thoughts bouncing around in my brain for it to be working right. I remember hating Radans more than I ever had, but I also remember thinking that being blesséd wasn't such a good thing. Not if it meant Mom was so sick she couldn't get out of bed and everyone else was crying. Not if it meant Dad was so sorrowful he wouldn't talk for days. Not if it meant I'd never see my brother Adam again, never skip stones with him, never joke around with him.

I knew the blesséd were right up there with God, and that He smiled upon them, but that didn't seem enough—at least right then it didn't. I'd always wanted to be blesséd some day. Heck, we all did. But I didn't know if that's what I wanted anymore. Not if it meant tearing at my family like this.

For the funeral, we all got dressed up, and everyone said lots of nice things about Adam. Our preacher said Adam was with God, that he was among the blesséd, and that his name would forever be hallowed. Mom and Dad stood there looking as proud as could be, but I knew they didn't feel like they looked.

I'd had a couple of days to think about everything, and the more I thought, the madder I got. I wanted to do something, but I didn't know what. I did think of one thing. When the preacher said Adam's name would be hallowed, I knew what I needed to do.

After the preacher was done and they laid Adam in the ground, everyone wanted to say their sorries to Mom and Dad. No one paid much attention to me, so I slipped away to the barn. I found Adam's chalk piece, took a deep breath and added his name to the list. Adam had told me only he was supposed to add names to the list, and I wasn't supposed to touch it. But I figured, now that he was gone, someone had to do it.

I stood there staring at the list for some time. I don't know how long. But I wasn't just standing there. I was thinking—thinking about as hard as I figured any ten-year-old could. I thought so hard it hurt my head.

I was so angry they'd taken my brother away from me I wanted to cry, but I remembered how Adam had made fun of me when I cried, so I didn't. Instead, I closed my eyes and prayed to God, asking Him what I should do.

"Joshua, are you okay?"

I was praying so hard I hadn't heard anyone come up. I turned and saw Uncle Ed. I knew right then that God had been listening in to all my thinking and praying, and that He sent Uncle Ed to me for a reason.

"Are you okay, boy?"

I nodded, and replied, "Uncle Ed, I want you to show me how to make a bomb."

A documentary about the ongoing strife between Israel and Palestine, and the way the children of each nation are passed the hatred from the previous generation was part of the inspiration for this story, as was the current red state/blue state divide in the U.S. At the heart of this turmoil—in both parts of the world—is religion. No surprise there, as most religions have spewed hatred, intolerance, and violence for centuries. "Bles-séd" is published here for the first time.

# GOD KNOWS

I'd been summoned, and this time it wasn't just some archangel with a burr up his wing about something I'd written. It was the Man Himself. I mean the Big Man, the Numero Uno. So, I was walking as fast as I could while trying to keep my feet on the ground and recall what it could possibly be I'd done wrong now.

I figured it was something serious, because I'd never been called before His Omnipotence before, but I had no idea. You never knew when a certain assortment of words, aligned just so, was going to rattle someone's cloud.

The closer I got to His offices, the more the ivory halls shimmered with terrifying celestial incandescence. By the time I heard a voice calling my name, I was nearly blind.

"Mr. Bain. Mr. Bain."

At first I thought the voice was coming from above. (Hey, it happens sometimes.) But the glare dimmed, and I saw a vision. I mean the girl standing there. She was exquisite—a knockout. Dressed simply in a formal white robe trimmed in gold (the prevalent regalia in these parts), blond tresses dancing across her shoulders, and blue eyes that said "come hither" while, at the same time, flashed "keep your distance."

"Mr. Bain."

"Yes, uh, I'm Bain."

"He's waiting. Follow me."

I followed, and was so busy admiring the preliminary view I almost missed the main event. The room was populated by women—gorgeous women, petite women, voluptuous women—women of all hues and ethnic stripes. They were all very busy, quietly going about a variety of tasks only some of which made any sense to me. Most seemed to be involved in long-range communications.

In the middle of all this activity was an average-looking fellow—a bit on the thin side, somewhat large nose, short black hair, noticeably bushy eyebrows. He was wearing what could only be described as pajamas—dark purple satin pajamas. He was sitting in something that was part throne, part easy chair drinking a strawberry margarita.

"Sir," said my escort, "Alex Bain."

"This is him, huh?" He looked me over, and a shiver ran down my spine and through my belly. "Alright then. Thanks, Miriam."

Miriam turned and headed back the way she'd come. I tried to resist the urge to watch her go—I really did—but it was in vain. I literally could not help myself.

"Amazing, isn't she?" He placed His drink on a tray that vanished as quickly as it had appeared. "She was Miss Marshmallow Nineteen-forty-nine. Soft in all the right places, if you know what I mean."

I nodded, managing to wrench my gaze from Miriam's departing derriere.

"I understand you're a writer of some renown, Mr. Bain. Is that true?"

"Well, uh, I guess that's true, sir."

His tone turned serious, and His voice nearly boomed, "I've been told some things about you."

I thought, *Uh-oh, here it comes. Whatever I did, He's not happy about it.*

"It's my understanding you'll say or write just about anything, with no regard to the consequences." His thick eyebrows arched as He said this. "Is this true?"

"Well, I...uh, it's true to an extent. I mean—"

"I've got some things I want to get off my chest. Actually, it's an almost infinite list of things, but I'm going to depend upon your literary skills to keep my thoughts manageable. There seem to be quite a few misunderstandings about what I want, and what I don't want. I'm looking to set the record straight.

"I want to write a book, Mr. Bain, and I want you to help me."

My trepidation did a one-eighty and ran smack into my insecurity.

"What do you think? Are you game?"

"I'd...I'd...I'd be honored, sir."

"Of course you would," He exclaimed, His words echoing in an unearthly way no one else seemed to notice. "But knock off the 'sir' crap. We're going to be working too closely together for that. Call me God—everyone does."

"Yes, sir. I mean, okay, God."

"Great! Can I call you Alex?"

"Yes, of course." I stammered. "When...when did you want to start?"

"Now!" He declared, His voice echoing again. "We're going to get started right now. What do you need? Pencil, pen, typewriter, computer, stenographer?"

"To start with, some sort of recording device would be fine."

No sooner did the word *device* escape my lips than a recorder appeared, along with a chair and a strange-looking dwarf.

"Sit, sit. We're going to be here a while. This is Dweezil, he/she's my publicist-slash-agent-slash-bookkeeper-slash-lawyer. Dweezil's my right-hand hermaphrodite, as it were." He bellowed with laughter, slapping His thigh, as if it were the funniest thing He'd ever heard.

The dwarf, meanwhile, didn't think it was so funny. He/she ignored his/her boss and shoved a fistful of papers in front of me.

"Sign here," he/she directed, handing me a pen.

"What's this?"

"Just a few legal technicalities," said God. "The most of important of which is that you'll be ghostwriting this book. Your name will not appear on the published copy, or in any of the PR. Your work will be subject to a confidentiality clause. I assume that's alright with you."

"Well I've never..." I looked up and saw both God and His dwarf staring sternly at me. "Sure. Of course. It's fine."

"Sign here," said the dwarf again.

I took the pen and signed.

"And here."

"The rest of it's the usual legal mumbo-jumbo about film rights..."

"And here."

"...interplanetary distribution..."

"And here."

"...penalty clauses, that sort of thing."

"And here."

As soon as I signed the last page, the dwarf vanished, along with the paperwork.

God rubbed his hands together. "Okay, where shall we start?"

"Uh, why don't we just free-flow."

"What's that?"

"You just start talking about whatever's on your mind, and I'll ask questions as we go along."

"Sounds great. I like you already, Alex. There's nothing I hate worse than being boxed in by some rigid dogma. I like the sound of it—*free-flow.*

"Okay, first of all, it's true, I am the Alpha and Omega, the beginning and the end, the first and the last. But it's more of a burden than people realize. Don't believe what you might have heard about me. I don't create chaos as a hobby, and I don't have a big ego. I'm way too cool for that. The truth is, though, if I didn't exist, it *would* be necessary to invent me.

"Still, being me isn't as easy it might sound. Sure I'm omnipotent and all that, but being all-knowing and all-seeing isn't always a picnic. Do you have any idea what I see? And if you knew what I knew—well, let's just say I'd have to put you on suicide watch. I've got that whole immortal thing going on, so self-annihilation's not an option for me."

It's safe to say God wasn't exactly what I expected. And it wasn't just me. I doubted He'd fit into any religion's notion of a supreme being. But, so far, I kind of liked the guy.

"I know what you're thinking. But it's not me—I never asked for all that prostrating and praying. I mean, I worship my creator, too. Of course, I'm a self-made man." He chuckled at His own witticism. "But really, think about it. What kind of self-respecting omnipotent being would want that? People dying for me—worse, *killing* for me? Crusades, jihads, it's insane.

"I blame the clergy. Priests, prophets, soothsayers—they all have the ability to pack the largest number of words into the smallest of ideas. Worse, they've decided they know what I want.

"Well, they don't. It's a fraud perpetrated on the masses. Most of their 'divine beliefs' began as just a way for some smart cookie to control others. That's right. Most religions began as power-plays. That evolved into a great majority of humanity doing whatever they think will help them attain nirvana, or get a free pass into Heaven, or Valhalla, or Shangri-La. What they don't understand is that I already gave them paradise—it's called Earth—and instead of making the most of it, they've wasted it, ravaged it, sullied it."

105

No question, this guy had issues. My earlier doubts began to fade. Maybe there *was* a book here. God rants, raves, and spills all. It had possibilities.

"Most men have all the virtues I dislike, and none of the vices I admire. Yeah, Winston Churchill said something like that. I gave it to him."

"Excuse me, sir," said one of His lovely lieutenants, pulling a large video screen into view. "I'm sorry to interrupt, but we've got breaking news."

"What have they broken now, Heather?"

"It seems the United States has invaded Venezuela."

"What? Why in the universe would they do that?"

"Their president says he wants to bring democracy to the people of Venezuela."

"Oh, great, like that worked so well for them last time."

"What are your orders, sir?"

"I'd like a cheeseburger, two tacos, a strawberry shake, and some seasoned curly fries. What about you, Alex?"

"I, uh..."

He waved her away. "I'm not going to get involved with this, Heather."

"This might be a good time to get your thoughts on war," I interjected.

"War? What is it good for? Absolutely nothing. The fact that mankind is inherently violent is one of my biggest failings. Bloodthirsty, territorial, intolerant...I'll tell you one thing that rubs my ass raw. I go to great lengths, stretch my powers to the utmost, to make everybody different. We're talking billions of people here. And what do the vast majority of my minions do? They do everything they can to be like everyone else. By the millions, they dress the same, eat the same crap, and spout identical ideology no matter how inane.

"You know, I could have made everyone look exactly the same, speak the same language, wear the same funny little hats. But no, I went out of my way to give them individuality. And what did they do with it? They put a pillow over its face and smothered it.

"Most of them can't stand it when they find someone who's different. Different color? Hang 'em high. Different nationality? Keep those tanks a-rolling. Different belief system? Crucify 'em. Blame me, I guess. I was way too thrifty with tolerance."

"Isn't there anything you can do about it? After all, you're God."

"You know," He replied, looking at me so seriously a vein swelled across His forehead, "people are always asking why I don't change the world. I'll tell you why. I keep thinking if I just toilet-train it, I'll never have to change it again."

He punctuated His quip by jabbing an elbow in my direction. He was too far away to actually reach me, but I felt it anyway. I was beginning to suspect God was a frustrated comedian. (Which would explain quite a bit.)

"Seriously, how do you *give* someone democracy? Isn't that something you have to strive for yourself? I mean, if you really want it. I'm not so sure it's that great, anyway. Have you seen the kind of politics you get with a democracy?

"I don't get the point of going to all the trouble to reach a position of power if, when you get there, you're no longer yourself. You've sold out to so many special interests, made so many promises, told so many lies, bastardized your own beliefs so much you don't even remember who you are. I mean, why bother?

"Isn't the whole point of power to be able to do what you want to do? To effect change and rule according to your convictions? If you don't have any convictions, if you're not you anymore, then who are you, and what in the slimy fountains of Hades are you trying to accomplish?

"Speaking of slimy, here comes my vertically inconvenienced adjutant."

Indeed, the diminutive hermaphrodite had chosen to use the main entrance this time.

"Hey, Dweezil, I got the results of your IQ test. They were negative."

I felt another jab to my ribs, but Dweezil seemed immune to God's sense of humor.

"Sir, I've just spoken with your publisher," he/she said with a pronounced East Indian accent. "She's upset that you've missed another deadline."

"You see Alex here, don't you? We're working on it, Dweezil, we're working on it. Tell her life isn't always going to throw her fastballs down the middle. No, tell her life is a situation comedy that will never be cancelled. No, no, tell her—"

"I'll take care of it, sir," interrupted the Dwarf as if he/she'd had his/her quota of platitudes for this millennium.

"Before you go, Dweezil, tell Alex your ideas for the book's title."

The dwarf looked at me and said matter-of-factly, "*God Damn It.*"

"*God Damn It*—get it? And what was the other one?"

"*Take This World and Shove It.*"

"*Take This World and Shove It.* I love that one."

"May I go now, sir?"

"Sure, sure, Dweezil. But find yourself a sexy companion of one sort or another. You're always alone, and I worry about the company you keep."

"Oh, ha-ha, that's a good one, sir," he/she responded and vanished.

"Hermaphrodites, you never know whether they're coming or going—even if you're all-knowing"

I took another invisible elbow to the ribs and figured enough was enough.

"God, if you don't mind, I'm developing a bruise."

"Sorry, I get carried away sometimes."

"Why don't you tell me about that? About the times when you've been carried away."

"Well, there was that time with the Egyptians—I was really pissed—and then there was the whole flood thing with Noah."

"Those were actual events?"

He stared at me as if angry I would doubt Him then broke out in a grin and laughed.

"Nah, but they make good copy, don't they? If it's one thing I love about humanity, it's that they know how to spin a good yarn. I did alright with the creative juices, don't you think?"

I nodded but decided to change the subject.

"I notice...I mean, just looking around, it's obvious you have an appreciation for beauty."

His face lit up like a little boy at Christmas. I made a note to ask Him about family holidays.

"Yes, yes, lovely, aren't they? I must say, at times I find it difficult to tear myself away from them. Why, if it wasn't for this book, I'd be appreciating an assortment of feminine charms up close and personal right now."

"So you...you actually engage in sexual relations?"

"Of course I do. You think those little blue pills just fell out of the sky? Sex is my finest creation. How in the name of the seven shopping malls of Hell humanity managed to screw that up, I'll never know. I create this perfectly wonderful, absolutely heavenly means of combining fun and procreation, and they turn it into either a sideshow act or something dirty and shameful. They've even got the nerve to use my name at the forefront of their priggish crusades. As if I would give them passion and then want to punish them for it. It's enough to make a supreme being cry.

"Not everyone has made a travesty of it, though. There are some who get it, like my pal Hef." He winked conspiratorially and added proudly, "I've got a standing invite to the Mansion you know. Have you ever been in the grotto? Now, *that's* divine.

"Speaking of which, I've got my own grotto of sorts. Okay, so I copied Hef's." His attention wandered then, his gaze moving from angel to angel. "All this talk is giving me an itch I need to scratch." He turned and said, "Heather, round up the girls, and tell Miriam it's time for her lunch break. Care to join us, Alex?"

"I uh, well..."

I was debating the pros and cons of engaging in an orgy involving my Creator when Dweezil reappeared, this time in mid-air. He/she had what looked liked bits of tomato splattered on his/her brocaded vest.

"We've got a bit of a crisis situation, sir. It seems Lucifer has rallied her troops again. They're marshaling outside the pearly gates. It's the usual. They're carrying signs, shouting slogans, throwing rotten produce, demanding new housing, better working conditions, equal rights, blah blah blah."

"Damn, Dweezil. You sure know how to take the edge off an erection."

"Shall I dispatch Gabriel and a host of negotiators?"

"No, I'd better handle this personally."

"Are you certain, sir?"

"What can I say, Dweezil, I'm a prisoner of my own charisma."

This sounded like a whole chapter itself.

"I take it you have quite a few problems with Lucifer."

"Yeah. Her buns always were screwed on a little too tight. She and her people just don't seem to get it. I mean, it's Hell, what did they expect?"

"Should I come with you?"

"No, Alex, this could get a little messy. You can review the video later if you think you must. In the meantime, why don't you go over what we've laid down so far, get it in some kind of order—think chapter titles—and come up with some more questions for me. I'm sure Miriam would be glad to help."

He winked and threw another elbow that I tried unsuccessfully to dodge.

"Oh, yeah, I've already got the book's last line written. I figure if someone's reading a book by the Almighty, they're going to want a big finish. I'll leave it to you to figure out how to lead in to it. It goes something like this.

"If you're looking for the key to the universe, I have some good news and some bad news. The bad news is, there is no key to the universe. The good news is, I left it unlocked."

The character of Dweezil originally appeared in the story "Between Iraq and a Hot Place" (page 231), only there he was working for the opposite team.

# MUSEUM PIECE

He could hear the tune—he could almost see its lyrics written capriciously across a saffron-tinted sky—but he couldn't remember its title. It distressed him that he couldn't remember. It nagged at him. Try as he might, he couldn't concentrate. His recollection was an empty slate.

Then, as imperceptibly as it had deserted him, consciousness reasserted itself. The vivid kaleidoscope that was his dream, and the song that scored it, expired. Yet with consciousness came only darkness and silence.

No chirping birds or barking dogs greeted him. He felt the early morning sunlight splash across his face, but he couldn't see it. It was the dull ache of his polyethylene, chrome-cobalt alloy knees and the dryness of his throat that alerted him to the new day's arrival. It had been that way for years—waking not with a bang but with a creak and a whimper, discomfort the daily reminder of his continued existence.

He'd never grown accustomed to regaining consciousness blind and deaf.

As he disengaged from the cobwebs of slumber, awareness gradually returned, and he recalled his place in the universe. For Benjamin Edward Glucorde, that awareness was not wholly gratifying. Although half-forgotten decades had dulled its razor sharpness and diminished its capacity to conceive, his mind was still his. Whether that was a curse or a blessing was a debate his inner voice never fully resolved.

His fingers inched across the cool Lycra sheet until they brushed the familiar texture of the rubberized control pad. The head of the bed began to elevate. With the first upward movement, his optic array activated, revealing daylight in progressively brighter increments. There was, however, nothing incremental about the stiffness in his back. It carped grievously against the change of position, drawing attention away from the complaint emanating from his titanium-plated hips. The pain came and went at its own discretion. He had few body parts that didn't whine and squawk from time to time.

He ignored the pain as best he could. There was little else he could do, since he refused to dull his senses with drugs.

When the bed reached a forty-three-degree angle, his cochlear implants became fully operative. As was often the case, the first sound he heard came from a passing aerocar. Damned flying gewgaws, he thought. They were always swooping over his place like they were on some kind of bloody bombing run. He was almost glad his ears shut down when he slept.

Lately, though, the volume control was all over the place. One moment he could hardly hear a thing, the next he was listening to a gnat walk up the wall.

At exactly seventy-six degrees, the bed halted. Using a technique honed by repetition, he slowly shifted his legs over the side and planted his feet on the carpeted floor. He took a deep breath and started to rub his eyes. He checked himself. There was something about rubbing his eyes he was supposed to remember—something about fracturing the lenses.

Standing required greater effort, but once his weight was equally distributed what he liked to call his "bionic knees" made walking easy, if not pain-free.

He had a sullen agreement with his body—at least what there was left of the original equipment. If it could go about its business without making him look like Mr. Roboto, he would resist the temptation to do the Highland fling.

He hobbled into the kitchen to see if he could find anything other than the Easy-Digest Nutrients swill he'd tried the day before, but the phone chime diverted him. He triggered the display and saw a stern-faced old man dressed in a dark suit. Of course, "old" was a relative term.

"Grandfather, it's me, William. Can you see me? Can you hear me okay?"

It took a few moments before he recognized the face.

"I can see and hear just fine, Billy. What do you want?"

"I know you don't want to hear this, but if you're going to insist on living in that place all alone, I should have some SecureVision cameras installed. That way, if anything happened to—"

"You're not spying on me with no cameras!"

"Not spying, Grandfather. They just alert the medtechs if you fall or—"

"I don't need anyone to babysit me."

"Well, anyway, that's not why I called. I wanted to remind you that Amber is coming to visit you tomorrow."

"Amber? Is that one of my grandkids?"

"No, Grandfather, *I'm* your grandson." There was impatience in his tone only somewhat disguised by a look of concern. "Amber is *my* granddaughter. She's your great-great-granddaughter."

"Oh," Ben muttered, chagrined. "So, you say she's coming to visit?"

"Yes, don't you remember? She's coming to see you tomorrow. And I wish you'd try to talk to her."

"About what?"

"Her mother says she's been spending time with some university extremists, reading prohibited books, that sort of thing."

"Prohibited books?"

"We thought maybe she might listen to you. She's always liked you. She won't listen to her mother or me. Will you do that? Will you talk some sense into her?"

"I'll take her for a ride in my car."

"Your car? Grandfather, that automobile's almost as old as you are. You shouldn't be driving that thing."

"What are you talking about, Billy?" Outrage fortified his voice. "Driving my car's the only thing I got left in this miserable life!"

"That antique is dangerous. You should get rid of it."

"Maybe then you ought to get rid of me, too."

"Grandfather, don't be ridiculous."

"Then don't be a dickhead, boy. I was driving that car before you were toilet-trained, so don't be telling me to trash her like she was some worn-out old shoe."

"All right, we'll talk about it some other time. Just remember that Amber will be there tomorrow."

"I'll remember."

"And, Grandfather, I'm seventy-six years old. Nobody calls me 'Billy' anymore. My name's William."

Ben was still staring at the phone display as it went black.

"You're still little snot-nosed Billy to me," he said to the blank screen.

Grumbling, he made his way with some effort to the side door.

"Thinks he can tell me what to do just because he's an old fart now. Let's see how bossy he is when he's a hundred." The door dilated at his approach. "Talking like a crazy man—get rid of my car. Sure...something's old, it must be useless. Just dump it, replace it, get some newfangled flying thingamajig." He stepped into the garage and the lights came on.

The sight of it calmed him. He stood steadfast, staring. It was a dazzling blue vision trimmed in shimmering chrome and carved with sleek, dynamic lines that conveyed the quality of motion even while it was stationary. Just seeing the old Ford was enough to alleviate the grumpy aftertaste left by the conversation with his grandson.

He limped around to the driver's side, inhaling the lingering scent of oil and exhaust. His fingers trailed across the hood, relishing the cool, soothing metal. So many years together, so many memories. How could his grandson understand? How could anyone understand when they made such a ritual of replacing the old with the new? It didn't matter if the oven still cooked properly, the stereo still sounded good, or the clothes weren't worn. What mattered was that there was always more money to spend—fresh styles, novel gadgets. Toss out the used, buy the up-to-date.

He peered through the driver's window. A strange face stared back at him. It took a moment to recognize his own reflection, disguised as it was by rucked rows of mottled skin and wispy wild strands of white hair. His face reminded him of a shirt that had been left in the hamper too long.

How different he'd looked the first time he gazed through that glass. He'd been a dashing young rogue of forty-something. He could have bought a brand-new car, but he'd chosen this one instead. Already a classic, it had been on the road more than three decades. He picked it because it was like his first car, the one he'd bought with his own money as a teenager. He'd loved that car, too, until he was drafted into the army and had to sell it. When got this one, he vowed never to part with it.

He grasped the chrome handle and pressed the button that opened the door. Not a console pad or touchscreen but a real mechanical button. The immaculate white vinyl beckoned him, but bending down and sliding into the seat was tricky. He managed it, though, resting his hands on the steering wheel.

The hard resin finish was smooth as a woman's thigh. He stroked it lovingly, his hands coming to rest on its chrome centerpiece, where a silver horse galloped ever in place across a red-white-and-blue field.

He pumped the accelerator once, twice, three times then released it—a routine ingrained in him by his father more than a century ago. He turned the key and felt the eight-cylinder beast rear up, its 289-cubic-inch engine roaring through dual exhausts. Twice more he pumped fuel into the four-barrel carburetor. She pulled at the reins then hushed as he lifted his foot and routinely checked the gauges. He needed to order more gas.

The garage door activated, and he drove out into the sunshine.

He could still handle her as long as he didn't push it, his reflexes not being as prompt as they once were. He drove past Cecilia's place. She was outside messing with her plants. She smiled and waved. He gave her a cursory wave back.

The woman had designs on him—he was sure. It didn't seem to matter to her that she was young enough to be his granddaughter. Hell, twenty or thirty years ago he might have taken her up on it and given her the thrill of her life. But now he just humored her because her son was some fancy engineer who liked "antiques," and was the only one Ben knew who could work on the old Ford when some part needed replacing.

He took his usual route, an old paved road that ran down by the sea cliffs and got little use these days. He was glad he lived far from the city proper, teeming as it was with what they called "people-movers" and "urban-cycles"—not to mention all the crazy flying contraptions taking off and landing all over the place. He didn't want to maneuver through those streets. He'd tried it once. It was like being a potato bug in a swarm of bees. No, he was content to cruise his back roads, reveling in the stares he provoked.

She still drove like a dream—smooth, steady, yet with get-up-and-go when he felt like testing her. He was sure she could outrun any of those flying cars...if they stayed grounded, that was.

"Yes, sir, they don't make 'em like this anymore," he said aloud, smiling at his own inanity. "Hold it together, Benny, don't start talking to yourself."

He glanced in his rearview mirror and thought for a moment he saw something. He looked again, but nothing was there. Nothing but an empty road and the hundreds of thousands of miles he'd left behind. That's the way life was, always trailing behind, memories always back there a ways, just beyond the vanishing point.

Off to his left now, far down the cliff wall, was the ocean. It was a balmy day, and the waters were tranquil; he couldn't see a whitecap or a single vessel all the way to the horizon. The only thing that marred the view was a phalanx of rusted old wind turbines, plumbing the depths offshore.

When he decided to turn around and drive for home he noticed the engine was running hot. Worried she might overheat, he babied her the rest of the way. As he approached Cecilia's house, steam sprayed up from under the hood. He stopped, turned off the engine and got out.

It was a struggle to open the hood, and he cursed himself for the decrepit old cripple he was. When he finally pushed it up, a cloud of steam billowed out, scalding his face and forcing him back. He cursed some more, until he tired of it, and started walking. Fortunately, his place was just up the way a bit.

He saw Cecilia as he rounded the corner and tried to call out, but when he opened his mouth nothing but a gurgle came out. He became dizzy, then uncomfortably warm. His optic array began to malfunction. Everything grew blurry.

Panic gripped him. A chill raced through his body. Was this it? Was it finally going to end? Conflicting emotions cascaded and collided—fright, dread of the unknown, regret, acceptance, relief. He'd wished for it more times than he could count. Now that it seemed near, he both feared and welcomed it.

He couldn't breathe. His chest was on fire. He felt himself falling and heard Cecilia scream.

"Benjamin!"

—⟡⟡⟡—

He opened his eyes. He didn't know where he was, but he knew he was alive. He knew because he could feel his body—his old, worn-out body. Anger surged through him. He'd been so close, so ready. Why wasn't he dead? Why wouldn't they let him die?

"Why did you do this to me?" he asked, his voice a hoarse whisper.

"Did you say something, Mr. Glucorde?"

He turned his head and found himself staring up at his doctor—Dr. Hooten, a woman with all the bedside manner of a servodroid.

"How are you feeling, Mr. Glucorde?" she asked without taking her eyes off the various monitors she surveyed. "Can you hear me all right?"

"Why does everyone want to know if I can hear them? Of course I hear you. You don't have to yell."

"I'm not yelling, Mr. Glucorde, but sometimes when the body shuts down like that, it can affect certain implants."

"Shuts down?"

"Yes," she said, turning to look at him for the first time. "That's what happened. One of your artificial kidneys malfunctioned, and when your nano-sensors discovered they couldn't correct the problem, they shut everything down. The trouble is, some of your artificial organs are so old their technology doesn't interface properly with the nanites that now regulate your system. It's like sticking a self-heat packet into an old microwave. They both have the same function, but together they're counterproductive."

"What if I'd been driving? Those damn nano bugs could've got me killed."

A nurse walked in, smiled her nurse-smile at him and handed the doctor a pad.

"Those 'bugs,' as you say, saved your life, Mr. Glucorde," the doctor said as she read the pad. "Besides, you shouldn't be flying. Your medical—"

"I said *driving*, not flying! Are you deaf?"

"You shouldn't be driving, either, Mr. Glucorde." The doctor stood. "Now, we've given you a new kidney, one that will exchange information, if you will, with the dominant nanites. As for your remaining outdated organs, I hesitate to —"

"So, when can I go home?"

"Why, you can go home right now, Mr. Glucorde. Your hearing and vision seem fine, but if you experience any problems with those implants have someone bring you back in. Just promise me no jitterbugging for a week."

"You're a funny lady, Doc," he said as she walked out. "Except the jitterbug was already extinct when I was born."

—⁓◦≼⁍⁌≽◦⁓—

He detested flying—especially the takeoffs and landings—but as the medvan descended he caught a glimpse of her. The sight relaxed him. She was parked out front, looking as resplendent as the day he bought her. Now when, exactly, was that?

He couldn't remember what year it had been, although somehow he could still picture the place. Too bad they didn't have an implant to boost his memory.

He ignored the medtech's dry insistence that they wheel him up to his front door like a sack of potatoes. Instead, he made his own way slowly over to the car. By the time he reached it, the medvan had taken off.

"She's as good as new." It was Cecilia's boy, Steve. "Glad to see you are, too." He opened the hood, and Ben felt a prick of jealousy. "The problem was your water pump, Ben. I don't know how long it was in there, but it was rusted through. Don't worry, though, I fabricated a new one—one that won't rust. I altered the design a little, so it should—"

"I don't want some fancy new pump. I just want the same old kind I've been using for years."

"Sorry, Ben, but they don't make pumps like that anymore. They probably haven't for decades. I don't know where you managed to find the last one."

"Junkyard," Ben replied gruffly.

"Well, anyway, she should drive fine now," Steve said, closing the hood.

"Didn't mean to sound ungrateful. I appreciate all the work you do helping me keep her in shape."

"Don't worry about it. I know she's more to you than just wires and pistons. But I'm afraid I've got some bad news. I've been transferred to our corporate headquarters in Osaka, so I won't be around to help you anymore. I'll miss it. I love working on this old relic. It's probably the only one of its kind still running."

"Yeah," said Ben, "we relics have to stick together."

Steve chuckled and said, "Looks like you've got company."

Ben turned and saw a hovering aerocar.

"I'm going to get going. Best of luck to you, Ben."

"Thanks for all your help, Steve."

The aerocar landed, and both hatches lifted. Out one side popped a little pixie of a girl. She had on a pink-and-white T-shirt and white shorts that revealed skinny legs.

"Grampa Ben!" she screeched and threw her arms around him.

He held on just to keep his balance as she hugged him with puppy-like zeal. She smelled of lilacs, or some kind of flower, he thought. He felt the silky smooth skin of her arms and the soft pressure of her breasts against his stomach. She was a tiny thing, not more than five-two or five-three.

Truthfully, he didn't recognize her. There was something familiar about her—that light-red hair, the slightly upturned nose. He was sure she looked like someone he had once known.

"Amber?"

"It's so swanking to see you again, Grampa Ben."

Someone else emerged from the aerocar—a young fellow carrying two small bags. He was neat and clean, and sort of serious-looking, except half his head was shaved nearly bald, with a tattoo of a featureless mask under the stubble. The other half had a full shock of wavy blond hair. The odd-looking young man stopped a few feet behind Amber.

"Grampa Ben, this is Shon. Shon, this is my great-great-grandfather, Grampa Ben."

"Jell to face with you, Mr. Glucorde," the boy said formally, but even as he spoke, his eyes were drawn to the car. "Scan this, Am. This is swanking," he said, as he circled it. "Must be at least fifty years old—a real museum piece."

"Hmmph! It's a lot older than that, boy. This is a nineteen-sixty-five Ford Mustang."

"You're jacking me? Did you file that, Am? This ob is more than a hundred years old."

"Sure, Grampa Ben's had that forever. I swoon for the color."

"Acapulco Blue," Ben said, and as the words left his mouth he was brushed by a vivid recollection. The woman with the red hair. He remembered now. She'd looked like Amber. How could he have ever forgotten her?

The lapse angered him. Through the disgust with his faulty memory he saw her clearly now. He recalled the time he'd taken the car to have it painted, and how she'd insisted on that color because its designation reminded her of their trip to Mexico. From then on, it was never just "blue." It was the blue-blue of the clear blue water off the beaches of Acapulco.

"Does it actually pow' up?" Shon reached out and tentatively touched the car as if its metal skin might come to life.

"If you mean does she go—damn straight!" Ben growled, his fragile reminiscence shattered. "She'll blow the Turtle Wax off that contraption of yours."

"Turtle wax?"

"Yeah, Turtle—oh, never mind. It's fast, boy, real fast."

"You'll have to take us for a ride, Grampa Ben."

"Sure, sure. But right now I've got to go inside and take a nap. Just got myself a brand-new kidney, you know."

—⚜—

From the senseless void where he slept, consciousness returned, and he groped for the control pad. As the bed elevated and his vision and hearing returned on cue, he recalled fragments of a lingering dream.

He was young again. He was running—running as fast as he could. Not chasing or being chased, just running—the sheer freedom of it exhilarating. The dream shifted, and he was driving his car, a young beauty in the passenger seat, her red hair flying wildly in the air stream from the open window. He couldn't see her face, but he remembered her laugh and the engine's sound as it accelerated.

He had felt a chill. A familiar, disturbing sensation of being overcome by cold. It had driven him from his dream and back to reality.

Now he heard another sound—not from the dream, a real sound. The sound of lovemaking. Unmistakable moans of pleasure, labored breathing, a rapturous cry—sounds he had not heard in...he couldn't remember how long it had been. He realized it must be Amber and her fellow.

Why not? They were young, full of life. He wished he still could, but he hadn't for a long time. The drugs were "incompatible" with his nano bugs, and he refused an implant. He imagined that would be as much fun as poking somebody with a stick. Yet he still had the inclination—dry and dusty as it was.

He waited a while after the sounds of passion ceased then made plenty of noise of his own before he came out. He found Amber and Shon sitting at his dining table. They'd made a meal out of what they'd found in his fridge and were going at it with youthful exuberance.

"Hi, sleepyhead." Amber jumped up from her seat and kissed him on the cheek. She was all aglow, bubbling over with enthusiasm. She almost made him feel guilty about being such an old curmudgeon. Almost.

"Are you hungry?" she asked. "I hope you don't mind—we helped ourselves. We were fammed."

"I told you to make yourselves at home, girl, and I meant it."

"It's swank and plenty, Mr. Glucorde," spoke up Shon. "Ease-on and face."

"You kids *are* speaking English, aren't you?"

They both laughed.

"I'll eat later. I'm just going to have some juice. You two go ahead and finish, then I'll take you for that ride I promised."

"Are you sure, Grampa Ben? You'd better eat something."

"Don't be trying to mother me, girl," he said, admonishing her with his finger. "You don't have the wrinkles for it."

The refrigerator door slid open at his touch, and he chose a plastic container. He steadied himself as his vision blurred momentarily. Must not be awake yet, he thought.

"How long you two planning on staying?" he asked as he filled a glass.

"I don't know, Grampa Ben," Amber replied hesitantly. She glanced at Shon with a look that said there was a disagreement. "We haven't decided. We don't want to impose for too long."

"Hell, girl, I don't hardly ever get any visitors. You both stay as long as you like. I'm sure you'll get bored with an old fossil like me long before I get fed up with you." He took a drink from his glass, frowned, and made a noise as if to spit out what he'd swallowed. "Damn! Tastes like metal. They can put a man on Mars, but they can't make a decent glass of lemonade. I don't envy you kids—having to live in this screwed-up world."

"Screwed-up?" asked Amber.

"You know," Ben replied, "messed up, made into a mess, disgusting, like that juice."

"Some of us won't input the mess," Shon said. "We're going to change things."

"*Shon,*" said Amber, censuring him.

"Good for you." Ben poured the remaining juice into the sink. "I was all fired up to change the world when I was your age, too. Yeah, we thought we could stop a war by singing songs and handing out flowers. We found out the hard way the world didn't want to change. Maybe you can do a better job of it."

—❧❦❧—

"This is swanking, Grampa Ben." With the wind playing through her hair, and a big smile on her face, she reminded him of someone. At the moment, though, he couldn't remember who. "I've never gone so fast this close to the ground."

"After all these years, she can still move. It's starting to get a bit chilly, though, we'd better roll up the windows."

"Roll up?"

"Yeah, like this." He cranked the handle on his side until the window closed. Amber followed suit.

"You control this automobile real jell," Shon said from the backseat.

"You mean for an old man, don't you? Well, this car and me, we've been together a long time. I can remember driving her to the Grand Canyon with my son when he was still little, crossing the Hoover Dam late at night when no one was around. It was eerie—like we were the only people left alive in the whole world. Funny how I can remember that, when I can't even recall what I had for dinner last night." He glanced to the side, trying to remember, then capitulated with a shake of his head. "You've heard of the Grand Canyon and Hoover Dam, I suppose?"

"Sure, Grampa Ben, we input a virtual trip last summer."

"Virtual? That's not the same as being there. You need to see it firsthand." Ben paused, lost in thought. "Now, what was I talking about? Oh, yeah. We've got a connection, this car and me." He clutched the gear shift as if to demonstrate. "I can feel by the vibrations of the tires and the surge of the accelerator if everything isn't just right. There's a rhythm to driving her, an awareness. It's like making love. Yes, sir, she's an ode unto herself, and every street's another stanza. Heck, when it's my time to go, I want to be buried in her."

"You're jacking us, aren't you, Mr. Glucorde?"

"I'm as serious as a heart attack."

"Bizarrama."

"Bizarrama? You mean like that half a head of hair you're wearing?"

"That's a political statement," Shon replied quickly, as if the comparison wasn't valid.

"Just what are your politics?" asked Ben, slowing to take a sharp turn.

"We're SADIR, Grampa Ben."

"Sadder than who?"

"No, SADIR," Amber replied. "S-A-D-I-R, Students Against Digital Image Recognition."

"What the hell is that?"

"The Face Recognition System," Shon said. When Ben gave no sign he understood, Shon continued. "They've got SecureCams everywhere—haven't you seen them?"

"I...don't remember. I don't think so. I don't get into the city much. The only camera I've seen is the one the doctor stuck up my ass."

"But you've seen casts, haven't you, Grampa Ben?"

"I don't watch the news anymore. It's a bunch of illiterate, pre-programmed smiley faces spouting politically correct platitudes. Can't stand to listen to it."

"They scan you wherever you go," Shon said, the emotion evident in his voice. "The cameras upload your image, the system contrasts and compares, selects and categorizes. Once you're identified, your movements are codified, your tendencies profiled."

"Big Brother's watching, huh?"

"Privacy deleted," added Amber.

"We're not citizens anymore," said Shon. "We're potential security risks."

"Well, if there's one thing I've learned," said Ben, "it's that complaining about it won't change anything."

"We're going to do more than complain." Shon started to say more, but a look from Amber shut him up. Something passed between them, so Ben didn't pursue it.

Instead, he focused on the road ahead. The steady hum of the engine was the only thing they heard for the next few miles.

Soon Ben found he was having trouble seeing. He thought his vision was blurring again. He eased off the accelerator and noticed the windshield was beginning to fog up. He flipped on the defroster.

"You know, Grampa Ben," Amber said, breaking the silence, "I think it's swank you want to be buried in your Mustang."

—⊸⧉⊸—

"You kids get yourselves something to eat if you want."

He walked to the bathroom to relieve the bloated walnut that was his bladder. As he did, he heard the muffled sounds of an argument. Futilely, he shook his head, trying to kick his implants into a higher gear. Damned super-hearing never worked when he needed it.

When he came out, Amber didn't seem too happy.

"Mr. Glucorde," Shon said, "a friend from the city wants to pow' down and face with us. Is that jell?"

Ben looked at Amber, but she'd turned away.

"Sure, you kids have a party if you want—God knows it's been years since I've been to one of those."

"No parties, Grampa Ben, just one friend. That reminds me, though, I need to face with Grandfather. He's in a swoon for me to come to Grandmother's birthday party."

"Yeah, the old sourpuss told me the same thing."

"He thinks cause my father's dead he can edit me and that I'll just input it. He's certain he files what's jell for me."

"You're not the Lone Ranger, girl. He treats me the same. As if I wasn't already a man of the world when he was just an itch in his daddy's pants. Well, enough rambling. There's the phone over there."

"The phone?"

"Yeah, the telephone. The whatchamacallit—the com display. I'm going to lie down and rest for a while."

He turned for the bedroom, but his left leg didn't turn with him. He almost collapsed.

"Grampa Ben! Are you okay?"

"I'm fine, I'm fine. Sometimes I just move too quick. The old muscles get cranky and freeze up on me. I forget I'm not a young buck of fifty anymore. I'll be okay."

He closed the door behind him and maneuvered himself onto the bed. Before he could lower it, his ears popped, and he heard voices from the next room like they were right next to him.

"...doing fine, Grandfather. He's jell. He even took us for a ride in his old car."

"What do you mean 'us?'"

"A friend's with me."

"Who's this friend?"

"Does it matter, Grandfather?"

"Well, you two better not be bothering your grampa Ben. He shouldn't be out driving that old piece of junk."

"The drive was his idea. And you should know, he wants to be buried in his car when he dies."

"Buried in it? That's crazy."

"I don't think it's so crazy. It's what he wants."

"Do you know what it could cost to buy a plot that large? I don't even know if such a thing would be legal. And even if it was, what would people say? The truth is, I should put him in a full-care facility where—"

Then, as suddenly as his implants had picked up the voices, they were gone, leaving the anger to sour in him like moldy scraps in a drainpipe.

*He's the one who's crazy if he thinks he's putting me in some kind of home.* He didn't care if snot-nosed Billy *was* in his seventies. He was going to take him over his artificial knee the next time he saw him and paddle his ass raw.

—⳥⳥⳥⳥—

When he woke from his nap he found he was hungry, so he ambled into the kitchen to make himself a sandwich. Not your ordinary everyday sandwich. He was going to pile on as much crap as he could find that was suitable for sandwiching. It was going to be a festival of pre-processed meats, pseudo cheeses and vinegar-soaked garnishes the likes of which would give his doctor a stroke.

As he worked on his grand design, he heard voices from the living room. Amber and Shon and another voice he didn't recognize. He continued to put together his meal, but the eavesdropping slowed him.

"...downloaded into the system in under an hour." That was Shon. "Even with backups where the worm can't mode, it'll take days for a system rinse."

"I still say we blow the whole Security Center into microts," said the new voice.

"That's more wank than swank," his great-great-granddaughter replied. "This is supposed to be a nonviolent, symbolic protest. If we start blasting everything, no one will input our message."

"I file. I'm just swooning for an upmode."

"This won't delete it," said Shon. "It'll take multi-tasking to input any real change. For that to click, we have to avoid confinement. That's what's faulty with this plan. Your employ codes can get us in, but even if we get out before auto-security locks down the building, alert mode will have the gops tracking the power signatures of every aerocar in range."

"We can walk it," the other voice replied. "I know a hackshack a few miles from the Security Center where we could pausemode till the gops sign off."

"Miles?" Shon didn't sound hopeful. "The gops are going to wall it off quick-time. We wouldn't make it."

So his great-great-granddaughter was up to her pretty neck in some revolutionary scheme, was she? He didn't know much about this "face recognition" system, but he didn't like the idea of the government spying on its own people. Hell, he'd been incensed when they forced national ID cards on everyone. He'd railed against that, for all the good it had done.

Now little Amber was trying to throw a monkey wrench into the works. Well, good for her. What was a monkey wrench, anyway? He tried but couldn't remember. It didn't matter. What mattered was what Amber was doing.

He got an idea. He would help them with their little plot. He found the notion invigorating. It had been a long time since he'd done anything really foolish—had any real fun. He was long overdue.

Ben walked into the living room carrying his three-inch-thick sandwich on a plate.

"I've got the answer to your problem," he said, sitting gingerly in his favorite seat.

Amber, Shon and another young fellow, coiffured with the same "political statement" as Shon, stared at him with various degrees of surprise.

"I hope we didn't wake you, Grampa Ben."

"Nope. I was in the kitchen making myself this Dagwood, and I overheard you."

"What did you hear?" Shon asked, apprehension tainting his voice.

"You're planning on breaking in somewhere, planting some kind of computer virus, and then breaking out. I assume it has something to do with this SADIR thing of yours, and those cameras you told me about. Am I right?"

"That deletes it!" The newcomer shot out of his chair.

"I think it's great what you're doing. At least, what you're trying to do. It won't do any good in the long run, you know. Despite their unflagging acclaim for freedom, most people don't have the gumption to stand up for it—to accept the risks, to do what it takes to be free." Ben took a bite of his sandwich. "But that doesn't mean I won't help you," he added with his mouth full.

"How can *you* help?" Shon asked.

Amber stood. "Grampa Ben is *not* getting involved!"

"Ease-on a microt, Am. Input what he has to say first."

Amber glared at Shon, but Ben continued.

"As I understand it, the glitch in your plan is the escape. Well I've got three hundred horsepower of getaway car, and no power signature that the...*gops*, as you call them, can trace."

"He's right," Shon said. "We could use the museum piece, and there'd be no way for them to track us."

"I don't file," the other fellow said.

"Mr. Glucorde here has this old gasoline-burning automobile that's still operational."

"Jesus, boy, you make it sound like a toaster. It's a nineteen-sixty-five Mustang with a high performance V-eight engine. And if we're going to be co-conspirators, don't call me Mr. Glucorde. I'm Ben or Benny."

"Grampa Ben, you're not going to do this," Amber said firmly. She turned to Shon. "We'll find another way."

"I program this cell, and I say we let him help." Shon tried to sound authoritative, but Ben noticed how quickly he mellowed when he made eye contact with Amber. "There's no other way, Am."

"He shouldn't be involved."

"Dammit, girl, I sit in this house every day, doing nothing of any substance, stagnating in a swamp of decrepitude and boredom. I'm a hundred and nineteen years old, and my dance card is blank. I don't just want to do this, I *need* to do this."

"It's a swank idea, Am," Shon said. "And with…Ben's help, it should be jell for me to file how to operate the ob."

"Whoa, there! I didn't say anything about that. Nobody drives that car but me. This isn't amateur hour, boy. You're going to need a good wheel man. Hell, you don't think I'm letting you kids have all the fun while I stay home do you?"

"Grampa Ben, you—"

"Amber, you hush now. You're not talking me out of this, so save your breath. Now, what's the plan? I want to see if this little cabal knows what it's doing."

—◦◦◦◦—

It had been a gray day, given life only by intermittent drizzle. Periodically, moonlight stole through the clouds, and everything glistened. When it did, one slender beam of soft white light managed to find its way through the city spires and onto the car's hood. Ben noticed how the water there beaded up in little Acapulco Blue droplets.

He'd been waiting for more than twenty minutes. His hip ached, and a new, sharper pain ran down his left leg. He needed to get up and move around, but he was afraid to. They'd said it would be less than half an hour when they left him there, wearing their rubber masks. He'd thought it was a nice touch, wearing facsimiles of the Homeland Security director's face.

However, the longer he waited, the more he began to doubt the whole scheme. What if something happened to Amber? He'd never hear the end of it from his snot-nosed grandson. But hell, she would have gone and done it anyway—or something equally rash. He convinced himself that at least this way he was here to help.

He looked out his side window and, as he did, caught a glimpse of something that rankled his nerves. Was that a chip in the paint—right next to the mirror? In the dim light, he couldn't tell for sure, but it looked like a scratch. How the hell did that get there?

123

He was about to open the door to take a better look when, out of the raw silence, an alarm shrieked. His heart battered his chest. He reached for the ignition key but didn't turn it. He thought he saw something. Was that them? His eyes blurred. For a moment, he couldn't see a thing. The alarm continued to blare. He started to sweat. His vision cleared, but he still couldn't see them. Where were they? Were they caught? Were they...?

A shadow opened and closed, and three figures hurried towards him. They pulled off their masks as they threw open the passenger door and climbed in.

"Let's mode!" cried Shon.

"Go, Grampa Ben, go!" encouraged Amber.

He started the engine, racing the motor in his anxiety, and pulled it into drive. Again he hit the pedal too hard, and the rear wheels spun and screeched against the wet pavement until they grabbed hold and took off.

"Did you do it? Did it work?" Ben asked.

"The worm is served," replied Shon.

"Watch out!" Amber yelled.

Ben swerved to miss a street-cleaning droid.

"You almost deleted us, old man!" the nameless subversive carped.

"Oh, don't mess your diapers, sonny. I'll get you there."

"Just be careful, Grampa Ben."

Careful wasn't what he was feeling. He felt robust, simultaneously fearless and fearful. He sensed his nano bugs working overtime, pumping out the adrenaline. For the first time in a long time, he felt alive. Careful didn't have a chance.

"There's where we get out!" Shon called.

Ben pulled up next to the designated building.

"Okay, we're just kids out having a swank time now," Shon said, winking at Ben.

They piled out. Amber ran around to the driver's side.

"Thanks, Grampa Ben," she said, kissing him on the cheek. "I won't ever forget what you did for us."

"Ever's a long time," replied Ben. "Even longer for some. You just keep marching to the beat of your own drummer, you hear? Don't take any guff from no one—that includes Shon boy." He paused, studying her face. It was a face he remembered from long ago. A face he had known so well once upon a time. "You know, standing there, your cheeks flushed with excitement, you look just like your great-great-grandmother. *Exactly* like her."

He saw Amber smile but hoped she couldn't see the tears welling up in his eyes.

A light passed over them. Ben looked up to see a pair of airborne searchlights.

"Get going, now. I'll distract them."

He turned the wheel, and his tires screamed for traction. Amber called to him, but he couldn't hear what she said. He had to get going, get that flying bloodhound to follow him. When the searchlight settled on the Ford he hit the accelerator. He figured if he drove like a madman, it would stay with him. But he didn't plan on letting it stay with him for long. He had a few fancy moves left in him. He grinned. It was glorious to be thumbing his nose at the man again.

Tires screeched as he turned sharply—first left, then right. Maneuvering under an overpass, he figured he'd evaded his pursuer. Then he saw another light up ahead. They'd called in reinforcements—good! The more attention he attracted, the less likely they'd bother with Amber.

He turned another corner and accelerated again, hoping to lose the aerocars in the dark of a smaller street. But they didn't shake that easily. They were tracking him somehow.

Amidst the swirl of excitement, he felt something in his chest—a flutter. For a moment, he had trouble breathing. His vision blurred. Not now, he thought, not yet.

He glanced in his mirror. There were even more of them. He'd never lose them all. They swarmed above and all around him like mutant fireflies, targeting him with their pallid, probing lights. He approached the turn. He had to decide. He had to make up his mind now.

He could stop. They'd question him. Probably fine him. Maybe even arrest him for speeding. But they couldn't connect him to the break-in, to the kids. Could they?

Or he could keep going. Take the turnoff and head for the ocean. Ignore the flock of federales overhead. Drive straight to sunrise.

He slowed to make the turn. Gripping the wheel a little too tightly, he accelerated, and as the Mustang roared off, chasing the light of its headlamps, a mishmash of old song lyrics bobbed through the murk of his memory. Something about taking the highway to the end of the night, riding a snake to the lake, and a blue bus. Yes, he remembered now. *The blue bus is calling us. Driver, where you taking us?*

He glanced down at the green glow of the dashboard instruments. The speedometer's toothy grin and the unwinking orbs of the fuel and temp gauges smiled back at him. Then, as if sensing his awareness, a red warning—the oil light. She'd blown a gasket, or worse. He was pushing the old girl too hard. Just a little longer, he coaxed her, just a little farther.

Through the windshield, the first hint of dawn flaunted itself along the horizon, and beneath the illumination he saw the ocean's dark expanse. He could even make out the wind-tossed whitecaps playing along its surface, and the gulls soaring above. He was where he wanted to be.

He was also afraid. That familiar chill coursed through his veins. It reminded him of the pain, the aching complaints, the sameness of the days. He didn't belong anymore. What was left? Let them put him in a home and junk his car? He welcomed the chill. He embraced it. As he did, he dropped the hammer—pressed the accelerator to the floor and rolled down the window to feel the wind rush by. He'd take her with him. Drive into eternity. Let the gods watch with envious eyes as he cruised by.

Downward he drove. Down towards the rocky cliffs. Down a bumpy incline of shallow gullies, through parched weeds, racing towards the precipice.

In one awkward instant, the old steel horse was airborne, graceful as a zephyr. Once a demon of cerulean speed, it began its descent in slow motion, as if resigned to its fate but still not wanting to go. In that split-second of soaring exhilaration, Ben felt something clutch his heart—a burning, ripping pain. As consciousness faded he heard the engine die, its last piston thrust withering to a conclusive silence before man and car drove through the surface and disappeared into the sea.

This story is near to my heart in that it's inspired, in part, by the first car I ever owned as well as the car I've now been driving for more than 25 years—each a 1965 Mustang. (Ben Glucorde is even an anagram for my own moniker.) Another impetus for "Museum Piece" came when my friend Carolyn said I should be buried in my car when I die, and always referred to it as "the Museum Piece." I'm happy to say this story is published here for the first time.

# YEARS LIKE WINE

Big Apple's seed
Westward blown
On wings of rock
And rolls of dough.
Sage fruit
Plucked & pleasured,
Bottled spirits
Moist & measured.
She's now
She's then
A feast
A friend.
Succulent & satisfying
Her years like wine
Sprung from the vine.


Living
Breathing
Breathing—ah yes
Until out of breath.


Sunburst tresses
Disguise in part
Her cloudburst heart
And worried obsolescence.
Monday morning Methuselah
Approaching,
Stumbling
Over a wandering Moses,
A floating Noah,
Ali's thieves
And the winks in a nap.

Merely symbols
Drying mortar
Twenty million minutes
Just life's third quarter.

Are they gone?
Are they lost?
Full the memories
Part the cost.
Refused the rule
To walk the line.
A yearning for
Years like wine.

No antique
This fair torso
The gods' delight
Mere mortal's morsel.

She reaches for the brass ring
And comes away with gold.
A Golden scepter
To ride in night's cold
And drowned in dreams
Foaming hot and wet
Between her legs
Brimming spice.
Pristine legs
Full of life.

A whispered pause
At surrender's sign
Still wanting more
Years like wine.

When a lover bemoaned the fact she was turning forty, I wrote
this ode to both express my feelings and ease her worries. (The
clues are all there—read it again.)

# RITE OF PASSAGE

Cruces stole soundlessly behind the mew tree, his fingerclaws instinctively unsheathing to grip the russet bark. The scent of the poyollo was almost overpowering. He felt the familiar rush of primordial hormones coursing through his body. His heart raced. His ears tilted one way then the other, listening for betraying sounds.

The sun had yet to emerge from the overcast, but time sense told him his father was waiting for him. Before that encounter, however, he needed to consume the anxiety that weighed on him. The thought of what he must do, what he was *expected* to do, was like a parasite gnawing at his psyche. Of late, it seemed as if he could think of nothing else. That's why he was here, in the sanctuary of the wildwood. The raw passion of the hunt would cleanse his mind. A clean kill would calm him.

He slid around the tree and heard a rustle of dead leaves off to his left. He congealed at once, holding a rigid pose as he probed the breeze for evidence of his quarry. It was there, not far to his right—a mother hen. It must have sensed his presence, for it had sent its chicks scurrying into the underbrush. Now it just stood there, motionless, waiting.

Its dim brain reasoning that neither flight nor fight would save it, it instead opted to act as decoy to save its hatchlings. Cruces understood this. It was true to the path of the Great Wheel.

As his muscles tensed for the endgame, his mind leapt to another time—the time of his first hunt. He remembered how his father had instructed him to rein in his fervent desire to strike straightaway, how he had taught him to assess the situation. Which way was the telltale wind blowing? Was his prey aware of his position? Had he judged the speed of his target—a rodinko squirrel—and gauged it against his own? What were its defenses? He recalled his father being stern but encouraging.

He had caught and killed that squirrel, and he couldn't recall ever feeling prouder. His father, however, wouldn't let him wallow in euphoria. He pointed out several flaws in his approach and kill techniques. At the time, Cruces couldn't understand why his father wasn't entirely pleased. But as he grew older, he came to appreciate his father's attention to the little things, and the time he took to hone Cruces' skills.

He had been a remarkable father, one whose love and devotion evaded traditional attempts at concealment.

Cruces eased forward, down on all fours now, careful where he stepped. The poyollo smell beckoned him, instinct cried *Run quickly!* but his intellect held sway. Another step, halt, assess his prey, then another step closer...closer...

The desperate bird suddenly flapped its obsolete wings and ran squawking in fear. Cruces bounded forward and in two full strides caught the poyollo, its neck snapping abruptly in the grip of his powerful jaws.

The exhilaration of the kill invigorated him. He stood upright and thrust his prey into the air above his head, bellowing his triumph in a roar that echoed frighteningly across the mist-shrouded valley.

The razor edge of a single fingerclaw sliced open the bird's plump belly. Cruces felt the warm blood run over his hands. He could smell the tender meat, and for a moment, he considered it, his golden whiskers twitching, the snowy fur on his chin wet with anticipation.

But a moment was all he needed. He dropped his kill, leaving it for the wildwood to consume, and hastened away to meet his father.

Through the pouncemelon vineyards and over the aqueduct, Cruces trotted at a steady pace. It was some distance from his favorite hunting grounds, but he didn't slow until he came to the Fountain of Renewal. There he stopped under the swirling beryl sky for a long drink and a brief rest. The water was crisp, cool against his tongue. He lifted his head and shook the droplets from his whiskers.

He would rather have been hurrying home to see Tabeth, but his father must be attended to first. The notion of seeing his father was always tainted with guilt—guilt that he didn't visit more often. Today he felt certain he knew why his father had summoned him. That was the reason he tarried. He didn't want to hear what his father had to say.

However, he couldn't delay the inevitable. The time would come—maybe it already had. That was what he was afraid of.

Cruces rose from the fountain's parapet and continued, much more deliberate now. He saw a group of children playing hide-and-hunt, and recalled the carefree days of his own youth. The district had been less crowded then, life less complicated. He gazed at the endless tawny arches of the dens he passed. There were so many more than when he was a child.

He approached the Great Library of Palonius, admiring the mammoth bronze statue of the learned warrior as he always did. His father had taken him to the library often when he was young. Books were the old stalker's passion, and he had made certain Cruces knew about his heritage and the accomplishments of his people.

His father's domicile was just the other side of the Great Library, but Cruces found his pace slowing as he drew closer. Again he reminded himself of his duty. The memory of his first hunt resurfaced, along with the recollection of how his father's scent had reassured him when he became disoriented in the wildwood and thought he was lost. His father had always been there for him. He could do no less in return.

130

"I was beginning to think you had not received my summons," said his father as Cruces stepped from the sunlight into the gloom of the den. The familiar aroma of brewing mewleaf tea greeted him. "I am gratified to know you still respond when your elderly father calls."

"You're not that old," replied Cruces.

"I am old enough."

Cruces saw the truth of it, saw how the ravages of time had diminished his father. The once great Onus, his mane now shot with silver-grey, his fingerclaws dull and deformed, his tail tuft drooping in the dust of the floor. The proud, robust father he had once looked up to was now a wizened figure barely strong enough to cross the room.

"The essence of the hunt hangs upon you, my son. How was it?"

"Satisfying, Father."

"I am certain it was more than that. Do not take for granted these times, Cruces. Glory in your strength, your speed, your skills, your youth." Onus turned and looked longingly at the painting of the wildwood that hung on the wall. That antique artwork had been affixed to the same spot for longer than Cruces could remember. "I miss the hunt more than you can imagine," continued Onus. "Did you eat your kill?"

Cruces squatted on the vermilion laze rug next to the table. The texture of its familiar weave bolstered him.

"No, Father. You know the old ways no longer prevail."

"Yes, so you have said." Onus turned to his son. "However, I know that many young stalkers still consume their prey. Why have you—"

"We've discussed this many times, Father. Do we need to once again? Yes, some conclude their hunts in the traditional way. I choose not to."

Onus didn't reply right away. When he did, he raised his arms in a gesture of futility.

"It is the path on which rolls the Great Wheel, Cruces. No modern thinking will ever change that. But that is not why I have summoned you. I hope, for my sake, you will not turn your back on all of our beliefs."

Cruces made no response.

"The time has come," Onus said flatly.

Cruces stood, avoiding his father's gaze.

"Surely, it's too soon. It can't be time yet," he protested without conviction. "How can you be certain?"

"I know, Cruces. I feel it in my bones. Just as you will some day. Just as you will tell your own son when that day comes."

"It doesn't seem...necessary—not yet. I know it must be done, but..."

"You will not deny me, will you?"

Cruces looked at his father and saw the proud pleading in his rheumy eyes.

"No, Father, I won't deny you. But not now, not today." He turned and hurried to the door. He stopped there, under the arch, looking outside. "I have to go see Tabeth now," he said without turning.

— ❦ —

"...not now, not today."

131

Onus heard the anguish in his son's voice. He watched the taut muscles of Cruces' back ripple beneath his pale fur as he strode to the door and paused there.

"I have to go see Tabeth now."

Then he was gone.

Alone, the tension within Onus seemed to melt away. He had tried to stand tall in his son's presence, but it had required great effort. Now that Cruces was gone, he slumped. Slowly, deliberately, he made his way to the kitchen where his tea was brewing.

Mewleaf tea always revitalized him, helped clear his mind. However, even the tea had its limits. It would not erase the blur that afflicted him when he tried to focus on the pages of his books. It would not turn back the seasons, nor put the spring back in his pounce. It would not change the way his son looked at him now—that look of lament. Onus despised that look.

He remembered how his son had once looked at him—with awe and veneration. On the day of his first hunt, Cruces had listened with respect as he instructed him. The child treated every word as a thing to be cherished. It did not matter that his initial hunt was crudely executed, and culminated in one of the clumsier kills Onus had seen. What mattered was that he had tried his best, and paid close attention when Onus reviewed his flawed technique.

That had been many winters ago. Ages, it seemed. His son no longer cherished his advice. He no longer curled up next to him by the fire. He was grown now, with offspring of his own. The Great Wheel had turned. His lineage would live on. What else mattered?

Only one last thing.

Onus poured the tea and stirred it with a gnarled fingerclaw. Its warmth soothed him.

He looked round the den that had been his home for so long. It had been a good home, a good life. He would stand proudly in front of Leus when the time came for him to be measured.

A chill ran through Cruces as he hurried home under the sunset sky. Leus had already begun His ascent above the horizon, and the songbirds were tuning in preparation of their nightly operetta.

Still several strides from his den, he recognized Tabeth's scent. It served as a balm to ease his agitation. She had proved to be a more than suitable mate, combining the best traits of lover, mother, and spirit guide. He could discuss anything with her, and she was never hesitant about sharing her feelings. But this—this was something with which females had no experience, no communal bond.

She did know Cruces, though, sometimes better than he knew himself. When he entered he could tell she discerned his unease with a single glance. However, all she said was, "The meal will be ready soon. Cronus and Edipeth are anxious to see you."

He found his progeny locked tooth and claw in a playful embrace, rolling this way and that across the floor in mock combat. Their energetic romp reminded him of his own carefree youth. When they became aware of their father's presence, they parted like the contrary poles of a magnet and scampered to him. Their bodies pulsed with joy as they rubbed back and forth against his legs.

He bent down, dug his fingerclaws gently behind their ears, and rubbed their bellies. They were still too young to speak, but their exuberant greeting told Cruces everything he needed to know. They were happy, as offspring should be. The surge of the hunt, the first flush of the kill, the burdens of custom were unknown to them. Some day, though...

Some day Cronus would be faced with the same task that now faced Cruces. Would he stand up to his obligation, obey tradition? Or would he struggle with his duty as Cruces now struggled with his?

"Soon they will be up off all fours and pleading with their father to teach them the path of the Great Wheel."

Tabeth entered the room behind him.

"Too soon," replied Cruces without turning to look at her.

He stood, and the little ones scampered off to continue their play. His mate rested her hands on his shoulders.

"What is it?" she asked. "What troubles you?"

Cruces turned to face her. "My father has informed me the time has come. He stated it simply, as if he were telling me to clean his cup and throw out the old tea bag."

"Is he certain?"

"As certain as that the night will descend when the sun withdraws."

"Then the rite must be carried out."

"You make it sound so easy," said Cruces, moving away.

"Not easy, but a thing that must be done."

"Why?" He turned back to her, his amber eyes imploring. "Why must it be done?"

"Oh, Cruces, you *know* why. Dwelling on it won't change anything. It's our way."

He stared at her, started to speak, to assert his feelings with logic and reason. Instead, he left her without a word and walked outside, letting the night envelop him.

What could she possibly know of such anxiety, he thought. Females were short-lived. Tabeth, and Edipeth like her, would never face such a trial. They were fortunate. Like his own mother, they would die long before age ever conspired against them.

The full face of Leus soared high in the sky, gazing down at him with stern eyes. It was later than he'd realized. Late enough that Leto and Lia had joined their father in His celestial domain, each shimmering with familiar azure light, phased like two halves of the same whole.

For an instant, Cruces wondered if Leto faced the same harsh burden as he then quickly dismissed the profane notion that he could compare his trivial life to that of a deity. He looked up at Leto following his father majestically across the sky and considered the world as it was.

His place in the Great Wheel was so meager as to be insignificant. Why, then, did he persist in magnifying it? That only made his troubles loom larger. His insistence on reasoning had given birth to a hulking, slavering apprehension. Who was he to question the way of the world?

With a sense of clarity, though not completely cleansed of doubt, Cruces went back inside and joined his family for their evening meal.

— ⟨⟩ —

Onus noticed a change in the light as a gray shadow was cast across the floor of his den. He had just finished his morning meal when a figure appeared in the doorway. It was Cruces. He stood, unmoving, under the archway. Onus was not sure if his son was afraid to enter, or simply demonstrating the hunter's patience he had taught him.

"Good day, Cruces."

"Is it, Father?"

Onus shrugged and turned back to his domestic chores. As he moved the dishes and cleaned up the crumbs, his memory came alive with a day similar to this one. A day so long ago he wondered at his ability to recall it.

He was in his own father's house, but his father was not aware of him. His father's awareness had become sporadic. Onus remembered the vacant stare etched upon his father's face. That stare had haunted his dreams for many seasons. He recalled the guilt he'd felt then the resolve. Afterwards, he never forgave himself for his reluctance. He did not want Cruces to suffer the same regret.

— ⟨⟩ —

Cruces watched his father continue to tidy up, cleaning as if it were just another day. The inanity of it made him want to laugh...and cry. He felt like climbing to the peak of the highest butte and roaring in protest. But protest of what, and to whom?

Instead, he remained silent. As he stood under the arch of the entryway, his muscles tensed. Reflex unsheathed his fingerclaws, restraint retracted them. Automatically, he assessed the scene. His father seemed preoccupied, and Cruces had no wish to disturb whatever thoughts he was dwelling on.

He had come here filled with decision, but now his determination wavered like a puffweed in the wind. He had never known his father to falter. Onus had always been strong, fearless. Like the time he had grabbed young Cruces by the scruff of the neck and pulled him from the all-consuming fire that had destroyed his birth home. Had Onus hesitated then, Cruces wouldn't have lived. And he wouldn't be charged with the obligation that now faced him.

"The Great Wheel has turned," said his father abruptly, without pausing his labors. "Have you achieved peace with the wisdom of acceptance?"

"Peace?" replied Cruces. "There's no peace in my heart, no contentment in my soul."

"You must be content with who you are, Cruces—with who we are. Since the time we rose from all fours and achieved the enlightenment of sentient thought, it has been our way. There is a purpose to even the seemingly harshest of traditions."

"A method to our madness, Father?" said Cruces, taking his first two steps into the den.

Onus turned to face his son, anger evident in his twitching whiskers.

"Madness? Madness is what we seek to avoid! Raving loss of reason and insidious decrepitude—that's what you should despise!"

Onus turned, staggered, and leaned against the archway for support. Cruces saw this and took several steps to his father's side. But Onus steadied himself, and Cruces, who had reached out to help, dropped his arms.

Moving with measured restraint, Onus ambled over to one of the many bookcases that lined the den and lovingly ran his fingerclaws over the volumes arrayed there. Calm now, he said, "I fear uselessness, my son. I fear it more than the rodinko squirrel fears the cry of the hunt. More than the sun fears the coming of Leus. I fear the time when I will no longer fear at all, when the blood coursing through my veins quiesces and stagnates."

Cruces had never known his father to be afraid of anything, yet now he could hear the dread, the pleading in his voice. He could smell the cowering uncertainty. He placed his hands on the old stalker's back to comfort him. He felt a slight trembling beneath the grizzled fur. His own heart raced.

"Surely, you would not dishonor your father by allowing him to fall prey to the disgrace of the vacant stare?"

"No, Father, I would not."

Without hesitation then, Cruces threw his left forearm around his father's chest, holding him tightly. He reached across with his right hand, punctured his father's neck with a single fingerclaw and quickly drew it across his throat. The wrinkled flesh yielded readily.

Reflex cried for Onus to resist, but reason maintained control. He relaxed in his son's grasp.

Cruces' own body shuddered with revulsion. He embraced his father with both arms, as much to steady himself as from despair, and held tight as crimson pooled around them.

Coming of age can mean radically different things in different cultures. In this tale, it comprises not only a beginning, but an ending. Set in the same alien world I originally created for my story "The Apocryphist" (on page 259), I've considered constructing a novel around this milieu (it's on a long list of book ideas).

# THE COLOR OF SILENCE

The Southern California sun showered the expansive yard with a welcome late-autumn warmth, while a gentle breeze scarcely bothered the treetops. Uninterrupted blue sky and a well-manicured lawn of green grass framed the picture-perfect day.

A little girl with curly blond hair and a smile as bright as the afternoon stretched out on a lavender blanket next to a floppy-eared cocker spaniel. The dog rested, its panting tongue a testament to its struggle to capture the slobbery ball that lay safely between its paws. The little girl patted the dog's head and chose a new crayon to continue her drawing.

Several yards away, the girl's parents sat apart beneath the shade of a canvas patio umbrella. The mood of their conversation was less relaxed than the setting.

"She seems so happy, so content," said the girl's father, watching his daughter.

"She'll never be content—not like that," responded his wife. "She'll never be able to listen to a symphony or hear the words 'I love you.'"

"Crystal knows we love her, and she knows how to sign the words."

"It's not the same. You know it's not. But it could be…if we try again."

He'd seen that hopeful look on his wife's face before, only to have it dashed with misery.

"It could also be like it was before. Do you want to put her through that again? The bleeding, the dizziness, the pain? You know what Dr. Stiller said about the first implant. Her body rejected it—wouldn't heal around it. He wasn't even sure why, except that maybe her system saw it as an intrusive foreign object. What makes you think it won't happen again?"

"He told me there was another option—a new kind of surgery."

He heard the hope in her voice. Hope salted with desperation.

"And what if it does work? Are you ready for the years of rehabilitation? The time it'll take for her to learn to understand what she hears, to learn to speak?"

"Yes, yes." She was on the verge of tears. "That's why we need to do it now. She's almost four. The longer we wait, the harder it'll be."

Even had Crystal been able to hear her parents, she would have been too preoccupied. She was playing with Rupert. She didn't know his name was "Rupert," although she had learned the sign for *dog*. But she knew Rupert. She knew he liked to chase his ball, as he was doing now.

However, each time he was about to grab the ball, a gust of wind blew it in another direction. First one way, then another. He could never quite catch it. Crystal laughed and clapped her hands in delight at his unshakable determination. She liked playing ball with him.

Her father stood and walked to the edge of the stone-lined patio. He looked at Crystal. He didn't pay any attention to the dog's bizarre, futile chase, but he heard his daughter laugh and saw the joy on her face.

"I don't know, Coral. I just don't know," he said without looking back at his wife. "Maybe her body was trying to tell us something when it rejected the implant. Maybe...maybe sometimes nature composes its own symphony."

Crystal, tired of the "keep away" game, turned her attention back to her drawing, and Rupert finally captured his ball. She found a new crayon and began adding another vivid arc to the rainbow she'd created. She was determined to use as many colors as she could.

—❧—

She knew this place. She knew it and didn't like it. It smelled. Everything was white, and everyone had pretend smiles. When the door they were waiting outside opened, she tried to run away. Her father grabbed her and picked her up.

"I don't know what's wrong with her, Doctor," said her mother. "She's been fussing ever since we got to your office."

"She keeps signing *No*," added her father. "Nothing else, just *No*."

"Here you go, Crystal. How about some sugarless candy?"

Dr. Stiller handed her an orange lollipop. Crystal hesitated, then took the offered treat.

"How is her signing coming along?"

"She has regular lessons, and Ginger, her tutor, says she's doing well, even though she started late. But she doesn't seem to want to sign much," said her father. "At least, not with us. We stopped the sessions after the surgery, and with all the recovery problems she had...well, I think it was hard for her to get started again."

"And what about you two? Are you learning to sign as well?"

"I sit in on her lessons whenever I can," said her mother. "Alan's been too busy."

"I see."

Her father shifted uncomfortably in his seat.

"So, Coral tells me she's talked with you about a new procedure that may work better for Crystal."

"Yes. It's still fairly new, but there's less chance of rejection. We could try another cochlear implant on the left ear, but..." The doctor held up his hands as if he wasn't very optimistic of a better outcome. "However, this new procedure completely bypasses the auditory nerve."

He held up a graphic illustration that was a cutaway of the auditory canal.

Crystal saw it and didn't like it. She didn't like it at all. She climbed down from her father's lap and went to the window. It was sunny outside, but an array of clouds had begun rolling in. They were as dark as her mood.

"Even though the nerve on her right side was damaged when we removed the implant, we could use this technique on that side. We'll still use a tiny microphone behind the ear to pick up sounds, but we bypass the auditory nerve and transfer those sounds straight to the brain stem."

"How successful has this operation been?" asked her father.

"It's only recently advanced from the testing phase, but the results have been excellent, even though the procedure itself is more technically demanding. Of course, I have to tell you, as with the cochlear implant, there's always a chance Crystal may not respond well."

"You mean her body could reject this, too?" Before the doctor could reply, her father continued. "We don't want her to have to go through all that again. It was too much."

"I'm not pushing this on you, Alan. It's a decision you're both going to have to make. But I think the odds of a favorable outcome are good, and certainly out-weigh the risks."

Crystal continued to stare out the window. The sun was gone now, blotted out by a menacing troop of steel-gray clouds. It had even begun to rain. She wanted to go home, where she was happy, where it was sunny, where she could play with Rupert.

"I'll give you some more information to read. Go home and take some time to think about it. We don't want to wait too long, but we don't have to decide this today."

"Are you drawing another picture?" Her mother placed a hand on her shoulder to get her attention. She didn't know how to sign the words but pointed at her eyes and then the drawing. "Can I see?"

Crystal understood. She handed her mother the drawing.

"Is that you?" she asked, pointing at the stick figure with long blond hair. She asked again, pointing at the figure, then at her daughter. "Is this you?"

Crystal didn't respond.

"Is this Rupert? It looks like a dog. Here's a tree, and the sun, and a rainbow. You like rainbows, don't you? There are so many colors in your rainbow. Let me see what colors you have here." She picked up some of the crayons and began reading their names. "You've got Sugar Plum, Yellow Sunshine, Magic Mint, Sky Blue, and even Atomic Tangerine."

Her mother tried to sign something but grew frustrated and gave up.

"I wish you could understand me, Crystal. If only we could talk together."

Crystal looked up and saw tears blooming under her mother's eyes. She held out a finger and caught one. She held it close to her own face, examining it, then stuck her finger in her mouth to taste it.

Still crying, her mother pulled her close and hugged her. Crystal hugged her back and smiled.

Crystal threw the ball, and it rolled until it hit the wood stacked inside the red-brick fireplace. Rupert chased it down, paused to sniff the wood then grabbed the ball and ran back to her. She yanked the ball away from him and threw it again. She laughed as he chased it.

"Are you playing with Rupert?" asked her mother, walking into the room. She knew Crystal couldn't hear her, but she couldn't get out of the habit of trying to talk to her. But soon...

Soon she'd be able to hear everything. After much talking and arguing, and many tears, she and Alan had decided to try the new operation. She'd had to convince him, but in the end, he agreed. Dr. Stiller was right. It was worth the risk.

Crystal saw her and signed something. Her mother tried to remember. Crystal signed again.

"Cold? Are you cold? Alright, I'll go get you a sweater, and then maybe we'll start a nice fire," she said, pointing at the fireplace.

On her way, the doorbell rang. She'd forgotten it was time for Crystal's lessons.

Like Crystal, Ginger had been deaf since birth, but her implant had been successful; and except for an occasional odd inflection in her speech, her impairment wasn't noticeable. That's what Coral wanted for her daughter. She just wanted her to have a normal life.

"She's very talented," said Ginger, looking at one of Crystal's drawings displayed on the fridge. "I've worked with many children, and this is more like the art of a ten or eleven-year-old. Her use of color is very original. She definitely has an artistic side."

"Yes, she loves her box of crayons. But we've got big news, Ginger. Crystal's going in for a new kind of surgery that will help her hear. Isn't that great?"

Ginger looked thoughtful but didn't say anything.

"What's wrong? I would think you, of all people, would be happy for her."

"I am happy for her. I hope with all my heart the operation's a success." Ginger hesitated, then asked, "What does Crystal think about it?"

"Oh, she's too young to understand," said Coral with a dismissive wave.

"There are those within the deaf community who think any child, no matter what age, has the right to choose whether or not to have such surgery," said Ginger. "To them, it's not so much an accident of birth as a variation of life. They believe being deaf is just a different human experience, not a disability."

"That's silly. Of course it's a disability. I'm surprised you'd say such a thing. You had the surgery. Didn't you want it? Aren't you glad you had it?"

"Yes, yes, I'd do it again. I was older than Crystal, but I did want it. I'm not saying it's wrong, but even with the surgery I'm still a deaf person. I'm still dependent upon a device to hear, and I don't hear everything the same way you do. I'm still different. I don't really fit comfortably into either the deaf community or the hearing one. In a way, my implant makes me more of an outsider."

"Well, I think that's nonsense. Who wouldn't want to hear if they could? And Crystal's too young to understand what it will mean for her life. She can't make that decision for herself, even if we were able to explain it to her."

"I guess that's true," said Ginger, although she didn't sound convinced.

"I was just going to get Crystal a sweater. She's in the den, if you want to go in."

Ginger found Crystal curled up next to her dog. They were both lying by the fireplace. Crystal had her head propped on the dog's tummy and was staring into the crackling fire.

Ginger bent down where Crystal could see her and signed as she spoke. "There's nothing like a good fire on a chilly day, is there?"

Crystal signed *Yes* then looked back into the fire. She was trying to pick out all the different colors she recognized within the flames. She had her own name for each and every one.

—⌀⟨⟩⌀—

She didn't know why her parents were so serious, so glum. It was a bright sunny day, and Crystal was happy in the back seat, looking out the rear window. She saw one lonely little cloud in the sky. It almost looked like a dog. She thought of Rupert and subconsciously snapped her fingers—the sign she'd learned for *dog*.

As she stared at the cloud, the wind played with it, moving it, molding it until she was certain it looked exactly like Rupert.

When the car came to a stop she looked around. She wasn't happy anymore. She didn't like this place. She hated it. She was so angry she didn't notice when the wind reshaped her cloud into something unrecognizable—something ugly.

She kept signing *No, No, No,* but her parents only kept moving their lips like they always did. She struggled as her father pulled her out of the car and held her against his shoulder.

"She remembers the hospital," said Alan. "She doesn't want to go inside. I don't know if I can do this, Coral."

"What do you mean? We have to do this."

"She's having a fit. I don't want to force her."

"It's for her own good." Her mother stroked her hair and tried to calm her. "It's okay, darling. It's going to be alright this time."

Crystal was still crying and struggling as they walked into the enormous glass entryway. The farther they went, the more she struggled. She was so upset her body began to tremble.

Tears dampened her father's eyes as he held her in his arms. He wanted to sit and quiet her.

But before he reached the waiting area, the ground beneath him began to move. He could barely keep his balance.

"Earthquake!" someone yelled.

Before anyone could react, the tremor ceased. Still shaken, Alan put Crystal down in a chair and sat next to her. Everyone in the room was buzzing about the quake, some trying to guess its size, as Californians are wont to do.

"My God, that's the last thing we needed." Coral tried to sign *It's okay,* but wasn't sure if she got it right. Crystal stopped crying, but her look of dread didn't fade. "She's so scared."

"We can't blame her. She associates this place with the surgery and all the pain she had afterwards. It's only natural she's scared to be here. Let's give her a few minutes."

"Okay, I'll go check in," said Coral.

"It's going to be alright. No one's going to hurt you." Alan knew Crystal couldn't understand, couldn't even hear him, but he felt like he had to say something. He hoped his contrived smile would calm her.

When her mother returned, Crystal had settled into her chair and stopped crying.

"They're ready for her."

"Alright, Crystal, we're going to get up now." He stood and took her hand, but as soon as they began walking toward the front desk, Crystal began crying again.

The brilliant sunlight filtering through the tinted glass of the entryway faded so abruptly that Alan looked up. A billowing storm cloud swept over them, shuttering the sun and darkening the sky before his eyes. The downpour that followed was instantaneous and emphatic, stridently pelting the glass.

Those who'd been watching the little girl's tantrum glanced up at the sound as a bolt of lightning streaked overhead. They were blinded by the flash. Belatedly, they covered their eyes as thunder exploded in their ears.

Free of her father's grip, Crystal turned and ran toward the exit.

"Crystal!" he yelled, but could barely hear himself. It was only seconds before he could see again, but when he looked around she was gone.

His ears still muffled by the thunder, Alan grabbed Coral's arm and motioned for her to follow him. They ran for the exit, pausing only for the automatic doors. Once outside, their initial panic gave way to wonderment. They stopped in their tracks, rigid with disbelief.

Crystal had run only a short distance away. She was swirling about, almost dancing, looking as if not a single drop of rain had fallen on her. Several yards on either side of her, the rain continued, although diminished, but directly above her the clouds had parted, and yellow sunshine was cascading through.

Crystal twirled around and around, laughing, her arms outstretched toward the heavens and all the colors of the rainbow shimmering there against a backdrop of sky-blue.

Inspired by a writing contest with the theme "The Color of Silence," this story is published here for the first time. (I'm not sure if my entry made it to the judges on time.)

# COMMON TIME

He stepped through the pandemonium of vines and hulking water-rich leaves as if walking on shards of glass, planting each step with caution, straining to see beyond the wall of vegetation. Shadows mocked his imagination. Every gargantuan outgrowth became another monster in his path.

Ignoring the pain as another barbed branch reminded him of the wound in his thigh, he scanned the foliage and listened to the distant but crisp sounds of battle. Through a break in the emerald canopy, he saw a burst of crimson light streak across the cloud-covered sky like the herald of some great storm.

What was he doing here? He, Willie Solman, who used to go out of his way not to step on even a garden snail. What the hell was he doing here, in the astromarines, trying to kill creatures he'd never even seen, except in some grainy vids? It was crazy.

The whole thing was crazy—the hate, the killing, a war over some godforsaken sector of the galaxy. It had nothing to do with him. It was none of his business. At least, it hadn't been until the government dusted off an antiquated conscription act and snatched him away from his life. It was lunacy. He didn't belong here. He belonged back home, on stage at The Bad Penny playing the blues.

Instead, he was...well, he didn't know exactly *where* he was—not where in space, not where on this planet. An ambush had separated him from his platoon. The chaotic images still blazed fiercely in his brain. Blood everywhere, weapons fire punctuated by screams, meaningless shouted commands. Gilmore and Fitzgerald and little Jose all fell with the first blasts, holes burned through flesh and bone. He'd dropped to the ground and covered up at the first sound of attack. Rigid with fear, he didn't move until he heard an order to withdraw. But withdraw where?

So, he crawled, the fighting all around him, crawled over the dead, burnt body of Doc McGee, crawled until he collapsed from exhaustion. He didn't realize he was wounded until later. His first firefight, and he hadn't even taken the safety off. For all he knew, everyone else was dead, and he still hadn't seen one of the things he was supposed to be fighting.

He'd heard stories, though. Stories like the ones Sergeant Bortman told about killing "slugs" on Vega 7. He called it "exterminating." He described their blue-slime blood and hideous features, and how they would eat their own dead. Willie didn't know how much of what Bortman had told them was true, but the stories alone had been enough to make him want to go AWOL. But where could you go in the dead of space?

The tactical com in his helmet had been spitting nothing but static for a while, so he'd switched it off. His visor display was inoperative, as was his GPS. The heft of the M-90 in his hands didn't make him feel any more secure, but at least he'd taken the safety off now. If only he could be sure which way to go. Toward the sounds of combat? Away from them? He wasn't even sure if he could tell which direction the sounds were coming from. But anything was better than just sitting and waiting—waiting for God-knows-what.

Another ragged flicker illuminated the sky, and the ground beneath him trembled with a distant rumble. A moldy stench saturated the air, and Willie's mouth tasted of his own sweat. The humidity clung to him like a second skin, and with each step green mud clutched at his boots as if to pull him down into the bowels of this alien world.

He pushed aside another elephantine leaf with the barrel of his weapon and stretched to step over a rotting log. His thigh was growing numb. He hoped that was a good sign.

Before he could swing his other leg over the log, something lashed out at him. Only a reflex duck prevented him from getting hit. He swung his weapon around, ready to blast whatever it was, and saw a long purplish whip recoil like a party favor. The tendril vanished inside a hulking, frog-like creature the size of a cow and as green as its environs. It had no visible eyes or legs, just a bizarre crown of prickly thorns atop what appeared to be its head. Willie wasn't sure if it was animal, vegetable, or enemy booby trap.

He kept his weapon poised as he edged around it, staying what he hoped was out of range of its tentacle tongue. It made no other movement, and although it was soon behind him, he was now wary of running into one of its cousins.

The distant battle sounds had faded, but that only rendered the pounding of his heart that much louder. He found a relatively dry patch of ground and squatted to rest. He even let his eyes close for a few seconds.

That's when he heard it. His fatigue vanished, and his eyes opened with the alertness fear brings. He didn't move, he just listened. There it was again.

Music!

A hallucination? Had an alien virus infected his wound? They'd been warned of the high risk of infection and delirium. Willie shook his head and listened again. It was still there—distant but real. The strangest-sounding melody he'd ever heard. Light and airy like he imagined the pipes of Pan yet hauntingly sad.

At first it sounded like a flute. Then he could have sworn it was a throaty sax. It reverberated through the jungle, each note creating its own echo. Willie found it both beautiful and bewitching.

He didn't hesitate. He stood and began tracking the sound like he was tracking game back in Louisiana. He was drawn to it—no longer concerned with threat to life and limb. Music was the only thing that still made sense to him, and he didn't care if the devil himself was playing it.

It grew louder, convincing him he was moving in the right direction. When he stepped out of the tangle of thick bush into a small clearing he saw it.

The thing was leaning against a twisted tree and playing a queer-looking instrument shaped like a trio of snakes, intertwined at a single mouthpiece but separating into three distinctly different tubular openings. The instrument's oddity, however, couldn't compete with the thing that played it.

It stood on two legs, manlike, and was even dressed in military garb similar to his own, but that's where the similarity ended. Its face was a discolored, gelatinous mass, given life only by the two bulbous eyes that seemed ready to burst from bloated, quivering cheeks. Even several yards away, Willie could see the veins pulsing through its nearly translucent skin. It had no nose to speak of, but three cavernous nostrils where a nose should have been. The thing was hairless, as far as he could tell, and its mouth was a lipless orifice wrapped obscenely around the base of the instrument.

Willie comprehended all this in the instant he stepped into the clearing—the same instant he froze, paralyzed by fear, enticed by the music.

The same moment the alien thing saw him.

Its own shock was evident. It ceased playing, lowered its instrument and stared. Reality replaced wonderment in a heartbeat, and both soldiers took aim with their weapons.

He was supposed to fire. Willie knew he should squeeze the trigger, get off the first burst and dive for cover. It had been drilled into him over weeks of intensive, shove-it-down-your-throat training. He knew he should fire...

But he didn't. So, he waited, waited for death to flash at him. Yet death never came. The creature held its weapon ready to fire...but didn't.

Willie decided to play the moment for all it was worth. Moving as slowly as he could, he shouldered his weapon. Almost simultaneously, the thing standing across from him lowered its own. They stood looking at each other, examining more closely their dissimilarities.

Willie wanted to speak, to say he hadn't fired because he had no stomach for killing, and because...because of the music. He wanted to ask the creature why it had *not* burned him, and what was that strange instrument called?

Instead, he reached carefully into his shirt pocket. When he pulled out his harmonica, the thing reacted defensively, raising its weapon once more.

Cautiously, Willie lifted the harmonica to his lips and began playing. At the first note, the alien relaxed. It propped its weapon against the tree and listened.

It was a slow, sad blues number that mingled easily with the dreary rain forest, the small clearing contained in it like a living amphitheater. Partway through, Willie stopped, looked at his adversary and grinned.

The alien retrieved its own queer instrument and began the same seductively eerie melody it had played before. Willie was amazed at how the creature's flabby puce fingers squirmed up and down the instrument's shafts as if it were playing some three-dimensional game. Watching the performance, he found his eyes as mesmerized as his ears.

He listened a while longer, trying to decipher the notes, the melody, then joined in with his harmonica. He played softly and tried to follow along. Just as he seemed to be getting it, the alien stopped. Willie stopped, too, and let loose with a big grin. He wasn't sure, but he could have sworn the thing smiled back at him.

The creature took a few plodding steps closer and motioned toward Willie with its triple-pronged instrument. It wanted him to do something. A noise escaped its mouth, but it was gibberish to Willie.

"I haven't a clue what you're saying, bub."

It kept pointing at him as it lumbered closer. Willie realized it wasn't pointing at him but at his harmonica. It held out its own instrument, and then he understood.

As they made the exchange, Willie's hand brushed the creature's, and the clamminess of its skin filled him momentarily with revulsion. The sensation faded as he ran his fingers over the smooth finish of the alien contraption. He couldn't tell if it was made of highly polished wood or some synthetic polymer.

Willie raised it to his lips, hesitated before touching it, then shrugged off the thought and tried to play. The noise that squeaked forth was anything but harmonious. After two audibly painful attempts he stopped. Meanwhile, the alien had fastened its own wide mouth onto the harmonica, but it took several attempts before it made any sound at all. When it finally discovered the proper method, the notes it created made them both laugh. At least it sounded to Willie like the thing was laughing.

Before the echo of their laughter faded, an explosion rocked the jungle clearing and knocked them both to the ground. The alien scrambled to its feet first and headed for its weapon. Stunned, Willie struggled to sit up as an armored juggernaut lumbered through the thick growth and emerged into the clearing. Behind it swarmed a platoon of marines. Like angry insects they opened fire. Blasts of red-yellow heat crackled around the alien in its ungainly dash for cover.

Willie staggered to his feet and looked at his fellow marines through a daze of colliding emotions. Before he could think to call out, the alien disappeared into the bush. Then the jungle exploded in a concussion of shredded leaves and flying mud. The creature's weapon twirled end over end through the air, in dreamlike slow motion within the shower of debris.

"Keep moving! Stay alert, stay close!" The platoon leader added a wave of his arm to his commands and moved in behind the treads of still-rolling vehicle.

Willie stood mute; a stupefied glaze plastered his face. His arms hung limp, his weapon in one hand, the alien instrument in the other.

"Hey! You okay?" A baby-faced marine tried to get his attention. "I said are you okay?"

Willie nodded in the affirmative, and the marine moved on. As quickly as it had stormed the clearing the attack force moved out, the only evidence of its passing the mangled vegetation.

Still standing, still staring off towards the jungle where the alien soldier had disappeared, Willie tried to breach the haze clouding his brain. He lifted the strange instrument in his hand, astonished to discover he still had it. His other hand opened, and his M-90 fell to the mud. With both hands, he raised the queer mouthpiece to his lips and...

...he played. He played it with the familiarity of an old friend. His hands were a pair of hummingbirds that fluttered up and down its shafts. The piece was one of his own creation, a fusion of scalding jazz licks that steamed to a crescendo then cooled and precipitated a more classical interlude. Rising, then falling, then rising again. By the time he had driven the tune to its summit, even the full orchestra backing him had fallen into respectful silence.

He played it like no man had ever played it, because no man ever had. No one else on Earth had an instrument like it. Others made copies after his fame had grown, but no one had come close to duplicating its unique resonance. He was the one man with the one-and-only sound.

The finale came all too soon for the audience. They stood en masse and applauded with fervor. Willie bowed slightly in recognition of their appreciation and blew them a kiss. After six years he'd become accustomed to the adoration—jaded, really. He brushed back his long hair, styled at extravagant prices but graying at the temples, and waved to the audience. Those in the first few rows could see the forced smile he flashed them, but the stage lights washed out the wrinkles.

He backed off-stage with the applause still thundering in his ears and wasted no time heading for his dressing room. Close on his heels was a short, heavyset man who smelled of cigars. He had a hard time keeping pace.

"Great show, Willie," he huffed, "just fabulous. They're going crazy out there."

Passing through the dressing room door, Willie pulled at the tie around his neck. He plopped down in front of his makeup mirror. An older woman handed him a towel and took his tripet.

"You sounded just lovely tonight, Willie," she said as she helped him off with his coat.

"Thanks, Georgeanne."

Willie wiped the perspiration from his face and began unbuttoning his shirt.

"Yeah, they love you, Willie," said the fat man, having caught his breath from the brisk walk. "Listen, you can still hear them. What about an encore?"

"Not tonight, R.J. I got nothing left."

Georgeanne brought Willie a glass of water, and he took a long drink.

There was a knock on the door. A stagehand stuck his head in the room and inquired, "Is he coming out again?"

"No, he's not," Georgeanne told him firmly.

Before retreating the intruder took a quick look at Willie, who offered him no solace.

"That's okay, Willie," said his manager, clapping him on the back, "save it for Sunday. Sunday's the big one. The whole world will be listening. Hell's bells, more than the whole world. You're going to be hooked up to every station and colony in the system. It'll be the biggest show of the decade, or my name isn't Robert Joshua Bottfeld." He pulled out a big cigar, flashed open a platinum-plated lighter and lit up.

No sooner was the cigar smoking away than Georgeanne snatched it from his mouth and extinguished it in the water.

"Not around Willie!" she snapped with a piercing stare.

"Oh, yeah."

Willie ignored the exchange, oblivious to everything but the face that stared back at him from the mirror. Success had put him in that chair, a preposterous kind of success that exceeded his wildest dreams. So, why was that face so sullen? How could he spread so much joy with his music yet find so little himself?

"Guess what, Willie," said R.J., twitching excitedly. "I heard from Dream-Works again today. They still want to do the movie. Did you hear me?"

"Yeah, I heard you. Look, you're a great manager, you've always done me right, but I told you before, I'm a musician, not an actor."

"Hey, for seven mil plus a soundtrack deal you can be ham and eggs on toast!"

"It's not about the money, R.J., it's about the music. You've never understood that."

"I understand all right. I understand you like your limos and your ladies, your house on the Riviera and all your toys. It's always about the money, Willie, and this movie gig will give your lagging music sales the boost they need."

"I'll think about it," replied Willie as if he wouldn't. Before his manager could extend the argument, he changed the subject. "How's your boy, Georgeanne?"

Her matronly smile dissolved into worry.

"Not too good. He heard they're going to start drafting young people into the military again, and he wants to go to school and study engineering."

"Yeah, looks like the government's gearing up for another fight with them slugs," said Bottfeld.

"But there's been no fighting for years," said Willie. "We've got a treaty and —"

"Treaty-shmeaty, those alien bugs are up to no good. Don't you keep up with the news? We should have wiped out every last one of them instead of letting them surrender. Hell's bells, they even let the slimy things on Earth now. Shoot, Willie, you know. You were out there fighting them yourself, back before the treaty."

Willie didn't reply.

"Maybe Georgeanne's boy will go back and finish the job you started. Good riddance, I say."

Georgeanne looked even more worried.

"Willie, do you think...?"

But Willie wasn't listening. He fled to the bathroom, closed the door behind him and stood over the sink.

Another war? More people dying? For what? For territorial rights? For steaming jungle planets? We were more civilized when we just raised our legs and pissed on trees.

He felt bad about Georgeanne's son. The kid probably didn't have any idea what he was in for. Willie knew, though. His own memories were too vivid, too close to the surface.

Still, he couldn't change the past, so why worry about it? Why not enjoy his success? He activated the faucet sensor. He'd made it—he'd made the big time. Did it matter how?

He scrubbed his hands with soap and began splashing water on his face. Call it chance, fate, karma, whatever you wanted—it wasn't his fault, was it? It was time to move on. Regrets were for chumps.

Willie grabbed a towel and wrapped it around his face. He sat on the toilet lid, leaned his head back and tried to empty his mind. He relaxed, endeavoring to unburden himself of all emotion. He needed a rest. Maybe after this next concert he'd take a vacation, no matter what R.J. had planned.

Then he heard it—that song he'd first heard nearly seven years ago. But he didn't hear it so much as it was in his head. Forlorn and ephemeral, the same tune that had called to him in that faraway jungle. He'd never played it himself—he didn't even want to try. But lately he'd been hearing it more and more, until he wasn't sure what was real and what was only a ghostly recollection.

He yanked off the towel and shook his head. He thought of other songs, other instruments. He hoped it would go away. It wasn't his fault. Why was he...?

Then it was gone as suddenly as it began.

Willie exited the bathroom, his hands shaking.

"Are you all right?" asked Georgeanne.

"Yeah, you look a little pale, there," added Bottfeld. "Come on, let's get going to the party."

"I'm not feeling much like a party tonight, R.J., I've got a headache. You go ahead without me. I'm going for a walk to get some air."

"But, Willie, there's going to be—"

Before Bottfeld could even finish, Willie was out the door.

"He's been getting those headaches more and more lately," spoke up Georgeanne, "and nightmares, too."

"Nightmares? What kind of nightmares?"

"I don't know. He won't talk about it. I wonder if it has to do with what you were saying. You know, about when he was in the war."

"That was years ago," said Bottfeld, reaching into his pocket for another cigar. "Why would that start bothering him now?" He lit the cigar and exhaled. "Of course, those damn slugs would give anybody nightmares. It's not enough they've got to invade our part of the galaxy, now they're messing my golden boy's head."

"There's something else," Georgeanne said hesitantly. "I don't know if I should be saying this, but you being his manager and all..."

"What is it?"

"I overheard him once, talking to himself. I think he's hearing things...in his head."

Bottfeld exhaled a large blue-gray cloud and replied with a hint of derision, "Let's hope it's material for a new album."

⌁⌁⌁

It was cold and damp out, but he didn't care. He had wandered into a familiar neighborhood but didn't notice a group of derelicts sizing him up. He also paid no attention to some late-night revelers who ridiculed him for sport. He focused on the bottle in his hand and not much else. He knew how to get rid of uncertainty—drown it.

He'd always thought being rich and famous was the end-all, but now, now that he had more than he needed of both, he wasn't so sure. It had been great at first, but what did it all mean now? Was he happy? Was he satisfied? Damn that tripet anyway. He hadn't asked for it. Now he had it though, and...

He realized too late that thinking about it had been a mistake. The tune that wouldn't let him forget slipped back into his head. It began softly, like a gentle breeze. Steadily, though, it grew, until it was a howling gale lashing his tattered brain. That song, that memory. It was so real.

"No!" screamed Willie, flinging the half-empty bottle against a wall. The shattering glass and his own rage silenced the haunting melody.

He felt exhausted and drunk, but not drunk enough. He looked around, noticing for the first time where he was. He remembered a dive nearby. A place he used to play, long ago, back before it had all gotten out of control. He could go full circle, finish himself off there. The idea appealed to him.

The rest of the night was a drunken haze. Willie recalled a band playing for a while. He remembered them because one guy, a strange-looking dude, was playing the harmonica, and not doing too badly at all. He remembered the guy looking funny because, in addition to a long overcoat and a big floppy hat, he wore gloves. Musicians don't wear gloves, especially harmonica players.

Willie also remembered falling out of his chair and arguing with the waitress over how much more he still should drink. A tip of significant denomination convinced her he was right, but after she brought the drink he didn't want it.

Sometime after the band stopped for a break, Willie passed out. It wasn't until the music started up again that he came to. There was something familiar about the song that woke him. Something...

A chill ran through him. That song, that curse of a melody. At first he thought he was dreaming, because it wasn't just in his head anymore. It wasn't a tripet he heard, it was a harmonica.

He opened his bleary eyes. The harmonica player stood alone onstage, performing that tune that had become a tempest in Willie's head. He listened intently to every note, every inflection, and still couldn't believe his ears. It wasn't possible. It was his imagination.

Determined to know for sure, he got to his feet when the song ended. He could barely focus, let alone walk. He took half a dozen erratic steps toward the stage, collided with someone and went sprawling. Before he knew which way was up, someone had grabbed hold of his shirt and hit him. There was much yelling and confusion. Willie felt himself being pulled away.

"You're out of here, buddy. I don't care how much dough you got."

Willie saw the bartender had come around to help the bouncer restore order. He reached into his pocket and tossed him a wad of bills then looked to the stage. It was empty. The harmonica player was gone.

They hustled him outside and pushed him towards the street. He fell and didn't try to get up. He lay there wondering—wondering what was real and what wasn't, and whether it even mattered anymore.

People poured into the concert hall like the streams from a mountain thaw. Even backstage, Willie found their discordant murmurings deafening. Tripet in hand, he paced his dressing room like a caged animal. He paused to massage his throbbing temples and paced some more.

"Willie-boy, settle down," said Bottfeld when he saw his client's nervous look. "Save it for the show. You know they're going to love you. They always do."

"Yeah, but am *I* going to love me?"

Bottfeld's phone beeped for attention.

"Yeah...What?...Well, make sure security clears him out...All right."

"Problem?" asked Willie.

"Nothing for you to worry about. Security had to chase off some old guy playing his harmonica out by the rear exit near your limo."

"What?"

"Don't get excited. It's no big—hey! Where you going?"

Willie was out the door already. "I'm going for some air."

"Wait!" called Bottfeld. "Hell's bells, don't be too long, Willie. You go on in twenty."

Willie exchanged nods with the security guard at the rear exit and started down the alley. There was another guard next to his limo.

"Do you want me to go with you, Mr. Solman?" said the second man.

"No, thanks, I'm just stretching my legs a minute."

He didn't walk far before he heard it—the phantom song that wouldn't go away. For some reason, though, the sound didn't terrify him anymore. It had become inevitable. He accepted it calmly, like an old friend who came to visit and wouldn't leave.

He continued down the starlit alley, following a tune that wasn't there. Only when it faded away did he stop. He listened, lost because it wasn't there anymore. The silence was filled with uncertainty. Momentarily, he was overwhelmed by apprehension. What should he do? Which...?

Then he heard something else. The very real, very ordinary sound of someone playing the blues.

He didn't have to go far to find the harmonica player, dressed as he had been two nights before. The stranger was half-hidden in the shadows, covered in clothing. Willie couldn't really see the fellow, but he didn't have to.

The stranger stopped playing, and Willie lifted the tripet to his lips. He began the same, slow, sad song the stranger had been playing, stopping after only a few bars. The harmonica player responded in kind.

"It's you," said Willie. "You're alive."

The stranger limped stiff-legged a few steps closer.

"Yes, it is me." The voice had a lisp that wasn't quite human.

"I thought you died on Vega Seven. There was an explosion and then..."

The stranger limped closer, as if to demonstrate his disability, and removed his hat.

"Only part of me died there."

The creased, rubbery features of the alien startled Willie momentarily, even though he knew exactly what hid beneath the hat.

"How did you know where to find me?"

"The great Willie Solman? Who on this planet has not heard of you? Tonight's performance has been well promoted. 'Songs of the Galaxy,' I believe they're billing it." The thing made a sound that was part belch, part cough, then continued. "You have mastered the tripet, as you call it, quite well. Much better than I ever did."

Willie lifted the instrument. "I always wondered what it was really called."

The creature made a weird-sounding noise that welled up from deep inside it.

" *Hgs-doushk.*"

"I don't think I could pronounce that," said Willie. "You know, you haven't done too badly yourself with that mouth organ. I heard you the other night. Those were some mean blues you belted out. I bet you've got quite a following where you come from."

"I am afraid the victors are more tolerant than the defeated," the alien said, then spat and coughed roughly. "After your military drove us off our settlement on *Klidcki-sh*—Vega Seven, you call it—your kind became the scourge of my world's existence."

The alien held up the harmonica.

"Yes, I learned to play it. I was fascinated with it. But my people hated anything remotely connected to humans with a passion I doubt you could understand. Your race, your technology, your culture, your music, even, became an anathema." The creature hesitated, remembering. "The more I played the harmonica, the more of a disgrace I became. I loved the sound, but I had no audience. They tolerated the crazy, wounded 'war hero' only so long, then…"

"How long have you been on Earth?"

"A few years, ever since they began allowing *my* kind here. The reception, for the most part, has not been very warm, but at least here I could play my music. Carnivals, sideshows, roadhouses—I played wherever I could. The locals are never too fond of my staying long, but I have my music, like you have yours…or is it the other way around?"

Willie laughed, and the creature responded until its own unearthly chuckle ended in a vile cough. When the cough subsided Willie held out the tripet.

"I guess this belongs to you."

"Not anymore," the alien said, and held up the harmonica. "After all, it *was* a fair trade." An inhuman smile formed on its quivering face, only to be interrupted by another uncontrollable fit of coughing. It gagged and gasped for air.

"What's wrong? Are you sick?"

"I am dying." It paused for a moment as if composing its inner self and gathering strength. "The greater force of your planet's gravity, its fouled atmosphere, have taken their toll on my life force. That is why I came. I hoped to see you before I—"

Another spasm interrupted, and Willie knew it was fighting for control of its own body.

"Look, I've got more money than I know what to do with. There must be a doctor who can—"

"No, there is no doctor on your world or mine who can alter what is to be. My race recognizes the end when it comes. It is instinctive. We prepare for it."

"It's not right—none of it," said Willie angrily. "I'm sorry I—"

"Do not play the blues for me, Willie Solman. I meet death with no regrets. I lived for my music and shall die for it, as shall you some day. But our music will live on. Maybe, one day, our two races will make music together."

Another wheezing attack staggered the creature. Willie caught it before it fell.

"Willie! There you are."

Willie turned to see Bottfeld huffing down the alley like he was three strides from a heart attack.

"For cripes sake, Willie, hurry up. You're on in thirty seconds."

"Guess what, I'm going to be late. Go tell them I'm on my way. Go on," he said, waving his manager away.

The alien being stood on its own, gesturing to Willie that it was okay. Willie lifted the tripet and tried to sound upbeat.

"Come on. I'll show you how to *really* play this thing."

The creature put its floppy hat back on its head, pulled the collar of its overcoat up closer to its face, and said, "Certainly, for *Cripe's* sake."

The crescendo of applause reached new heights as Willie walked onstage. Smiling to the audience, he put his hands up, pretending their adoration was unexpected. He bowed, held out his tripet to the multitude and encouraged more applause for the instrument.

Then, laughing, he raised his other hand to signal for quiet. The ovation died stubbornly.

"I want to..." he started, then waited for the noise to fade. "Since this concert is titled 'Songs of the Galaxy,' and is being broadcast system-wide, I want to dedicate tonight's music to galactic peace. Peace among all races, all beings."

The call for peace was met by enthusiastic applause.

"Now I've got a special treat for you. Backstage is the musician who gave me my first lesson on this thing," he said, holding up the tripet once more. "Let's bring him out here and see if he remembers how to play it."

Willie clapped to start a polite round of applause and motioned for the creature to join him. It hesitated, pulling its collar up as high as it would go. With Willie still encouraging, and the audience still clapping, the shrouded alien hobbled on stage. Its weather-beaten wardrobe inspired a few chuckles, and Willie heard someone in the audience call out, "It looks like a slug. I think it is!"

He had no doubt the bright lights had revealed his mystery guest's identity to those nearest the stage, and to the cameras feeding the satellite uplinks. He didn't know for sure how they'd react, and he didn't care.

He handed the tripet to the alien, and its gloved hands fondled the instrument with familiarity. Willie gave it an encouraging nod, and the creature began to play.

It played the same seductive melody that had led Willie through the jungle to his encounter with destiny. The same song that had haunted him since that day. Only now, for the first time since then, it was beautiful again—no longer a specter of guilt.

When it came to a natural pause in the piece, the creature reached into its pocket and handed Willie the harmonica. Then, to the audience's delight, and a smattering of applause, they played together. Two musicians, in a world of their own, oblivious to everything but their music...until the sounds of choking brought Willie back to reality.

The alien clutched futilely at its chest, as if trying to rip open its own lungs, as it fell to the stage floor. Its hat rolled off, and a collective gasp rose from those in the audience who hadn't already noticed its inhuman features.

Willie knelt down and cradled the grotesque head in his lap. The thing sputtered and coughed before it was able to speak.

"They liked my music, did they not?"

"You were sensational. They loved you."

The alien handed the tripet to Willie, then held out its gloved hand in expectation. Willie looked unsure, started to ask then realized what it wanted. He handed over the harmonica, and the creature clasped it close to its chest.

"I don't even know your name," said Willie, fighting unexpected tears.

"You could not pronounce it."

"That's a funny-looking case you've got there."

"It's custom-made."

"What you got in there?"

"Just an old instrument."

"Instrument?"

"I have a reservation in the name of Solman."

"Okay, one moment, please." The purser completed his file search, raising his eyebrows in surprise as he did. "You're going all the way to the Outlands?"

"That's right."

"That's dangerous territory, mister, what with them slugs on the warpath. You've got all the necessary permits and travel visas, so I guess you must know what you're getting into. I don't know why you'd want to go way out there, though, unless you've got some kind of death wish."

"Not a death wish. Let's just say I want to see how good I really am, and there's only one place to find out. Can I go aboard now?"

"Yes, sir. Your stateroom has been prepared and personally coded for you. Enjoy your trip."

"Thanks, I will."

Inspired by a short film about an encounter during the Vietnam War, "Common Time" has a rich backstory, beginning in 1986 as a very short piece of fiction. Soon after, I transformed it into a twenty-minute teleplay specifically for Steven Spielberg's television show *Amazing Stories*. Through a minor miracle (by Hollywood standards), I got an agent to read it. He liked it and passed it on the producers of the show. They liked it as well, but before any transaction could be made, *Amazing Stories* was cancelled.

I used the teleplay to write a longer version of the story, and in 1988, I entered it in the L. Ron Hubbard Writers of the Future contest, where it was awarded an honorable mention as a semi-finalist. After that it lay entombed in a drawer until 2003, when I pulled it out, rewrote it with a new ending, and sold it to *Palace of Reason*, where it was published for the first time.

A few years later, I put on some polish, cut some fat, and sold the tale to the British magazine *Farthing*, where it was published in 2006, twenty years after its conception. Since then it has been published in the magazine *Brutarian*, in the Canadian H.G. Wells tribute anthology *War of the Worlds*, translated into Greek for the publication *Ennea*, and translated again for the Romanian almanac of science fiction *Sci-Fi Magazin Almanah*, where it resides alongside stories by Robert Heinlein, Theodore Sturgeon and Poul Anderson.

# MUSINGS OF A TOWER JOCKEY

The whine of a straining engine,
The jolt of a familiar rut in the road,
Bodies sway and strain for balance
Each time the road curves
And the truck's tires slide.
Someone's steel pot
Batters aimlessly about.
There's a new face among us,
His expression taut with fear,
Eyes wide in disbelief
As the truck swerves
Around another corner.
He hasn't yet learned
To be unafraid of the knowledge
That the driver is stoned,
Or drunk,
Or just plain pissed.

A jarring stop.
I jump out.
A facsimile in green fatigues
Walks by without greeting.
I pass through barbed wire,
Pull the gate,
Snap the lock,
Glance up at steel girders,
Wooden planks,
And begin to climb.
On top I shed my ammo belt,
Drop my helmet and M16,
And squat on the sheet metal floor.

How many hours
Have I perched on that chilly surface,

Squinting at paperbacks
Smuggled under my shirt,
Or hunted for roaches among the dust
To roll a number,
Or read the bitter graffiti
Scrawled on walls
Battered by angry rifle butts and boots,
Or slept away the time
Knowing a rock thrown to the catwalk
Would be my alarm?

Better the fantasy of dreams
Or words
Or weed
Than time spent wondering
The reality or reason
Of my position,
Standing watch high above the world
In my tower,
Overlooking bunkers
Of bombs and missiles
In a foreign land,
And watching for the enemy.

It was my wretched fate to be one of the last citizens of these United States drafted into the military (at least to date), in violation of the 13th Amendment to the Constitution (look it up). After enduring the ordeal of basic training and the inanities of military police school, I was shipped off to the Republic of South Korea. There I spent most of my time in a maximum-security area inside the six-by-six box of a guard tower a hundred feet off the ground.

The Tower Jockeys of Camp Ames were an infamous lot. Though the TJs were technically MPs themselves, the command structure of the US forces in ROK once ordered a company of military policemen stationed more than a hundred miles away to fly in via helicopter and pull a drug raid on the TJs. Most were forewarned and cleaned out their lockers. When the MPs arrived they found the halls of the dormitory-style barracks strewn with bags of marijuana.

# PROFILE OF A PATRIOT

They shoved him into the room, hands bound behind him, and forced him onto a cold metal chair. He lost his balance, and someone he couldn't see grabbed him and jerked him upright. Before he could orient himself, the door shut, leaving him alone and in total darkness.

What was going on? What did he do? His only attempt to question the men who had grabbed him was silenced by a curse and threat of physical violence. Why were they so angry? He hadn't done anything. Why had they taken him? Was he under arrest? No one had said anything to him. They'd just stared at him with loathing.

He'd been at home, watching television—watching the president's address. He had rushed after his date home to see it, hoping he wouldn't miss anything. He remembered being relieved when he activated his wall set and found he was just in time.

Yet halfway through the speech, a loud banging shook his door. A voice shout something he couldn't make out; and before he could even think to react, his door burst open, wood-frame splinters showering him like shrapnel.

"On the floor! On the floor! On the floor!" Overlapping voices screamed at him as a flurry of uniformed men and women rushed into his apartment, their weapons threatening, their expressions vehement, hostile.

Shock welded George to his chair. He hadn't even time to consider responding to their demands when two of the intruders yanked him from his seat and slammed him face-first onto the floor. The impact stunned him so, he barely felt the handcuffs as they squeezed his wrists. Moments later, he was hauled outside under the accusing stares of his neighbors, only vaguely aware of the search-and-destroy whirlwind laying waste to his home.

Now, waiting in the dark, he'd lost track of time. He almost called out but thought better of it. He should wait calmly. He should cooperate. Everything would be straightened out. He hadn't done anything.

Just as he realized he was going to have to relieve himself soon, several ceiling-mounted lights burst into brightness. Momentarily blinded, he heard the door open. Someone walked in.

"Where are your shoes?"

"My shoes?"

So much had happened he hadn't even considered that all he had on his feet were socks.

"What's a matter, don't you believe in shoes?" asked a second voice, its tone full of sarcasm.

"No—I mean, yes, of course I—"

"Is it some kind of cult thing? Some religious perversion?"

"What are you talking about?" He was confused, but his vision was clearing.

"We're talking about shoes, George. Don't you wear shoes? You got some kind of shoe phobia?"

He could see well enough now to make out two distinct figures. One was wearing a tan jacket and tie, the other simply a white shirt with sleeves rolled up. The latter fellow was a hulking brute with a scowl stamped on his face. In contrast, his partner seemed nonchalant.

George didn't recognize either of them, and he saw nothing in the room that would tell him where he was. All he saw beyond the light's glare was an empty chair positioned across from him and a camera mounted high in the corner.

"Who are you? What's going on?"

"We'll ask questions here, Georgie," said the big fellow. "George McGrath—is that your real name?"

"Of course it is."

"What kind of name is that? Sounds Irish-Catholic to me. Or maybe Scottish. Are you a kilt-wearing Scotsman, Georgie?"

"No, no, I'm an American—a good American."

"So, why don't you wear shoes, George?" asked the one in the jacket, examining his fingernails.

"I do—I do wear shoes. It's just that when—"

"What kind of shoes do you like, George? Do you like loafers, George? Brown loafers or black ones? Or do you like shoes you can tie up?"

"What are you talking about? I don't understand what this is about."

George tried to swallow, but his mouth was dry. The big guy whirled around and thrust his face up close enough to give George a rancid whiff of sausage.

"Do you pick your toes, Georgie? What do you do with the toe jam, Georgie?"

"I don't do anything with it."

"Come on, George." It was the other one now. The way they were both at him, he didn't know who to look at. "We all get our fingers into some toe jam every now and again. There's nothing wrong with that. The question is, what do you do with it, George?"

"I don't—"

"Tell us about your fetishes, George. What kinds of things do you like?"

"I don't have any fetishes." The pressure on his bladder was becoming uncomfortable.

"Come on, George. We've all got our little quirks. Tell us what you like. Tell us about your peculiar appetites."

"I, uh, I don't have any."

Without warning, the brute roared in frustrated rage and smashed his forearm against the bare wall. George twitched involuntarily. The big man glared at

160

him and stalked across the room. His partner eyed him, shaking his head, then turned to George.

"Give it up, George. We know all about you. What we don't know is what you know about what we know. Those are the known unknowns, George. What we're really concerned about are the unknown unknowns—the things we don't know we don't know. That's what we want you to tell us about, George."

"I, uh, I don't know what you're talking about."

What could he have done? What were they getting at? George couldn't think of anything. He hadn't done anything. All he'd done was the same thing he did every day.

He thought back to when he'd gotten off work. He remembered a Homeguard copter passing overhead and thinking nothing of it. He remembered being relieved when he reached the tram before it left the station. He was so relieved that, for once, it didn't bother him he had to stand, packed in elbow-to-elbow with his fellow passengers. What had concerned him was he didn't know whose elbows he was rubbing.

Who was standing behind him? What kind of person was the dour-faced woman next to him, wearing a print dress and holding a big basket purse that kept jouncing against his thigh? Was she a party member? A subversive? A mother grieving for a son lost in battle?

He was still looking for telltale signs, trying not to stare, when the heat and confined space had overcome him. He felt woozy and grabbed hold of the railing to steady himself. He closed his eyes and with his free hand wiped his clammy brow. It was so hot, so stuffy in the tram, yet with air conditioning proscribed as a power conservation measure, there were few cool places anymore. A drop of perspiration beaded at the end of his thin, beak-like nose and fell free.

Heat and humidity had always bothered him, even as a child. Once, while playing soccer with his whole family watching, it had been so hot, and he had been so tired, that at a crucial moment, just as he had a rare chance to take a shot on goal, he grew dizzy, tripped and fell. That was his last soccer game—his last sports-related endeavor. His father wouldn't let him join any teams after that.

The heat always reminded him, always brewed the reluctant memory of how, when they got home that day, his father wouldn't let him come inside. Over his mother's weak objections, George's father had made him stay outside—made him stand in the sun until he passed out. Things at home were never the same after that. Not for him, anyway.

To take his mind off the heat, George looked for the nearest screen. Instead, on the panel above him was a familiar poster—the one with New Glory waving in an imagined breeze and a Continental soldier, braced on his musket, reminding citizens to "Buy Patriot Bonds." The sight of it encouraged him to stand straight. His chest filled proudly, and he reached up to touch the New Glory pin on his collar—the one that had come when he'd purchased of his own bond.

Mounted next to the poster was a standard security cam. Its presence soothed him. It was comforting to know you could be seen almost everywhere you went. George turned to make certain the camera lens could focus on his pin.

He spotted a screen, and though the audio levels were low, the sound reverberated up and down the tram. If he listened closely, he could make out the words.

"...a charge of treason in a closed proceeding. Dr. Leonard Jefferson faces life in prison for, among other disloyal acts, ranting against public policy while on a speaking tour at the University of the Republic in New Haven, and referring to President Anwell as a "despot." Excerpts from the secret court will be released after evaluation by the National Security Agency."

George didn't know exactly what a "despot" was, but he knew it wasn't something you called the president. Obviously this Jefferson fellow wasn't a true Republicrat. No doubt he had ties to any number of odious factions.

"...at the top of the hour with a look at how a woman in San Francisco is challenging federal contraception laws. Until then, good day and God bless America."

The tram lurched to a stop. George looked at his watch—only nine minutes behind schedule. He'd have just enough time to get ready for his date. He let himself be pushed toward the exit by the press of humanity flowing all around him, trying as best he could to ignore the stifling odors.

Two men stood on either side of the exit, examining face after face. They wore no uniforms nor any other official insignia, which led George to believe they were Homeguard. They had that look, and lately they'd been prowling the tram station. Last week he'd seen a group of women taken into custody after protesting federal restraints on travel. There were still people who felt they should be able to go wherever they pleased, *whenever* they pleased.

George shook his head condescendingly at the memory. Some people just didn't get it. They just didn't understand America was at war, that unregulated freedom was anarchy. Well, soon they'd—

Suddenly, the two intent men took hold of a disembarking passenger and said something George couldn't hear. He strained to get a good look at the man before they hustled him away. Dark eyes, puffy cheeks, weak chin, ragged haircut—yes, George was sure the man was an Episcopalian. The thought made him shudder. Episcopalians were known carriers of UMV, and this fellow had been in the same tram car as George. He might even have had contact with him.

Yet hadn't he heard the Upper Mississippi virus had been contained? Maybe the fellow was just another exposed homosexual being taken off to the reservation. The weak chin certainly fit. Come to think of it, his eyebrows looked trimmed as well. That was probably it. No reason for him to start worrying over nothing.

He looked away. He'd ignore the whole incident.

It was a short walk to his place, but once the crowd thinned he didn't waste any time. He was going on his first date with the woman from the grocery store, and he didn't want to be late. He'd had his eye on her for some time. Before he'd even dared to speak to her, he'd watched surreptitiously as she sorted the prepackaged meats or washed down the fruits and vegetables. She was a bit plump, certainly no beauty, but she had these large, round, grapefruit-like breasts George couldn't take his eyes off.

He was halfway home when he came to an unexpected assemblage along the roadway. He cursed them all under his breath as he pushed through, and then saw why they were there. Coming down the street was a phalanx of military vehicles. Each one was packed with troops returning, no doubt, from Finland, where their pacification of the radical leftist regime and restoration of democracy had been a success.

As the first group of soldiers motored by, George drew up rigidly and saluted, his thumb against his chest, right hand steadfast, perpendicular to his heart. The sight of New Glory, its stripes and lone star waving staunchly from the rear of each vehicle, filled him with pride. The United Republic of America had triumphed once more, and the world was a safer place because of it.

He searched the soldiers' faces for smiles of victory but saw only dull eyes and vapid expressions. They must be exhausted, thought George, which only prompted him to hold his salute that much firmer. Someone near him mumbled "God bless America." He nodded his head in silent agreement then observed, not ten feet away from him, a teenage couple canoodling there on the street, oblivious to the parade of American military might. The disrespect infuriated him.

"You—you there!" he declared in a tone that demanded attention. "Eyes front. Stand up straight. Show some respect." George narrowed his eyes with stern regard, gesturing toward the progression of troops.

The lanky, thin-lipped boy stared at him, but he and his girlfriend turned to face the parade. They didn't salute, but George was satisfied he'd gotten their attention.

Instead of saying anything else, he committed their faces to memory. Probably Oregonians, from the look of them—maybe even Californians. That would explain it.

A modest sense of accomplishment bolstered him, even though he'd only done what any good American would. It was a small thing but also one that had likely been captured by street security cams. Maybe he'd receive a notation of recognition from the party. Or maybe not. It didn't matter. It just felt good to belong.

But he didn't belong here. Not here in this room with lights glaring in his face, a camera bearing down on him, and these men questioning him as if he were some kind of...

Some kind of what? Had those teenagers concocted something? Had they borne witness against him?

The smallish interrogator scratched his head, as if he needed to take a different tack.

"Tell us about your dreams, George. Everybody dreams. What kinds of things do you dream about?"

"I...I don't know. I guess I dream about different things. I don't usually remember my dreams."

"Do you masturbate, George?"

"Do I *what*?"

"You heard me. Do you, George? Do you play with yourself? What do you think about when—"

The door to the tiny room opened, cutting off the question. A woman wearing a gray pinstriped suit and carrying an oversized pad entered. The pad's screen was lit, but George couldn't see what was on it. The woman sat in the empty chair. The two men remained standing, deferring to her.

"George McGrath," she said, reading it off her pad but ignoring him. "Yes, I've got your complete record here."

George took a breath and braced himself.

"Why am I here? Who are you people? Police? Homeguard security? I have a right to know."

"I thought you were a good American, George," said the smaller fellow. "A good American, a *patriotic* American, wouldn't ask, wouldn't cry about his *rights*. He would just cooperate."

"I'm *trying* to cooperate. I just don't understand."

George strained to think back. What could he have done? He remembered walking home, sidestepping a pile of uncollected refuse and feeling something brittle and sticky *crunch* under his shoe. He'd wiped the remnants against a broken chunk of concrete. One had to be careful where one stepped these days, what with city services being cut back to support the national security effort. Even his own building was somewhat dilapidated, although it had hot water twice a day. That was more than some places, or so he'd heard. Dreary as it was, it was good enough for him, and all he could afford.

Several of the building's residents had been gathered outside to escape the heat. Some talked, some just sat in their plastic chairs and smoked. Most he recognized, although none by name. He nodded to them in tacit acknowledgment as he passed under the security cam mounted over the entrance and made for the stairs. No use trying the elevator, it hadn't worked in months.

He'd trudged up the bleak steps, oblivious to the ever-present smell of mold and boiling rice. Fumbling with his key, he saw the old black woman across the hall crack her door and eye him suspiciously, secure behind her double chains. He returned her stare in-kind before closing his own door behind him. He didn't like the way that woman looked at him. He'd always wondered about her. Maybe he should prompt a background check. It couldn't hurt.

Idly, he turned on his screen while he cleaned up and got dressed for his date. He wished he'd been able to find some deodorant, but it was one of those things that had grown scarce. Shortages were part of life. He understood. Everyone had to make sacrifices.

He glanced at the solitary family photo that adorned his dresser, remembering how his older brothers Joe and Gerald used to get ready for their dates. They had both been popular with the girls, excelled in school, sports—just about anything they tried. His father loved them, doted on them.

And why not? They were the kind of sons every father wanted. When they'd both joined the marines, his father had been so proud. He'd bragged to everyone until...

Until the day they were both killed in the same skirmish. It had been seven years now since the preemptive action against Liberia. The mission proved to be a success, eventually, but it had left his father bitter.

George tried to enlist as soon as he was old enough, hoping to fill the void left by his older brothers and maybe, finally, gain his father's approval. But even that wasn't to be. A childhood bout with rheumatic fever had left his heart valves thick with scar tissue. Induction doctors rejected him on medical grounds—unfit for duty to his country. There were times, even now, he lamented that he'd never been allowed to serve—never allowed to join.

"Georgie says he doesn't have any fetishes," the big guy said, addressing the woman.

"I heard," she responded. Her expression was noncommittal, but George sensed stern disapproval behind the chilly professional facade. "Is it true, Mr. McGrath, that you own but a single Patriot Bond?"

"Yes." George's hand sought out his Patriot pin and discovered it was missing. It must have been torn off when he was taken into custody.

"Why is that, Mr. McGrath?"

"Why? Why is what?"

"Why do you have only one bond?"

"It's all I could afford. I want to buy more. I—"

"I see no record of military service here," she said, scrutinizing her pad. "Why is that, Mr. McGrath?"

"I, uh, have a heart murmur. The doctors said I was medically unqualified."

The brute snorted in disgust.

"Are you a closet Constitutionalist, Mr. McGrath?"

"No, no, I'm Republicrat. I have been my whole life—a proud Republicrat."

George felt his bladder about to burst.

"Uh-huh."

"Do you believe in individual rights, Mr. McGrath? In the right to say anything you want, believe anything you want, do anything you want?"

"Uh...no, no."

"Why the hesitation?"

"It's just that...I don't know...I mean, I know we can't just say anything. It depends on—"

"Depends on what, Mr. McGrath?"

"I...I guess it depends on what you say, or what you do."

"Oh, come on, enough of this," the burly fellow practically spat out. "Look at him. Green eyes, narrow chin, diamond face, wispy build—and look at the nose. As aquiline as I've ever seen."

"He fits the profile, that's for sure," said the other man.

The woman nodded, checked her pad again, and continued. "I see, Mr. McGrath, that you've never been married. Why is that?"

"No reason, really. I just haven't—"

"Do you like women, Mr. McGrath?" she asked, studying him. "Are you attracted to women?"

"Of course," he stuttered.

Did this have something to do with his date? Did that woman say something about him? How could she? She didn't know anything about him. All he knew about her was her name, Dorothea, and that she'd worked in the same store for three years now.

He'd taken her to a café he frequented—not too expensive, but not too cheap, either. They were seated next to the window, which was nice, because she commented on the vivid sunset. He tried to talk politics, about the war, the ongoing security threats, but he could see it bored her. From what he could tell, *he* bored her. She showed all the signs of having no interest in him whatsoever.

He knew those signs. He'd seen them before. She wasn't any different from all the other women. She wasn't so special. She was lucky he'd asked her out.

"So, Dorothea, may I ask why you've never married?"

She looked at him as if the question were rude.

"You can ask whatever you'd like," she replied, her words coated with annoyance. After a pause that left George feeling awkward, she decided to respond. "I was married once. It didn't work out. But that was a long time ago. What about you?"

"Me? No, I've never been married," responded George. "I've never met anyone who...anyone with the same interests, I guess."

She nodded her head knowingly and looked out the window. Unable to formulate anything else to say, he did likewise. It was twilight—not quite dark, but the striations of pink and orange had turned dull and gray, like his expectations. He should have gone to the party meeting instead. At least there he'd be among friends.

Well, not friends really, but people more like himself.

Suddenly, like something out of a coarse docudrama, a wild cub pack blustered by the café, making faces at them through the window. They were a filthy lot—at least a dozen of them. A couple of the bigger ones slapped their grimy hands on the glass. George turned away as if they weren't there. His date, however, stared and clucked her tongue sympathetically.

"Look at the little one. It's so sad."

George looked back to see one of the younger strays lingering next to the window after her cohorts had moved on. Her hair was stringy, knotted, barely blond, and dirty like her face. He couldn't categorize her features, but he noticed her eyes were the same shade of green as his own. Those eyes stared wistfully at the remaining food on their plates.

"Go on," George said, waving his hand like he was shooing a troublesome insect. "Go on, get out of here."

The fragile waif looked at him, tilting her head, trying to make sense of his words through the glass. With a faint shrug, she walked away.

"The poor thing. You didn't have to scare her."

"I didn't scare her."

"I could have given her some of my dinner. I'm done with it anyway."

"If you feed them they'll just keep coming back."

Dorothea shook her head. "She couldn't be more than five or six. A little girl like her shouldn't be on the streets. It's just awful. There are so many of them these days. Someone should do something about it."

George made a noise of contempt. As he did, he caught sight of Dorothea's cleavage—a single inch of exposed flesh. He stared long enough to feel a swell in his loins.

"I don't know why they don't round them all up," he said. "Who knows what kind of mischief those runaways are up to."

"Oh, not that little one. She's too young to have run away."

"Well, then, her parents were probably criminals or, worse yet, Libertarians."

"It's so sad, all the homeless children you see these days. Sometimes I wonder if it wouldn't be better if they were never born."

Astonishment slapped George in the face. No wonder this woman wasn't interested in him. She sounded like she wasn't even a Republicrat—not a true patriot, anyway. Who knew what claptrap she believed in.

"Are you saying you want to go back to the days of abortion—the wholesale slaughter of fetuses?"

"No, no, of course not. It's just that—"

"Then you should be more careful what you say," he replied curtly. "Someone's likely to hear you and think you're a godless Constitutionalist or something." George looked around, worried someone had overheard *him*. "People shouldn't rut like animals anyway," he said, lowering his voice. "Then the streets wouldn't be full of their unwanted spawn."

Dorothea didn't respond, but her expression lacquered the silence. George turned away, watching the cafe's security cam as it swiveled in perpetuity.

"I think I'd like to go now," she said, firmly aloof.

"Fine."

Despite her chilly demeanor, George was determined to walk her to the tram. He figured he still had time to get home and see the live broadcast of the president's speech.

They started down one side of the street until George saw the same pack of strays malingering up ahead, near a public safety booth. The dingy little girl with the green eyes was staring at them.

Something about the look in her eyes rankled him. He pretended not to see her—not to see any of them. He guided his date to the other side of the street. No sense in taking a chance the strays might actually touch them. Who knew what kinds of diseases they carried.

"Do you like little children, Mr. McGrath?"

"What do you mean?"

"Just answer the question, Georgie. Don't make me beat it out you," the brute added, his casual tone belying his words.

"Why did you choose to work as a custodian at an elementary school, Mr. McGrath?"

"I don't know—I mean...it was all I could get."

"What are these for, George?" The smaller man pulled a pair of latex medical gloves out of an oversized envelope. "Do you like to play doctor, George?"

"Those are for cleaning. You know, for paint and chemicals and—what are you saying?"

How could they think such a thing of him? As hard as he worked, picking up after other people's children without complaint. Cleaning classrooms wasn't just his job. He'd always been proud to be part of a place where the republic's future was being groomed, where children were taught proper values, where they learned to put country first and respect tradition. Remembering that had always made it easier for him to overlook the grime and clutter.

He'd stood, broom in hand, that very afternoon, waiting for the teacher to dismiss her class, hearing her cue the children, listening as they recited in unison.

"I pledge allegiance to the flag of the United Republic of America, and to the values for which it stands: one nation under God, indivisible, with security and justice for all."

The final bell echoed through empty corridors, and the exodus began. A gaggle of third- and fourth-graders swarmed outside, chattering like magpies, their prim uniforms, replete with colorful New Glory patches, not so crisp as they had been that morning. He watched as the multi-colored mélange merged into a swelling sea of younger and older children, flowing en masse toward the exits.

George observed the scattering of expectant parents. He examined their faces, idly matching them with the children they claimed. He looked for questionable styles of clothing, dubious grooming practices, suspect physical and racial features. He noticed one family of Nordic descent, another grouping he labeled Hispanics, and a swarthy man of obscure lineage bending down to the tie the shoe of a much lighter-skinned little girl of mixed race.

George found himself wondering how many were actually clandestine Constitutionalists. He thought he could pick them out if he had to. But were there any extremists among them? Maybe even a radical insurgent? George couldn't be certain. If only he'd taken that class in profiling they'd offered at party headquarters. Then he'd have a better understanding of what to look for. He might even be able to identify a suspected subversive and collect a cash reward. He could certainly use the money.

As it was, he had to content himself that the school's security cameras were recording every face, every action—storing visual data that would be catalogued and analyzed by experts. If any of the faces were wrong—and George had been certain there must be some—they'd be found and dealt with. They always were.

"Mr. McGrath, our BEA has provided us with probable cause to—"

"BEA? What's BEA?"

The woman frowned, annoyed at being interrupted. "Behavioral Evidence Analysis, Mr. McGrath. Our BEA, in combination with the psychogenic inventory we've conducted, has determined the likelihood you are a pedophile, Mr. McGrath, a pervert who preys upon innocent children." For the first time her professional facade withered, and George saw the wrath she'd held in check. "I have children of my own, Mr. McGrath, and I plan to make certain they're safe from you and all the degenerates like you."

"No, no, you're wrong. I would never...I couldn't. What evidence could you —?"

At that, the brute lunged at him, and they both hit the floor. George's kidneys were pressed painfully against the chair's metal supports, his cuffed hands crushed beneath their combined weight as the enraged interrogator strove to choke the life out of him.

Just as suddenly, the brute was pulled off him and maneuvered out of the room, leaving George lying there, soaked in his own urine, gasping for breath. He closed his eyes to avoid the glare of the lights and tried to think, but denial clouded his mind. This wasn't happening. He hadn't done anything. All he'd done was turn on his television, settle into his overstuffed chair, and take off his shoes.

He remembered wondering what the president would talk about in his address to the nation. Would he detail the glorious victory over Finland, or maybe

168

announce an improving economy? Perhaps he'd unveil the new five-year plan George had heard about. It didn't matter. Whatever the president said, George knew he would be reassured. Things would be better. The republic was in good hands.

On the screen, he saw the commander-in-chief pass through a gauntlet of New Glories, looking healthy, sharp, fearless. The assemblage of dignitaries, generals, and journalists stood as one, and George did likewise. When the president assumed his position behind the podium, everyone, George included, sat back down.

"My fellow Americans, tonight I come to you with an important message. That message is...the nation is strong."

Applause erupted, and the president waited for it to subside before continuing.

"We are strong, not only at home, but around the globe, where American military might is feared by the enemies of democracy. We are strong because we are one nation under God, undivided in our purpose—our resoluteness to crush the malevolent minions of iniquity."

Again he waited through the applause, punctuating it with a booming declaration.

"Nevertheless, the war against insidious terrorism and autocracy is far from over. It's a battle in which we must remain ever-vigilant, like the Colonial farmer, musket in hand, watching for redcoats crossing the Potomac. Like the army tank commander waiting for the Nazi Panzers to come rolling over the hills toward Bastogne. Like the marine sentry gazing eagled-eyed over the ruins of Fallujah, on guard against the next wave of marauding Islamic fundamentalists.

"Eternal vigilance is the price of security. Yes, my fellow Americans, we are strong, we are vigilant, and we understand the rules have changed. The world has changed, and we must change with it. There are limits to freedom, limits necessitated by the war in which we find ourselves—a war of ideologies. To counter foreign influence and domestic insurgency, we've had to suspend certain rights for the good of the nation...for the good of us all.

"Good Americans need to be watchful against all possible threats. Look around you. Do you see something suspicious? Do you know what that person over there is doing? Did you hear something that didn't sound right? If you're not sure, if you have doubts, report it.

"Be alert. Be observant. Bear witness."

The familiar credo echoed through George's head even as the president recited it.

"Remember, too, good Americans need to be careful what they say. This is no time for dissent. Dissent is a sign of weakness. This is no time for weakness. This is a time for—"

"Help Mr. McGrath back onto his chair," said the woman in charge as she and the man in the tan jacket came back into the room. The big fellow wasn't with them.

"It looks like George has pissed himself," he said, pulling George up from the floor.

"Did you wet the bed as a child, Mr. McGrath?" asked the woman.

169

"No...no. I never—"

"Is that what your mother's going to tell us when we ask her, Mr. McGrath? Or is she going to tell us an entirely different story?"

His mother? What did she have to do with this? Was it a coincidence his mother had called him just the other day, for the first time in months?

"How are you, George?"

"I'm fine, Mother. I'm just fine."

"Are you still working at the school?"

"Yes."

"That must be nice—working with children."

"I don't really work with the children, Mother. How are you?"

"Oh, well, not so good, George. You know my bad feet. They're still bothering me. And now my back is acting up."

"What does the doctor say?"

"We can't really afford to see a doctor now...you know, since our Social Security was cut."

George's head lurched back in exasperation. "It wasn't cut, Mother, it was progressively abrogated."

"Well, whatever you call it, it's been hard making ends meet since. Your father's had to go back to work at the mill, and I've been doing some sewing when I can. It's just been hard."

"I'm sure it has been, Mother. It's hard everywhere you know. The president did the right thing. He was exactly right when he called Social Security a relic and an icon of socialism. It was draining government resources. We've got higher priorities now, like national security. You don't want terrorists blowing up your church, do you? Or a bunch of leftist Hindus halfway around the world telling you how to live."

"No, no, I guess you're right."

"The economy will turn around—you wait and see. I'll try and send you some money when I can."

"You don't need to do that, George. I know you don't have much, either."

"I said I'll try." George hesitated. "Is Father there?"

Now it was his mother's turn to waver. "Yes, he's here."

"Do you think he wants to...?"

"George, you know how talking to you upsets him—reminds him of your brothers."

"Yeah, I know."

George knew. He remembered, too. He remembered how his father used to take his brothers to ballgames and on fishing trips, and leave him at home with his mother. There was always a different reason for excluding him. Sometimes no reason at all. Sometimes they'd leave without a word. Often he didn't even know they'd gone until they came back. It got to where he paid no attention at all to their comings and goings. If he didn't look, he couldn't see.

"Are you still with us, George?"

"What are you thinking about, Mr. McGrath?"

"Daydreaming, George?"

"Nothing. I wasn't thinking about anything."

170

"Uh-huh," the woman said, making no attempt to hide her disbelief. "We're going to release you, Mr. McGrath—for now."

"You mean I can go?"

"Yes. However, your travel permit is suspended. Make no attempt to leave the city."

"We'll be watching you, George."

He wanted to tell them if they'd been watching him they'd know he's innocent, but he didn't. All he cared about was getting out of there—getting home. He just wanted to put it all behind him. A mistake had been made. That was it. It was over.

At least, he thought it was over until he reached his building and saw the looks of suspicion and hostility on his neighbors' faces. Their silence was thick with innuendo. One woman hurried to scoop up her toddler, and he couldn't help but think it was because of him. Had someone told them? Did they think...?

His apartment, his home, was a collage of chaos. Nothing had escaped the search, nothing had been restored to its rightful place. Even his favorite chair had been ripped open, as though it might have contained some damning bit of evidence. George slumped down on loose bits of stuffing. What was he going to do? What *could* he do?

He felt better once he got back to his normal routine the next morning. However, immediately after arriving at work, he was called to the superintendent's office. No one spoke to him as he passed through the building. The only acknowledgment of his presence were looks of repugnance and an exchange of whispers.

"Sit down, McGrath," the superintendent said, glancing over the tops of the papers he was perusing.

George sat and waited through an extended silence.

The superintendent placed the papers on his desk and signed the top sheet. "We're letting you go, McGrath."

"Letting me go?"

"Yes, your services are no longer required by the school district."

"I...I don't understand."

The superintendent shot a look of indignation at him. "*You* don't understand? *I* don't understand how you could betray our trust in you, McGrath. I hired you in good faith. How do you think this is going to make me look? How do you think it's going to make the school district look?"

"I don't know what you mean. I haven't done anything!"

"I think you know we can't have someone like you working in one of our schools," he said with finality. "You'll be escorted off the premises immediately. Your termination file will be forwarded to you. That's all."

George opened his mouth to protest his innocence, but the denial died in his throat. What could he say that would be believed? What words would matter? He stood, dazed and dizzy. He steadied himself and turned to the door where his escort waited.

George didn't know what he was going to do—how he was going to reverse this wrong. He headed home, thinking there must be some government agency he could appeal to. A good American, a good Republicrat, couldn't be treated this way. There must be some recourse. Did he dare bother his congressional representative? Was there a lesser official he could approach?

He was still struggling to fully accept the reality of his situation when a mobile police unit cruised by. His stomach knotted. His insides were like broken glass. The police unit disappeared around the corner, but the discomfort didn't go away.

Beset by indecision, he found it difficult to concentrate. Everything concrete had turned to quicksand. What could he do?

He was so distracted he failed to notice the surly bunch lingering near the entrance to his building.

"There he is," called out a voice accusingly.

Only then did George realize they were coming at him. He held up his hands as if the motion would hold them back.

"Wait, you don't under—"

Someone hit him, and he staggered back. Several hands seized him, and he struggled to get free. More blows pounded him—his head, his back, his stomach. Someone kicked at his legs, but the press around him was so constricting that many of the punches lacked intensity.

The adrenalin of desperation surged through him, and he broke free, stumbling away. His attackers followed. He hurried to the nearest security cam.

"Help! Help me!" he pleaded to the camera.

Something heavy struck him from behind. As he fell, he caught a glimpse of a baseball bat with an imprint of New Glory on it. More blows inundated him. The pain was overwhelming. He was crying as he passed out.

~─⊶⧉⊷─~

He woke to discomfort so intense he tried to slip back into unconsciousness. But he couldn't ignore his bruised body any more than he could his battered spirit. As he lay there, hurting, doubt poisoned his resolve. Could he, without realizing it— could he have done something and not known it? Could he really be a...?

No, no, he wasn't—he couldn't. It was lunacy to think so. He had to get up. He had to tell someone.

Yet even if he could induce himself to stand, to disregard the pain, where would he go? Who would he tell?

George opened his eyes. It was dark, although he thought he saw a hint of daybreak stealing through a mottled pane. He didn't know where he was, but it wasn't the street. As his eyes adjusted to the faint light, he made out a ragged Patriot Bond poster hanging askew next to the window.

"He's awake."

George flinched at the sound of the voice then located its source. Two others were in the room with him—no, three. He could see them now. Two men and a woman.

"Where am I? Who are you?"

One of the men moved closer and squatted next to him.

"Let's just say we're kindred spirits."

"Yeah," responded the woman, "Homeguard-haunting spirits."

George scooted back despite the pain, and propped himself against a wall.

"Are you Constitutionalists?"

The woman laughed.

"No, George, we're not Constitutionalists."

"How do you know my name?"

"We have our sources, George. We know all about you. We've read your *profile*." He said the word with loathing. "You were one of their own—a good Republicrat, weren't you?"

George nodded. "What...what do you want with me?"

"We don't want anything, George. You needed help."

"We figured, after what they did to you, you might want to join us."

"Join you?"

"Us—others like us. There are hundreds in this city alone. More across the country. We're going to set things right. No more totalitarianism and intolerance. We're going to end the tyranny and bring back government *by* the people *for* the people, George."

"You're subversives."

"We're Americans," the woman countered.

"We're freedom fighters, George. We're fighting for the freedom to be different, the freedom not to be categorized because of our religion or our hair color, the freedom to disagree."

George grew dizzy. He grabbed his head with both hands. What were they talking about? Americans were already free. Security and justice for all.

"I know you've been through the wringer, George, and this is a lot to take in. So, you just think about it. You're pretty banged up, so you stay here and rest. We've got somewhere to go. We'll bring you some food as soon as we can.

"In the meantime, you think about it. Think about what they did to you—what this government is doing to thousands of others every day with its paranoid mania and wars of aggression. Just think about it."

—⁘—

A short time after they'd gone, the pain subsided. It didn't hurt much, as long as he didn't move. However, he now felt a different kind of distress. Trying to make sense of everything that had happened caused his head to ache. He considered what the strangers had said. Maybe there was some truth to it. He could see, from his own circumstance, how things could get twisted around. Where was the justice in that?

Still, they wanted him to become a subversive, to fight against the government—*his* government. How could he? It was contrary to everything he believed. Yet, how could he go home? How could he go back to a life that had been turned so upside down? What could he do? What should he do?

He wasn't sure how much time had passed when he finally struggled to his feet and found the door. Dawn had chased away the dark, and he could see more clearly now. Slowly, painfully, he lurched out into the still-empty street. He spotted a public safety booth and limped over to it. Once behind the dark glass of the enclosure he hesitated, trying to subdue the fragmented notions still troubling him. He picked up the phone, banishing his wayward thoughts.

173

A voice responded immediately. "Homeguard. What is the nature of your call?"

George cleared his throat and said, "I need to bear witness."

From the moment the post-9/11 hysteria began, I stood aghast at how my countrymen were reacting. I was never on-board with the whole "fear" thing, but I watched with my own personal horror as a majority of Americans gave carte blanche to an egomaniacal president to wage war and edit our constitutional freedoms as he deemed necessary. I know our history is filled with many atrocities, but when we summarily invaded Iraq for no legitimate reason, I was ashamed to be an American. The America I know just doesn't do that—we protect our allies but we aren't imperialist invaders.

"Profile of a Patriot" was my way of warning what might become of America if the ultra-conservatives who ran the Bush Administration continued to tighten their grip on this nation years into the future, creating a country where a "good citizen" is someone who's careful about what he says, doesn't question authority, and is always ready to bear witness against his neighbor.

# OUT OF HIS LEAGUE

Bats slammed into lockers, cleats scraped the floor, and frothy spittle stained the walls. An influx of uniformed combatants filed into the room, some mumbling, others grumbling—the sure sign of another loss. In moments, the place smelled of dirty socks and planetary jocks.

As if to alter the mood, one of them began revolving around the post-game spread, waving his arms.

"I say we put this one behind us," called out Saturn in an upbeat tone. "I say we go out and find some bodacious local asteroids in need of a good fertility rite. What do you say?"

His idea was greeted by a colorful array of expletives. No one was in the mood to party. By the time little Mercury showed up with the really bad news, the room was already subdued.

Most had changed out of their uniforms, and were already in and out of the showers. Mars noticed the normally peppy infielder appeared usually glum.

"What's wrong? You look like you've seen a black hole."

"Did you hear what happened to Pluto?" the speedster asked the room in-general. "They cut him."

"What?" Mars slammed his fist against the wall. "Damn it! I knew something was up."

"Are you sure?" asked Jupiter, scratching his oversized head with sausage-like fingers.

"Yeah," replied Mercury. "He's in with management right now. I hear they're sending him down to the dwarf league."

"I bet it was Terra's fault," groused Mars. "He's always stirring up trouble. No telling what he told management behind Pluto's back."

"Well, Pluto's always been a little erratic," said Saturn, fresh out of the shower and adorning himself with his usual bling. "He's not the fastest guy in the galaxy, either."

"Maybe," said Mars, "but he's a scrappy little player, and he was always there for us, eon after eon."

Jupiter stood, stretched his massive arms, and yawned. "I'm going to miss the little guy."

"What's this going to do to team chemistry?" wondered Venus.

"Management doesn't care about chemistry," carped Mars. "All they care about is astronomy."

"We should tell the others before he gets here," suggested Venus.

Saturn volunteered, "I'll get Neptune, he's still in the shower."

"That figures," responded Mars. "Hey, while you're in there, get Uranus out of the head."

Before Saturn returned, Terra walked in and said excitedly, "Did you guys hear what happened to Pluto?"

That was all Mars needed. He grabbed Terra by his uniform and slammed him up against a spate of lockers.

"What did you do, you prissy, waterlogged, rodent-infested little—"

Jupiter and Mercury moved quickly to intervene, separating the pair.

"What did you tell them?" Mars ranted as Jupiter held him back.

"What are you talking about?" Terra seemed stunned by the attack.

"Mars thinks it's your fault they're sending Pluto down," explained Venus.

"What? I didn't have anything to do with that. How could I? Why would I?"

Before Mars could continue his diatribe, Pluto walked in. He was already in street clothes but went straight to his locker. The room hushed noticeably, and for a moment, everyone acted as if nothing were amiss.

But when Pluto began emptying out his locker, Mercury put an arm on his shoulder.

"Sorry, my man. We all heard. It's a bum deal."

Pluto shrugged. "It's part of the business. I didn't get the job done." Then, mustering a bit of bravado, he turned to face the room and added, "I'll be back. Don't you worry about that. I'll go down, I'll get my game together and then I'll be back. It's just a slump. You'll see, I'll be back up here in no time."

Jupiter nodded his big head and his bassoon-like voice bellowed, "That's right. You'll be back in no time at all. You go down there and give them a good showing, Pluto, old bud."

"Yeah," called out a couple of other voices with less than genuine enthusiasm.

Unable to hold back the tears, Venus turned away. Mars looked like he wanted to break something.

Searching his rather voluminous cranium for something else to say—something inspirational—Jupiter came up with, "Just remember, you can't steal first base."

"Yeah...right. Thanks, Jupe," responded Pluto. He knew the big guy well enough not to waste time puzzling over anything he said.

But Jupiter wasn't finished.

"Did I ever tell you how I could have been a star?"

Venus waved him silent.

"Not now, Jupiter."

Pluto finished bagging up his stuff and started out. Terra stepped up and shook his hand.

"Good luck, Pluto."

"Yeah," said Mercury, "knock 'em dead down there."

Pluto looked like he wanted to say something else but couldn't get the words out. Instead, he glanced away and walked out.

Mercury stared at Jupiter.

"You're a real gasbag, you know that? *You can't steal first base?* What kind of idiotic thing is that to say?"

Jupiter shrugged his mammoth shoulders. The gravitational effect of the movement pulled Saturn back in from the showers with Neptune and Uranus in tow.

"What happened?" asked Neptune, still dripping.

"They cut Pluto. He's gone."

"Cut him? Why?"

"Why do you think?" Mars replied sarcastically. "He wasn't orbiting up to expectations."

"It's not why that matters," offered Mercury. "It's who—who will they cut next?"

When I was growing up, there were always nine planets. Pluto was always number nine—that little planet way out on the fringes of our solar system. But when astronomers decided it could no longer be deemed a full planet, nine became eight, and I wrote "Out of His League" to satirize Pluto's plight. It was published in *OG's Speculative Fiction*, *Polluto*, and in *Postcards from Uranus* under the title "Nine Minus One." It was also converted into an audio tale by Drabblecast.

# PLUTO'S LAMENT

Too mild, too meek, too small,
Giving astronomers fits.
"Dwarfed" by the gang of eight,
Desperate for some Hollywood glitz.

Scrutinized—
Its orbit an eccentric case.
Ghettoized—
Too far out in space.
Subcategorized—

Defined out of place.
Under the sway of Neptune,
Say stargazers, picking nits.
Just a mistake once made,
Now in need of a media blitz.

Written about the same time (and for the same reason) as "Out of His League," the poem "Pluto's Lament" was published in *Space and Time*.

# I FOUND LOVE ON CHANNEL 3

Okay, I admit it. I had this...this affair with a cartoon...I mean, an animated babe. I don't mean she was hyper. I mean she was a drawing, an illustration—you know, not real.

No, that's wrong. She was real, all right, but she was a real cartoon, like Mickey Mouse or Roger Rabbit.

I don't expect you to believe me. I wouldn't believe it myself if she wasn't the best thing that ever happened to me. But she was more than that. She was this vibrant, tough, intelligent woman. Alright, she was a cartoon, but she was still a woman. A woman I fell in love with.

You can choose to believe me or you can laugh it off as one man's perverted fantasy. I don't really care what you think, because I lived it. I know it happened.

That first time it was late, like most of my nights were. I had the TV on, and I was a little drunk and a little stoned. Hell, there wasn't even a decent old movie on, so I was flicking the remote like I was getting paid by the channel. On top of my boredom, I was feeling a little lonely and more than a little horny. It had been a while.

Life, of late, had dealt me a rather putrid hand. I won't bore you with the insipid details, but I was as low as a lizard's belly. Half the time I walked around in a daze, like I'd been hit by a bale of hay. One more straw, and it wouldn't be just my back that broke.

I was flipping from station to station when this one program caught my eye. Something I hadn't seen before—a whimsical mixture of science fiction and fantasy. I didn't know if it was a regular series or some obscure animated film. I'm about to zap the remote again when  she swings into my picture. I mean literally swung in, on some cable right into a cluster of Brand X bad guys.

She had high cheekbones and long hair as deep, dark red as the merlot I'd been drinking. A thin silver headband kept it out of her tempestuous green eyes. The black leather strips she wore were just enough for the modesty of the censors, and the flesh it did expose was every comic book artist's ideal of sinewy, supple perfection. In other words, she had it all.

Her boots pounded the head of yet another generically depraved minion as she drew her rapier from its ebony scabbard and began dealing death to and fro. She'd feint to the left as her blade licked out like a serpent's tongue to the right.

Leap and parry, roll and thrust. Her battle dance was as deadly as it was seductive.

Waging war with my own lethargy, I found myself imagining what it would be like to get naked and do the nasty with this voluptuous heroine darting across my high-definition screen.

This, of course, is where you're going to think I've totally lost touch with reality. You'll probably write it off as drug-induced, or maybe severe manic-depression. I know I did...at least at first.

I was still fantasizing about what it would be like to be deep inside such a powerful woman, tempering her pleasure with every stroke, when she comes flying boots-first through the television screen and lands with a distinct *thud* on my living room carpet.

What did I do? Well, I did what any red-blooded American male would do in that situation. I froze. I sat there with my mouth hanging open and my hand clutching the remote as if it were a high-tech crucifix that would ward off televised apparitions. For the first time in my life, I thought I'd blown a fuse.

There was something odd about her that added to my understandable amazement. She no longer looked like—well, like a drawing. In becoming three-dimensional, her flesh tones had taken on depth, her emerald eyes the spark of life. But there was still something not quite right about her color—about the corporeality of her presence. It was as if she were only part human, and still part the pen-and-ink of someone's imagination.

At that moment, however, with her standing there flashing the look of a trapped panther, blood dripping off her sword onto my coffee table, I had no doubt of her existence.

"What wizardry is this?" she demanded as both the look in her eyes and her blade threatened my very existence. "Who are...?"

Before she could get the *who?* out of the way, the big *where?* popped into her head. She scanned the room as if she'd just gotten off the bus in Bizarreville. My black-and-white photo of Leonard Nimoy seemed to intrigue her, but she didn't know what to make of the stuffed Alf doll.

Then she saw the television and almost freaked. The show, *her* show, was still on. She recognized the villainous hordes she'd been doing battle with and spun into a fighting stance, knocking over my Tony Gwynn-autographed baseball. The bad guys were searching for her, looking everywhere. But it wouldn't do them any good, because she was in *my* living room.

"It's all right," I found myself saying, "nobody's going to hurt you here."

"Where is this?"

"You're in my house. I don't know how you got here, but you're obviously here."

"Where is this house? What strange world is this?"

"Well, until a minute ago, I thought this was the   real world. Now I'm not sure what's real. But you can put your sword down. I swear no one is going to hurt you here. Please."

She regained some of her regal composure, surveying the room and deciding there was no immediate danger. One look at me cowering against the cushions of my couch made it obvious I was no threat. She sheathed her sword and turned her attention back to what was on the TV screen.

"That's...my world?" It was part statement, part question.

"That's where I was watching you, until you popped in unexpectedly."

"This is a window between worlds?"

Not only heroic and gorgeous, she was bright, too.

"Yeah, I guess it is. Actually, it's a window to many worlds. Watch this."

I aimed the remote at the TV and changed the channel to CNN, which was airing a report on a new electric car.

That, as I discovered, was a mistake.

As I watched her watching the television, she began to change. Her colors weren't as bright, her presence not as imposing. She was dwindling away, becoming transparent. When I finally what realized was happening, she had all the substance of a ghost.

As fast as I could fumble with the remote, I switched back to her show, but it was too late. She had vanished—at least from my living room. I saw her there, back on the screen. She looked disoriented for a moment, and that moment was enough for the bad guys to drop a wire-mesh net over her.

That was it. That's where the episode ended. They rolled credits over scenes from previous shows, and I dove for my *TV Guide*. The name of the show was *Phaedra, The Warrior Princess*, and it was on Channel 3 five nights a week.

—◦◦◦◦◦—

I couldn't get to my TV quickly enough the next night. I left it on Channel 3 more than an hour before the show was due—just in case. Instead of working, I had spent the day worrying. Worrying what might happen to her in the hands of the villain—although I told myself she was the show's star and nothing really bad could happen to her.

I also worried I'd never see her again, except on television. And I worried plenty about my sanity. Who wouldn't, after what I'd seen?

So, I waited, but this time I didn't have anything to drink or smoke. I didn't even want to eat. I was damn sure going to be in my right mind if it happened again. Even though I'd convinced myself it wouldn't.

When the show started, I learned she was, indeed, the title character, and that she now lay at the mercy of the grotesque Dark Prince, who intended to use an odd amalgamation of science and magic to make her his love slave. She had been stripped naked and strapped to a table somewhere deep in the bowels of his citadel. The straps, of course, were strategically placed to cover her more feminine parts.

As the episode progressed, there appeared to be no rescue for Phaedra. The Dark Prince was only minutes away from reshaping her mind, and I didn't see any way for her to escape. I couldn't help but wonder if it was all my fault. If I hadn't started fantasizing about her and sucked her into my world, she probably never would have been captured.

Yeah, I know—it was schizoid reasoning at best. On one hand, I was sure I'd imagined the whole thing, and on the other, I felt guilty. There was only one way to find out for sure, and only one way to rescue her.

I stood, closed my eyes and began thinking about her as hard as I could think. I thought about her straps coming untied. I thought about her cutting the prince's throat and escaping. I even thought about her beaming into my living room like something out of *Star Trek*.

Nothing worked. I was such a dismal failure I couldn't even hallucinate properly. She was doomed to become the mindless bride of that villain now, unless...

I tried to remember exactly what I had been thinking about the night before. That was easy—the same thing I was usually thinking about—sex. So, I envisioned making love to Phaedra—the passion of her kisses, the power of her thighs, the deep, dark red of her hair, and...

*Wham!* I felt a rush of cold air that nearly knocked me back, and suddenly I felt *her*. I opened my eyes and she was there—right there—in my arms, as naked as she'd been on that table.

"*You*," she said, actually sounding relieved.

I, of course, was my usual eloquent self. Standing there with this incredibly beautiful naked woman in my arms, I replied, "Hi."

"You have saved me from the clutches of the Dark Prince," she said.

"It, uh, was the least I could do."

That's when she kissed me. And it wasn't just any kiss. At least, it wasn't like any kiss I'd ever had from a real woman. It was a kiss that seared my lips, assaulted my insides, and rendered my legs immobile. It was a TKO.

Have you ever been in a situation like that? Of course, not exactly like that. But a situation where you thought, "This is too good to be true." Well, at that moment, that's what I thought, and I wasn't about to waste a second of it.

I kissed her back. One thing led to another, and we proceeded with the most passionate, most ferocious lovemaking I have ever, or will ever, experience. On the floor, across the couch, in the shower, over the kitchen sink—she couldn't get enough. And who was I to argue?

Somewhere between unbridled lust and rubbed-raw passion, she wore me down. We were lying on the couch, and I realized the TV had been on all this time. I let go of her to sit up and check out what was on. Her show was long over, and some infomercial had usurped the channel. When I turned back to look at her, she'd already begun to dissipate.

"Phaedra!"

She opened her eyes and sprang to her feet like an adrenalized cat then realized what was happening. I tried to grab her, but it was too late. She faded from my arms like a misty day and vanished.

—◦◦◦◦◦—

From then on, I was by my television set every night, five nights a week. My weekends were one long holding pattern, waiting for the arrival of her show late Monday.

Although she was staying with me longer and longer after her show ended, we discovered the only sure way to keep her from dematerializing was continuous lovemaking. That led to some marathon sessions I will not elaborate on here. She relished escaping from her violent, barbaric world into mine, and I relished her—the feel of her, the sound of her, the scent of her.

It was the perfect love affair. Perfect, that is, if you fail to consider the fact she was the figment of someone's imagination. But I no longer worried I was losing my mind. I didn't care. I was immersed in a cascading pool of bliss. Every night with her was ecstasy, and "reality," whatever that was, be damned. Hell, she called me her "hero." What more could a guy want?

Then, one Monday night, after a particularly long and boring weekend, I turned on my TV and waited for her. I had a bottle of semi-expensive champagne and a new kind of chocolate for her. In the few weeks we'd been together, she was always wanting to try something different from my world.

I no longer had to concoct elaborate sexual fantasies to make her appear—we had established some kind of preternatural link. One quick thought was all it took now.

And you could see it in her face. No matter what the creators of her show had her doing in a particular episode, her heart wasn't in it. I could tell she was waiting for the moment when I would whisk her away from the fighting and into my arms.

I never waited long, and the more often she disappeared, the more the show's minor characters began to take center stage. In fact, her "mysterious" disappearances had become part of the plotline, with both her allies and her enemies left to wonder where she had vanished to, and what "magical powers" she had acquired. In the opening of one show, I actually watched as Phaedra confided to her maidservant that when she disappeared she flew into her lover's arms.

So, there I was, waiting for her, when I see the opening sequence to an episode of *Gilligan's Island*. I started messing with the remote, figuring I've got the wrong channel. But I don't.

Now, I like Ginger and Mary Ann as much as the next guy, but at that moment, pure panic clutched my throat. I flashed through the TV listings and there it was—*Gilligan's Island*, right where *Phaedra* should've been.

I spent the rest of the night looking at every single show in that week's listings, figuring maybe she'd been moved to a different time-slot. I frantically stabbed at the remote until my fingers grew numb. But I couldn't find her anywhere. Finally, I drank myself into oblivion with the champagne I'd bought for her.

The next day, I called the station and found out *Phaedra* had been cancelled. I'm sure I sounded desperate, but I guess they get a lot of crazies calling about their favorite shows, so the woman on the other end took it in stride. I asked if the show had only been cancelled locally, and whether it might still be on other stations around the country. Even before she answered, I was contemplating what I'd have to do if I relocated to a new city.

No, she said, the show was an independent that had ceased production, and as far as she knew, there would be no new episodes. I asked her about reruns. Yes, she said, in time, some station somewhere might pick up the show for reruns. Would her station? She sincerely doubted it.

It seems viewers had been complaining about the show's change in focus from its heroine to other characters. Its ratings had plummeted. Could she give me the address of the production company? Sure.

―❧―

185

For a long time after that, I wrote letters to the company that had distributed *Phaedra, The Warrior Princess*, and then to the creators of the show. I begged, I pleaded, and in one particularly deranged moment, I even threatened. They thanked me for my interest and my praise, empathized with me, and eventually told me, in so many words, to get a life.

After the third letter, they did send me a DVD copy of one episode, but there was no magic in it. No matter how much I fantasized, no matter how much I conjured up images of the nights we had spent together, Phaedra no longer left her world for mine.

Like any great love affair that's ended, I'm left with wonderful memories, memories that widen the cracks in my heart when I dwell on them.

Of course, if you're reading this, you're more likely to think I'm cracked in other places. That's all right. I don't care. I know it was real. I know *she* was real. I know I touched her, kissed her and, on occasion, even transformed that stoic warrior look of hers into a childlike smile.

She was real, all right. She was the love of my life.

Engendered by the fantasy many (most?) guys have had when watching a sexy cartoon character, and created after viewing the animated series *Aeon Flux*, "I Found Love on Channel 3" was the winner of *Speculative Fiction Reader*'s 2003 Firebrand Fiction prize. It has also appeared in *Aberrant Dreams, Man's Story 2, Leafing Through, Emerald Tales,* and the Canadian and Australian anthologies *North of Infinity II* and *Scary Kisses.* However, before it won the short story contest, it collected 43 rejections over 87 months. It taught me you just never know who's going to like what. One editor might think it's garbage, while the next believes it's the best thing since glossy paper.

# SAINT MARGARET

The storm was relentless. For hours, the ship swayed and jerked until she was sure she'd be sick. Her brother and sister had already succumbed to the constant pitch and roll, heaving their suppers across the sodden decks. She was determined not to.

There had been lulls in the gale, but each time she thought it might be fading away, the wind resurrected and the sea resumed its onslaught against the battered vessel. She beseeched God to save them from the tempest, and although she felt guilty for it, she also implored Anya to not let her family's fate be to drown.

She was alone, for the moment, uncertain where her mother had gone. Likely Mother was ministering to her brother and sister on the other side of the hold, although the squall was much too loud for her to hear them, or anything else.

It was bad enough they'd had to flee their home in Wessex, but her mother had insisted they must do so right away, in the dead of night. Margaret had overheard her uncle tell her mother and brother that the armies of "William The Bastard" were on the march and would be at his door the following day. He said it wasn't safe for them. Their royal blood would be sure to adorn the executioner's block if they stayed. William of Normandy had defeated the armies of King Harold at Hastings, and he was not likely to let anyone with a claim to the crown live to stir up rebellion.

So they fled, although her brother Edgar foolishly wanted to stay and fight. Fight with what? The English were a conquered people now. They'd have to bend knee to a Norman king.

Margaret didn't care who was king, even though Edgar thought he had every right to the throne. She only cared that she'd found a home in the courts of Wessex. Her family had traveled so much, and now they were off again.

Even before she was born, when her father was but a baby, he'd been banished from England by Canute, the Viking who seized the throne when Margaret's grandfather King Edmund died. Canute shipped her infant father to Sweden, where he was to be murdered. But someone took pity on the child and spirited him away to Kiev. He grew up there then spent years traveling across the continent before finally settling in Hungary, where she was born. They called her father "Edward The Exile"—although never to his face.

After Canute's reign ended, England was torn by various factions. When one group of nobles learned her father was alive, he was sent for. His claim to the throne was expected to have a stabilizing effect on the fractious nation. So, Margaret and the rest of the family left Hungary and traveled with him to England—which to her was as foreign a place as the godless halls of Persia.

But not long after they arrived, her father died. She heard whispers it was poison, but no one would tell her. She didn't think anyone really knew for certain.

The years after her father's death were happy, for the most part. She enjoyed life at the court—the pomp, the merriment, the gaudy feasts. However, despite the luxuries, she and her sister Christina had vowed to one day become nuns and devote themselves to the Church.

Now, they were forced to leave, running away like thieves in the night. Her mother wasn't sure where they'd go—Burgundy first, then maybe Franconia, where her mother had family. Maybe they'd even return to Hungary. It didn't matter to Margaret. She'd seen the world and didn't think much of it. It was a man's world. Women weren't allowed much. She wanted to do things with her life, not just become some man's wife.

She wondered if all her childhood friends in Hungary were married now. They probably had children of their own, while she had spurned many a suitor. They all seemed to be dilettantes, philistines or vulgar boors. Now, more than ever, she was certain the only bride she'd become was a bride of Christ.

"You never know what fate has in store for you."

Margaret turned at the sound of the voice. Sitting next to her, seemingly impervious to the swaying of the ship, was a tiny gray mouse.

"Anya?"

"I see a man, a powerful man with golden hair and a voice rich like molasses."

The voice Margaret heard was that of a young girl, although it emanated from inside her head rather than in her ears. Yet she knew it was coming from the mouse. It wasn't the first time—Anya appeared to her in many forms.

"Oh, Anya, I beg you to save us from this awful storm. Please, at least save my family. Even if I must die, please spare them."

"Their fates are not my concern. I am only for you, Margaret. Your destiny lies not in the sea but in being seen."

"Seen by who?"

The ship rocked violently, and Margaret tumbled over backwards. When she regained her balance, the mouse was gone.

"Anya? Anya, are you there?"

She was alone again, but no longer afraid. Anya had said her destiny did not lie in the sea, and her *dola* had never been wrong—not since she'd first appeared to her those many years ago in the Hungarian forest. But she wondered what Anya meant? To be seen? And who was the man with golden hair and a voice rich like molasses?

She woke to a calm that belied her fitful night of half-sleep. The deck no longer rolled beneath her. The ship was still.

Margaret rubbed her eyes, pulled off the cloak she'd used as a blanket and stood. She was sore, bruised by the battering of the storm. She straightened her robe skirt and tied it at the waist with a gold-embroidered silk belt. She threw the cloak over her shoulders and fastened it with her silver brooch—the one her father had given her just before he died. She pulled her wimple over her hair and tied it under her neck before climbing the stairs to the main deck.

The ship was docked to a ramshackle pier. Looking seaward, Margaret spied a number of small fishing vessels already underway, sailing out of the harbor. Inland, a quaint hamlet dotted the coastline, and beyond that was a range of rolling hills so green they might have been painted. In the distance loomed nature's counterpoint, a range of jagged black mountains. None of it was familiar to her.

She spied her mother walking on the pier and wondered where her brother and sister were. A man on horseback cantered down the pier toward her mother. When her mother reached the man, she curtsied—which was not at all like her. Having come within a hairsbreadth of being Queen of England, her mother did not show deference easily.

The rider was a powerful-looking man with a rich mantle across his shoulders, sword at his side and braes bound at the knee over forest-green tights. Although she couldn't hear his voice, his hair and full beard were golden.

The ship's captain strode up to the railing where she stood.

"Is this Burgundy?" she asked him.

"No, milady. The storm damaged our foremast and blew us off course. It's alright, I've harbored here before. This is Scotland."

Her brother and sister appeared at her side.

"Where's Mother," asked Christina.

Margaret simply pointed.

Their mother bowed again and turned back toward the ship. The man turned his horse and galloped away.

"Who's that fellow on the horse? Why is Mother bowing?" wondered Christina.

"I recognize him," said Edgar. "That's King Malcolm. I saw him at Wessex once."

Margaret had heard of Malcolm, King of Scotland, but all she knew of him was that he was her uncle's ally and had visited Wessex years ago. Unlike her brother, though, she had no memory of ever having seen him.

Her mother drew close and called to them.

"King Malcolm has granted us safe haven and invited us to his castle. Come now, he's sending for a wain."

—◦⟨⟩◦—

Their ride was more rustic than royal, and its driver had to quickly construct some makeshift steps for the ladies. King Malcolm watched the proceedings from his horse, ordering his retainers to load their luggage.

Margaret prepared to follow her mother and sister up the steps into the rear of the wagon while Edgar took his place on the driver's seat in front. As she stepped up, a strange urge overcame her. For a moment, she felt as if she had no control over her own body. She pulled her skirt off the ground so as not to trip but raised it much higher than was necessary, baring a length of her leg. As she did, she looked up.

King Malcolm was watching her.

She continued up the steps and sat in the wagon, only then feeling as if the loss of control had passed. When it did, she was overcome by embarrassment. What had caused her to do such a thing?

As the wagon pulled away, she chanced a glance. The king was still looking at her.

— ⊚∽⟨⟩∾⊚ —

Margaret found the Scottish castle dreary and damp compared to the colorful halls of Wessex. Even Castle Réka in Hungary, where she'd played as a young girl, was a nicer place.

Like the rest of the manor, the room where they gathered to eat was less than spacious, poorly lit and badly in need of a tapestry or two to adorn its colorless stone walls. Much too austere, she thought, for a king's dining hall.

Still, they could be worse off. They could be eating scraps in William's dungeon. She chastised herself for her lack of graciousness. She should be thankful to King Malcolm for taking them in.

The food, at least, was delicious. There were helpings of mutton, pork and a kind of fish she couldn't identify. The bread was tasty, though coarse, but the dates were not nearly as good as the ones she remembered eating in Hungary. She tried the ale in her cup and found it much too bitter.

The king was an older man—she guessed him to be in his late thirties—more than a decade her senior. A touch of gray streaked his beard, yet he was handsome; and there was a thick brogue in his voice Margaret found charming.

Now that she knew he was a king, he seemed more regal than he had on horseback. A ring of brass fastened a fur-lined mantle across his shoulders, and a single eagle's feather hung from the side of his long blond hair. She'd never seen a man wearing a feather like that before.

The king sat at one end of the table, her mother at the other—which made Margaret wonder where his queen was. Across the table from her, Edgar, and Christina were the king's three young sons, the eldest of whom was only eight or nine. They did not speak but demonstrated hearty appetites.

"It grieves me, Lady Agatha, to hear of the Bastard William's invasion of England."

"Look to your own borders, sire," warned her mother, "for he might not be content with the lands he's already conquered."

Malcolm pulled the dirk from his belt and jabbed it more forcefully than was necessary into a serving tray full of pork.

"Aye, he may try, milady, but he'll likely find Scottish meat a bit too tough for his liking. So says I, Máel Coluim mac Donnchada." He cut off a piece of pork. "Still, it's passing strange that a Norman now sits on the throne of England."

"He's an interloper, not a king," spoke up Edgar. "I'm the rightful King of England."

For a long moment, Malcolm regarded the skinny teenager who was her brother.

"That may be, young prince, but a man who would be king must have followers, an army. Royal blood isn't everything. Your grandfather Ironside would have told you the same."

Malcolm bit into his hunk of meat. He stared at Edgar as he chewed, waiting for a reply. Edgar looked vexed but remained silent.

"I was in much the same state as you, Edgar Aetheling, when I was a boy. After the betrayer Macbeth slew my father, my mother spirited me away for my own protection. But when I reached manhood I made allies, gathered my forces, killed Macbeth and his son Lulach and took what was rightfully mine. It wasn't easy, but being a king isn't as simple as saying you're one. What is yours is only yours if you can take it..." Malcolm grabbed a fistful of air. "...and hold it."

Margaret thought it sage counsel, although she doubted her brother would embrace it. She'd had no idea Malcolm had been exiled, much like her father. She couldn't imagine what ordeals he must have gone through to regain his crown.

She glanced at the king. He was staring at her. She averted her eyes and reached for a piece of bread.

"I was sorry to hear of the death of your wife, milord," said Agatha. "She was known in Wessex as a gracious woman."

"Aye, she was."

"It will be lonely for you now, and hard, with three young boys to raise."

"They're good lads...most of the time." Malcolm stared at his sons as if they'd recently committed some transgression. They avoided their father's gaze.

"When do you think you'll remarry?"

Margaret was appalled at her mother's lack of propriety. The king simply shrugged and took a drink of his ale.

Boldly, her mother continued.

"What a fine union it would be if the King of Scotland were to marry a granddaughter of King Edmund the Second. If the royal house of Scotland were to unite with the royal bloodline of England, it would forge a powerful alliance."

Margaret blushed but kept her head down, eyes on her food. She didn't know if her mother was referring to her or Christina, but the blatant nature of the suggestion was mortifying. It wasn't unusual for her mother to try and find them husbands but speaking thus in their presence was outrageous.

"You speak true, milady," responded the king politely. "It would make for a fine union."

Although she dared not look at him, Margaret was certain she felt the king's eyes upon her as he spoke.

Margaret was alone in the chamber she and her sister had been given. Christina had gone out riding with Edgar, and she didn't know where her mother was. But that was alright. She was happy propped against the bed, doing her needlework, although she kept thinking about King Malcolm. She tried not to—even to the point of reciting holy verses in her head. But thoughts of the king would not be vanquished.

Something brushed against her, and she looked down. It was a cat with thick orange fur. It was purring and rubbing against her. She'd seen this cat before, but that had been a world away.

"Anya? Is that you?"

"You must catch his eye before you can capture his heart." It was the familiar voice of the young girl that Margaret heard in her head, but she wasn't sure who or what Anya was speaking of.

"What do you mean, Anya?"

"The king needs a wife. You need a husband. There are children to be born."

"The king? No, no, I can't," replied Margaret, bemused by the idea. "I'm to be a nun. I am for Christ. God calls me."

"Fate is stronger than faith." The cat rubbed against her once more. "There are children to be born."

Even though her *dola* had never been wrong, Margaret protested, "That can't be, Anya. I've promised—"

"Beg your pardon, milady."

Margaret looked up to see King Malcolm at her door. She hastened to her feet and bowed.

"May I enter?"

"Of course, Your Grace."

"Who were you talking to, lass?"

"I...uh...I was just talking to the cat."

"There are no cats in this keep, milady. My dogs would tear it asunder if they saw one."

Margaret looked round, but of course Anya was gone.

"Who is Anya?" asked Malcolm.

Margaret hesitated, wondering what to say, nervous because it was the king who questioned her. However, it was not in her nature to lie.

"Anya is my *dola*, Sire."

"Your dola? What, may I ask, is a dola?"

"A dola is a protective spirit, the embodiment of one's fate. It can take the form of an animal or a person."

"So, you pray to this pagan sprite?" wondered Malcolm.

"No, Sire, I am a good Christian. I pray only to the one true God. But Anya has been with me since I was a little girl in Hungary. She guides me. I believe God sent her to me."

"I see," said Malcolm, walking over to her small stack of books and picking one up. "I am not so good a Christian, milady, although I make allowances." He opened the book and looked inside. "I've never told anyone this, but as a child, I believed in the *Ghillie Dhu*—little folk in clothes woven of leaves and grass. I even saw one of these benevolent forest elves once, or so I thought. But that was before Macbeth killed my father and the world changed. On that day, I could no longer lend myself to such flights of fancy."

Malcolm continued to look through the book, tracing the lettering with his fingers as he did. Watching him, Margaret couldn't help but think about what Anya had said to her.

"This is a work of great craftsmanship," said Malcolm. "I've never seen a book with golden letters and precious stones on its pages."

"I like to embellish my books. Would you care to borrow it?"

"I'm afraid I don't have the knowledge of reading, milady. But I do find books a thing of both beauty and mystery. I suppose if I could read them, they wouldn't be so mysterious, would they?"

Malcolm chuckled, but Margaret was surprised at his admission. A king who couldn't read?

"Reading is not that difficult, milord. I could teach you, if I had time."

"Speak you true?" Malcolm appeared intrigued by the possibility. "Then I pray God grant us the time. "However, I have other demands upon my time now. I must depart, and beg pardon for interrupting your needlework."

"Not at all, Your Grace. As your guest, I am at your bidding," Margaret said with a curtsy.

"Your presence in my home does me honor, milady," said Malcolm with a brief bow of his head.

When he was gone, Margaret looked for Anya, but she wasn't likely to return now. Yet what the dola had said kept returning to her. *There are children to be born.* The king's children? Her children?

After supper the second night in Dunfermline Castle, Margaret was unsettled. She begged leave to go to her room as soon as was polite and stayed there for some time. During the meal, Malcolm had made a point of speaking to her several times, asking her opinion and seeming to gauge her answers. He all but ignored Christina, and did not seem that enthralled with engaging either her mother or brother in conversation.

It was his manifest interest in her that was troubling. Not that she didn't find Malcolm an intriguing and handsome man, but that was something she didn't want to dwell on. Instead, she wanted to pray. She felt the need to commune with the Holy Spirit.

However, she found it difficult to clear her mind of the king.

"Go to the chapel."

Startled by the sound, Margaret flinched. She turned to see a familiar face. A young girl of only twelve or thirteen years.

"Anya. Oh, Anya, I'm so glad to see you. My mind is in disarray. Tell me what to do."

"Go to the chapel," repeated the dola.

"Yes, yes," agreed Margaret. "I'll be able to clear my mind and pray in a house of God."

By the time Margaret had collected her cloak and put on her wimple, Anya was gone. But Margaret hardly noticed. She hurried out, down the stone stairway and outside the castle. The soldiers there paid her no mind.

The night air was thick with fog, but she knew where the little chapel was. She'd seen it just across the courtyard when she first arrived. Still, she went slowly, careful of her footing, her skirt sweeping the ground with every step.

She heard a noise and discovered a trio of waifs so poorly clothed they must have been chilled to the bone. They were huddled inside a small shed next to the chapel.

"What are you children doing here? You should go home."

The oldest of the three, a boy of maybe ten, replied, "We have no home, milady. We're orphaned, we are."

The poor wretches were as scrawny as scarecrows, and Margaret could only think of feeding them. She reached into her robe and pulled out what coins were there. She gave them to the boy.

"Get yourselves some food. I'll speak to the priest about finding you shelter."

The boy accepted the coins, but replied, "The priest runs us off when he sees us, milady."

Margaret couldn't imagine anyone being so cruel to children, especially a man of God.

"I will speak with the priest. Go on, now, feed yourselves."

The children ran off, and Margaret found the entrance to the chapel. She didn't know what she'd expected—certainly not the splendor of the churches in Wessex—but she was surprised by the extravagance of the tiny church. There were rich tapestries of velvet and ermine along the walls and adorning the altar, upon which lay chalices of gold. A golden crucifix hung on the wall above it.

Given what she'd witnessed just outside its doors, the opulence was anything but devout, to her way of thinking. Praising God was one thing, ignoring poverty was another. Someday, she would work to change that.

She refrained from approaching the altar, choosing instead to kneel in the rear. She began to pray, asking for clarity to end her confusion.

Before long, her silent communion was interrupted by voices coming from the front of the chapel. At first Margaret tried to ignore them, continuing to pray. When the voices grew louder she had no choice but to listen, although she kept her head down and continued to kneel.

"...and if I aid you in this plot against the king, what is my reward?"

"My dear priest, isn't the removal of this heathen king enough? He's never been a true Christian."

"That may be so, but neither does he interfere with the church's business. What you propose is for the church to intercede and support your claim to the throne. Some might call that treason."

"Treason to right the wrong? I, Máel Snechtai of Moray, am the rightful King of Scotland."

"Perhaps, but—"

"Don't pretend you have qualms, priest. We both know you can be bought. The only question now is the price."

"Yes, well...how much gold are we speaking of?"

The men continued to move as they spoke, and for a moment, Margaret was afraid they would happen upon her. She shifted her position, trying to see where else she could hide, and slipped.

"What was that?"

"Someone's in here."

Hearing she'd been discovered, Margaret stood in plain view of the men and ran for the door.

"Stop her!"

She heard them give chase as she pushed open the chapel door and raced through the fog. She was frightened and disoriented. She could only pray she was headed in the right direction, running like she hadn't since she was a young girl.

A voice ahead of her, to her left, called out, "This way, this way." It was Anya.

Her heart pounded as though it would burst from her chest when she reached the castle. One of the soldiers she had passed earlier came running. She could hardly catch her breath to say, "The king—I must speak with the king."

———————

The guard outside the king's chamber stopped her.

"I must speak with the king. It's urgent."

"The king has retired for the evening, milady. He mustn't be disturbed."

"He must be," insisted Margaret, "for I have news that is more than disturbing. You must allow me—"

"What's this all about?" bellowed Malcolm, appearing at the entrance to this chamber.

"Sire, I'm sorry. The Lady Margaret insists upon speaking with you."

Malcolm looked at her, and she realized what an unflattering figure she must present. Between the damp of the fog and the sweat of her own exertion, she must look like so much flotsam.

"Please enter, milady."

Margaret stepped inside but couldn't contain herself.

"Your Majesty, there is a plot against you."

"There usually is." Malcolm smiled. It almost seemed to Margaret as if he found her state amusing.

"Sire, this is no jest. There are those here in Dunfermline who would see you cast out or worse."

"Did your dola tell you this?"

"No, but she led me to where I heard it with mine own ears. Your own priest plots with a man named Snechtai—Snechtai of Moray he called himself."

The name struck a chord with Malcolm. His expression darkened.

"Snechtai is the son of Lulach, whom I dispatched to reclaim my throne after I killed his stepfather Macbeth. You say the priest is in league with him?"

"The last thing I heard, Sire, was the priest discussing how much he'd be paid for his treachery."

To his guard, Malcolm commanded, "Gather the men and conduct a search. Bring me the priest—and Snechtai of Moray, if he's still about."

The guard hurried off, and Malcolm took Margaret's hand, leading her to a chair within his chamber. By now, several servants had been roused and stood waiting.

"Please sit and rest yourself, Lady Margaret." To the servants he said, "Bring us some warm broth and bread."

Malcolm paced as he spoke, and Margaret saw the concern on his face.

"I must thank you for your forewarning, milady. A king must always beware of assassins."

"I simply wanted to pray, milord. It was Anya who sent me to the chapel. I think she must have known what I would hear."

"Then I thank Anya as well as your piety. It is unfortunate that many of the Christian faith only feign to follow their own teachings."

"It is a sorrow, but true, Your Grace. I have seen such time and again."

Malcolm stopped pacing and looked at her.

"Your brother tells me you and your sister are determined to join a nunnery."

Margaret felt herself blush, although she didn't know why.

"Yes, Your Grace, I hope to someday right such wrongs within the church, and to work for the further glory of God."

"A solitary nun would find altering the course of the church quite difficult, I imagine. Perhaps you would be in a better position to right those wrongs if you were a queen."

It took Margaret more than moment to absorb the implication. She blushed all over again.

"Sire?"

"You should know, Lady Margaret, that, with your permission and that of your family, I intend to pursue your hand in marriage, and to make you my queen."

His words left her dazed, speechless. Although her grandfather had been king, and had come from a long line of kings, Margaret had never considered, even for a moment, that she might become a queen. Such fanciful thoughts were for little girls who knew nothing of the real world.

She didn't know what to say, let alone what to think. Malcolm was right. As queen, she would be able to help the less fortunate, to change the church for the better. It would not be easy, but at least she could try.

Yet she didn't know how to be a queen—or, for that matter, a wife. She'd long since given up on the idea. Perhaps it was time to consider new ideas.

—⊱❦⊰—

Less than a year after their chance meeting in 1070, Margaret and Malcolm were married. They would have eight children, including a daughter Edith, who would go on to become the Queen of England when she married Henry I, and three sons who would all become kings of Scotland. Christina would, indeed, become a nun, but Edgar never became king.

Though Shakespeare's Macbeth was a work of dramatic fiction, there was, in fact, a real Macbeth. However, he didn't murder King Duncan. The king was killed in battle against Macbeth's forces, and years later, the king's son Malcolm killed Macbeth (as King Malcolm relates in this tale).

Queen Margaret was known to attend to orphans and the poor every day before she ate. She is said to have risen every midnight to attend church services every night and was known to work for religious reform. She was considered to be an exemplar of the "just ruler" and influenced her husband and children to be just and holy rulers.

Margaret was canonized in the year 1250 by Pope Innocent IV in recognition of her personal holiness, charity, fidelity to the Church, and work for religious reform. The spot where she and her family first landed in Scotland is still known today as Saint Margaret's Hope.

In 1093, Malcolm was killed in battle after reigning as King of Scotland for 35 years. Margaret, who was already ill, died just a few days later—some say from sorrow.

Among the direct descendants of Saint Margaret and King Malcolm were King Henry II, King Edward III, Sir Ralph Neville, and the author of this tale, who has no title to speak of (royal or otherwise) but is their great-great-great-(27x)-grandson.

"Saint Margaret" was a tale that grew out of a sudden interest I developed in my family heritage. After trying to determine all the bloodlines of my granddaughter Savannah, and looking at the genealogical information my aunt Barbara had previously assembled, I caught the bug, spent many hours discovering research others had done with connections to my family lines, and ended up with a very complex family tree that, for a couple of lines of descent, predated the 10th century. While information that far back is often sketchy, the tale of Saint Margaret and King Malcolm is based on all the historical information I could glean, along with my "what if" addition of the Hungarian imp/spirit of the *dola*.

# RECKONING

Two down, sacks loaded, three and one—I knew I had to throw a strike. I figured I could throw one by him. Nothing fancy...go with the heat...muscle up and blow it by him.

Ruiz, my catcher, he gives me the sign for a yakker. I'm thinking he's crazy. No way I'm risking a breaking ball three-and-one. Anyway, I knew I could throw it by this guy. He was nothing. He was meat on a stick. So, I shook off the sign.

He puts down three fingers for the change. I'm thinking screw him, I can blow this guy away. I shake him off again.

Finally, he gives me the number-one, my bread and butter. I figure I'll throw it by him, then three-and-two and he's mine.

I wind up, put a little extra juice on it, and let fly....

Next thing I know I'm listening to the PA guy.

"It's a graaand slaaam, folks. Rusty Storr's thirteenth homer of the season."

He slammed me. I couldn't believe it. How'd he catch up with that pitch?

I knew when I saw Maggio pop his ugly head out of the dugout and start my way I was screwed. I was in no mood to listen to his crap, but I knew that wasn't gonna stop him.

"What kind of pitch was that? You call that pitching? My grandmother could've thrown that fat one."

"Bring in your grandmother, then."

"You're outta here. Give me the ball."

"It's all yours," I said, flipping it to him as I walked away.

"Hey! Get back here and wait for your relief."

I thought of several clever comebacks, but I kept them to myself. Maggio, though, wasn't gonna let it go that easy.

"Yeah, well, just keep on going. You're washed up anyway, yuh bum."

I flashed him the international symbol of disrespect and kept going. It wasn't that I disagreed with his evaluation of my skills. I just didn't cotton to his managerial style.

It's funny the things you notice at a time like that. The first thing I focused on during that long walk back to the dugout was the moths dancing around the light towers. Then I saw the mascot trying to drink a beer he had begged off some fan. Most of it was dribbling down the front of his costume. And although it was the last thing on my mind at that moment, my eyes fastened on to this annie with a chest like two softballs—the giant mushball kind they use in the Sunday beer leagues.

But she wasn't paying any attention to me. She was checking out Donner at first base.As casual as I tried to act, by the time I got to the bench I was ready to puke my guts out. It had become a familiar feeling. Six years in the minors, and my arm wasn't getting any younger. I wasn't no poet laureate, but I could read the writing on the wall. In big, bright letters, it spelled *LOSER*.

—⚬✥❧🙘⚬—

When I finally woke up my mouth felt like I'd been sucking on a resin bag. My head was ringing so loud I might as well as have been beaned by one of my own fastballs. I didn't want to open my eyes, but I knew I'd have to eventually.

I thought back to try and figure out what had left me in this condition, and what I might find when I did risk a look. All I remembered was the big dinger I'd given up, and a lineup of empty shot glasses.

I took a peek and realized I wasn't alone. Had the pounding in my head not been so heavy, I probably would've noticed someone was lying on my arm. So, I had no choice but to open my eyes and take a good look.

God, she was an ugly one. I mean, don't get me wrong, she had a great body, if you like the pillowy look, but her face belonged in a manual explaining why catchers wear masks. It wasn't the first time I'd woken up next to a bowser, and I figured it probably wouldn't be the last, but this one was going for the record. To get away without waking her, I would've chewed my arm off right then and there, but it was my pitching arm, and there was at least a slim chance I might still need it.

Fortunately, it wasn't long before she rolled over, freeing me to get the hell out of Dodge.

Once outside, I found myself in some part of town I didn't recognize. I started walking, hoping I'd find a taxi or something. By then, it was all coming back to me, and I'm wishing I was still asleep. It didn't take much remembering to recall my pitching career was on the fast track to Nowheresville, and last night I'd punched my own ticket.

I knew I'd be lucky to last the season. At my age, they wouldn't even bother sending me down. It would be *c'est la vie* and *sayonara*—thanks for the memories. I had to face facts. I was never even gonna get a cup of coffee in the bigs.

It was still early, a Sunday morning, I think. There wasn't even nobody on the street for me to ask where the hell I was. Then I heard this *guh-thump* noise. Then again, *guh-thump...guh-thump*.

I figure whoever's making the racket can tell me how to get back to the ballpark, but when I turn the corner I see it's some kid, maybe ten or eleven. He's got his cap on ass-backwards like the kids do today, his pointy little ears sticking up like flags, and he's throwing a ball against this cement wall—*guh-thump...guh-thump*. He's trying to pitch, but his follow-through has all the grace of a drunken giraffe. Speaking of which, by now I'm close enough that the *guh-thump* is echoing inside my hangover.

*Guh-thump.*

"Hey, whatcha doing?" I yell to him.

*Guh-thump.*

"Practicing," he answers without stopping.

*Guh-thump.*

Then, cause I can't take any more *guh-thumps*, I grab the ball on the rebound before he can glove it.

"You'll never throw strikes like that, kid. You gotta bring your arm over the top like this, and follow through across your body after you release it."

"How would you know?" he says, real smartass, like.

"Cause I'm a pitcher, kid. Here, try it like this."

I wound up and let one go, easy-like. It hit dead-center inside the chalked circle the kid had drawn on the wall. I saw he was impressed, so I worked with his form for a few minutes, just till I'd smoothed it out enough he wasn't practicing any more bad habits. He was a quick learner.

"Try one more."

The kid wound up and fired...dead center, right down the heart.

"There, just like magic."

He gave me a quick smile, retrieved his ball, and shot me one of those glances kids do when they've got a serious question.

"You believe in magic?"

"Me? I believe if you work your butt off you might—just might—be lucky enough to make it. But if you don't, all the magic in the world won't do you no good. That's what your pitching needs now—lots of work. Just keep practicing until you can throw nine out of ten inside your target."

"Nine out of ten?" he repeated, as if I'd asked him to memorize the Bill of Rights.

"Hey, if you want to be the best, you gotta be willing to pay the price."

"The price?"

"Yeah, whatever it takes. Everything's got a price. You gotta sacrifice. You gotta give to get. There's always a reckoning. Didn't anybody ever teach you that?"

"Are *you* the best?"

"Yeah...right. Hell, I'd give anything to be the best—even for a day."

Then he says to me, real grownup-like, "I guess you didn't sacrifice enough, huh?"

He froze me for a second with that, like a southpaw with a real good pick-off move.

"Hell, you're a kid, what do you know?"

He just flashed me this big grin.

"Now, tell me how I get out of here. Point me in the direction of the ballpark, kid."

He grabbed my arm and pointed down the street. As soon as he touched me I felt this electric tingle, kinda like when you smack your funny bone and things go numb for a second. It ran from my fingers all the way up through my shoulder.

"You can go that way there," he said, "or you can take the shortcut."

"Give me the shortcut, kid, I'm in a hurry."

—◦◦◦◦—

My next start I pitched a one-hitter. I followed that with a no-hitter—yeah, no bull. My arm felt like it was nineteen again. I can't explain it—it just came out of

201

nowhere. All of a sudden I'm hitting my spots, my curveball's breaking like a mother-trucker, and my heater's in the mid-nineties. I mean, I'm throwing some serious gas.

About the same time, the big club got a little desperate. They were in a pennant race, and one of their starters went down with a bad wing. So, they looked around, and there I was. They gambled and jumped me from Double-A all the way to the majors. That's how I finally made it to the Show.

I get my first start against the Cards, and I'm one nervous rookie. I'm standing there on the lip of the dugout, soaking it all up. The stands full of people, the scoreboard with my name in the starting lineup, my teammates getting pumped for the first pitch, and I'm thinking this is the same field where Musial played...the same mound where Gibson pitched. Swear-to-God, I'm tingling all over—when I see the kid.

The same kid I was showing how to pitch a couple weeks back. Only that was on the other side of the country. But I'm sure it's him—same hat on ass-backwards, same pointy ears. I stare at him, but he's just sitting there in the stands, field level.

Number 16 pats me on the behind on his way to take the field, and I snap out of it. I decide to figure out the kid later, cause I got a game to pitch.

—❧—

Despite a case of the shakes that has me walking the lead-off man on four straight, everything's still working, and I pitch my way out of some trouble. I'm holding them scoreless through eight and am getting ready to go out for the ninth with a two-nothing lead. The guys are slapping me on the back, telling me to close it out, and I happen to look over to the stands.

What do I see but that damn kid again. This time he looks right at me and flashes that little grin of his. I'm still trying to figure out how he might've got there when it's time to take the mound.

I strike out the first guy, but then I give up a bloop single. While I'm worrying about the guy on first, the next batter drives one into the gap. Now I really got something to worry about. It's second and third, and I can see them scurrying around in the pen. I decide to go from the windup but fall behind three-and-one.

The catcher calls for Uncle Charlie, and I shake him off. Then he puts down three fingers, but I want to come with the heat so I shake him off again.

Strike two. Strike three. I blow the guy away with a couple of pills.

Now I just need one more out for the win. I come with another fastball and... *crack!* Suddenly, a line shot's coming right at my head. I swipe at it with my glove as I'm falling to get the hell out of the way. It hits me somewhere, and I hit the ground. The next thing I know, the crowd is dead silent, and my teammates are pulling me up.

Talk about luck. The ball was jammed into the webbing of my glove. The game was over, and I had my first major league win.

On my way off the field, I'm high-fiving, low-fiving, and then I remember the kid and look over to where he was sitting, but he's not there anymore. At this point, I don't really care, cause I got a W.

—❧—

I didn't stop there, no, sir. I threw a one-hit shutout at Cincinnati my second start then a five-hitter against the Cubs at Wrigley. Before you know it, I'm getting more press in the clubhouse than an ironing board. Oh, yeah—they also signed me to a three-year Major League contract, big bucks. If I told you how many zeros, you wouldn't believe me.

Not long after that, I met Sonja, the kind of classy woman I never figured would go for me. In less time than it takes to play a four-game series, we fell in lust, in love, got crazy, and got married. Then, believe it or not, the day after our 48-hour honeymoon, I no-hit the Giants. Was I living a charmed life or what?

I didn't stop to worry about how long it would last, I rode that puppy for all it was worth. I rode it all the way into the last game of the season. A win would put us into the playoffs, and I drew the start.

In the clubhouse before the game, the guys are all pretty loose. Someone's got ESPN on the tube, and I'm trying to look like I'm not listening, even though I am, cause the guy's talking about me.

"...Of course, he hasn't proven it over the course of a whole season."

"That's right, Dan. No one knows if he's just fooling hitters because they haven't seen his stuff enough, or if he's the real thing. But right now, he's the best pitcher in baseball."

"That would be tough to argue with. As for the rest of the staff..."

It was a tough game. I threw the hell out of the ball, but these guys were no pushovers. By the top of the ninth it was 3-3, and I was just about out of gas. On my way out to the mound, something catches my eye, and I glance into the stands. It's funny how, in that sea of faces, I would spot him—looked right at him and didn't even notice anyone else.

It was the kid again. Different city, same kid. He kind of waved to me with this serious but dopey look on his face. Not knowing what else to do, I nodded to him and took the mound. While I'm warming up, I get curious and look back at the kid, or at least where he was. Now I can't see him.

Anyway, I got two quick outs, but the next guy plays pepper with the outfield wall and my left-fielder kicks it around. So, I've got the go-ahead run on third, and the way they're heating up in the pen, I know this is my last batter. Which is just as well, cause my arm is dead.

I start him with a curve then come in with the change. He's oh-and-two before he knows it and hasn't a clue what to look for. I decide to throw a BB on the outside corner. I wind up, let fly, and *crack!* Only it's not the sound of the ball hitting the bat, cause I just whiffed the guy.

I've got enough time to see him swing and miss before the pain knocks me to the ground. That's when I see my pitching arm dangling like a piece of cooked spaghetti.

If you follow the game, you probably know I never pitched again. But I did see that kid once more. It's crazy, but I'm sure it was the same kid. It was eight or nine years later, long after the cancer had gotten so bad they had to amputate.

I was sitting there, watching Sam play. Yeah, Sonja had stuck with me, and we had a little boy. Well, I'm watching him play ball. He's out at shortstop, and he makes this great stab and throw on a grounder in the hole. I'm talking Major League play here. So, all the parents are clapping and whistling as the team runs in, and that's when this kid comes up to me.

I don't recognize him at first. Why should I? The kid I remembered should've been full-grown by now. But this kid holds out a baseball card, and I see it's mine—the only one they ever made of me.

"Could you sign this for me?" he asks, real polite-like.

Now, you gotta know I don't get that many requests. I was such a flash-in-the-pan not many even remember me, especially a kid like this, who should've been in diapers when I made the bigs. So he's catching me off-guard, but I take the card from him.

"Sure, kid," I say, using the pen he hands me.

"It's too bad about your arm," he says right out, which surprises me again, cause most people are afraid to even mention it.

"Yeah, life's tough."

"But you were the best once, weren't you?"

I finish signing the card, look up to hand it back, and that's when I recognize him. It's the same kid I stumbled on that day I was lost—*the same kid*. I knew it was him, but I also knew it couldn't be, 'cause this kid looked *exactly* the same. I mean, he hadn't aged an inning.

"Yeah, kid, I guess I was the best...for a time."

He takes the card, glances at the signature then looks back up at me, with his cap still on ass-backwards, his ears pointing up at the sky, and asks, "Was it worth it?"

I knew right away where he was coming from.

"Sure was, kid. Hell, yes."

Much to my amazement, this is my most popular story with editors—it has been published twelve times prior to its appearance in this collection. Originally published under the title "The Sacrifice" in *Palace of Reason*, "Reckoning" has appeared in *Doorways*, *Twin Cities Magazine of Science Fiction & Fantasy*, *Dark Discoveries*, *SB&D*, Peridot Books, Scrybe Press, *Leafing Through*, *Wily Writers Speculative Fiction*, and the anthologies *Love & Sacrifice*, *Stories of Myth, Legend, and Future*, and *The Magazine of Fantasy & Science Fiction*.

This tale was inspired, in part, by the travails of former San Diego Padres pitcher Dave Dravecky, who lost his pitching arm to cancer. I dedicate this story to him, and to my son Eric, a great pitcher in his own right.

# THE BIRTHDAY GIFT

Everyone was there—Aunt Gertie; Uncle Roy; the cousins from Chicago whose names I could never remember; the triplets, Pat, Pam, and Priscilla, whose names I could remember but never knew which was which; even Great-uncle Bob—they were all there. Them and more that I had never even heard of.

It was 1969. The country was still recovering from a pair of shocking assassinations, young men were being torn from their loved ones and sent to Southeast Asia to die, and man had just set foot on the moon.

I knew about Neil Armstrong's one small step, but I was too young to think about much else but myself—especially on that day my entire family gathered at Grandpa and Grandma Easterly's ranch outside of Winslow, Arizona. I didn't recognize half the faces, but my mom said they were all relatives in one way or another.

I thought of them all as ducks congregating to quack at the same pond. The idea made me laugh—especially when I pictured Aunt Gertie waddling like one. Of course, I was just a little kid at the time, one with a notoriously wild imagination.

The big family reunion had been called to celebrate two birthdays, both of which fell on November 1st. The truth was, the big to-do was really only for one special birthday. Great-Grandpa Easterly—Gramp Jack, I liked to call him—was celebrating his 100th birthday. That was the real reason why my mom and dad had driven all the way from San Diego, and why the rest had flown in from all over the country, including Hawaii, where Second- (or was it third?) cousin Bill lived. And even though it was also my birthday, eight years weren't much when compared to a hundred.

I didn't care that everyone was fussing over Gramp Jack instead of me. That just meant more time to play. Not that I had anyone to play with. I was the only kid—if you didn't count cousins Amy and Erin, who were just babies and no fun to play with. Everybody else was a teenager or grownup; I didn't see much difference.

So, as soon as we finished lunch and unwrapped all the gifts, I wandered off into the neat trees that grew all around the ranch. I'd grown bored listening to old family stories, and besides, my mom kept telling me to "stop making all that racket." The racket being caused by my favorite birthday present, the one Gramp Jack gave me.

It was the kind of battery-powered toy machine gun they had back then that shot sparks and fired off half a dozen caps every time you pulled the trigger. It was shiny black, plastic-smooth, and fit right in my hands. It was just what I had wanted. That, and the skateboard my mom and dad had got me. But a skateboard wasn't much good on a ranch.

*Rat-tat-tat-tat-tat-tat!*

Another evil alien invader appeared from behind a tree and met his doom. I moved deeper into the off-world jungle of my imagination, stalking creatures with one eye and four arms. Each time I wheeled and aimed the toy weapon there was another one—*rat-tat-tat-tat!*

I felt a little guilty that I hadn't gotten Gramp Jack anything for his birthday. But nobody had told me to, and besides, Mom and Dad had put my name on their present, so that was from me, too.

I sprang from my hiding place, hit the dirt sliding on my belly, rolled across the ground, and came up firing. *Rat-tat-tat*—it jammed! I unlocked the clip and pulled it out. Nope, it wasn't jammed, I was just out of ammo. I pulled a spare roll of caps from my pocket and sat—calling for a temporary truce with the enemy.

Now, how had Gramp Jack put that in? I fiddled unsuccessfully with the roll, trying to feed it into the tiny slot so it could get started. Darn! Why hadn't I paid attention when Gramp Jack had showed me? Stupid thing!

My fiddling led to frustration, and I kicked at the ground. The kick sent a stone flying into one of the many small ravines lacing the woods, and the echo of its fall came back to me. But the echo seemed to go on and on, as if coming from farther away.

It was then I realized I was hearing something else. Something that sounded like distant screams. Not like calls for help, but wild, threatening screams like... like a bunch of Indians. I listened some more until I was sure. I'd seen enough old movies to know the cries of an Indian war party when I heard them.

I closed the machine gun, still in disrepair, and stood. The sounds were getting louder, coming closer. I heard the sounds of horses and gunshots, and that was all I needed to hear. I started running as fast as my size-three tennies would carry me. I ran straight for the ranch house. But where was it?

The rush of adrenaline had left me confused. I was no longer sure in which direction it stood. I had gone so far into the forest I couldn't see it anymore. Panic fueled the pumping of my little legs. The war cries were right behind me. I could hear the pounding of hooves. I didn't dare look back. I just ran, clutching my birthday present, unwilling, even in that moment of terror, to abandon it.

When it seemed I was so scared I'd swallow my own tongue, I broke through the trees and saw the ranch house. I didn't stop, even though the sounds of pursuit had faded. I didn't stop until I burst through a throng of relatives most impolitely and was corralled by my mother.

"Matthew! What are you doing?" she said angrily. "Quit running around like a wild—"

"Indians!" I had caught my breath and didn't hesitate to interrupt. "Indians...they're coming!"

Most of the family members standing nearby smiled and laughed, and remarked on little Matthew's Hollywood potential.

"Matthew, I don't want you running around people like that. You're going to knock someone over. Now, if you can't play nice—"

"But really, Mom, there *were* Indians! I heard them and they chased me and—"

"All right, that's enough, Matthew Easterly. I don't care if it is your birthday. If you can't behave, you'll have to go sit in the house."

I started to say something else, but one look at my mother told me it was useless. I looked back toward the forest. There was nothing there. I listened, but didn't hear anything.

"That boy has such a vivid imagination, sometimes I don't know what I'm going to do with him," said my mother to whomever. Then she turned to my dad. "I don't know why your grandfather had to buy him the noisiest toy in the store."

My dad shrugged and turned to me.

"It was probably just the wind you heard, Matt," he said, putting his arm around me. "The wind can make some awfully strange noises blowing through those trees. I know, I played in those woods when I was a boy."

"But, Dad, there were gunshots and war cries and horses and—"

"Matthew." It was the stern voice of Gramp Jack that stopped me. The old man was sitting in his favorite rocker, on the porch of what used to be the hired help's bunkhouse. It was his little cottage now. "Come here, boy."

My dad smiled and gave me a gentle boost in Gramp Jack's direction. He motioned for me to sit on the porch.

"Boy, did I ever tell you the story 'bout how my folks—your great-great-grandparents—was killed by Injuns?"

I shook my head.

"Didn't think so," said Gramp Jack, tapping his new birthday pipe against the railing to free the ashes. "Well, listen up.

"My folks was headed for Californee in a small wagon train out of Texas. I was 'bout four at the time, and dumb as a three-legged jackass. Well, the wagons had stopped to rest and water the horses, so I'm wanderin' off playin'. It was just over that way not too far." Gramp Jack pointed beyond the woods where I'd been playing. "That's when the Injuns hit. I guess they figured we was trespassin' on their land. They come screamin' out o' them woods with warpaint streaked 'cross their faces, firin' arrows from horseback like there was no tomorrah. Apaches, they was, the coldest, bloodiest killers that ever lived."

By then, my eyes were as wide as they could get. From the first mention of Indians, my attention was locked on my great-grandfather's every word.

"My pa and ma and the others never had a chance. Every one of them was slaughtered by them red devils. So, I never got to Californee. When I was old enough, though, I came right back to this spot and decided this was where I was gonna build my own spread. No Injuns was gonna scare me off the land, no, sir. Why I—"

"But how'd you get away from the Indians?"

Gramp Jack leaned back in his rocker and slowly refilled his pipe with tobacco. I waited patiently as he lit the pipe, inhaled, then exhaled a cloud of smoke.

"That's the strange part of the story. As soon as I saw them Injuns, I knew I was in trouble—even bein' as dumb as I was. I lit out for the cover of them trees just as fast as I could. But one of them braves saw me and whooped and hollered like he'd found a prize pig. He turned his pony so hard it nearly broke a leg."

"What did you do, Gramp Jack?"

"What did I do? What did I do? Damn, boy, I did what any little brat, dumb or 'telligent, would do. I ran like hell. But you can't outrun a horse. I made it into them trees and turned around. The injun bearin' down on me was so fierce-lookin' I froze, starin' at death thunderin' towards me.

"Then, from I-don't-know-where, this boy—not from the wagon train, mind you, 'cause I'd never laid eyes on him before—this boy who was a little older than me pops up on the ridge. If it weren't for that boy in them woods, I wouldn't be here now, tellin' you this story." Gramp Jack laughed at some private joke and added, "I guess you wouldn't be here, neither."

"What happened then? How did the boy save you?" asked Matthew.

"Well—"

"Happy birthday to you, happy birthday to you..."

Gramp Jack stopped his story as the whole Easterly clan moved in around him singing. My mom carried the cake, ablaze with what looked liked all 100 candles, and Uncle Roy had his Bell & Howell 8-mm camera out, filming the event for posterity. I eased back as the relatives crowded around their senior member, and wound up being pushed back by sheer force of numbers.

I blocked out the singing and wondered about Gramp Jack's story—wondered if he'd made it up—wondered if he'd remember to tell me how he got away. I walked off, sat down and, after a while, figured out how to get the fresh roll of caps into my gun.

"Want some cake, Matt?" my dad asked between mouthfuls.

"Not now, Dad. I want to go play."

"No cake? I can't believe it."

"Dad, when you played in those woods when you were a boy, did you ever hear any Indians?"

"Sure, hundreds of times. I must have killed off a thousand Apache warriors and at least a dozen chiefs in my day. Of course, I had a good imagination—like you do."

"Oh," I said, disappointed.

I got up, locked my fully loaded clip into the gun and started back in the direction I had run from earlier. After just a short distance, I slowed, hesitated and decided to go back. One of my teenage cousins saw me and called out.

"Watch out for those Indians. Just whistle if you need the cavalry."

I turned back towards the trees, ignoring the chuckles.

Part of me—a big part of me—was afraid to go back into those woods. But another part, fueled by curiosity, thought about discovering something beyond belief. The farther I walked, the harder I listened and the less I heard, the more I was convinced it was just another one of Gramp Jack's tall tales, and it *was* only the wind like my dad had said. Even if the story was true, that had been almost a hundred years ago.

I tried to remember the sounds I'd heard. They'd been so real. I'd even felt the beat of the horse's hooves on the ground beneath me. I wished I hadn't been too afraid to turn and look. Then I would have known for sure.

I tried to picture the Indian warrior Gramp Jack had described. Embellished by my own imagination, I saw a trio of eagle feathers perched above a terrifying red face streaked with black and yellow warpaint. I envisioned a necklace of human bones and bear claws draped over a buckskin vest. I even imagined a savage scream and a stone tomahawk slicing through the air.

I could almost see the—"Ah!"

My daydreaming and a hazardous tree root sent me sprawling, and a shower of dirt and rocks flying over the ridge in front of me. I lay there a moment as the echo of falling rocks faded. I got up, dusted myself off, and heard it again. Not the echo, but the screams, the war cries, the gunshots. The sounds were very close and very real.

I jumped up, ready to run, thinking in the same instant no one would believe me again. I stopped in mid-stride and thought about Gramp Jack's story. I thought of the people in the wagon train and the little boy who was Gramp Jack. At the same time, fear tugged at me, pulling me toward the ranch house. But I didn't budge. Something inside me wouldn't let me. Instead, I clutched my plastic machine gun and made sure it was ready to fire. I eased my way over the ridge as the sounds drew closer. All the while a baseball-sized knot swelled in my throat.

It wasn't until I saw him that the knot dissolved. Him—my Indian, complete with war paint and tomahawk, astride a horse that was galloping towards me. No, not me—towards a little boy standing just below me.

It happened so fast, I didn't know what I was doing. I just reacted—raised my gun and fired.

*Rat-tat-tat-tat-tat-tat-tat!*

Sparks flew, and twenty caps burst in rapid succession. The horse reared so hard the Apache brave was thrown to the ground. The younger boy recovered from his shock, took a look at me then turned and ran like a scared rabbit.

The horse raced off, and I looked where its rider had landed. The warrior staggered to his feet and looked at me. Our eyes met for only a moment, but the savage fury I saw in that moment hit me like a thunderclap.

I ran. I ran for real—no game, no imaginary enemy. The brave whooped a victory cry on seeing me flee and gave chase.

I practically flew over the ground, leaping every obstacle, knowing one misstep would be the end of me. All the while, the howls of rage from behind screamed that death was gaining on me.

I wanted to believe that if I reached the edge of the tree line and broke into the open field of the ranch, I would be safe. It wasn't a belief fashioned by reason; it wasn't a moment of reason. I could only hope.

But hope couldn't make me run any faster, and I realized my pursuer would be on me before I could reach that sanctuary.

What I did next was pure reflex. I didn't think it out. I couldn't have if I'd wanted to. I stopped, wheeled around and, with my eyes closed as tight as they would go, fired my toy machine gun.

*Rat-tat-tat-tat-tat-tat!*

I squeezed that trigger for all I was worth and tried to imagine pretend bullets tearing into my savage attacker.

Though my finger never let up, a tranquil silence eventually replaced the frenzied cracking of the caps. I waited with eyes closed, waited for the end to come. When it didn't, I peeked out from under my eyelids and saw only trees, trees and more trees.

When I got back to the ranch house the party was winding down. Feeling shaken, and older than a mere eight years, I passed through a dispersing flock of relatives towards my great-grandfather. He was still in his rocker on the bunkhouse porch, puffing away on his pipe.

I stopped in front of the porch but didn't speak. Gramp Jack stared at me for a moment, real serious-like.

"You've been there, haven't you?"

I nodded.

"Then you know the rest of the story, don't you?"

"Yes, Gramp Jack."

"Well, boy," said Gramp Jack, still very serious, "the way I figure it, you gave me the best goldarn gift of the day." The old man smiled as big a smile as someone with that many wrinkles could manage. "Happy birthday, boy, to the both of us."

Loosely inspired by an old *Twilight Zone* episode and written as an exploration of the paradoxes of time travel, "The Birthday Gift" was a Writers of the Future quarter-finalist, and has been published in *Coyote Wild* and *Emerald Tales*.

# DINNER FOR ONE

Though his eyes routinely adjusted to the dimly lit basement, Karl's nose never did. The stench was inescapable. Even his nose plugs didn't help much. But dealing with garbage was his job now. He cleaned it up, he dumped it, he hauled it. Better the garbage down here than the squalor up above, he thought.

Up there, in the courtrooms and detention blocks of the Hall of Justice, all manner of filth and human carrion flourished. Scumbags and gangsters, predators and panhandlers, mutants and misfits—they were everywhere. They inundated the streets, invaded the entrails of residential complexes, spilled over into the libraries and the markets. Karl loathed them all.

The sound of more refuse sliding down one of many chutes disrupted his inner litany of grievances and, like the echoing of a gong, sent him grudgingly back to work. He unlatched the catch-all from its position, pushed it aside and wheeled an empty into its place. A hunk of sodden paper and a half-eaten piece of rotten fruit were stuck to the chute's mouth, so he climbed up to scrape it off. Up close he saw it was a peach and what looked like wads of wet tissue. Even through his glove he could feel the slime as he stretched up to wipe away the congealed mess. He clenched his teeth and grunted a curse, half-wondering who above could afford a fresh peach.

After a while, he became lost in the monotony of his work and the basement gloom. Even the putrid odors surrounding him seemed to recede. He knew it must be late afternoon, and that meant only a few more hours before he would be home, where a rare treat awaited him. He was going to eat steak tonight—real beefsteak, not soy byproducts or compressed vegetable matter but real meat. He hadn't had a real steak in...

He couldn't remember exactly when it had been. The failure of so many farms and ranches made such delicacies expensive. This one time, though, he had saved enough to indulge himself.

He could almost hear it sizzling under the broiler. He imagined the aroma, and the flavor of the meaty juices as they flowed over his tongue. He had some seasonings somewhere. He'd—

"Leander? Where are you?" A familiar voice interrupted his culinary reverie. "It's always so darn dark down here. Karl, are you down here?"

It was Walt, one of the roving security monitors. He came to the basement whenever he wanted to take an unofficial break. He was a misguided oaf who jabbered incessantly, but Karl endured his visits because...well, because they helped break up his day. Besides, he didn't have much choice.

"Of course I'm here, Walt. Where do you think I'd be?"

"I don't know," Walt said, lumbering down the stairs. "Sometimes they got you cleaning upstairs. Oh, there you are. It takes a while for my eyes to adjust."

Walt sat at the foot of the stairs, as he usually did, and pulled out a candy bar. Karl was continually amazed the stench never affected his appetite.

"It's sure a hot one today," Walt said as Karl continued to work his mop. "You're lucky you're down here where it's cool. It's a zoo upstairs. They're always busier when it's hot. The crooks come out of the woodwork when the weather's like this—God forgive them.

"You know, this world would be a better place if everyone found God. You, too, Karl. You'd look at things a whole lot different if your spirit hooked up with the Holy Ghost."

Karl ignored Walt's spiel, as he always did. He strained to visualize the steak again but couldn't concentrate. It wasn't long before he found himself tuning into the pious windbag's diatribe.

"...ozone's getting worse. Them radiation levels, or whatever they call them, are going up. I heard a report there'll be even more mutants being born because of it. As it is now, Beth and I don't let the kids out till after sundown. But where's it safe to let kids play after dark with all those hunger riots?

"Hey! I've got a new family photo, one of them three-D jobs. Here, take a look."

Karl stopped his mopping and pretended to glance at the picture, but he didn't want to see Walt's family. He didn't want to be reminded.

"See, that's little Timmy and Peggy Ann, and me and Beth, of course. You got any family, Karl?"

"No!"

The terse reply silenced Walt for a moment, but it didn't keep him quiet long.

"Yeah, I guess I asked you that before. You know, children can be a real blessing, Karl. Of course, Beth and I thought long and hard before we decided to have kids. What with all the mutants being born, and the Antarean refugees crowding in everywhere. Our alien brothers do tend to be extremely prolific, God bless them.

"But we prayed over it and decided God put us on this world to be fruitful and multiply, so what the heck."

"Damn aliens and their droids are everywhere," spoke up Karl. "You can't walk down the street without bumping into one. It's not as if we don't already have enough immigrants from all the gutter countries."

"I know what you mean, Karl. Though it's not very charitable of me to say, I'm sure our off-world visitors are contributing to all the shortages. It seems like our monthly allotment is never enough. Just last week one of them random blackouts hit Timmy's school, and they sent all the kids home.

"You used to be a teacher, didn't you?"

Karl flashed him a look that said he wasn't going to answer, so Walt went on.

"You know, I understand some of those Antareans have heard the Word of God. Born again right here on Earth. It's enough to make a man get down on his knees and shout 'Hallelujah!' I truly believe in live and let—"

Walt's com-flap squawked with static, and Karl was tempted to thank a deity himself.

"Walt, you there?"

"Right here. What's up?"

"We've got a toilet gone berserk on the fifth floor. The whole place is flooded. Go down to the basement and get Leander up here."

"I'm on it." Walt stood. "Well, you heard him, Karl. Looks like they need you upstairs, and that means my break is over."

He started back up the stairs, and Karl jammed his mop into the water bucket. The only thing he hated more than cleaning up garbage was cleaning up after filthy degenerates.

Emerging from the Hall of Justice, Karl traded the reek of garbage for the grimy smell of smog and the stink of dried urine. Outside, a familiar billboard greeted him—a monstrous sign, eighty feet above ground and a good fifty feet across. It featured a well-covered citizen, a blazing sun, and the warning "Mega Watts Not Mega Burns." It was an old sign, one that seemed superfluous now.

The real sun was about to drop below the horizon, and the tableau of reds, yellows, and oranges combined with the smoggy haze to give the city a hellish hue. To shield himself from its lurid glare, Karl covered his eyes with dark glasses and stepped out into the teeming multitude.

Compared to his basement's quiet seclusion, the clamor was almost deafening. It was all he could do not to cover both ears with his hands and shout for silence.

The streets reminded Karl, more than anything else, of where he was and what he'd lost. Sidewalks swarming with humanity and its galactic offshoots, streets choked with bikers, skaters and all manner of rollerboarders. He despised them all.

The crush of bodies was even more overwhelming, considering only those who had to be out would be. Those who could, would remain inside the safety of their homes. Streeters would be seeking shelter in whatever shady refuge they could find. They wouldn't come out until dark, when hunger drove them like rats.

It was still hot outside, much hotter than Karl remembered the June evenings of his childhood to have been. He wondered if it was the dwindling ozone or only his fading memory. But there were things he didn't want to remember, so he didn't wonder for long.

Street vendors and pedi-cabbies and beggars called to him. He ignored their mercenary cries and hurried to catch the next solarbus. As he pressed through the wall of bodies to get in line, his skin began to itch, as it always did in such proximity. Too many people. Too many germs. A festering population of cranks and freaks and wireheads. He cursed them and wished they'd all go back to where they came from.

Ahead, he saw a woman with sunken nostrils and no lips. He thought she also might have a third breast, but he couldn't be sure. The sight of the mutant was all the reminder he needed to turn up his coat collar. Like everyone else on the street, he was fully covered despite the heat. Hats, umbrellas, overcoats had all become commonplace with the rise in solar radiation.

He reached under his tattered cap and scratched at the itch behind his ear. As he did, someone bumped into the mutant woman, or perhaps she tripped and fell on her own.

She didn't say a word or make a sound, and the dense flow of pedestrian traffic kept moving around her, creating a momentary pocket. Karl hurried by, pretending not to notice.

He got into line as a group of children who'd disembarked from the solarbus passed by. He scanned their faces a bit too eagerly, trying to see through the shadows created by their little parasols. He didn't see who he was looking for. He never did.

He scratched his neck and shuffled forward a few feet as the line gained momentum. He tried to concentrate on what awaited him at home, tried to ignore the stifling throng. It's what he did every day. Even those days when he had nothing to go home to.

—❧⸻❧—

Karl took a deep breath and released it, closing the door behind him. His hunched shoulders relaxed as if he were tired of holding them up. He activated the door's locking mechanism and set the alarm.

The day had faded, and very little light flared through his solitary window, so he reached up and furiously rubbed the glowbulb in the wall next to the door. The friction soon built up enough of a charge for some faint illumination.

The heat inside was oppressive, but he couldn't afford the air conditioner's drain on his allotment. He began peeling off layers of clothing, all the while trying to convince himself it wasn't that hot.

He thought about the meal awaiting him, the steak he would broil to perfection. As he disrobed, he walked to his tiny bedroom and dropped the clothes onto the bed. He looked at the picture frame on the wall, as he always did. It was a nice frame, with an intertwining black-and-gold design—an expensive one, and an empty one.

He kept meaning to take it down, but he could never bring himself to do it. Each time he looked at it, he tried to imagine Kevin's face, but with each passing week the mental picture he carried of his son grew less vivid.

A crashing clatter from outside his window, followed by the bellow of an argument, caught his attention. Most of the time he was able to block out the steady hum of street noise, but at times it was too loud to ignore. He decided to utilize a portion of his allotment on some music. That wouldn't expend much energy. He chose a soothing ensemble of woodwinds and waterfalls and went to the kitchen.

He rubbed up another glowbulb until it had a good static charge and opened the refrigerator. There it was, not too large but worth every dollar he'd spent. He began unwrapping it, inexplicably gratified by the thick texture of the butcher paper. His nostrils caught the faint, almost-forgotten smell of beef, and he imagined how it would taste with the salad and red potatoes he'd saved to go with it. It was the first steak he'd had since...

Since Helen had taken Kevin and gone away.

She'd told him the city was too crowded, too infested with criminals and perverts, but he'd insisted he couldn't leave his job. He told her teaching positions were hard to come by, and that his job gave them some security. He hadn't realized how determined she was, how little she must have cared about him. Damn her! She'd taken everything, even all their pictures.

The grim joke was, he'd been so distraught over losing his wife and son he'd lost his coveted job. That was more than two years ago, and he was still looking at empty picture frames and keeping the world at a bitter distance.

A little garlic salt, he thought, some pepper—a dash of cumin, if he had any. Most nights he wouldn't bother much with dinner. He'd radiate some prepackaged ready-to-serve meal and be done with it. Tonight, though, would be different. Tonight it would be a labor of love.

When he was done preparing the steak he placed it gently in the oven, punched the broiler setting, selected medium rare and turned to prepare the rest of the meal. Almost immediately, the music stopped. A familiar dying whine issued from the refrigerator. He'd lost power.

A quick glance out his window told him it wasn't a regional blackout, so Karl hurried to his residential powerpack and discovered his last cell completely drained. He cursed the world and slammed the powerpack as if he could bash it back to life. Still two more days until he'd get next month's allotment, and without refrigeration, the steak would spoil. Even if it wouldn't, he didn't want to wait two days. He'd thought of nothing but that steak all day, and he was going to eat it tonight if he had to break up his furniture and burn his books.

He was angry enough to do it, but the building's flame sensors would have doused his cooking fire and sounded an alarm for which he would pay a sizable fine. You couldn't even burn a candle in the city anymore without special dispensation.

He wanted to lash out and break something, hurt someone. Life had become a multi-limbed miscreation that bound and suffocated him, whipped him until the pain made him numb. It was the numbness that reminded him how useless his outrage was.

There was only one thing he could do. He figured he might have enough money to buy a power cell. He'd never bought a black-market cell before, although he knew it was a common, if illegal, transaction. He wasn't sure exactly where to go or whom to ask, but he knew someone on the street would be selling.

He hated the idea of going outside. It was bad enough during the day. At night, it was no place for a civilized person. But he was going to eat that steak if it was the last thing he ever did.

<hr />

The sun had retreated, and the low-pressure sodium lamps lining the streets had begun to shed their orange pall over the city. There were still plenty of people out, but most were streeters with nowhere else to go. More and more emerged from their daylight havens. As their empty bellies began to growl, Karl knew they would gather and grumble and fume. Emboldened by numbers they would spread through some unlucky neighborhood, demanding food that was not theirs, food they had not worked for. He didn't have much, but at least he earned what he had.

It was a warm night, like so many nights seemed to be now, and most of the people Karl saw had shed their protective daylight apparel for less modest garb. Now that they could display their wares, a host of tawdry hookers had taken up positions along the sidewalks. From what he could see, business was brisk.

Squads of police began arriving at standard staging areas, encased in protective body armor, carrying tear gas launchers and stun weapons. They ignored the hookers. They had more volatile problems to deal with.

Maybe Helen had been right. Maybe he should have quit his job and left this festering hellhole of humanity. Maybe...but it was too late for maybes. She and Kevin were gone, and he was here.

The moon peeked over the horizon, bright with the promise of cool radiance. With sunlight now toxic, the moon's glow had become a symbol of purity. It was even the focal point of a new religion. Just what the world needed, Karl had thought scornfully when he read about the Lunarians and their rituals, more crazies.

He fought against his own repulsion to approach several strangers, but the conversations proved fruitless. They either couldn't help him or wouldn't. He was ignored or brushed off or threatened. They were animals, and he detested them all.

Just when he thought his spite might get the best of him, a woman walked out of the shadows, adjusting her minimal skirt. It was obvious to Karl she was selling it...or *he* was. One look at the size of her arms, and Karl wasn't sure. Another pervert.

"Hi, honey," she purred, "want to have some fun?"

"No, thanks," growled Karl, still trying to decide what might be under the skirt. "I'm looking to buy a power cell. Do you know where I can, uh, get one?"

"You don't need no juice, handsome. I can give a charge right here." She moved closer as if to touch him.

Karl did a quick backpedal.

"No, sorry, no."

"Okay," she said, her sugary inflection replaced with one of boredom. "You want Roblevo. He's always got juice for a price."

"Where can I find this Roblevo?"

"Down there, honey," she said, pointing, "corner of Mollison and Third. He always shows up there sooner or later."

—⚬⚬⚬—

When he arrived at the intersection he saw a street vendor unsuccessfully promoting his wares to a passing couple. Karl hesitated then walked up to the vendor.

"Are you Roblevo?" he asked.

"No, can't say that I am," replied the vendor jauntily from behind his portable stand. "The name's McCloud—Big Loud McCloud to my friends and clients. The Roblevo you seek does hang in these parts. No doubt he'll be along soon. But in the meantime, friend, let me show you the latest in solar-powered timepieces." He held up a wristwatch that didn't look much different from any watch Karl had ever seen.

"I don't need a watch," said Karl sullenly.

"This isn't just a watch, sir. No, this is not the antiquated sundial of your glorious ancestors. This is a chronometer of the finest caliber, featuring the latest technological advances acquired during mankind's quest for the stars. This scientific wonder not only calculates the time for any time zone on or off planet, it can do so in four different languages. Meanwhile, it's keeping tabs on your heart rate, blood pressure, body temperature, and—"

"I said I don't need a watch," Karl interjected abruptly. He wished this Roblevo fellow would show up soon. He was getting hungry, and he didn't like being outside so long.

"I understand, friend," the vendor continued undeterred. "You're obviously a man who isn't ruled by time. Not to fear, I have a wide assortment of items for your perusal. Perhaps a pocket pouch made of the finest synthetic leather, or one of these handcrafted dolls for your child? No? I have concert tickets, theater tickets, tickets to balls and ballgames. I have—"

"Do you have any power cells?" asked Karl, interrupting the spiel again.

"I am shocked and chagrined, sir," the vendor said with as much sincerity as he could muster. "Surely you know the unauthorized sale of P-cells is illegal. Big Loud McCloud is a reputable merchant who adheres strictly to all civil and moral codes.

"Perhaps, though, I can interest you in the power of the Lord, good sir. I have some pocket Bibles printed on the highest quality paper, guaranteed to provide you with spiritual enlightenment up until the day you receive the call."

Karl shook his head and impatiently shifted his feet.

"I'll tell you what, friend. With any purchase, I will give you, free-of-charge, a personal aura reading. Surely I must have something you'd like to take home with you."

"Aura? What aura?"

"Your aura, friend, is the light of your soul. During a spiritual journey I once took through Tibet, I learned how to read and interpret the aura that envelops each of us. And I must say, friend, the dark-gray hue of yours is a might distressing. Are you ill?"

"I don't want anything, and I don't want my aura read!" snapped Karl. "I just want to find a power cell and get home."

"You lookin' for juice?"

Karl turned at the sound of a bellowing voice. A hulk of a man stood there, his long, thick arms dangling at his sides. A dull expression tempered his face, and his clothes looked like something a streeter would throw away.

"Well, you lookin' for juice or what?"

His size and demeanor made Karl apprehensive.

"Yes, I need a power cell. Are you Roblevo?"

The expressionless giant didn't reply, but he motioned for Karl to follow him.

As he trailed behind the brute, wondering if he were being foolish, Karl noticed the dark street getting even darker. He looked up. A thick cloud bank was moving in, blanketing the sky and blotting out the moonlight.

The giant stranger led him a short distance to a spot where there were few people about. Waiting for them was an Antarean. It was shorter than Karl, although its diamond-shaped head gave it the appearance of being taller. It was leaning against a wall, smoking a cigar.

The fact it stood on two tentacles and waved the other two about like arms didn't make it any more human in Karl's eyes. He fought back an impulse to turn and flee, and choked off a cough when he got close enough to smell it—not the cigar, the Antarean. They all had that same smell.

"Lookin' for juice," said the giant, taking up position behind and to the left of the Antarean.

"*Roblevo*," said the voice from the alien's mobile translator. "*What may I do you for?*"

"I need some wattage for a residential power pack," said Karl.

"*How much you need?*" asked the Antarean, its grotesque mouth wrapped about the cigar as its translator did all the talking.

"Just one power cell."

One of the thing's thick black tentacles reached into its pouch and pulled out a cell. It extended the cell to Karl, who took it gingerly, cringing when his fingers brushed against the clammy, scaled appendage. He looked it over.

"How do I know it's fully charged?"

The Antarean stared at him for a moment, its two black eyes burning with what alien emotions Karl couldn't begin to guess.

"*How does...*" Static squawked from the translator. The Antarean reached up and slapped it. "*How does the wind know which way to blow? How does a chicken know how to fly?*"

Karl shifted his feet uneasily. "Chickens don't fly," he said.

The Antarean moved closer, slightly tilting its pointy skull towards Karl.

"*How do you know I won't have my friend Geek here cut your throat and take your money?*"

Karl glanced nonchalantly to his left, trying to determine a direction in which to run.

"How much?" he asked, his voice trembling.

"*Twenty.*"

"Twenty?" complained Karl. "For one cell?"

"*It's primo juice*," said the Antarean, seeming to shrug its version of shoulders.

Karl didn't want to argue. He paid for the cell and moved on.

In his haste to get away from the Antarean and its henchman, he didn't pay attention to where he was going. It wasn't long before he realized he was lost. He wasn't used to being on the streets, especially at night, and now he was completely turned around.

As he searched for a familiar landmark, he heard something behind him. Had the

Antarean sent the one called Geek to follow him and take the rest of his money? It would be just like an Antarean. Well, the joke would be on it, because what he had left wasn't worth stealing.

Maybe they were lunatics who'd kill him for sport. Or maybe it wasn't the Antarean at all. Maybe it was some desperate streeter, or one of the mutant gangs he'd heard about.

There was another noise, louder and closer. Karl panicked at the sound and took off running.

He hadn't gotten far when he hit a dead end—a wall scarred with graffiti phrases like "Mutants Suck" and "Feed me or Kill me." He searched the darkness for his pursuers, listening to the silence, tasting his own sweat. Hearing and seeing nothing, he retreated until he found a way he hoped would lead him out of this hostile maze.

He moved carefully, avoiding the piles of refuse in his path. He thought maybe he'd lost whoever was after him. Yeah, he thought, the street trash would be the type to give up easily. They'd lose their appetite for trouble if it became too much work.

He followed a chain-link fence for some time and began to relax. He still wasn't sure where he was, and was trying to decide which direction to take, when something came at him out of the blackness. A massive dog, barking bloody murder, threw its forepaws against the fence, making clear its intentions to tear out his throat.

Karl backed off from the fence and ran. He knew he had to move fast. The barking would attract the scum who were after him. He ran until he was gasping for air, until he saw lights and heard the clamor of shouting. He ran for the lights.

As he got closer, the pandemonium grew louder. Suddenly, as he emerged into an open area, he collided with someone and went sprawling. Momentarily stunned, he struggled to his feet and found himself being swept away by a mob of angry streeters. It was all he could do to maintain his footing as he was pushed and bumped from every direction.

It was bedlam. A swell of noise engulfed him, distraught screams punctuated by angry shouts. He saw some people making a futile attempt to organize the mayhem, but they were swept away unheeded. Glass shattered nearby, and he ducked out of reflex.

"*You are ordered to disperse,*" bellowed a machine-like voice. "*All those not leaving the area at once will be prosecuted to the full extent of the law. You are ordered to disperse immediately.*"

Karl couldn't tell where the voice was coming from, but he had to get away. He knew what would happen next. He'd seen the video reports all too often.

"We want food! We want food!" The shouts began somewhere off to his right. There were only a few voices at first, but in seconds the cry spread virus-like through the rabble, and thousands were chanting, "We want food! We want food! We want food!"

He heard several explosive *pops*, and the crowd surged. Panic created a domino effect, and a wave of bodies slammed him and dozens of others to the ground. Those who weren't knocked down began to run, although no one seemed to know which way was safe.

Once he was back on his feet, Karl saw the gas clouds and the brilliant eruptions of flash grenades. All around him was disorder and confusion. Before he could decide which way lay escape, an excruciatingly bright burst of light materialized at his feet.

Karl grabbed at his eyes and cried out. He fell backwards but bumped into something that kept him upright. His eyes burned and his head pounded with a rogue rhythm. He tried opening his eyes, but all he saw was light—a blinding, brilliant glare and nothing else. The pain and the loss of sight unhinged him. All he could think of was that he was blind. He staggered off, calling out, "I can't see. Help me. Please, I'm blind, help me." But his cry was one of hundreds.

He kept moving as best he could, and after a short time the chaos shifted away from him. He realized he was easy prey now. The thought fed his hysteria, and when he tried to move faster, he stumbled over some unseen hazard.

Exhausted, his head and eyes still throbbing, he kept going, prodded by the dread of his own imagination. The longer he couldn't see, the worse it became. He stopped calling out, afraid of whom his cries might attract. He was sure someone would see him soon, but who would that someone be?

Using a wall he had come to as his guide, he felt his way along, taking one step after another until, abruptly, he took a step into nothingness. He plunged downward, hitting hard and tumbling headlong over uneven concrete. When he hit bottom he was only partially conscious.

He lay there for a long while, assessing his injuries. He hurt but wasn't sure if he'd broken any bones. He tried to open his eyes. The painful flash was still there.

"Hello?" It was a child's voice. "Are you okay?"

"I need help. I'm blind," called Karl. "I fell down here, and I need help getting up."

"I'm not supposed to talk to strangers."

"I'm not a...Please, I need help."

He waited and listened, but there was no response.

"Are you there?"

Nothing.

"Where are you?"

Damn little rodent has gone off and left me here, thought Karl. Probably an ignorant streeter kid, a wild little animal. He tried opening his eyes again, but instead of one bright blaze he now saw several brilliant dots. In between there was only blackness.

"See? Down the stairs. He says he's blind." It was the child's voice again.

"You down there." This time it was a woman's voice. "What's wrong?"

"Something blinded me, a flash grenade or...I don't know. Then I fell down here."

"Can you get up?"

"I don't know. My ankle might be broken."

"Well, see if you can get up. I'm coming down there, but don't try anything or I'll gut you. Iris, you stay here."

Karl managed to get to his feet, and when he did he thought he saw something moving. He was banged up, but he didn't think any bones were broken.

"Okay, there are stairs right in front of you," she said. He felt her next to him now. "Step up, and I'll help you."

It was slow going, but when he reached the top he could tell his vision was returning. The glare began to subside, and despite the spots, he could see more clearly. He looked up, saw the clouds pulling back from the moon and breathed a sigh of relief.

"I think my eyes are clearing up."

"That's good," said the woman.

"I was scared I'd never see again," he said, still looking at the moon through blurry eyes. "Thank you for your help."

"Don't thank me, thank my daughter Iris. She's the one who found you."

Karl looked at the little girl. Even through his fuzzy vision he could see her imperfections. She had no hair, not even stubble, and both her ears were swollen and disfigured. Her mother appeared normal enough—a streeter, from her clothes, but the genes the woman had passed on to her daughter had obviously been damaged. Too much exposure, thought Karl.

"Thank you, uh, Iris. I don't know what I would have done if you hadn't come along." He turned to the mother. "If you could direct me back to Third Street, I won't bother you anymore."

"It's right down there," she said, pointing behind him.

Indeed, he'd gone almost in a circle. He could see the street vendor still in place, hawking his wares.

"Well, I, uh...Thanks again."

He checked his pocket as he walked away, limping only slightly. The power cell was still there. It had been a long, hellish night, but he'd have his steak after all.

He passed by the vendor, who recognized him and called out, "Get your juice, friend?"

Karl nodded.

"Well, good night and good living to you, then."

He had anticipated having to dodge another hard sell, but the vendor had apparently given up on him. Like Karl, he knew a lost cause when he saw one.

Lost causes—that's what he was. That's what this world was, his world, empty and barren.

An odd feeling came over him. It was an urge he hadn't felt in a long time. It was so unexpected, he didn't even question it. He turned back towards the little stand and eyed the vendor's merchandise.

"Change your mind, friend? Something I can show you?"

"How much for one of those dolls?"

"For you, only three and a half."

"Oh. I've only got two."

"Two it is. Sold to the power seeker with the limp." The vendor made the exchange, looking at Karl as if trying to be sure of what he saw. "Your aura, it's altered. Very unusual for it to happen so fast. I see some color in it. Looks like you might be a healthy blue with a little work."

"Yeah? Well, thanks."

Instead of turning towards home, Karl made his way back to where he'd fallen. A short distance from there, he found Iris and her mother. They seemed surprised when he approached but didn't move.

"This is for you, for saving me," he said, handing the doll to the little girl. Then he asked the mother, "Are you two alone?"

"Just us," she replied warily.

"Well, uh, my name is Karl—Karl Leander." He held out his hand, and she hesitated before lightly shaking it.

"Selene Eos."

"Selene, I'd like to find some other way to thank you and Iris. Who knows what would have happened to me if someone less charitable had come along."

"We are who we are," she said, shrugging.

Karl thought about it for a moment and then asked, "Do you like steak?

The idea for "Dinner For One" began germinating after a power blackout, and warnings from authorities that such occurrences would increase in the future. It was first published in *Palace of Reason*, and later reprinted in Peridot Books, SB&D, and re-written with a female protagonist for the anthology *Warrior Wisewoman 3*.

# WAITING FOR GRIM

One sat cross-legged, the other two propped against an outcropping of granite. A trio of horses stirred restlessly nearby, tethered to a dying sycamore. The half-eaten remains of a jackrabbit hung on a spit over the withering fire. Overhead, a lone buzzard circled, undeterred by the menacing swarm of nimbi looming in the western sky.

"Come on, it's your turn," urged the first one, scratching a septic rash on his arm.

Ignoring the nag, his heavily-scarred companion groused, "When's he going to get here? I'm tired of waiting."

"Yeah, I'm getting hungry," said the scarecrow-thin third fellow.

"You're always hungry," complained Scar. "Eat some more rabbit."

"It tastes like rat."

"You would know."

The expressive but rheumy eyes of the first fellow said he'd heard it all before. He scratched some more and coughed. Spitting, he said, "He'll get here when he gets here. Make your play, already."

"Alright, alright. Hold your pus. Here."

Scar tossed aside his scarlet cloak, leaned over the four-sided board situated between them and placed his inscribed chips just so.

Rheumy turned his head sideways to read. "*Strife.*"

"You always use that one," mocked Scarecrow.

"I can't help it if I always draw those letters."

"A couple of triple-letter scores, two, three—that's eleven points," tallied Rheumy.

"*Eleven,*" chuckled Scarecrow derisively.

Scar raised his gauntlet-covered fist as if to backhand Scarecrow's cracked lips but restrained himself.

"Let's see what *you* can do, scrawny."

Scarecrow fingered his chips contemplatively but withheld his move.

"Did you see the latest M. Night Shyamalan movie? I laughed so hard I nearly cracked a rib. It was a hoot."

"A *hoot*? Who talks like that? What in the seven fiery torments of Hades is a hoot?"

"Damn, you're cranky today," said Rheumy. "That's what happens when you sleep with your sword."

Scarecrow sniggered. "He woke up on the wrong side of his sword. Get it?"

Scar shot Scarecrow a look that would have melted the armor off a Panzer.

"It's a joke," said Rheumy, as if tired of playing conciliator, "just a joke."

Scar sheathed his gaze and mumbled, "Yeah, you guys are funnier than a barrel-full of fuming nitric acid."

Quicker than Scarecrow could riposte, Rheumy farted explosively, and all three burst out laughing.

"Okay, here we go," said Scarecrow, his bony fingers placing five chips to intersect the R of the last word. "Read it and weep, boys. *Drought*. Triple word score. That's thirty-nine big points."

Scar made a noise signifying he couldn't care less and stood up to scan the horizon.

"Where the hell is he? He's always late. We're always waiting on him."

Rheumy didn't bother to answer. Instead, he studied his own chips.

"You guys want to catch a flick later?" asked Scarecrow. "I can already taste that butter-drenched theater popcorn."

"Films are irrelevant," responded Rheumy. "Give me a good poetry reading anytime."

Scar snorted, startling the horses.

Rheumy went on. "Celluloid, videotape, laser discs—they'll melt. Books will burn. An entire book can't be memorized—with apologies to Ray Bradbury—but a poem can be. Poetry is truly eternal." He spread out his chips on the board. "*Scourge*. That's twenty for me."

Scarecrow nudged Scar. "Who do you think would win in a fight between Adolf Hitler and Charles Manson?"

"Manson," Scar replied assuredly. "He's one crazy bastard. He'd crush Hitler."

"I don't know, Hitler was awfully wiry."

"They say Manson had twice the strength of a normal man when he went berserk," added Rheumy.

"Who's *they*?" groused Scar. "Everyone's always saying *they say* this and *they say* that. Who are *they*?"

"Well," began Rheumy, "nominally, 'they' refers informally to people in general, or those regarded collectively as being in authority, or in-the-know."

"What the blazes does—"

His retort was interrupted by the approach of pounding hooves. Scar stood immediately, his hand reaching for the ruby hilt of his sword.

"It's about time," he said, recognizing the incoming rider. "I'm ready to kick some ass."

The rider approached, slowing his ebony horse to an unwilling trot. Skeletal fingers gripped the long-handled scythe resting across his saddle. His grim face was shadowed by the hood of his coal-black cloak, but his eyes were white-hot. He yanked on the reins. His horse reared.

"Mount up." His voice echoed as if from a tomb.

The trio complied. Scarecrow yanked his pitchfork from where he'd planted it. Rheumy pick up his bow and quiver, leaving a trail of maggots in the dust. Scar strode across their unfinished game, scattering the inscribed chips, and pulled himself atop his anxious red-eyed sorrel.

"Where to?" he asked.

"Somewhere gluttonous, I hope," responded Scarecrow.

"I prefer a healthy clime," replied Rheumy, barely getting the words out before he began to cough. He covered his mouth with a gangrenous hand, but not before his pale horse stamped and whinnied.

They followed Grim, guiding their steeds to the edge of the spectral mesa where they'd camped. Their leader took his scythe and gestured with it through the void toward a blue sphere in the distance.

"Them again?" Scar said, shaking his head.

"You'd think they'd learn," added Scarecrow from atop his malnourished beast.

"It's their nature," said Rheumy. "They'll never learn."

Scar drew his sword, the blade shrieking from its scabbard.

"Let's get to work."

Grim turned in his saddle and flashed a murderous gaze at his comrades.

"Actually," he said, his jagged teeth showing in a malevolent grin, "I was thinking of blowing off work today and going bowling. Who's with me? I say we go knock some pins to hell and back again."

His black horse reared high into the air; then, as one, the four horsemen spurred their mounts and galloped into the void.

After researching the Four Horsemen of the Apocalypse for possible inclusion in an upcoming book, I decided to make use of the gruesome foursome in a brief bit of satire. "Waiting For Grim" has been published in *OG's Speculative Fiction* and in *Untied Shoelaces of the Mind* under the title "The Continuing Adventures of the Four Horsemen." It was converted into an audio tale by Drabblecast, and won first place in the *Whispering Spirits* short story contest.

# THE WITHERING

I lay here, as I have lain for so long, like a crumpled fetus, waiting for an end that will not come. I beg for it...I pray for it. But even as I wait for a cessation to my terrible existence, I know it is only a seductive fantasy. I imagine release, escape, blissful freedom—for imagination is all I have left. How perversely ironic that the cause of my damnation is now my sole salvation.

The air reeks of disinfectant, as it does habitually, and the only sounds I hear are distant murmurings. There's a chill in the air, so I clutch futilely at the lone coarse sheet that covers me and open my eyes to the same austere wall, the same mocking shadows that greet me in perpetuity.

This time, though, I see a slight variation. Something is there. Something I can barely discern in the feeble light. A tiny, quivering wiggle of activity. I strain to focus and see a caterpillar laboriously weaving its cocoon. Somehow, it has made the Herculean trek to where the wall and ceiling intersect and has attached itself in the crevice there.

As I lay here, I wonder what resplendent form will emerge from that cocoon.

But even this vision is eventually muted by the despair that possesses my soul. I struggle not to reason, because there is no reason. Guilt or innocence, fact or fiction—they are concepts that no longer matter. All that matters are the gray ruins of my memories, memories that play out across the desolate fields of my mind. I cling to them the way a madman clings to sanity. In truth, I'm but a single, aberrant thought from slipping into the murky, swirling abyss of madness myself. So, I try to remember.

I remember the carefree excursions I took to the ocean as a child—the warm sand, the cool water, the waves lapping at my ankles. I remember the university, in the days before reformation. The camaraderie of my fellow students. The give and take of creative discourse. Soaring over the sea cliffs on a crude hang glider built by a classmate. The girl with the bright red hair for whom I secretly longed. I remember many things...but always there is one tenacious, tumultuous recollection that intrudes.

It's always the same. The same thunderous sound of cracking wood as my door bursts open. The same flurry of booted feet violating the sanctum of my thoughts. The same rough hands that assault and bind me.

I remember the looks of hatred and repugnance, the shouted threats of violence from unfamiliar voices. The relentless malice focused on me was like a living thing. Time and space became a rancorous blur as I stood in the center of an imposing room, still bound, surrounded by more strangers. I was on display, the accused in a courtroom where only the degree of my guilt seemed subject to debate.

Much of what occurred that day is lost in a haze of obscurity, but I clearly remember the prosecutor's embittered summation.

"The facts are incontrovertible, Honorable Justice," I recall him stating with restrained assurance. "A routine intruscan of the accused's personal files disclosed numerous writings, both prosaic and poetical in nature, which can only be described as obscene and disturbingly antisocial. Public decorum prevents me from detailing the improprieties here, though the complete volume of these degradations can be found in the articles of evidence.

"In addition to the *possession* of these heinous works of pornography, the accused fully admits to authoring them. I say he stands guilty of counts both actual and abstract. I request that no leniency be shown by the court, and that he be sentenced under the severest penalties allowed for such crimes."

I distinctly remember the prosecutor, indifferent but confident, returning to his seat as the presiding justice contemplated the charges.

Turning a stern glance towards me, the justice methodically asked, "Does the accused have any statement to make before judgment is passed?"

I remember standing there, befuddled by the ritual of it all, unable to accept the realization that it was *my* fate they were discussing. When it seemed I wouldn't reply, the justice opened his mouth to issue the verdict, and I quickly stammered the only thing I could think of.

"I...I admit I wrote things that may be considered inappropriate by some, but they were simply meanderings of a personal nature, never meant for public dissemination. In no sense was I propagating the enforcement of my ideals upon society. They...they were simple fantasies, scribblings of an unfettered imagination, nothing more."

"Surely," boomed the justice, "throughout the course of this trial, if not previously, you have been made aware that, under our governing jurisprudence, thought *is* deed." When I failed to respond, he went on. "If you have nothing further to say in your defense, I rule, by law, your guilt has been determined within reasonable doubt. I hereby sentence you to the withering."

I remember the clamor of hushed voices swelling like a balloon about to burst as the words were repeated throughout the courtroom.

*"The withering."*

The sound reverberated inside my skull, but terror and denial colored my reality. The withering. It was something spoken of only in whispers. No one I had ever known knew the truth of it. There were only rumors, grisly tales with no substance yet having the power to invoke dismay and horror.

Much of what happened next is a void of innocuous bureaucracy, but I remember the room where it took place. I was still bound, this time by sturdy leather straps that embraced my wrists and ankles. Except for the straps, I was naked. Lost in the surreality of the moment, I felt no humiliation at my nakedness but was overwhelmed by a pervading sense of vulnerability. I remember a chill in the room. There was a draft blowing from somewhere nearby. A single bright light was positioned so that it blinded me with its glare.

Three others were in the room—one I designated the "doctor" and two men who assisted her. They went about their business with systematic efficiency, seeming to ignore my obvious presence. Then, without really acknowledging me with her eyes, the doctor began explaining the procedure.

Paralyzed with fearful anticipation, I failed to absorb much of what she said. I remember only bits and pieces. Something about *hormonal injections, osteo and rheumatoid mutations, effects that bypass the brain.*

The technical details of her explanation became a mere backdrop when I spied the row of hypodermics. Its length extended beyond absurdity, and when she reached for the first one I braced for the pain to come. However, after a few minor stings, I felt only a pinching sensation as needles were inserted with care into my thighs, my forearms, my neck...and on and on until each violation of my body no longer mattered.

I must have passed out at some point, because when I awoke I was in another place.

I have no idea how long I was asleep, but as I weaned myself from unconsciousness, I felt a stiffness that convinced me I had been lying there for some time. I tried to move but couldn't. I saw no restraints holding me down, so I tried again. I was successful, briefly, if you consider inducing a stabbing pain somewhere in my back a success. The pain convinced me to forgo any further attempts at movement. So, I shook off the vestiges of slumber and tried to recall with more clarity what had happened.

Oh, that it could only have been a horrible dream, but my reality had become the nightmare, one I hadn't yet grasped in its fullness. I know now nothing could have prepared me for what I was about to learn.

After I lay motionless for some time, a white-coated attendant approached me and bent over to engage in some sort of interaction with my bed.

"Where am I?" I asked, my voice cracking with dryness. "What's wrong with me? Why can't I move?"

The attendant made no sign he heard me. Instead, he pushed my bed into a corridor that stretched on without end. The wheels churned below me as we passed cubicle after grim cubicle. In the dim light, I saw other beds, beds occupied by inert bodies. The shadows and the constant jog of movement prevented me from seeing more until we came to a halt.

The attendant departed, leaving me as naked and helpless as the day I was brought into this harsh world. The alcove where I had been left was much brighter, and it took time for my eyes to adjust. Unable to turn my head without great pain, I could look in only one direction. Facing me was a metallic wall or door of some sort. The metal's sheen was highly reflective, and in its mirrored surface I saw myself.

Rather, I saw what I had become.

I have no idea how long I screamed before my cacophonous lament attracted a swarm of attendants, who quickly sedated me. But I'm sure I wasn't the first, or the last, to wail in terror inside those somber halls.

229

I try not to remember what I saw in that hideous reflection, but I can't forget that my fingers are now gnarled deformities, my arms shrunken and folded against my chest. I know the slightest attempt to move my legs will cause indescribable agony that writhes up through my hips and assaults my spinal cord. I can try to forget that my once-wavy hair has been shaved to a coarse stubble, but my lips are ever dry and cracked, and too often my skin is aflame with a devilish itch I cannot scratch.

Warehoused like a spare part that no longer serves any purpose, my days passing into years, I suck sullen gruel through toothless gums and wait for the impersonal touch of an attendant to wipe my body clean. It is a morose whim of fate, indeed, that even such routine maintenance is a welcome diversion to an otherwise monotonous subsistence.

Trapped in a useless husk, perched on the precipice of lunacy, I turn inward for deliverance. From a place deep within, I rise and soar high above other lands, gliding lazily into other times. They don't know about my journeys. They think I'm a prisoner of this room. They don't know I become other people—bold people, curious people, people who commemorate their adventures in rhyme. I don't tell them about the rhymes or the improper thoughts that creep into my head. I still dare to imagine the unimaginable, but no one knows.

They won't find me in here. In here, I don't allow myself to dwell on past transgressions. I seek no pity nor submit to reproach. And, no matter how seductive its siren call, in here, I resist the longing for sweet death.

Instead, like the caterpillar, I wait to emerge from my cocoon, spread my glorious wings and fly.

As I related earlier in this collection, my mother's body began to deteriorate at a relatively young age due to extreme cases of osteoporosis and rheumatoid arthritis. Although her mind remained sharp, it was soon trapped in a body that had become a useless husk.

Impelled by her horrific decline to write something, I recalled the works of Edgar Allen Poe I'd read as a youngster, and in that style wrote "The Withering." It was originally published in the anthology *Top International Horror 2003*, reprinted in the British publication *Nemonymous*, the American publication *Wrong World*, the anthology *Neverlands and Otherwheres*, translated into Greek for the science fiction magazine *Ennea*, and recorded as an audio tale for *Parade of Phantoms*.

# BETWEEN IRAQ AND A HOT PLACE

"I don't want excuses, Dweezil, I want perversion, I want hostilities—I want conflict and I want plenty of it!" Nick ran his long, perfectly manicured fingers through his hair as if his head hurt. The thinning gray strands didn't provide much resistance. "Milksops and Dainty Marys—that's what you've been scheduling."

Dressed in his favorite black suit, shirt, and red tie, Nick was camera-ready and in full-speed mode when his producer caught up with him backstage. The shorter Dweezil had trouble keeping pace. Every few steps, he/she had to perform a sort of hop, skip and jump to stay in range.

"When was the last time you got me a contentious psychopath or a hardcore religious fanatic? Huh? Or even a habitual peeping Tom? I can't remember the last time I was able to goad so much as a sincere obsessive-compulsive shopaholic. Let's face it, Dweezil, you've been shooting blanks."

Looking chagrined, the producer replied, his/her East Indian British accent cracking defensively.

"I am aware there has been a rather insipid stench related to our most recent programming. However, I have several *non compos mentis* candidates queued for next week."

"Next week!" Nick threw his hands above his head. "This show's running on a wing and a curse as it is! We're near critical mass. We could go down in flames before next week's even on the calendar—and you know I mean *flames*." He snapped his fingers and pointed his bony index at Dweezil. "We need depravity. We need pugnacious, spiky-haired deviants. We need the cream of the corruptible and incorrigible. We need some flaming head-cases, and we need them *now*, Dweezil. This is no time for one of your fastidious surgical strikes. It's time for you to bite the bullet and bring out the big guns."

They passed two grips raising a bank of lights and practically trampled an assistant producer who was re-taping scorched stage marks. The chaos of pre-show preparation was all around them, but Nick didn't notice.

"Another thing—it's as cold as a frost giant's butt in here, Dweezil. Could we *please* turn down the air?"

The little producer wiped the sweat from his/her forehead.

"You are aware we must maintain a temperature no higher than seventeen degrees Celsius for the video apparatus."

"You won't care about the cameras when I come down with pneumonia. I can feel it creeping into my pores now. See my eyes? Look at my eyes."

Still trailing behind, the diminutive producer couldn't see his boss's eyes.

"They're all red. See, I'm getting sick. Of course, my eyes make a good match for my gray hair, don't you think? You see this hair, Dweezil? My hair was black when I started this show—mostly black, anyway. Look at it now. Look what this show's done to me."

"I recall when I was in the employ of Madonna, we—"

"Madonna?" Nick stopped abruptly, snapped his fingers and pointed at Dweezil. "Madonna is immaterial. You don't work for Madonna anymore, do you? You work for me." He started forward quickly then stopped just as suddenly. He put his arm around a stagehand, and his tone softened.

"Charlie! How you doing? How's the family?"

"Oh, hi, Mr. Mammon. They're fine, everyone's fine, thanks."

"Good to hear, Charlie. Keep up the good work."

Then he was off again at a breakneck pace, Dweezil still in his wake.

"There's always time to rally the troops. Remember that, Dweezil."

"Sir, there is one item I neglected to—"

"What do you think about my jaw, Dweezil?" asked Nick, patting under his chin. "I've been thinking maybe I should get some work done. It's a little saggy, don't you think?"

"I am not certain, sir. However, a personage from—"

"It wouldn't hurt me to lose a little weight, too. The last thing this show needs is a paunchy host."

"Sir, a woman from the network—"

"Wait till we get inside, okay?" Nick opened the door labeled *Nick Mammon Executive Producer*, walked in and found himself face-to-face with a prim-looking blonde. She was such a remarkable vision there amidst the dingy trappings of his office that she seemed all aglow. The sight of her made him think of a bawdy jazz number. Inexplicably though, what he heard was a melodic harp.

He shook off his initial stupefaction and inspected the intruder. She had on a pearly white business suit that coalesced with her alabaster skin and an unusual but tastefully stylish silver headband. Her curves were in all the right places, but her face showed no signs of a smile.

"Gabrielle Goodman," introduced Dweezil, "this is Nick Mammon. Sir, Ms. Goodman is the network censor."

"Censor?"

"Actually, we prefer the term 'envoy of compliance.' Mr. Mammon, I've—"

"Call me Nick," he said, making his admiration for her physicality obvious.

"As I was saying, Mr. Mammon, I've been assigned to scrutinize your production, observe your show, and report any findings I deem prudent to the network's Director of Pacification."

"Speaking of the show, excuse me a moment, Gabrielle—mind if I call you Gabrielle, or do you prefer Gabby?" Before she could respond, Nick snapped his fingers and pointed. "Dweezil, get your little hermaphroditic ass out there and make sure everything's running as smooth as Gabby's inner thighs." He turned to the censor. "I hope I'm not presuming too much?"

Dweezil disappeared in a fount of steam, and Nick closed his door.

"You know, Gabrielle, you could have just as easily tuned in our little broadcast from Elysium Fields, or wherever it is you're stationed. You didn't have to come all the way down here. Perhaps you had something more personal in mind. If you're looking for a little divine inspiration, I'd be more than happy to introduce you to The Serpent," said Nick, patting his crotch. "That way you could combine a little business with an obscene amount of pleasure."

The lady in white didn't budge. She didn't smile. She didn't frown. Her stony expression was unmoved.

"Mr. Mammon, I assure you I have no interest in snakes, or in reptiles of any sort. I'm here because of complaints about your show."

"Complaints? Complaints from whom?"

"Let's just say complaints from on high."

"Really?" Nick seemed genuinely surprised.

"And, may I add," she said stiffly, "my initial impression of your conduct only serves to exacerbate preconceptions which, as a neutral observer, I've made every attempt to disregard."

Nick threw his hands up in a gesture of surrender. "Hey, what can I say? It's what we do down here. This is show business, Ms. Goodbody. I just give the people what they want."

"Hostility and havoc? Discord and distrust? Fear? That's what you think the people want?"

"Everybody loves a good train wreck."

She stared at him, keeping her emotions, if any, in check.

"Did you ever consider that harmony and reason might strike a popular chord, given the chance?"

"I've *considered* a lot of things. However, it's my experience there's no market for harmony, and the voice of reason is usually hushed by the tumultuous crescendo of the rabble."

The door opened, and Dweezil stuck her/his head in. "Two minutes."

"I'd love to chat you up more, sugar lips, but I've got a show to do. Grab yourself a good seat. Maybe afterwards I can show you around some of our darker corners, and we can discuss the ramifications of libidinous deprivation."

—⟡⟡⟡—

"And now, ladies and gentlemen, and those of you who deign to be categorized, live from Ocularis Infernum Studios, it's time to play..." Dweezil's disembodied voice cascaded through the cavernous studio with an unearthly resonance. His/her accent no longer distinguishable, he/she paused to let the audience finish with him/her.

"*The Hell You Say!*

"Here's your host, the Duke of Darkness, the Supreme Commander of Conflict, the Lord of Lust—*Nick Mammon!*"

Nick sprinted on stage through a mock fiberglass Stonehenge and was greeted by a salacious onslaught of applause. He wallowed in it momentarily then raised his hands for silence.

"Welcome, everyone. Welcome to the show that sticks its tongue out at placidity and prudery, and gives chastity a well-deserved slap on the ass." As the wave of laughter washed over him, Nick pretended to shield his eyes from the bright lights and scan the audience. "It looks like we have a particularly gruesome congregation tonight. Well, you won't be disappointed. We have for you one of the most belligerent and degenerate shows you will ever see, so let's get right to it!" More applause. "But first, let me introduce the she-beast that needs no introduction, the purveyor of pain and pleasure, my lovely assistant, *Mistress Erin!*"

A statuesque redhead wearing black leather straps and shreds of gossamer chain mail strolled out stage left. A malicious sneer adorned her harsh face. She smiled only briefly as she cracked her whip.

"Now, let's meet tonight's contestants." Nick paused for the disco-pop music to come up, then continued. "She's a former choir girl, now working as a spokes-model for the chemical warfare industry—a luscious thirty-eight double-D with a passion for hot oil massages and a penchant for guys with particularly hairy backs. Let's have a big hand for a real fallen angel—Sasha Dhum!"

Applause and scattered whistles greeted the voluptuous brunette with a dark upper lip that hinted at a testosterone imbalance.

"Our next contestant says he's a college dropout and proud of it. He's a card-carrying member of the NRA who works in his father's marketing business, has a thing for big butts and takes golden showers to relax. He not only has a minor criminal record but registered a truly vile score on our moral turpitude test. Meet a real flag-waving scoundrel—Jorge Chaparral!"

More applause and some screams as the smiling contestant plodded out—plodded until the hostess's whip kissed his rump and sent him scurrying.

"Looks like Erin's already got a thing for you, Jorge."

The audience laughed.

"Before we begin, tell them what they're playing for, Dweezil."

"You'll have a hot time in Hades without any nasty napalm burns wearing your Vulcan all-asbestos bodysuit!"

As the hermaphroditic producer's voice boomed through the studio, Mistress Erin batted the body suit with the butt of her whip to demonstrate its durability.

"Next, you'll think you're in Heaven after spending endless hours with your new Orgasmatron, Playco's latest prod of joy and anguish."

Erin ran her fingers lovingly over the appliance as Camera Four zoomed in for a close-up.

"Finally, our winner will spend two sin-filled nights at the fabulous Under-world Hotel, where he or she will be joined by Satan himself!"

Various stills of the hotel flashed across the monitors.

"There, they'll dine in the romantic Ember Room overlooking Acheron, the River of Sadness, and spend the day in a tortuous rock climb through the rarefied and smoke-filled air of breathtaking Fire Falls."

"That's one depraved package you've put together there, Dweezil," said Nick, returning to center stage. "I feel a bad case of satyriasis coming on, so let's get started with *The Hell You Say!*

"We begin by putting our contestants on the hot seat with some locked and loaded questions. Let's begin with Jorge.

"Now, Jorge, if Sasha had a really nice car—a car you really wanted—would you A) try to buy it from her, B) seduce her and borrow it, C) send a couple of goons over to stomp her and take the car, or D) suppress your desire for the automobile?"

"Well, Nick," replied the weasel-eyed contestant in a high-pitched drawl, "I'd have to think on it." He pondered the question as the audience barked out its choices like a pack of deranged jackals.

"Quickly, now, Jorge, I need your answer."

"Shoot, I guess I'd say C. I'd have someone stomp her and, uh, whatever else you said."

A raucous howl of approval rose from the audience, mingling with explosive sound effects.

"You nailed it, Jorge! Answer C was good for the maximum one hundred points on that question. Now, let's go to Sasha, turning that same question around.

"Sasha, if you had intelligence that Jorge had launched a covert act of violence against you, would you A) convert your assets to cash, deposit them in a Swiss bank account, and go into hiding, B) try to negotiate a compromise, C) set a trap for the goons and deliver their mutilated bodies to Jorge, or D) retaliate with a strike against Jorge's friends and family?"

Against the tumult of the audience, the bosomy contestant with the hint of a mustache blurted out her answer. "C, Nick, I'll take answer C."

Her response was greeted by rather watered-down sound effects.

"I'm sorry, Sasha," said Nick, as though he really wasn't. "While you did score thirty points with that answer, we were looking for D—retaliate with a strike against Jorge's friends and family. But you've still got plenty of time to catch up. Let's go to our next question."

—⁓∽⧉∾⁓—

Nick plopped down on his couch and was pulling the padding out of his pants as Dweezil slid into the room via a soft-shoe routine.

"Ninety seconds until we come out of break, sir," warned Dweezil, "and the network censor is proceeding in this direction."

"Do you think she likes me?" Nick pulled off his shoes and let them drop. "These new lifts are killing my feet. I think she's got the hots for me. What do you think?"

"Oh, I am certain you have stoked her carnal fires into a frenzy, sir."

"You know, Dweezil, you're so funny you should have your own show. Now, go keep an eye on mine, and don't let Erin get carried away with that whip. You know how she likes to abuse the audience. I'll be out before you can resurrect Barnum and Bailey."

"Mr. Mammon." The network representative struck a rigid pose in the doorway.

"I'm sorry, Ms. Goodthighs, but I've got only a few seconds before I'm back on."

"Mr. Mammon," she said without flinching, "you can't use the word *Heaven* on this show."

"What?"

"Your announcer said 'Heaven'—you can't do that."

"Why the hell not?"

"You just can't. We can't allow that. It's not appropriate, and there are proprietary and intellectual property concerns."

Nick shrugged and put his shoes back on.

"You know, Gabby, we're like oil and water, you and I—okay, more like unrefined crude and Evian, but I think we could be a good mix, if only—"

"Excuse me, sir," said Dweezil, materializing four feet off the ground as a ghostlike apparition. "As much as I detest interrupting a moment as splendid as this one—"

"Dweezil, when I want to hear from the wee people I'll kick a mushroom. What is it?"

"*He* is on the telephone for you, sir."

Nick cringed involuntarily.

"Is he in Washington?"

"No, sir, I believe he is calling from Baghdad this time."

"If you'll excuse me, Gabby, I need to take this call. We'll continue our little tete-a-tit later."

As soon as she left, Nick turned to Dweezil.

"Does he sound like it's bad news?"

"Is it ever *good* news when he calls?"

Nick didn't bother to answer.

"Mammon here," he said, picking up the bronzed goat horn on his desk. "Yes, your demonship...Sir?...No, sir, I wouldn't presume to make sport of you... Yes, I know the ratings have been down...They were down that much for our first segment?...Well, it's tough doing a show with this network censor hovering over me...Of course you don't want any excuses, and I would never...Yes, Your Unholiness...Yes, don't worry. The second half of our show's a killer. My producer stakes her/his life on it...I will, we will...Goodbye, sir.

"Dweezil!"

"Right here."

"Did you hear that? He's pissing brimstone about the ratings. He said he'll have my balls on a silver platter if we don't spice things up. You're my producer, what are you going to do about it?"

"Polish the silver, sir?"

—⊙≼≽⊙—

"...very well played, Sasha. Your victory in the Megatons for Megapoints round gives you the lead." Nick sidled up next to her and spoke conspiratorially, although his amplified voice could be heard by all. "I have to say, the way you bombed Jorge's cities back into the Stone Age was downright inspiring. Don't you agree, audience?"

The audience did—vociferously.

"It nearly brought a tear to my eye. Kind of reminded me of the way my dear old mother used to wallop the bejesus out of me.

"But I digress. Enough fond reminisces. Up next, your favorite segment and mine—*How violent-crazy-vicious are you?*"

Nick blew a kiss to the audience as Dweezil's voice droned, "We'll be back right after this message from Styx's Stigmata Salve, the new, improved way to fight off symptoms of sainthood."

236

— ❧ ❧ —

"Mr. Mammon."

The network censor moved into his office so sylphlike you would have thought she was walking on air.

"Ah, Ms. Goodbody, I knew you couldn't stay away for long. How do you like the show so far?"

"It is one of the most disgusting, licentious, reprehensible displays of debasement and aggression I have ever witnessed."

"Thanks, I thought it was pretty hot, too. I don't suppose you're a Nielsen family, are you?"

"Your attempts at levity are improper, irrelevant and inane."

"Brilliant use of alliteration, Ms. Goodframe."

"I must concur," added Dweezil, who suddenly manifested atop a bookcase wearing a kilted gladiator outfit.

"Do you realize," she continued, ignoring their comments, "that your bilious little show is creating such mayhem that it's having a ripple effect across the entire network? The fallout alone will mutate programming for decades to come."

"You know, Gabby, when I first saw you, I thought I was going to like you. I thought maybe you and I could enjoy a little innocuous indiscretion. But I've changed my mind. I'm tired of your holier-than-thou attitude. I don't think you grasp the true intellectual depth of this program—what it says about the sociodynamics of human emotion and desire, the psychogenic give and take of yin and yang, Scylla and Charybdis, Abbott and Costello.

"You know what? I'm not going to listen to your pseudomorphic, pedantic pessimism."

Moved by the timbre of his/her boss's rant, Dweezil began humming "The Battle Hymn of the Republic."

"No longer will I lie down with the downtrodden. I say, up with people! Down with seraphic totalitarianism! Are you with me, Dweezil?"

At that, The petite producer amplified her/his humming and took up a position behind Nick.

"No, I say we're as mad as hatters, and we won't take it anymore!" Nick began to march in place, and Dweezil joined him, still humming away. "Come, Dweezil, the disenfranchised multitudes must be unfettered." He snapped his fingers, pointed out the door, and together they marched from the room, both now humming the hymn.

— ❧ ❧ —

"Whooooa! That was foul! Would you like to see more of that next week?" Nick extended his microphone towards the audience, which responded with its customarily mindless enthusiasm. "Who'd've ever thought we could have so much fun with pugil sticks and rhino dung? I have to give credit to our loose cannon announcer for that bellicose bit. You really blew me away there, Dweezil.

"Okay, when we come back, our contestants will spin the Pentagram of Armageddon for weapons of mass destruction, conscripted armies and big bonus points. And we'll find out who'll be today's winner of..." The audience joined in. "...*The Hell You Say!*"

Over the sound of applause, Dweezil's rapid voiceover boomed formally, "All audience members will receive our *The Hell You Say!* home game! The producers of the show take no responsibility, incur no liability, and are indemnified against any trauma, emotional or physical, resultant conceptions, combat incursions, or loss of limb suffered by anyone playing the home game."

The stage lights were dark and the last of the audience had been herded out of the studio when Nick fell into his chair and plopped his feet on his desk.

"Whew! Glad that's over. I think it was a good show, though. What do you think, Dweezil? Dweezil? Where in the misbegotten bowels of Baal are you?"

The hermaphroditic gnome emerged through the back wall of Nick's office to the triumphant blare of trumpets, wearing a burgundy silk robe and smoking a stogie the size of a shotgun barrel.

"I rather thought the show went swimmingly, sir. I was especially fond of the moment when the automatic gunfire resulted in Ms. Dhum's incontinence."

"That was nothing compared to when the flaming chariot swooped down and carried Jorge away. I thought he was going to have a cow right there in his Satanic Majesty's favorite ride."

"Humorous, indeed, sir. Almost as comical as the time—"

"I hope I'm not interrupting," said Ms. Goodman, interrupting.

"Of course not, Gabby. Come right in. Great show, huh?"

"Certainly, assuming your tastes run to a blatant disregard for the supernal principles of peace and brotherhood."

"You're a real hellion, aren't you, Gabby? But piety ill becomes you." Nick swung his feet off the desk, snapped his fingers and aimed one digit at the censor. "You and yours, with your drive-by sermonizing, are hardly innocents in all this. You know this little skirmish isn't about ideology. It's about ratings—about who will stand tall in the eyes of the viewing public when the rain of fire and ash ceases to fall. This isn't a crusade for hearts and minds, it's show business. It's ground zero of a hard-fought campaign for the very souls of those loyal lap dogs who fondle their remotes like worry beads. Go ahead, go back to your cherubic coven and make your report. Why—"

Nick's rant was gathering momentum when his goat horn rattled for attention.

"Nick Mammon, what's your pleasure?...Sir, yes, sir." Nick sat up straight in his chair. "You didn't care for that?...Well, what about the...No, I guess it wasn't that original...Sir?...I'll fix it, sir. I'll fire my producer immediately. Better yet, I'll have him/her flayed alive...My previous job? Well, before this show I did a little stint as a succubus...I guess I was good at it. Why?...Oh...Yes, sir...Yes, sir."

Nick dropped the horn, looked at Gabrielle then at Dweezil.

"Apparently, the confrontational approach of our program is no longer in alignment with either the financial objectives or the philosophical goals of the network. We've been cancelled."

This satirical look at man's inherent need for conflict was written before President Bush invaded Iraq, but while he was beginning to rattle his rusty saber. As it turned out, the invasion was much more of a game show from Hell than any piece of fiction. "Between Iraq and a Hot Place" was published in *New Myths*.

# DEMONIC PERSUASION

Desmond was a conscientious, hard-working fellow. Within his cadre he was thought of as steady and reliable, if a bit standoffish. He always showed up for work on time, but he seldom took part in any extracurricular activities. While he put up a good front—tried to be one of the boys—the truth was...he was different.

Oh, he had the same splendid leathery, bat-like wings as the other incubi, the same fierce, glowing red eyes, the same diminutive nubs that would grow proudly into horns should someday he be advanced to the status of greater demon. But Desmond was conflicted. Despite his outward appearance, he questioned his demonic orientation.

For a long time, he denied these feelings. However, deep inside the putrefaction of his internal organs, he knew he didn't belong.

Each night, when Asmodeus inspected his legions, Desmond stood smartly wing-to-wing with the other incubi, feeling like an imposter. He didn't know why he'd been cursed so, but he knew he'd rather be on the opposite side of the ranks...with the succubi.

It wasn't that he was unable to gather sustenance when he invaded the dreams of his female prey, consuming their energy through a series of phantasmagorically aberrant sexual acts. It was that he felt like such a fraud in doing so. He had none of the natural enthusiasm for the work his fellows exuded. For him, it was a loathsome mechanical process, distasteful at best. Get in, incite the nightmare scenario, get out.

For millennia, he didn't know what to do. He spoke to no one about his discomfiture (his family would *never* have understood). He did his best to dismiss it. Yet, it wouldn't go away—this irrational impulse. So, during one nocturnal autumn raid, he gave in, flaunting the unholiest of regulations, and sought out a man. That's when his guilt commenced to fester with abandon.

His compunction, however, was balanced by the relief he felt. No longer was there a need to fabricate his relish. No longer did he have to let his imagination fly wild in order to stave off the revulsion. Instead, he pursued his occupation with rapacious diligence. For the first time he was happy in his work.

Everything was going fine, until one night when he came upon a particularly handsome fellow, fast asleep, his soul ajar, fully accessible. However, when he swooped down and tried to force entry, he encountered a succubus already hard at work draining the unsuspecting soul of his spiritual essence.

"What in the fiery hell of the seven pentagrams are you doing here?" she demanded.

"Oh...uh, sorry. I, uh...must have made a mistake."

"A pretty big one, I'd say." She was obviously perturbed by the interruption. "Wait a minute," she added, eyeing him suspiciously. "You're not bi, are you? One of those switch-hitters?"

"I assure you I am not," he replied with feigned indignation.

"That's too bad," she sighed. Desmond caught her look of disappointment before she abruptly shifted emotional gears. "I mean, that's good—good."

"Are *you*?" he asked tentatively. "Do you go both ways?"

Her leathery face drooped as if the deceit were suddenly too much for her.

"Yes, yes, I admit it! I like girls. Okay, there, I said it. I can't help it. Is that a crime?"

"Actually," said Desmond, "I think it is."

Shamed, she covered her face with a wing.

"You don't understand," said Desmond. "I'm guilty, too. I...I prefer men myself."

"You do?" Relief washed over her, and her red eyes sparked with a new glow. "Then you know what it's like, night after night..."

"Yes," said Desmond, nodding his nubby head, "I do. It's too bad we can't, you know, change places."

The succubus looked as if a devilish idea had occurred to her.

"Maybe we can," she said. "I know this necromancer who, for the right price..."

Even demons get shuffled sometimes when it comes to sexual orientation. "Demonic Persuasion" has appeared in *Raven Electrick, Emerald Tales,* and *Necrotic Tissue.*

# FROM TIME TO TIME

It began casually, a banal little tryst instigated by loneliness and happenstance. Then, it evolved into something more—more than Larkin could ever have imagined.

She would never have met Evan if they hadn't lived in the same building. It happened, in of all places, the laundry room. He didn't bowl her over with good looks or charm—it wasn't instant attraction—but he seemed nice enough. As the days rolled by, and she got to know him, she discovered he was fairly clean as guys go, punctual, and a grad student in philosophy, of all things. It impressed Larkin that, in his spare time, he volunteered at a hospice. Of course, his family had money, so he didn't have to work. However, they kept him on a tight financial leash. Hence, his residency in her rather rundown apartment building.

She met him after returning from one of her infrequent gigs as a fill-in flight attendant. She also worked at a little off-campus café while taking what classes she could. She'd been working on her degree for six years now, and was about halfway there. It had become a sort of mythic quest—something more to be endured than achieved. Often she questioned why she kept at it. Did she still want to be an elementary schoolteacher? Was it worth it? Was it a waste of time? Although she never rationalized it, she knew the answer. She knew why she wouldn't quit.

*Time will tell. You'll never amount to anything.*

That's what her father had said as she'd gone out the door—the last thing he'd ever said to her. It had turned out to be quite a motivational speech. Probably the best thing he'd ever done for her.

She didn't expect much from her spur-of-the-moment fling with Evan. Just a convenient little respite from loneliness and chastity. Besides, she had no time for a real relationship. Surprisingly, though, sex with Evan was...well, it was fantastic—almost from the beginning. Relatively inexperienced, contrary to her father's notions, Larkin soon mistook the intensity of their passion for something that transcended the physical. In a way—a way that would soon shake the foundations of her intellect—it did.

Although her encounters had been few, she'd always been somewhat "sensuously inclined"—as she termed it when her girlfriends' discussions turned to sex. With Evan it was more than that. It was streaming rapture—one climax after another, vigorous, unrelenting ecstasy. Sex had never approached anything like that for her. She wondered if it did for anyone. It was how she imagined perfection. So perfect it was unreal.

At first, she speculated it was something in her that had changed. Maybe she was just getting the hang of it. Then she thought it was all Evan. Finally, she decided it was simply the unique chemistry of their pairing. After a while, she stopped wondering—stopped trying to analyze it. All she was certain of was that the only thing that slowed them every night was the necessity for her to pause and catch her breath.

It wasn't just her. Evan admitted he was overwhelmed as well. He jokingly told her she was a sexual witch who'd cast a spell on him. He confided in her that several times during their lovemaking he reached orgasm without ejaculation—something he'd never experienced before.

One night, just a week into their relationship, as exhaustion propelled them towards one final animal surge of exaltation, time stood still. Although she wouldn't realize it until later, it was the first indication they were part of something even more extraordinary than boundless bliss. Not just part of it, she would come to believe, but the cause of it.

—◦◦◦◦◦—

"Is your clock broke?"

"I don't think so," responded Larkin. "Looks like it's working."

Evan rolled over but was too exhausted to get up.

"Then how come it says it's only ten-forty? I know we were going at it more than ten minutes."

Larkin caught her breath and covered herself with the sheet, as she had a habit of doing.

"So."

"I glanced at the clock, you know, when we started. It said ten-thirty."

"What are you doing, timing us?"

"No, no, of course not," Evan replied defensively. "I just happened to notice it."

"Maybe it just seemed longer because it was so good," she said and kissed his arm. "You know, time flies when you're having fun."

"Actually, that expression refers to more time passing, not less," he said. "You could be right, though. It could have just seemed longer. 'One would think that time stood still, so slowly does it move.'"

"What's that?"

"A quotation we were discussing in class," he said, sitting up and looking around for his underwear. "Something an old Roman philosopher/poet said centuries ago." He grabbed his clothes off the floor and started to get dressed. "I still say there's something wrong with your clock."

—◦◦◦◦◦—

Gradually their relationship bloomed over the days and weeks they spent together. Emotions, fueled by their lovemaking's intensity, began to play a part. Larkin felt herself wondering if Evan might be The One, which was strange in itself, because she'd never believed there was any such thing. She never bought into the romantic fantasy that there was "one true love" out there for her. More

244

likely there were thousands of potential candidates. That's what she used to think, anyway. Now, she wasn't so sure.

Likewise, it seemed Evan was falling in love with her. Not that she believed either of them had any real concept of what love was. Who their age did? Even so, Larkin was certain their feelings stretched beyond the incredible sex.

Still, no rush to judgment was necessary. For the time being, she was happy. That's all that mattered. She had all the time in the world to worry about such big picture things. Or so she thought.

"Did you ever notice that even when the leaves on the trees are turning red and brown," said Evan as they strolled through the park, "the grass here stays bright green no matter what time of year it is?"

"Green is good," replied Larkin, looking up at the moon, which had made an early appearance in the late-afternoon sky.

"No, seriously, why is that?"

"It's a rye grass mixture," she said, spying a row of swings. She let go of his hand and ran off. "Let's swing," she called back over her shoulder.

He followed her to the swings.

"How do you know that—about grass?"

"My...someone I used to know was a landscaper," she said, plopping down on a swing.

He gave her a push.

"I guess I'm used to snow, and the grass starting to die around Thanksgiving."

"Do you miss the snow?" she asked.

"No, not really. I've always gone home for Christmas, so I get enough of it."

Her hair blew across her face, and she brushed it away. It was the time of day when the wind picked up.

"I've always wondered what a white Christmas would be like."

Evan caught her swing and held it instead of giving her another push.

"Why don't you come home with me for Christmas break and see for yourself?"

"Are you serious?" she asked, several scenarios racing through her head.

He let the swing go with a shove. Larkin lunged forward, spent a fleeting moment suspended in space then fell back.

"Of course I'm serious."

"It's nice of you to ask, but I'm sure I'll be working. You know they always schedule me for the holidays."

"Tell them you can't work this time," he said, giving her another push.

"You know I can't do that," said Larkin. "Some of us don't have families to pay the rent."

It sounded like a putdown, and she regretted it as soon as she said it. It didn't seem to bother Evan, although he didn't pursue the topic. Probably because he knew how touchy she was on the subject of family.

Instead, he sat on the swing next to hers and pushed off.

"Say something philosophic."

"Something philosophic?"

"Yeah, you're the philosophy grad. Dazzle me."

"Okay." He looked up at the sky and thought a moment. "Did you know the ancient Greeks believed the world began with Eros, the god of desire? See the moon? For the Greeks, the fact the moon stayed close to the Earth was an erotic activity. They believed all the universe was connected by erotic principles."

"I know what's on *your* mind."

He laughed, and so did she.

They swung in silence for a bit before he said, "You know, I've got a line on a teaching job when I finish my doctorate. It's a little college in Oregon. Have you ever been to Oregon?"

"No," she said, sailing backwards as he surged forward, their swings out of sync.

"I went there once," he said. "It's nice, but only if you like green."

"Green is good." Larkin giggled as she soared.

He let his feet drag until he came to a stop. He stared at her as she swung past.

"You're right," he said.

"About what?"

She flew past him again.

"I can't wait to make love to you again."

She let her momentum fade until she'd almost come to a stop. She looked at him. He smiled, his eyes focusing on her so lovingly it unsettled her for a second. But only a second.

She planted her feet and responded, "There's no time like the present."

When they finally came up for air, her body was limp, drained, clammy with perspiration despite the cold outside. Before she could even gather her wits, Evan blurted, "I love you." When she failed to reply right away, he said, "Sorry, that just sort of slipped out."

"That's all right," she said. She understood his quick recant. Neither of them had used that word before. "I feel the same way...I think."

He laughed, and she joined in.

"Let's change the subject," she said. "What's on TV?"

He leaned back across the bed to check the time. "Your clock's messed up again. I'm surprised you make it to class on time."

"No, it's not," she said, rolling over to take a look.

The clock read 7:59. Evan was right. It must be broken, because earlier that evening they'd watched their favorite show. It came on at eight. That was a couple of hours ago.

"You're right," she said, "it's not working. I'll check my computer."

The screensaver vanished at her touch. She looked once, twice.

"So, what time is it?" asked Evan.

"It says eight o'clock."

"That can't be right." He grabbed the remote and turned on the TV. "At eight, we were watching *Survivor*. So it's got to be at least..."

He didn't finish. The opening of *Survivor* flashed across the screen.

Evan's voice wavered. "Am I crazy or...we saw this, right? Larkin?"

Larkin didn't answer. The more she tried to concentrate, the more her memory of the past two hours grew fuzzy. She remembered making love—that was clear enough—but what about before that? A moment ago she'd been certain, but now it all seemed hazy.

She turned her attention back to the show. Evan was right. They *had* seen this.

—⸎⸎—

"I checked the listings. Last night's programs all ran as scheduled," said Evan, taking another slice of pizza.

Larkin started to take a bite and stopped.

"Well, then, it was one wacked-out bit of déjà vu."

"You don't really think that's all it was, do you?"

"What do you think it was?"

Evan shook his head slowly side to side as he chewed and swallowed.

"I don't know. As absurd as it sounds, I'd say we relived two hours of our lives."

"But not the same two hours," said Larkin. "We didn't do the same thing."

"Yeah, I thought about that."

"We should...I don't know—tell someone."

"Tell them what?"

Larkin shrugged and bit into her pizza. It was already getting cold.

"It's not possible," she said, as if it were the final word on the subject. "There's got to be a rational explanation."

"What explanation?"

She didn't respond, and they finished eating in silence.

"I've got to study tonight," she said, wiping her mouth. "So, I guess I'll see you tomorrow."

"Okay."

She felt guilty, because she didn't really have to study. She just wanted some time alone.

—⸎⸎—

Larkin woke up the next day feeling fine. She looked at her clock. It was working fine. Everything seemed normal. She felt silly for worrying. She made up her mind to forget the whole strange incident. Just because she couldn't explain what had happened didn't mean she was going to dwell on it.

Later in the day, while killing time between classes, she ran into Evan. He made no mention of their odd little experience, so neither did she. He invited her to come over later, and she accepted.

That night it didn't take long before they were naked on the couch...and then the floor...the bed. The sex was as all-consuming as usual, and they topped it off with simultaneous orgasms so powerful Larkin was dazzled by a sudden, intense flare of light.

Well, she'd heard great sex described as "seeing fireworks"—maybe this was it. That's what she thought, anyway, until she opened her eyes and the bright light was still there.

She raised her hand to shield her eyes. The light was streaming in from the window. Evan was already sitting up in bed. He reached for his cell, looked at it then looked at her with a dazed expression.

"It's already tomorrow," he said dryly.

"What do you mean tomorrow?"

"I mean it's nine a.m. The sun's up."

—◦◦◦◦◦—

"What's happening to us?"

"I don't know," said Evan, "but it's something cosmic."

"Something cosmic? I don't even know what that means. What does that mean, Evan?"

He shrugged his shoulders.

"Why us?" A razor's-edge of hysteria tinted her voice. "Why hasn't anyone else noticed it?"

"Maybe they have, or maybe it's not happening to anyone else." He turned away, as if he didn't want to face her. "I've been thinking about it. I've been thinking maybe it's not really happening to us, exactly. It could be that...we're the cause." He turned back to her, and she saw he wasn't joking.

"What are you talking about?" she demanded.

"The sex—when we make love—it's so good, so intense, it's unreal. You know what I mean? Maybe...I don't know," he said in surrender and walked away as if he were done talking about it.

"No, you don't," said Larkin, following him. "You can't just say that and walk away. What does sex have to do with it?"

"It's going to sound crazy."

"Crazy?" she said, and then repeated, "Crazy? This whole thing *is* crazy. Whatever you're thinking can't be any crazier."

"Okay," he said, giving in. He covered his mouth with his hand momentarily, as if formulating what he was going to say. "We generally think of ourselves as living in three dimensions. But there's a fourth dimension—time. What if our lovemaking is somehow affecting time? What if our orgasms are creating a backlash—a ripple through the fabric of time?"

She wasn't sure whether to laugh or be angry at such nonsense.

"I'm not saying it's true," he continued, "but what if, somehow, we've transcended normal physical existence, and we're no longer subject to the limitations of the material universe. What if we've been caught up in a timeless existence where past, present, and future don't apply?"

She shook her head. It was meaningless babble to her.

"And you base this theory on...?"

He shrugged his shoulders again. "I told you it would sound crazy. But I think we should test it—tonight."

"I don't know," said Larkin, raising her hands as if to say hold it right there.

"Sooner or later we're going to have to."

The thought frightened her. Was it possible? Were their feelings for each other—their lovemaking—somehow altering the framework of the universe? No, no, there had to be some other explanation. It would be easier for her to believe she was going insane than to buy that.

But if she didn't believe it, why was she afraid?

"I can't believe I'm saying this, but what if you're right? What if it gets worse?"

She could tell by his expression he was thinking the same thing. What could be worse than what they were going through now—not knowing what was happening to them, not knowing when or if they'd lose another nine hours of their lives? Next time, it could be a whole week, or maybe they'd go back and repeat an entire year, perpetually bouncing back and forth through time.

"We have to try," he said.

—◦◦◦{◦◦◦—

That night They tried. However, they found they were both too self-conscious, too hung up on what *might* happen for it to be any good. Larkin kept looking at the clock. So, she noticed, did Evan. It was an act totally without passion—the least enjoyable sex they'd had. Finally, well short of any "fireworks," they decided to stop.

The attempt was a failure—or a success, depending upon how she looked at it. Nothing happened, nothing changed, everything was normal. Except she wasn't feeling like she usually did when she was with Evan, and that bothered her.

Strangely as it was, it was at that moment of disappointment she first admitted to herself she was in love with him. She hadn't said it out loud, not like he did—not even to herself—but she'd been thinking about it. Now, as she tried to cope with the bizarre nature of what had happened, she felt certain.

"So," said Evan, "I guess we're okay as long as the sex is tepid."

"I guess."

"We'll have to try and—"

"No, Evan, I can't. It's too much for me to deal with right now," she said almost apologetically. "Look, you're going home for Christmas in two days. Let's take a break from each other until you come back."

"What are you saying? Are you saying...?"

"I'm not saying anything except we should take a break until you come back, that's all." She saw the dismay on his face. "I think I'm falling in love with you, Evan—I really do," she said before realizing the words had escaped her lips. "I hate to qualify it like that, but right now, with what's going on, I can't think straight."

Her admission caught him off-guard, but he nodded his head.

"I understand. I love you, too."

"Maybe when you come back this...whatever this is...will be over, and we can be together again, like we were."

He smiled. She could barely tell it was forced.

"'A time to embrace, and a time to refrain from embracing?'"

Larkin returned his smile and responded, "Yeah, something like that."

—◦◦◦{◦◦◦—

It was the longest, deepest, most passionate kiss she'd ever experienced.

Evan surprised her, coming straight from the airport. They were in each other's arms without a word. She pulled him inside and shut the door.

"I've missed you so much."

"Me, too. I couldn't wait to see you."

"I want you so bad," he pleaded.

"I want you, too. But what if...?"

"Forget what-if," he declared and kissed her again.

He began unbuttoning her blouse. Even as she helped him, she said, "I'm afraid."

"Don't be."

Between his kisses and disrobing she said, "Being with you...you make it seem as if the world doesn't matter. But it does. It does matter. We can't, we—"

His kiss silenced her. He locked eyes with her, smiled and said, "'Tis better to have loved and lost than never to have loved at all.'"

Swept up in the overwhelming ardor of the moment, she forgot her fears.

Morning arrived in a timely manner, and Larkin stretched to greet the day. It was seven a.m. Evan was still asleep. She decided to get the paper and see if she had any juice to drink. It wasn't until she was halfway to the door it even occurred to her to wonder if everything was normal. It seemed so.

She retrieved the newspaper and went to the kitchen. There was still some OJ left, so she poured a glass and opened the paper. It was filled with the usual crime, politics and natural disasters—nothing that interested her much. So, she looked for the ads.

It took her a moment to assimilate what she saw. Why were they advertising a Labor Day sale in January? Shouldn't they...?

it struck her like a slap to the face. She turned back to the front page. Terror fought disbelief.

"Morning," said Evan, scratching his stubble. He must have seen the anxiety constricting her face. "What's wrong?"

"Look at the paper." She handed it to him. "Look at the date."

He stared at the newsprint. "It can't be."

"It is," replied Larkin. "It's happened again."

"It can't be August, it's only—"

"Look at the *year*." She wanted to shout, but all she managed was a hoarse whisper. "The year."

His expression said what he couldn't—or wouldn't.

Larkin tried to rein in the dread smothering her, but panic was evident in her voice.

"Evan...we've lost more than two and half years."

Slowly, he shook his head, incredulous. Larkin was more animated. She surged out of her chair.

"We've got to get it back. We've got to undo this."

"How?" he wondered.

"I don't know," she said, her whole body trembling. "I *do* know. We're going back into that bedroom right now and do it until we're back where we're supposed to be."

"Wait a minute. Calm down. There's no way of knowing what will happen if we do that. We could end up losing even more. Or we could bounce so far back down the continuum of time we wouldn't even exist anymore."

"I don't care," she said, grabbing his hand and pulling him. "We've got to try."

"Not like this," he said. "It won't work like this. You've got to calm down first."

"How can I calm down?" She felt the tears welling up in her eyes. "Why us, Evan? Why us?"

"I don't know."

"Tell me why." She was near hysteria.

"What do you want me to do—make something up? Tell you it has something to do with the meshing of our souls, the convergence of our unique bits of matter at this particular point in time and space? Whatever I told you would be bullshit. I don't have any answers, Larkin."

"Well, we've got to undo it."

"Let's wait...wait until tonight," he urged her, "after we've had time to absorb this and relax. I promise—we'll try tonight."

She hesitated, then relented. "All right. Tonight."

⁓ ⌁⟨⟩⌁ ⁓

She finished putting away the dishes and began sorting laundry. If she finished her chores in time, she might be able to get to that concert they were holding in the open air theater.

Soon she was filling the wash machine and thinking about vacuuming. She had another chapter to read, but she could do that while the clothes were in the dryer. She was hurrying and not paying attention. On her way out of the laundry room she bumped into another tenant.

"I'm sorry," she said.

He stooped over to retrieve his scattered laundry, and she picked up the book he'd dropped.

"I should watch where I'm going."

"That's okay," he said.

She couldn't help but notice most of his clothes were shades of the same color.

"I guess you like green."

He laughed. "I do have a lot of green clothes, don't I?"

"Green is good," she said. "I haven't seen you around here before, have I?"

"No, I just moved in a few days ago."

"Are you a student?"

"Yeah, grad student. My last apartment was converted to a condo, and this was the only place close by I could afford."

"Not exactly the lap of luxury, is it?"

"It's okay," he said.

She looked at the book, handing it back to him.

"*Being and Time* by Martin Heidegger. Science fiction?"

"Philosophy and physics."

"That sounds deep."

"It is. Up to here," he said, holding his hand over his head.

"You know, you look familiar." She tried to remember where she might have run across him. "I must have seen you around campus."

"You're a student, too?"

"Yeah, part-time. I also work at Rick's Café. Maybe I saw you there." She held out her hand. "I'm Larkin."

"Evan," he said, taking her hand.

"I've got to get going," said Larkin. "I'm sure I'll see you around."

"Sure."

She headed down the hall but got the feeling he was staring at her. She looked back over her shoulder. Sure enough, the new guy was standing there checking her out.

"Uh, Larkin, maybe, uh, you'd like to—you know—get together sometime?"

He wasn't exactly suave, but he seemed nice enough.

"Sure," she answered, "sometime."

This tale grew out of a very late-night premise—what if sex between two particular people was so incredible, so passionate, so orgasmic, that it transported them to another world or another dimension? In the case of "From Time to Time," it wasn't another world but another time they were transported to—time and time again. (While I won't claim to have experienced such erotic heights myself, neither will I deny it.)

# AFTER EVER AFTER

Once upon a time there was a young woman and a young man who were madly, passionately in love. Then they got married. They lived in a secondhand mobile home set on a patch of sparsely wooded bottom land, surrounded by piles of refuse and the back seat of a '63 Bonneville. Life was good...for the first few weeks.

But the years that followed did not unfold true to their fairy-tale expectations. Soon, their love was rusting away, much like their trailer.

—◦~◦⟨⟩◦~◦—

"When are you gonna get off your ass and start making some money—some *real* money."

She kicked the beanbag chair for emphasis, and her husband, who'd been dreaming about a monster truck with naked-girl-silhouette mudflaps, jerked awake.

"Dammit, Red, what did you go and do that for? What's wrong now?"

"What's wrong *now*?" she mocked. "What's wrong *now*? Three blind mice could see what's wrong. It's the same thing that's been wrong since we got married, Harley Hunter. We've got nothing—nothing but this beat-up old trailer and a yard full of scrap metal."

"That's all gonna be worth something someday." He struggled up out of the chartreuse vinyl beanbag and said, "What's got into you, anyway?"

"Well, it sure ain't been you," she said, hands on her hips. "At least not lately."

Not that she missed his clumsy groping and poking. She'd given up her schoolgirl Prince Charming fantasy years ago, along with her dreams of a big two-story house with plenty of closet space and all the fancy designer-name clothes she wanted.

Instead of a prince, she'd ended up with a toad. All she wanted now was a new air-conditioning unit so she didn't have to sweat like a hog all day long.

"Well, you're not exactly *little* Red Riding Hood anymore, are you?"

"*You!*"

She grabbed a beer can off the counter, disappointed to find it nearly empty, but hurled at him anyway. He ducked, and it glanced off his arm, splattering him with room-temperature suds.

"Dammit, Red! I was just joking. Now look at this mess. I'm gonna have to change my shirt."

"That'll be a first, won't it?" she said, still steamed.

"You're one to talk," he said, pulling off his shirt and using it to mop his armpits. "Look at this place. It's a sty. Why don't you spend more time cleaning, and less time bitching."

"Maybe if you'd ever get some work, I could buy some cleaning products, and maybe even a new vacuum cleaner that did more than blow the dust around."

"You know the landscaping business has been slow lately."

"Really? I thought it was just you that was slow."

He found a shirt in a pile by the bed. "You won't talk like that when I win the big Super Powerball lotto. I bet you'll be real sweet then. I'm gonna win it. You watch and see."

"Oh, yeah? It sounds like to me you've been smoking some of Jack's bean-stalk again."

She grabbed his jacket off the antler hook and started rummaging through his pockets.

"Hey, what are you doing there? I need that. I'm going to work."

"I thought you didn't have any work?"

"Well, that's how much you know. I got me a job to do today."

"Good for you," she said, finding something in one of the pockets. "I need ten dollars to buy cigarettes and some more Cherry-orange Wildfire Fruit Roll-ups." She pulled out a scrap of paper. "What's this?"

"That's the address for my job," he said, hurrying over to retrieve it.

"One-oh-seven Dwarf Drive," she read out loud, wondering why it sounded familiar. "Isn't that where Snow lives?"

"Yeah, so what? She wants her lawn mowed."

"I bet she does," said Red, her voice dripping sarcasm. She didn't care. The carpet was already stained.

He grabbed his jacket from her, but she held on to the scrawled note, glaring at him.

"It's just work," insisted Harley. "That's all. You want me to work, don't you?"

She held out the paper scrap. "If it's just work, then what's this little love heart here around the initials SW?"

"It doesn't mean nothing," he said, grabbing it from her. "You know how Snow is."

"Yeah, I know. I know every dwarf, troll, leprechaun, and hobbit in these parts has heigh-hoed that brunette coochie of hers."

"There's no call to be talking like that."

"It's the truth, and you know it."

"I gotta go to work."

As quick as the door slammed behind him, Red's anger turned to apprehension. For a fleeting instant, she was overcome by the notion he wouldn't be coming back—ever. She hurried to the window, pushed aside the strands of gold tinsel and saw Harley kick one of the empties that littered their front yard. The can ricocheted off the old car seat. Wistfully, she remembered how they used to sit outside together on that seat. She couldn't remember the last time they'd done that.

The sound of his battered pickup brought her back to reality. She retreated from the window, more angry than maudlin now, as Harley drove away.

In front of her mirror she turned side-to-side. Sure she'd put on a few pounds, but she wasn't all that unattractive, was she? It wasn't as if Harley was some prize bull, either.

She thought about cooking herself up a gingerbread man but remembered how unsatisfying that could be. Last time, the dough boy had crumbled before she'd even gotten warm.

She waded through the clutter to reach the sink, looked at the dishes piled there and began stacking them until she found one that was acceptable. She filled it with Lucky Charms and then wished she hadn't thrown that beer at Harley. She picked up another can, wondering if it was half-full or half-empty, shrugged and poured it over her cereal.

She sat down to watch her favorite soap, and wasn't yet to the first commercial when there came a knock at the door. She opened it to find a pair of fellows dressed alike in black pants, white shirts and plain ties. One wore a sheepskin jacket over his shirt, and they were both carrying these fat brochures.

Although she wasn't one to make fun of disfigured folk, she couldn't help but wonder if these weren't the two ugliest fellas she'd ever seen.

"Can I help you?"

"We wondered if you might have a few minutes to talk about the Lord," said the one with the jacket.

"Have you been saved, sister?" asked the other.

"I'm kind of busy right now."

"We won't take but a few minutes of your time."

"I don't know, that looks like quite a big pamphlet you have there."

"The better to inform you with, my child," said the one in the jacket. She decided he was even uglier than the other one.

"I hate to be rude," said Red, "but those are some awfully big ears you have there."

"The better to hear God's Word, my dear," he replied.

"And your feet, they're not exactly tiny, either.

"The better to walk over God's green earth and spread the word."

"Well, could you get your foot out of my doorway so I can close it?" Before he could respond she noticed something. "You know, you look awfully familiar."

"Grab her, Larry!"

"I'm not going to grab her, Harry. You grab her."

The one in the sheepskin snorted in disgust at his companion. Taking hold of Red, he forced his way in.

"What are doing?" cried Red. "Who are you? What's the—you're wolves!"

"That's right, sister," snarled the uglier one. "We're wolves. You know about wolves, don't you?"

She shook off his grip, but there was nowhere to run.

"I don't know what you're talking about."

"No? Think back—back several years. Think back to when you and your granny and that man of yours ganged up on a kindly, spindly old wolf and killed him. You remember now?"

255

"That wasn't my husband, that was his father, Old Man Hunter. I was just a little girl. And that wolf *tried* to eat me!"

"Well, we're sorry about that, miss," said the second wolf. "And we're sorry to barge in like this. But, see, that wolf was our father."

"That's right, that's right," said the other. "We've been doing time in the joint, but I promised my brother Larry we were going to break out and get our revenge someday. Well, today's the day."

"We're sorry for the inconvenience," said Larry, "but we're going to have to eat you and your husband."

"Yeah," growled Harry, "just like we did with that motor-mouth little chicken we ran across on the way here."

"I think that bird was on something, Harry," said Larry. "My stomach's starting to hurt. I'm sure that little chicken was tripping. The whole time she kept shouting, 'The sky is falling! The sky is falling!' Whatever she was taking is not sitting well with my tummy."

"Forget about it, Larry. You'll be okay."

"I think she gave me gas." Larry covered his mouth and belched. "Excuse me."

"Don't be excusing yourself to her," snapped Harry.

"I was only being polite," countered Larry. To Red he said, "Sorry, my brother is a tad antisocial. By the way, I like what you've done with your hair. But why do they call you 'Red' if you're a blonde? Is it because it's kind of a red-blonde, because you know I—"

"Shut up, Larry."

"You shut up."

"No, you shut up"

"Now you did it," said Larry. "Now my ulcer's acting up. I think I'm getting a headache, too."

"You're weak," grumbled Harry. "You've always been weak. Pop spoiled you. He always did like you better. He should have named you *Mary*."

"Yeah, well, I don't think Pop would have liked what we're doing, Harry. It's wrong."

"Listen to your brother," said Red, "he's making sense."

"Shut up, bitch!" Harry was about to slap her across the mouth when there was a knock at the door. He grabbed her, covered her mouth with his paw and said to his brother, "I'll take her in the other room. Get rid of whoever it is."

Red struggled, but the wolf was too strong for her. She felt his hot, fetid fowl-breath on the back of her neck as they waited in the bedroom.

They heard the door close and nothing else, so he eased her back out, still muffling her voice.

"Hold it right there, wolf."

Three pigs wearing badges and armed with shotguns had gotten the drop on Larry. Harry raised his hands in surrender, and Red scooted away, spitting hair.

"Homeland Security, ma'am." said one of the pigs. "Are you all right?"

She nodded.

"We've been tracking these two terrorists since they broke out of lockup. We've got a score to settle with them."

"That's r...r...right," said the second pig.

"We're not terrorists," claimed Larry, "we're grift—"

An elbow to the ribs from Harry silenced him.

"What do you mean, 'a score to settle?'" asked Red.

"One of these mean bastards huffed and puffed and blew down my brothers' houses," said the first pig. "If they hadn't been arrested for hijacking sheep, we would have hunted them down long ago. We're still looking for the third member of their cell."

"You'll never take Barry alive," taunted Harry.

"We'll see about that, dog boy."

Red sighed. "I appreciate your help, but if you could just—"

"What was that?" shrieked the third pig. "I heard a noise outside."

"It's okay. There's nothing out there," said the first pig. He shot a malicious look at Harry and Larry. "See what you did to them? You scared them so bad one stutters and the other's paranoid."

"I d...d...do not stutter."

"I never huffed and puffed nobody's house," claimed Harry. "It was Larry here that pulled that caper."

"I did not," said Larry indignantly. "I can't even blow out birthday candles without my inhaler. It was Harry who did it."

"We'll take them both back to the zoo and sort it out there," said the first pig.

"Yeah, back to the zoo with them."

"B...b....back to the zoo."

There was another knock on the door.

"See? See?" declared the third pig, "I told you something was out there."

His shotgun ready, the first pig cautiously opened the door. Three brown bears of varying size stood there.

"Go ahead, Papa," urged the middle-sized bear with a thick Slavic accent. "Go ahead already, ask."

The biggest of the three bears shuffled his feet as if he didn't want to be there. Reluctantly, he inquired, "Is here where lives Goldilocks?"

The pig moved aside as Red stepped up.

"There's no one named Goldilocks here," she said.

The middle bear eyed her suspiciously. "You look like her."

"Mama, she said here there's no Goldilocks. Home we go now, yes?"

"Home we're not going, Papa—not until we find Goldilocks," said Mama, eyeing Red up and down. "We've got bone to pick with that home wrecker, isn't that so, Baby?"

The third bear, who didn't look at all like a baby, sighed, stared at the sky and responded, "*Whatever.*"

"Look," said Red, "I don't have time for this. You can see I'm already dealing with three pigs and a pair of wolves here." Then she got an idea. "Goldilocks lives down at one-oh-seven Dwarf Drive. Oh, and by the way, she's dyed her hair and changed her name, so don't let that fool you."

"Okay, Papa, let's go."

"Can't we just go home, Mama?"

"Yeah," said Baby, "I want to go home and download some tunes."

257

"Not till the Goldilocks pays for damages—one way or other."

Baby sighed. Papa shrugged and shuffled his feet, but before he could move a burst of multi-colored sparks lit up the room, followed by a swirl of pink-and-puce smoke.

"What's that?" cried the third pig.

"Take it easy," said Red, "it's just my fairy godmother."

Before the words were even out of her mouth, a stocky middle-aged hermaphrodite in sequined tights and a frayed lace cape materialized.

"Damn, homegirl," said the androgyne, "what's this, a costume party?"

"Well, well," replied Red, making no attempt to conceal her disdain. "If it isn't the old FG. What's it been, an elf's age since you last made an appearance?"

"Yeah, my bad, Red. I ain't been able to boogie on out of the castle in a while. That damned Cinderella is such a little princess. I've never worked with a girl so needy."

"Like *she's* got problems," complained Red.

"Well, FG's in the house now. What can I hook you up with?"

Red held out her arms and looked around as if to say *Duh*.

"All right, everybody get to steppin'. Let's go, let's go. Head 'em up and mooove 'em out!"

"I beg your pardon, madam...uh...er, sir, but we're—"

"Talk to the wand, pork chop. Come on, everybody out."

When they were gone the FG rolled up its Lycra sleeves and asked, "You want me to get to cleanin' now?"

"Later," said Red, plopping down on the couch and motioning for the FG to do the same. "First, I want to hear the latest gossip from the castle."

"Well," said the FG, looking around conspiratorially, "I've got the four-one-one on Sleeping Beauty. You won't believe it, but evidently, there never *was* an evil queen. It was all just a hustle."

"No!" uttered Red in disbelief.

"Yes, it's true. Word is she's got a touch of the narcolepsy. Now I hear tell the little ho is sleeping around again. And wait until you hear why old King Cole is always so merry..."

For a long time I mulled over the idea of taking a fairy tale and doing something fun with it. "After Ever After" is what I came up with. It's published for the first time in this collection.

# THE APOCRYPHIST

I stood waiting at the entrance to the den, my few meager possessions stuffed into a satchel. I was here because I had been unable to summon up the courage to make a decision, and in not deciding, a course of action had been thrust upon me.

My father, who had never been too pleased with me, became angry when he learned I had applied for an apprenticeship. When he discovered the truth, his roar resounded through our den, his scent dominating every echo that careened through the cavern.

Of course, he wanted me to be a warrior like him. He looked with dignified disdain upon any other calling. My mother didn't offer her opinion; she simply assumed the traditional position of submission. I knew she wouldn't speak against my father, even if she disagreed.

Personally, I quivered at the thought of combat. I saw no sense in escalating conflict, and the idea of intentionally killing or even injuring another being made me ill. Leus knows, I would go out of my way to avoid stepping on a tong beetle.

So, my father cast me out and marked my departure with the formality of a ritual urination. The ceremonial display had been wholly unnecessary. I knew I could never return home.

The irony was, I didn't have any particular desire to become an apocryphist. I wasn't even sure exactly what it was those mystical sages did. I knew they were considered wise counselors, but I was a little vague on the details. I imagined some form of sorcery was involved.

By far the most noted apocryphist in the land was Grrrmon. It was said he had the ear of sovereigns and simple folk alike. He was very old and had reportedly been plying his trade for more than fifty winters. However, it wasn't his trade I was interested in, it was his daughter.

Ever since I'd first laid eyes on Tesla, I was unable to get her out of my mind. Her winter-white fur, her delightfully wicked green eyes, the playful way she wiggled her tailstub when she was playing a trick on someone. She had this look that said she was untamable, but I still dared to desire her. I would do anything to be with her.

So, I applied for an apprenticeship with her father. Of course, my fervent wish to escape the "honorable life" of a warrior had something to do with it as well.

You would be correct if you described my application as deceitful, yet applying for that apprenticeship was the bravest thing I had ever done. You see, I wasn't exactly known among my companions for my courage and strength of character.

I had survived sixteen winters, a piecemeal education, and endless taunts by my father's warrior compatriots when my petition for an apprenticeship was answered with a summons to appear in the presence of the venerable apocryphist. Fortunately, I had shown some aptitude for language and letters—the one requirement I knew an apprentice candidate must possess.

I arrived at the den at the exact time instructed then waited outside, as tradition required, for an invitation to enter. As domiciles went, it was a rather crude-looking den. No embellishments adorned its entrance, no markers of prestige, only a wood carving that read "Apocryphist."

I'd been waiting so long my legs began to wobble, and I'd shifted the satchel from one side to the other and back again. I whiled away the time staring up at the moons. Leus was bright and full, while Lia and Liet were phased like two halves of the same whole. I saw Leus's face clearly and imagined he seemed rather benevolent tonight. I took that as a good sign.

Finally, my presence was acknowledged. An elderly female motioned me inside, but just as quickly she disappeared, leaving me standing there to wait some more.

As I stood there, I couldn't help but notice the strange odors that blanketed the den. There were scents of tanglewood and mewleaf and other spices I couldn't distinguish. I could also hear the soft, melodious sounds of a slute echoing through the den's chambers. I wondered if it was Tesla who was making the music.

I'd never been inside her home before—we had only spent time together at school and in the forest, where we all gathered to stray and play. The thought I might actually be close to the place where she curled up and slept made me shiver slightly.

My romantic fantasy, however, was interrupted by a mocking voice.

"Not for you...not for you."

At first I couldn't tell where the voice was coming from. I cautiously took a few steps deeper into the chamber, not wanting to appear too bold.

"Not for you...no, no, no."

I didn't have to go far before I discovered the sound was coming from a simp. The household pet clung to its perch and scratched itself behind its oval ears. It looked at me and put its smooth little hand against its flat face as if it were thinking about what to say next.

"No, no, no...work, work, work," it jabbered as it fell from a polished limb, catching itself with its tail and swinging around to sit once more. "Not for you... no, no, no."

My mother had gotten me a simp when I was much younger, but something it said upset my father and he ate it. I never wanted any pets after that.

"So, you want to learn how to weave wit and wisdom out of thinnest air?"

It wasn't the simp speaking this time. I turned to find the ancient apocryphist standing there staring at me as if I were a hen he was preparing to pluck and roast. In contrast to Tesla, his fur was black, although flecked with silver-gray splotches. His fingerclaws were long but not particularly sharp. I could tell, because he was pointing them at me.

"Speak up! You are the apprentice petitioner, are you not?"

"Yes...yes, I am."

"Not many young stalkers wish to apprentice in the apocryphal arts. I recall only one other. I rejected him."

He stared at me with intense yellow eyes, as if to discern whether I might waver and run for it. Believe me when I tell you I wanted to. I was doubting whatever sense, or lack thereof, had led me to this place. My leg muscles were coiled, and I was ready to spring past him...except I realized I had nowhere to go.

"Do you know how to read?" he asked.

"Yes."

"Can you write?"

"Yes."

"While it's true brevity is often the soul of communication, can you speak any words other than *yes*?"

"Yes...I mean, I can speak...I mean, I know many words."

"What is progeny? Define genus...appellation...colloquy."

Of course, at the time, I didn't know any of those words, so I stood there like the simpleton I was, blurting out, "I'm not sure."

"I did not think so. What about your memory? An apocryphist must have a keen and voracious memory."

"I have a good memory," I replied weakly.

"So? What were the four words I just spoke of?"

I was so nervous and unsure I couldn't think clearly.

"Quickly! What were the words?"

"Genus, appellation, colloquy...and progeny."

"Hmmph," he murmured, continuing to look me over. I'm sure what he saw didn't impress him—a scrawny young stalker with a bent tailstub and dirt-red fur still spotted by patches of immature white. I was never more prepared for rejection than I was at that moment.

"It takes many winters of hard work and study to become an adept apocryphist. It is not an art, which is learned easily. There are subtleties and fine lines of distinction. You must study science and psychology, politics and social dynamics. You may spend a lifetime and still never master the craft and its arcane techniques.

"But if you are determined, you may stay and work as my apprentice."

It was not the response I'd expected. I had already shifted my weight in the direction I'd entered and was preparing something I hoped would sound intelligent, something I could say as I departed. Instead, I stood there dumbfounded, with my whiskers twitching and a look on my face that was probably making him second-guess his decision.

And that was how I became the apocryphist's apprentice...all because of a pretty tail.

He put me to work right away. However, it was not the kind of work I'd anticipated. Each household task he assigned me was more tedious than the last. When I wasn't seeing to his needs, I was studying. When I wasn't studying, I was cleaning pots and burying refuse. And what did he have me study? His life's work, of course. At least, that's what it seemed like.

Parchment after parchment of his scrawled, often illegible writings, consisting of biographies, anecdotes, a variety of individual forecasts, combat reports and directives, historical accounts, and other documents I couldn't categorize. He told me to memorize each piece and write down any words I didn't understand. However, he failed to advise me what to do if his scribblings were so poor I couldn't decipher them.

I was occupied thus when Grrrmon entered my chamber one day.

"Come, I have petitioners to see, and it's time for you to begin observing."

I followed him to another, much larger cavern where both the walls and floor were ornately decorated with many intricately woven rugs. Pieces of pounce-melon were set out in ritual fashion, and I noticed the powerful scent of mewleaf.

"Sit there." Grrrmon motioned to a stool in an inconspicuous corner, and I complied. "You're not to speak, only to observe and learn."

What I observed, in short order, was the arrival of an older female whose saffron-and-red coat was likely once beautiful. But now it was shabby, bare in patches and graying in others. She limped in, each step painful, and took no immediate notice of my master, who sat in the middle of the room in a grand chair woven from the clawbark of some ancient tanglewood tree. He said nothing and made no attempt to help her, despite her obvious discomfort.

She removed a piece of jewelry from her satchel and placed it in a bowl next to the simmering mewleaf. Taking two painful steps toward my master, she said, "A disease of the blood is ravaging my body, great apocryphist. I need your healing words to ease my pain and prolong my insignificant life. I pray to Leus you will look favorably upon my petition."

At that, she backed away, turned and departed.

I started to speak, but barely a sound had escaped my mouth when my master raised his fingerclaws for silence. So I shut up, sat and waited as he did. Soon, another petitioner walked gingerly into the cavern. From his dress, I guessed him to be a merchant, although not a particularly successful one. He did not place anything in the bowl but halted in front of my master and waited quietly.

"I have considered your petition," said my master after a calculated pause, "and have decided to grant it. Your business is failing and you wish to find a way to lure more patrons into your shop. In order to entice customers away from your competitors, you need something that distinguishes you from them.

"I advise you to tell everyone that your fowl tastes better than the fowl being sold by others because you have the happiest birds in the land. Make signs for your shop, both inside and out, that say, 'A happy bird is a tasty bird.'"

"But how do I know if they're really happy?" asked the merchant.

"How do you know they're not?" retorted my master. "Go. Heed my advice and be prepared for prosperity."

"Blessings on you, great apocryphist," he said, backing out of the cavern. "I will send you another bird, a very happy, very tasty bird."

When he was gone, my master rose from his seat and looked to me.

"Well, did you learn anything?" he asked, running his fingerclaws through his whiskers. "I...uhhh, I'm not sure, Master. What was it the female put in the bowl?"

"That was her offering. I will examine the offering, consider her petition, and decide whether to grant it."

"What do petitioners offer?"

"It is different for different petitions, different petitioners. The merchant offered several of his finest birds. It was a wise offering for what he asked. The female, obviously from an impoverished family, has likely offered a thing she prizes above all."

"Will you grant her petition?"

"You will learn that when she does."

"But how—"

"Enough talk now. You have pots to clean and errands to run before the sun rises."

It wasn't long before I realized that, in all the time I'd spent in the den of the apocryphist, I had still not seen the object of my desire. I was curious, but many days passed before I gathered the courage to broach the subject with Grrrmon.

The ragged furrow in his brow told me immediately it was not a subject he cared to discuss, especially with an apprentice. Tesla, he told me curtly, had run off with a warrior and was no longer welcome in his den.

I was surprised I felt no disappointment at the news. I'd gotten so caught up in my work and my studies, I'd spent little time thinking of Tesla. The realization sparked a quiver of guilt. However, I was actually beginning to think I had an affinity for the apocryphal arts. I liked learning new words and new ways to use them. I'd begun to think longingly of the day when my own voice might both aid and influence others.

"Nightdreaming again?" The old apocryphist had approached so silently I hadn't heard him. "Come, let's put your energy to work at more useful things."

I followed him into the petitioners' chamber and made the room ready as was my custom. Then I took my seat in the corner, prepared to observe the master at his craft and learn another lesson.

The old female who had claimed a blood disease limped slowly into the room. Her condition had noticeably deteriorated in the nights since she had first petitioned my master. I found myself hoping he would grant her petition, while at the same time wondering how he could possibly help her.

She had already made her offering, so she stopped in front of him and waited in silence. He looked at her sternly, as was his way, and rose from his chair.

"I have decided to grant your petition," he stated in ritual fashion.

Her eyes seem to spark with new life, her tired old ears erect with attentiveness.

"Be warned—my healing incantation only wields the power of the conviction that lies in your own heart. *You* must be strong to feed upon *its* strength."

She nodded, but when my master approached and spread his fingerclaws across her head, she looked frightened.

"The mind is strong, it must know the affliction is wrong. Let darkness into your soul, confine evil to its bright hole. Truth and goodness are the way. If not, the sickness will stay. Let your blood burn and boil—soon the disease will be foiled. Your health restored, your illness severed from your inner chord." As he ended his chanting refrain he removed his fingerclaws from her head. "Go now, be well and live life."

The old woman nodded again, almost a bow of respect, and turned to leave. I thought she moved a bit livelier than when she'd entered, but it was likely only my imagination.

When she had disappeared into the long cave my master turned to me.

"Will your incantation actually heal her?" I dared to ask.

"It might," he replied with uncharacteristic melancholy, "if she believes in it strongly enough. The mind is a source of great power, remember that."

"But how—"

"Grrrmon!" A great warrior, bedecked in lavish battle pads, strode into the cavern, interrupting my query. He didn't bother with ceremony, addressing my master as if *he* were the apprentice. "The sovereign approaches. Prepare yourself."

He turned and marched out.

"Sit and remain silent," Grrrmon commanded me, returning to his own chair.

Shortly, I heard several footfalls proceeding towards the cavern. Gruff commands followed a brief silence, and then the sovereign walked into the cavern. At least, I presumed it was the sovereign, never actually having caught his scent before. It was a scent I would have remembered. A powerful scent. One that made me want to run and hide.

But it wasn't the only thing that gave him an air of command. His fur was royal saffron in color and his bearing confident and brusque.

"Grrrmon, you old prevaricator, how are you?"

The sovereign made no attempt to comply with ceremony, walking past the offering bowl and straight to my master. I knew by the way my master's whiskers twitched that the omission irritated him.

"I'm well, Sovereign. But tell me, to come all this way you must have a problem only my skills can address."

The sovereign put his powerful arm around my master, increasing the old apocryphist's discomfort by visible degrees.

"Indeed, I do have a problem, old friend. One I hope can be solved with your counsel and your craft." The sovereign noticed my presence for the first time but promptly ignored me. "My warriors are howling and spitting demands to avenge the recent attack on our river-land province. However, I know the warriors of the Fangclan are well prepared for such an attack, and it would prove costly. How am I to avoid appearing weak before my own warriors without committing strategic suicide?"

My master thought for a moment before he replied.

"I can see it's a precarious position you've been placed in, Sovereign. I realize the political hold you have on your military is a tenuous one, and that any sign of weakness could prove fatal."

"As could a rash attack," added the sovereign.

"Let me contemplate this a moment," said my master, interlocking his fingerclaws and placing them against his mouth as he tended to do when deep in thought.

As he waited, the sovereign took notice of me once again.

"You, there, have you been sharpening your claws so you can join in the glorious hostilities against the Fangclan?"

"I? No, I—"

"He's my apprentice, Sovereign. His training is for a purpose even more glorious than battle."

"Hmmph. He doesn't appear to have the vocabulary for it."

"Sovereign, I believe I have a solution for you," said Grrrmon, thankfully shifting the sovereign's attention away from me.

"Yes? What is it?"

"First, you will relate to your warriors the historical tale of the Fangclan warrior who rushed into battle seeking revenge and made a fool of himself in defeat."

"I know of no such tale from history."

"That is because I have not written it yet. The tale will give your warriors pause. You will then turn your attentions to the Fangclan's sovereign. You will send him praise on his victory, and admit that, under an ancient treaty, the river-land province was rightfully his anyway." "Praise? Treaty? What treaty are you talking about? Have you lost your mind, old one?" "My mind is perfectly sound, Sovereign, I assure you. By praising your enemy and admitting the land is rightfully his, he will not expect a counterattack—at least not soon.

"The season of mating is almost upon us, and it could provide you with the perfect opportunity. When the bloodlust of both your warriors and your enemies has given way to a lust of a different kind, that is when you will order an attack and reclaim the river-land province."

"Yes, I see. It could succeed."

"It *will* succeed, Sovereign. I will prepare for you both the history and the treaty."

"Yes, yes. I knew you'd find a solution, Grrrmon. Excellent! Now I must go keep a clawgrip on my captains until you're done. I'll be anxiously awaiting your work."

The sovereign strode from the cavern with the same flourish with which he'd entered. Passing the offering bowl, he tossed in a bagful of what sounded like coins.

My master rose from his chair, his whiskers still agitated, and approached the bowl.

"War," he said with contempt, "is a game for fools." He reached into the bowl and pulled out the sack of coins, testing its heft. "Still, it keeps the coffers full."

"Master, I have a question."

My voice seemed to remind him of my presence, and he turned to look at me. "Yes?"

"How can you create history? Isn't history, by definition, that which has already taken place? The true course of past events?"

"History," he said, pausing to lock his eyes onto mine, "is simply the distillation of rumor. When necessary, it is the burden, even the duty, of the apocryphist to refine those distillations."

I wondered at this but couldn't make sense of it. He recognized my perplexity.

"History, young Siam, like truth, is whatever I make it."

—◦◦◦◦◦—

"...and when the flying machine finally descended, the young stalker emerged from its belly and discovered a queer sort of world. The sky was as red as blood, and the land barren and flat as far as he could see."

I was gratified beyond description to see their little faces fixed upon me in wonder. The more narrative I spun, the more their whiskers twitched and their little tailstubs wiggled. The group of youngsters gathered around me had grown from a mere trio to an even dozen as I spoke.

I'd begun with a simple idea, one intriguing flourish of imagination, but their wide-eyed interest had prompted me to expand the details until I was leading them on an adventure to a province they would find on no map.

"There were massive holes burrowed into the ground—like dens, only dropping straight down. Leaning to gaze into one of these holes, he caught an alien scent on the wind. It was a scent with such power it knocked him back. Before he could recover his balance, a monstrous creature emerged from the hole."

They were on their haunches now, clinging to every word. One little stalker who couldn't have seen more than five winters looked too frightened to move.

"The beast had eight legs and fangs the size of my arm. It raised up on its four back legs and reached out with its others to ensnare the—"

"Siam! Come here!"

It was my master, standing at the entrance to his den with that irate expression he was so fond of using with me. It was only then I realized I was late for my lessons. I had become so enthralled with my storytelling I'd lost track of time.

"I'm sorry, young stalkers, I must go." Their disappointed cries touched me in a way I found pleasing. "Don't worry, we'll finish the tale tomorrow."

They ran off, scurrying with ease across the logwalk that spanned the nearby ravine.

"Flying machines and eight-legged creatures? What are you doing, Siam?"

Grrrmon's vision may have been failing him, but his ears were as sharp as ever.

"I was only entertaining the small ones, Master."

"Entertaining? I have not taught you the arts so you can use them to amuse the masses. Your words are not to be given away casually like pieces of pouncemelon. They are a commodity of high value. Do not cheapen them on my own doorstep."

"I'm sorry, Master. I didn't think I was doing any harm."

"You've been under my tutelage for countless nights, yet sometimes it seems you have learned nothing."

"Actually, I have counted the nights. I have been here for—"

"Do not attempt to cross wits with me, fledgling! I will cut your words into pieces and gag you with them."

"Yes, Master," I responded meekly to appease him. I had never seen him so angry, and that was saying something.

"Inside now," he said and limped away without waiting for a response. His old bones had started to bother him, and he didn't move as quickly as he had when my apprenticeship began. I paused so as not to overtake him and followed him inside.

Instead of going to our work area, he stopped in the outer cavern next to the simp's perch and stroked the little brute.

"I'm afraid I have some news which may distress you," he said to me, although his attention was still focused on the simp. "You've undoubtedly heard of our sovereign's great victory in reclaiming the river-land province from the Fang-clan."

I'd heard the battle talk but had not paid much heed.

"There were many casualties in the combat, and I regret to tell you your father, the warrior Miam, was among them."

"My father is dead?"

"Yes, Siam. Regrettably, the clan has lost another hero. But it has been reported to me his death was glorious. By the tongue of his own commander, I was told the tale of how brave Miam withstood an onslaught of enemy warriors, protecting a strategic passage until reinforcements could arrive. He cut and slashed, growling his war cry until the very end, when he was finally overcome by sheer numbers, buried beneath a sea of Fangclan vermin."

My master proceeded to extol the Miam's virtues, describing the battle in detail, but I no longer focused on his words. All I could think of was that my father was dead. My father, who had cast me out of his home—my home. My father who thought of me as a coward, not worthy of his family. Yet, still—my father.

"...and when his fellow warriors had beaten back the crimson tide of the enemy, they found Miam still fighting for life. With his last breath, he told them to pass the tale of his death to his son, the apocryphist's apprentice."

It was a good tale, but even before its improbable ending I knew my master had embellished it in the telling—or more likely, created it whole from his bountiful imagination. My father would never have relented to recognize his banished son, even standing at death's den.

"Thank you for the telling, Master," I said with all sincerity. For I knew, in time, his prevarications became truths.

"Do not dwell on these sad tidings, young stalker," he said, mistaking my reflection for grief. "Look towards tomorrow. For an apocryphist, foresight is a much better thing than hindsight."

My master was right, of course. He was always right. But today, I would choose to reflect on the past. There was plenty of time tomorrow to look forward.

—⚬⚬⚬—

Over the next two winters, the remnants of my white fur matured into the dirt-red that was my family's color. Despite all my tedious and often mind-numbing work, I felt little closer to becoming a full-fledged apocryphist. At least, that was my perception of my master's opinion. It seemed no matter what I did, it wasn't enough. It wasn't good enough, correct enough, thoughtful enough, traditional enough.

In spite of his obvious scorn for my abilities, I truly believed I'd begun to excel. I decided I would not let his denigration of my talents sway my determination. I'd also come to believe the art of apocryphy could be used for something more valuable and enduring than misrepresentation and mummery. What that would be...well, I had an idea, but I was keeping it to myself.

My master hobbled outside the cavern one day, bumping into a clawbark tree that had been there long before I ever arrived. He'd grown feeble, and his eyes were as weak as a newborn's. However, his temper was as strong as ever.

"What's this? What's this?" he repeated loudly, waving pieces of parchment in the air. "What's this about a giant river on the moon of Leus where creatures travel on trees?"

Apparently his failing eyesight had not prevented him from discovering the story I was writing. However, I'd already decided I was not going to let him intimidate me anymore.

"These profane tales show how little you have learned in all your time here."

"I believe I've learned quite a bit, Master."

"Oh? Do you think you are an apocryphist now? Do you think you have the power to move sovereigns and change worlds? What do you think you know? Knowledge may arrive naked and alluring on a white stallion, young stalker, but wisdom lingers in its finery till the saddling of the deathbed. You'll never have that wisdom, Siam, because you were never meant to. I took you in and called you my apprentice because I needed a laborer, and that's all you've ever been...all you'll ever be. This isn't the art of apocryphy," he ranted, waving my story in the air and then tossing it away. "You've learned nothing of the true art."

The true art? What was truth? Was it true he'd only taken me into his home to perform menial tasks? It was certainly true I'd spent more time toiling than learning. Could it be true I had no aptitude for apocryphy? No grasp of what the art really was?

No. I believed old Grrrmon was only speaking out of anger. I knew what I'd learned and how my mind had expanded with time's passing. I was certain my writings were worthy. If my master refused to call them apocryphal then another designation would do.

"You are no longer my apprentice, foolish stalker," he said, his ears turning to focus on me because his eyes couldn't. "You never were."

He swung about in as dignified a posture as his aging limbs would allow and strode away toward the logwalk. I watched him go down the path, the same path I'd seen him travel a thousand times.

But this time old Grrrmon's failing balance and feeble eyesight betrayed him. Once atop the logwalk, he took a single misstep, teetered, clawed at the air for a grip that wasn't there and fell into the rocky chasm.

—⟲⟯✦⟮⟳—

I paused for dramatic effect; their little faces turn towards me in anticipation, their whiskers twitching, their eyes open wide.

"Then the great Grrrmon turned and hurled a magic incantation at the onrushing monster. The words he used were powerful, ancient words, and they struck at the heart of the creature, killing it even as it leapt at the old apocryphist. The beast's huge corpse hurtled through the air like a falling tree, striking

Grrrmon and knocking him into the abyss." I paused again, soaking in their wonder. "Though he was killed in the fall, crushed beneath the monster's body, the great Grrrmon had saved the province."

I don't know if my old master would approve of the way in which I'd memorialized him, but I had done so using all the skills he'd taught me, intentionally or not. It was true I would never be the apocryphist he was. Instead, I would be the one I was meant to be.

This idea for how the art of storytelling began on one particular world came to me one day when I went to the dictionary to look up the word *apocryphal* after hearing George Carlin use it in a stand-up routine. One of the few tales I've written that doesn't take place on Earth and feature humans, this bit of alien folklore has appeared in *Forgotten Worlds*, *Fantasy Today*, *All Possible Worlds*, and was performed as an audio tale by *SFZine*.

# THE NOT-SO-FINAL RESTING PLACE BLUES

He drifted out of Redemption Hall into the sublime sunshine and took a long last look at the heavy double doors closing behind him. He felt like a new man, and thanks to the divine guidance of the Holy Father's 1,012-Step Plan, he was. New as a rosebud about to bloom on a spring day. New as the first tinkling laugh of an infant. New as the glossy coat on a freshly painted '65 Mustang. New as...well, you get the general idea.

Yesterday's Jesse was gone, cleansed of his rancor, his negativity, his derision. No more would he ride the storm of discontent. He couldn't wait to embrace the world—the warmth of its breezes, the music of its soul, the puppy-dog playfulness of its children. He was also very hungry.

However, before he could decide if he finally wanted to try the Sacred Cow Buffet or just stick with the Celestial Cafeteria, his mentor approached. He fought off his demon first impulse to think *What now?* and greeted her with spurious enthusiasm.

"Hello, Priscilla."

"Good day, Jesse, and congratulations on your graduation. I thought you might want to take advantage of your new A-Three status and have a look through the Earthfinder."

He'd always been curious about the Earthfinder but hadn't been permitted to use it.

He was anxious to find out what wonderful and glorious things mankind had been up to over the last few decades.

"Far out," he replied, "let's go look."

She led him down the hall, where he thought he caught a whiff of lemon meringue incense, past the guardian, who didn't so much as glance their way, and right up to the edge of an enormous crystal sphere.

"Do you know what you'd like to see first?" asked Priscilla. "What do you miss most?"

"Well, I sure miss singing the blues. There's not a lot of call for that up here. I guess I'd like to see how the rest of my old group is doing."

"Then look."

Jesse looked into the sphere, and as the smoky haze cleared, he saw his old friends. They were all together, and they were jamming. That surprised him. He hadn't expected them to still be making music after all this time. He figured they would have found something else to do—gone on to bigger and better things in their old age.

They look ridiculous, he thought, with their gray ponytails and potbellies, trying to be hip.

The sphere's audio became more distinct, and he was able to hear them. They were playing one of his old songs!

"Look at them. I come out after three decades of soul-cleansing, and there they are, playing the same tired old tunes, looking like poster children for a geriatric jamboree."

"*Jesss-seee*," admonished Priscilla, "where's your sense of charity, your willingness to be tolerant towards others? Have you forgotten your lessons so soon?"

"Oh, yeah...I mean, no. I was just, uh...joking with you. I think the old farts are, uh...cute."

Priscilla was an A-2, only a cherub's breath away from being promoted to A-1, and Jesse realized he couldn't pull the wings over her eyes that easily.

"Until you've walked as many miles in their snakeskin boots as they have, you have no basis on which to judge them. Even then—"

"Judge not, lest ye be judged," Jesse replied as if by rote.

"That's right," she said, "but I think you need to do more than mouth the words you've learned. You need another kind of lesson."

"But I just finished—"

"Now, Jesse," she said before he could go on, "consider this the first step towards becoming an A-Two."

Boy, he thought, you'd figure they'd let a guy enjoy being an A-3 before they started pushing him out of the nimbular nest toward A-2.

"It's not about enjoyment, Jesse," she said, reminding him for the umpteenth time that she could hear his thoughts as plain as his speech. "It's about a willingness to learn.

So..."

So, wham, bam, thanks a lot, ma'am, Jesse found himself back on terra firma.

He realized right away how good it felt—walking on air with his head in the clouds had always made him a little queasy. He did, however, experience a brief sensation of claustrophobia. Four walls and a ceiling were a bit much after all that time in the infinite expanse.

He became aware Priscilla had outfitted him in his trademark black leather pants, and he was enjoying the smooth sensations when he realized he'd been transported into the recording studio where he'd seen the guys laying down some tracks. They were so busy arguing, they didn't notice him.

"Can't you guys ever agree on anything?" he asked, waiting for their reaction.

"*Jesse?*" they called out simultaneously in amazement.

"Rick, Joe, Rollie, good to see you guys again."

"But...how?" sputtered Rick.

272

"I know this must seem like a weird scene after all this time," said Jesse, "but don't worry, I'm still dead. I mean, I did die, you know, way back when. I'm just visiting."

"Where...?" asked Joe, and Jesse pointed up, anticipating the rest of his question.

"Why...?" began Rollie.

"My mentor thought it would be good for me," said Jesse.

"How long...?" queried Rick, but again the answer came before the question was completed. He was getting the hang of this consciousness-attunement thing.

"I'm not sure, exactly," said Jesse. "Probably not long."

"Well, you look great, man" said Rick.

"I should—I haven't aged a day in thirty years. Sorry I can't say the same about you guys. You know, when I saw you all, I thought you looked pretty ridiculous. I mean, you're all pushing sixty and still trying to be rock stars."

"Hey, some of us still have to make a living," responded Joe.

"Yeah," added Rollie, "not all of us got to be a dead icon."

"An icon?"

"Don't you know?" asked Rick. "Man, you've got more fans now than you did when you were alive. They think you're some kind of rock 'n' roll god."

Suddenly, a great rumble swelled from beneath the floor. The entire room shimmied and shook as they each grabbed hold of something to steady themselves.

"Another LA quake," said Joe when the rumbling ceased.

"No," replied Jesse, motioning upward with his head and eyes. "He just has a low threshold for blasphemy. But look, what I wanted to tell you is, what you're doing is cool with me. I mean, who am I to judge?"

"I'm glad you're in tune with that," said Joe. "I was afraid you came back to kick up a fuss about the pantyhose commercials."

"What pantyhose commercials?"

"We sold a few of our old tunes," said Joe, "and they're using them to sell pantyhose. It's not a big deal. They just changed a few of your lyrics."

"Changed my lyrics for *pantyhose*?"

Jesse tried to remain calm. They were only words. After all, he reasoned, who was he to criticize? Just to be safe, however, he inwardly recited several soothing mantras.

"The commercials aren't nearly as good as the lunchboxes," said Rollie.

"Lunchboxes?"

"Yeah, we got this great merchandising deal," Rollie continued enthusiastically. "I used my percentage for hair implants. Looks pretty real, huh?"

"I think the little figurines are kind of cute myself," offered Rick.

"Figurines?"

"Yeah, you know, like little dolls, only made to look like us. The Jesse doll is a real big seller. You are *so* like it, man."

"The Jesse doll?"

Jesse increased the pace of his mantras, but they weren't having much effect. He was smoldering inside, and the words that were coming to mind weren't as virtuous as he would have liked. He hoped his mentor was out of range.

"You okay, Jesse?" asked Joe. "I'm not getting very good vibes from you. You look like you've seen a ghost...so to speak."

"I'll be all right as soon as I get rid of this feeling that someone's stomping all over my grave."

"Uhh...speaking of graves, man..." Rick didn't finish but looked to his comrades for help. Neither of them wanted to elaborate.

"What?" demanded Jesse in the most spiritual way he could manage.

"What Rick means," said Joe, "is the lease on your gravesite in that French cemetery is about to expire, and the locals want to move you."

"Lease? Move me?"

"Yeah," chimed in Rollie, "it seems a bunch of your crazed fans have been dousing the place with booze, littering, and generally desecrating your final resting place, as well as the surrounding gravesites. The French authorities say they've had enough, so they're refusing to renew your lease."

"They're going to dig up my grave?"

"Hey," said Joe, raising his drumsticks in mock surrender, "you're the one who wanted to harmonize in the hereafter with all those seventeenth-century poets."

"There's talk of building a shrine for you here, man," said Rick, trying to find a bright side. "I think they've got a spot picked out in Burbank."

"A shrine in Burbank?" Jesse was seething now. "Are you dudes crazy? You're going to let them dig me up and replant me like so much mulch? I've never heard of such an asinine excuse for—"

"*Jesss-seee.*" It was Priscilla, suddenly at his side and looking very disapproving. The instant she appeared his former bandmates froze like wax figures. "Where's your angelic sense of forgiveness? Your compassion for those who lack your celestial insight?"

"In a hole, six feet down, just outside of Paris." Jesse plopped onto a stool like so much dead weight. "I've been kicked out of a lot of places, but I never thought I'd get booted out of my own grave."

"Look at it as part of life, or in your case, afterlife." Priscilla tittered at her own wit.

"However, I'm afraid this outburst means it's back to Redemption Hall for another cleansing. I'll have to revoke your A-Three standing."

"Another thirty years?" whined Jesse.

"Don't worry, you have all eternity. Besides, I have it on good authority your friends will have joined you by then."

"Can I at least say goodbye?" he asked, and before the last word was out of his mouth, she was gone and his old friends were reanimated.

"I've got to go, guys, but could you do me a favor? Would you see if you can talk them into renewing my lease? Promise them my pantyhose royalties or something. I'd hate to be uprooted now that I'm just getting settled in."

"We'll keep trying, man," Rick assured him.

"Hey," cried out Joe, as if a light bulb had exploded over his head. "Why don't you cut a song with us and improv some lyrics before you go? Maybe a little blues number. We'll call it 'Growls from the Grave.'"

"Right!" chimed in Rollie. "We'll make it the centerpiece of a huge concert like Live Aid or Bangladesh, only we'll be raising money to keep Jesse's room in the tomb!"

"It'll be a world event," agreed Rick. "Peace for a day...food for all...let sleeping rock stars lie!"

Jesse looked upward for guidance, and in his mind he saw the ethereal image of Priscilla nodding her head in approval.

"Far out," he said, "let's jam."

When I read that authorities in France were considering digging up and moving the remains of my favorite rock star and poet, I had to do something. So I wrote "The Not-So-Final Resting Place Blues" (although I changed the names to protect the interred). It was originally published in *Leading Edge*, and reprinted on ScienceFictionFantasyHorror.com, the anthology *Tabloid Purposes II*, and in the Australian publication *Ticonderoga* under the title "Let Sleeping Rock Stars Lie." Despite the furor caused by uncouth gravesite visitors, Jim Morrison's bones remain in their original plot in the Père Lachaise cemetery just outside of Paris—at least so far as we know.

# DANCE OF THE FURROWED GODDESS

Miranda carefully feathered the pencil across her right brow, fashioning a black arch to match the one on the left. She turned her head from side to side, checking herself in the mirror. It was a decrepit old thing, chipped and stained and spotted, with a crack running helter-skelter beneath a spray of synthetic ostrich feathers. She resented having to use such a cruddy mirror—despised what it represented.

She closed one emerald eye and lightly brushed her eyelid to a violet hue then likewise shadowed the other eye. She studied her reflection, grabbing a tissue to clean what she thought were water spots on the mirror. The spots wouldn't rub out.

She rested her fingers against the cool glass. In spite of the mirror's condition, there was no denying the face that looked back at her from it. The crow's-feet were certainly hers, hard-earned, as were the worry lines that chronicled her life. Father Time had deftly carved his initials there for all to see.

The wall behind the mirror pulsated with a bass beat. She felt the music vibrate through her toes. Did she need more foundation? She shrugged her shoulders and settled for some blush, catching a whiff of the dead flowers in the vase on her dressing table. For some reason, the odor reminded her she had to smile.

It should have been the easiest thing to do. She always used to smile, even when she didn't have any particular reason. Now, it was something she put on every night, like body glitter and mascara. Smiling's what drew them in. She had to remember to smile.

Miranda shook her raven hair and pursed her lips. She decided to add some gloss. It wasn't as if she didn't love what she was doing—she always had. There were other things she could have done, things she'd wanted to do, but she didn't dwell on regrets. She knew she was still good, even if the multitude of admirers had given way to the occasional inebriated come-on, and the deluge of cash had dwindled to a trickle that never let her ends meet.

She took one last look in the mirror, glancing this way then that. Dreadful old thing. She'd see if she could get Nardo to replace it. She stood and adjusted her outfit, pushing her boobs closer together. *Keep their eyes riveted where you want them, so they don't go wandering to your flaws.*

The air stank of stale beer and off-world smoke, but the music was loud and the customers well-oiled. They laughed and cursed, shoved each other and talked business, and occasionally even ogled the dancer. The lights were dim everywhere but on stage, where a flurry of reds and blues illuminated a buxom young blond beauty who, having littered the stage with her scant garments, wiggled in perfect unison with the techno-pop tune that reverberated throughout the club.

A disconsolate few sat around the stage, cuddled with their drinks, staring up almost wanly at the erotic exhibition just out of reach. Some even tossed money onto the stage. One dangled a credit chip, coaxing the dancer close enough to make a deposit in her cleavage.

The music ended unceremoniously, and the dancer swept her clothes and tips into a pile. She sauntered offstage, escorted by trifling whistles and half-hearted applause.

An amplified voice cut through the unruly din and, with a pronounced lack of enthusiasm, proclaimed, "Honey Moon, everyone. Let's hear it for Honey and her twin moons." More applause, more whistles, and the voice droned on. "And now, gentlemen and perverts alike, scotch your rocks and grab your cocks. Planet Raw now presents for your carnal pleasure, the mesmerizing Miranda."

Spotty applause and drunken whistles greeted Miranda as her music surged through the amplifiers and she undulated across the hardwood stage, timing her movements to the melody as if she were the music. She ignored the laughter emanating from one corner, remembering to smile as she swirled to an up-beat and then collapsed into a position of submission as the tune died and was reborn with a primitive tom-tom staccato.

Leisurely, Miranda raised her head and arms, swaying like a wind-tossed flower. Still on her knees, she removed her sheer golden cape and flung it across the stage. It caught a pocket of smoky air and hovered momentarily before collapsing into a withered heap.

The song's tempo raced ahead, and Miranda twirled and writhed, now possessed by the dance. Spinning round and round, she saw her likeness reflected in the shimmering sheet metal above the bar. It was only a glimpse, but the roving spotlight lingered on her thighs long enough to illuminate the dimples there. Inwardly, she cringed.

The club was populated with the usual dregs—mostly human but a few ETs. Many paid no attention to her—they were busy carousing with their friends or haggling with one of the floor girls over the price of a lap dance or boob rub. Accustomed to the indifference, Miranda continued to smile and dance, focusing on one customer up front she recognized as a regular.

When the moment came, she ripped off her lavender lace top and shook her breasts at him. He tossed a sawbuck in her direction as she twisted and fell into a perfect split.

Shifting to a prone position, face down, she executed a series of movements guaranteed to rouse the dead. Then, still lying on the stage floor, she squirmed out of her G-string like a snake shedding its skin. It was a silky move, one she'd choreographed herself. Fifteen years ago, when she'd first perfected it, it had brought the house down. They'd showered her with greenbacks. Now...

Now, she was just another naked pair of tits. An ass to shimmy and shake to distract the marks so the liquor kept flowing. So, why did she keep coming back? She wasn't some dumb cumrag. She could quit and do something else.

But what? What else was she going to do? Learn a new trade at her age? Go back to school?

"We want Cherry!" called out a voice from the dark.

"Bring on Cherry!" cried another.

"Yeah! We want Cherry Red!"

"Get this old hag off the stage."

Miranda spied the group of rowdies that had decided to focus its petulance on her. She ignored them and continued dancing.

"We want Cherry!" they cried out in unison. "We want Cherry!"

The catcalls soon became a chant Miranda found difficult to block out. She needed this like she needed—

"We want Cherry. We want Cherry."

She wanted so badly to get offstage she rushed her climax. It wasn't like her to let anything or anyone throw her off like that.

"Hey, honey," bellowed someone over the chants, "you can get more for that body at the biobank than up there."

A bouncer eventually stalked over and silenced the rowdies with a few quick words. Miranda didn't notice. She focused on the music, waiting for the finale she knew was mercifully near. When it came, she grabbed her costume and what little cash had been thrown onstage and made a hasty exit.

—⊙≈⟨≫⊙—

Backstage, after she'd scrubbed off her makeup and dressed, she cornered the club manager in his office. Nardo was a pretty fair guy. She'd worked for worse—much worse. But she needed more work. Twice a week was not going to put milk in Titty Kitty's saucer.

"Miranda, honey, you looked good tonight. I'm glad you stopped by."

Nardo shifted his considerable bulk uneasily in his chair, but Miranda didn't notice. She was used to shrugging off the catcalls, but tonight they'd left her with a full head of steam.

"Nardo, I need more work. Two nights, especially these off-nights, aren't paying the bills. How about you let me have Friday?"

"I can't give you Friday."

"What about a couple of more weeknights?"

He shook his head.

"Come on, Nardo, I'll take anything. I need more stage time."

Nardo cleared his throat and dropped his huge flabby hands onto his desktop.

"Miranda, honey, I can't give you any 'cause we've decided to let you go."

Poised to continue her pitch, Miranda was struck dumb. A dozen things raced through her mind, none very coherent.

"We've decided to go with some other girls."

"You mean *younger* girls, don't you, Nardo?"

He shifted uneasily again, and his chair squealed from the strain.

279

"Look, Miranda," he said, gesturing with his hands, "you know how this business works. Hell, you've been in the business longer than—"

"Don't say it," responded Miranda, cutting him off with a tone that threatened bodily harm.

Nardo slapped his hands together as if praying and sighed.

"It sucks sawdust, I know, but that's the way it is. What are you gonna do?" he said, throwing his hands open again. "Look, I happen to know they're looking for some dancers down at The Black Hole. Why don't you try there?"

"The Black Hole? Well, gee, thanks, Nardo. Why didn't you say so in the first place? Shit—a great place like that—who wouldn't want to work there?"

"Okay, okay, knock off the sarcasm," he replied angrily. "What do you want from me?"

Miranda looked at him and slowly shook her head. "Nothing, Nardo. Nothing at all."

—⚜—

She slapped her entry-card onto the sensor and waited for the identiscan to recognize her face. Her own image, tiny and distorted, stared back at her from the security lens. The door opened, the autolight switched on, and Miranda stepped inside. Immediately, she punched up her mail, scrolling through it quickly. Her mind was elsewhere—somewhere back on stage.

Nobody cared about the dancing anymore. It was all about bio-enhancements and cosmetic surgery. Hell, she could be younger if she wanted, and if she could afford it. But she couldn't—wouldn't if she could.

A loud *merouw* greeted her.

"Hi, there, Titty Kitty. Come to Mama."

A skinny little cat, white as milk, materialized on her lap the moment she sat. Its purr was instantaneous and loud.

"Did you have a good day, Tits? I'm sure it was better than mine."

Maybe I *don't* belong on stage anymore, she thought, absentmindedly scratching the cat's pink belly. Maybe it was time to hang up her G-strings and her flyaway bras. But if she didn't belong onstage, where *did* she belong?

Maybe she didn't. Maybe it *was* time to call it quits.

She'd seen and done plenty in her life. No family, no one who'd miss her, no reason to hang around. Nick would take care of Titty Kitty if she asked. It would be easy. A quick trip to the Euthacenter—

The door buzzer squawked with annoying familiarity. Before Miranda could get the cat off her lap, the door opened and Nick steered himself in. He wore an ultra-bright orange shirt and his usual burgundy beret.

"I hope you're decent because I'm coming in."

"Decent—that's very funny, Nick, but I'm not in the mood for any stripper jokes."

Nick positioned his wheelchair in front of her, using his joystick to propel himself, first up and then back. Garish black-and-red zebra-striped material covered the chair's seat, and a sticker slapped haphazardly across its back read "I brake for parties."

"I'm on my way to light up the lives of the artistically deprived masses. Verily, it is my mission in life to bring joy to the joyless heathens...and it's not like I have anything else to do. So, put on your best bonnet and let's boogie."

"Not tonight, Nick. I don't feel like it."

"Surely, you would not deprive the public of your ravishing presence? Come, let us roar off into the night, trumpeting our existence in brazen fashion."

"I said I don't feel like it!" Miranda responded with uncharacteristic irritation.

Her vehemence caught Nick by surprise.

"Okay, you don't have to tell me thrice," he said, engaging his wheelchair motor and heading for the door.

Miranda threw her hands up over her face and shook her head. Nick wasn't just a friend, he was someone she respected. Jesus, the guy had kept his head up and his mind right even after a hijacked transport had slammed into his shuttlecar, costing him not only an arm and both legs but his wife and daughter as well. Now here she was, raining on his parade when he was trying to march straight ahead. Hell, she was spitting on it.

"Wait! Wait, Nick. I'm sorry."

Nick maneuvered into the doorway and stopped.

"I got canned at Planet Raw tonight. That's why I'm such a witch."

Nick threw his chair into reverse and turned to face her.

"I'm sorry to hear that, Mira."

"Well, don't be. You showed up just in time. Give me three shakes of a tail feather to get changed, and we'll set this burg ablaze."

—⦿⧫⦿—

"You don't have to strip, Mira," said Nick, doing his best to bolster her spirits. "There are other things you could do if you wanted."

She wasn't so sure. Dancing was the only way she'd ever earned a living. What was she going to do—scrub floors? Sell vids? She was a dancer. It was the one thing she was good at.

They were sitting in a dim little club, an outgrowth of a gaudy Greek restaurant—itself a cultureless tumor on the city's backside. There were maybe a dozen customers, some in conversation, others nursing drinks, alone. One brave soul was up on the tiny block stage, singing away with the help of a prompter and an antique audio system. Her rendition would have solicited a cascade of howls had the establishment permitted canines.

"You know, I was going to be a teacher," said Miranda. "Can you imagine that? Me, a schoolteacher?"

"It's not so difficult to imagine," replied Nick. "What happened?"

Miranda laughed. "I discovered taking off my clothes was a whole lot easier than studying, not to mention more lucrative. But it wasn't just the money. I liked the attention, the power over men it gave me." She made a derisive noise under her breath that was more whimper than laugh. "At least, that's how it felt back then."

"There must have been men who were interested. Why didn't you ever get married?"

"There were plenty of men. They came, and they went. There were a couple that almost...but none worth crying over."

"You know, this glorious reality could have more in store for you than being an exotic dancer."

"I've told you before, Nick, the others can call themselves 'exotic dancers' if they want. I'm a stripper, just an old-fashioned stripper—with the emphasis on *old*."

"Bah and blattersnot! The redwoods of Yosemite are old. The cave paintings of Mars are old. You're a puerile fledgling who's about to be reborn into a whole new life. 'I'm too old' is a mantra for quitters." He grabbed her right hand with his. "You don't have to strip naked in front of strangers to be someone."

"You don't understand, Nick. When I'm on stage...it's the one time I *don't* feel naked."

Nick looked away, pretending to scan the club. "What a sorry-looking dump this place is. But it'll have to do until I can get my own place. I'm going to see if I can go next."

Miranda watched him steer over to the stage. He talked all the time about how he was going to get his own nightclub. They both knew it was a fantasy, an eccentric dream to help pass the days. But dreams were expensive, and so was buying your own club.

Watching Nick maneuver through the maze of tables, she recalled the night she first saw him. He'd come in while she was onstage. When the lights spilled into the crowd, she'd seen the guy in the wheelchair, the guy with the missing limbs and the horrible scars on his face. He got drunk, got rowdy then, later, started crying like a baby. She'd helped him get home because she felt sorry for him.

Now, she admired him. She admired his independence, the way he always held his head high, the way he kept his sense of humor. He could always find something to make her laugh. Nick was beautiful.

"I'm ready."

The sound of Nick's voice coming from the house speakers prompted her to look up. He was onstage, microphone in hand. The music started, and so did Nick, wailing some old ditty that asked if the audience would walk out on him if he sang out of tune.

Unfortunately, Nick's singing voice wasn't just out of tune, it was awful. He didn't let that stop him. Nick didn't let anything stop him.

—⚙❦☙—

The Black Hole was a wretched pit, a dilapidated, scum-infested hovel that reeked of sweat and semen. The stories told about it were enough to scare away most girls—those who could get work anywhere else. It was a den of outlaws, addicts, and alien riffraff. It wasn't strictly a place for ETs, but few locals patronized the joint. Why would they when there were better places to spend their money?

But there she was, onstage, bumping and grinding, stripped of her pride as well as her clothes.

She'd had to beg just for the opportunity to dance on off-nights. On top of that, she had to wait tables. She couldn't remember ever feeling so humiliated.

Now, though, after a couple of weeks, the humiliation had worn off. Only a bitter taste remained.

"Wiggles fat like Deneath worm," called out a hairy mud-groomed brute sporting a pair of stubby horns. His accent was so thick, Miranda barely understood him. The tone, however, was familiar. He jostled his friend, a red-scaled Nylean and pointed at her. "Much-used loose bags."

They snorted and guffawed, but Miranda ignored them, even when the Nylean stuck his long, prehensile tongue out at her, moving it obscenely up and down.

Nick had tried to dissuade her, but he didn't understand. He didn't know what it meant to her to be back onstage—even that stage, even with all the insults and lurid proposals, often in languages she couldn't even understand.

When she finished dancing, she changed to the skimpy pseudo-spacegirl outfit they'd given her. She was supposed to wait tables the rest of the night. She didn't want to, but as it was, she was having trouble with her credit flow. So, she took a deep breath and traipsed out, determined to coax some big tips.

Before she even reached the bar, a short, thin blue fellow held out a hand to get her attention.

"That was a beautiful dance, Miranda," he said with only a slight accent.

She noticed he was completely hairless, not an eyebrow or an eyelash on him, and his tiny hands had no fingernails. His clothes were obviously expensive, but the motif of his jacket was odd, even for an ET.

"You are a woman of elegant charms."

"Uh, thanks. Would you like to order a drink?"

"Actually, I would like to make you a proposition."

Here it comes, she thought as she caught herself staring at the ET's ears. They looked like a pile of rolled-up tubing.

"First, let me introduce myself. I am the Honorable Sesmon Jer Rhap Queesnat. I am a businessman—what you would call an entrepreneur—from the planet Epheme."

Miranda had never heard of the place, but that wasn't unusual. Since the creation of the transportals, they'd discovered more ETs and alien worlds than you could count. This guy was just another strange one.

He was too small, too slight of build to be a threat, so she looked him over good. His sky-colored skin was baby-smooth, not a wrinkle anywhere. Even his lips, so dark-blue they were almost black, were silky smooth.

"I would like to offer you a job," he said, his daffodil eyes gauging her surprise. "I want you to dance in my cabaret on Epheme."

"Get out of here. Don't fuck with me, buddy. I'm not in the mood."

"I assure you, Ms. Miranda, I would never fuck with you. Ephemerals never mate outside their species. In addition, I have passed the age of procreation."

Miranda looked him over again. He sure didn't look old.

"I think you are a fabulously talented dancer—one that would be fully appreciated by my clientele. You have a beauty that is rare on Epheme."

"Now I know you're screwing with me," said Miranda, turning to walk away. But she didn't. "Why would you want an old hoofer like me when there are hundreds of younger girls you could hire?"

"I do not want a younger girl," he said. "On our world, a woman of your experience and maturity is highly regarded. We are a short-lived race. We rarely survive much more than three decades, Earth time. We have a saying, which roughly translates 'Age is beauty, and beauty age.' A woman such as you would be appreciated beyond my ability to place a value on it.

"But since I must—if you would agree to dance in my establishment, I would pay you ten times your current wage."

"Ten times?" The disbelief was obvious in her voice.

"Please, take some time and consider my offer. I do not make it out of generosity. I make it because I believe I will profit enormously should you choose to dance in my establishment. Here is my comcard. Please think about it and advise me of your decision. I will remain in your city for another two days."

"Sure," said Miranda, taking the card, "I'll think about it."

The rain cascaded in sheets as they hurried inside the karaoke club that night. Miranda didn't know rain had been scheduled, but then, she had more important things on her mind. Two sips into their watered-down drinks she told Nick about the job offer.

He didn't respond.

"Well, what do you think?" she finally asked, breaking the silence. "Should I take it?"

"You mean traverse the galaxy with this ET? Relocate to another world, so you can continue to dance?"

"It's not just the dancing, Nick, it's the chance to be appreciated again."

"I appreciate you right here."

"You know what I mean. I can get out of The Black Hole and go somewhere I'm respected. Somewhere it doesn't matter how old I am. Do you know they have a saying there that age is beauty, and beauty age?"

"I could have told you that," responded Nick, staring at her. "You know, you don't always have to live your life according to someone else's standards."

Miranda ignored the comment, and the look he gave her. It was the same look of disappointment her mother used to give her when she was little—just before she told her how fat and ugly she was.

"And there's the money. I've never made that kind of money before, even when I was twenty. It's a fabulous opportunity."

"Maybe it is, but you're not hearing what I'm saying, Mira."

"What *are* you saying, Nick?" She didn't understand why he wasn't telling her to go for it. That's what she'd expected him to do. He looked so serious, and now he'd shut up again. "Well?"

"You don't have to go," he said finally, putting his hand on hers. His skin felt coarse, almost clammy. He flashed a timid smile. "You could always stay here with me. We could settle down together, raise kittens, and live happily ever after."

Kittens? What was he talking about?

"Do you really think there's a happily ever after for people like us?"

"Sure there is," responded Nick. "All you have to do is open your eyes and look for it."

They'd been good friends for so long, she'd never considered that Nick might have...other feelings for her. He deserved better.

"That's very sweet, Nick, but this could be the chance of a lifetime for me. Shit—it could be the *last* chance of my lifetime."

"You've already decided, haven't you?" he asked, staring at his drink and twirling the straw counterclockwise.

"I guess I have."

Nick slapped the table. "It'll be a fantastic adventure!" he exclaimed, his mood shifting radically. "Stepping through a dazzling cosmic gate into a strange world filled with wondrous new mysteries."

Miranda laughed. "I don't know if it'll be that exciting."

"Exciting? You want exciting? That's my cue." He engaged his wheelchair motor and backed away from their table. "You won't leave without saying good-bye, will you?"

"Of course not."

Nick flashed a grin, spun his chair and accelerated towards the stage.

Miranda wondered if he'd meant what he said. He always joked around, but tonight he seemed different. His attitude had changed as soon as she'd told him about the job offer.

It wasn't as if leaving him would be easy for her. He was the one person she could always count on. She watched him pluck the microphone from its stand and use it to push up his beret. His first few notes were way off, but that was Nick. He started singing something about rain and rhythm, but she wasn't paying attention.

Miranda pulled out the comcard the ET had given her. It read simply "The Honorable Sesmon Jer Rhap Queesnat." She slid the card into her phone and waited. Nick continued to croon away about a girl that went left him and took his heart.

The com connection was made. The alien businessman answered.

"It's Miranda. I just want to know one thing. Can I bring my cat?"

—⊶⧉⊷—

Miranda didn't know how far she was from Earth. She only knew it was farther than she could comprehend.

The trip itself had taken less than a minute. With Sesmon at her side and Titty Kitty in a carrier under her arm, she'd waited for the transportal operators to fold space or do whatever it was they did. When she was directed to proceed, she stepped into a gleaming corridor. Across its surface resonated her own image, contorted like something in a funhouse mirror. There was no sound, not even that of her own footfalls, but there was an ozone taste in the air. In what seemed like no time at all, she stepped out onto the surface of Epheme.

It wasn't all that different from Earth, except it had been cloudy and windy when she left, and when she arrived on Epheme it was sunny and warm. A good omen, she thought.

The buildings were on the small side, with a tendency towards peaked roofs, but she saw nothing so bizarre to be startling. She was almost disappointed the place wasn't more alien. Sesmon told her she'd feel a little lighter on Epheme, because of gravitational differences, but she never noticed it.

Miranda did notice all the looks coming her way as she and Sesmon boarded a monorail. She figured the Ephemerals didn't have many Earth visitors, and that they must have an extremely polite society, because everyone treated her like royalty. At least, until they arrived at Sesmon's "cabaret."

She didn't need a translator to interpret the cold stares the other dancers gave her. Except for some ET she didn't recognize, they were all Ephemerals. Apparently, they didn't care for the attention the new girl was getting.

The jealous stares were forgotten that first night when Miranda was overwhelmed by the audience's enthusiastic response. And what an audience it was. Sesmon's place was a true theater, not at all like the dives she'd danced in. The seating faced the stage in a semicircle, rising tier after tier. She had no idea how many people the place held, but from the sound of the applause it was at least several hundred.

The Ephemerals applauded by slapping handheld fans against their open palms. It was a distinctive sound, diluted by the polite but ardent cries of approval that gushed from the sea of soft azure faces. Whether those faces were male or female, she couldn't tell. She didn't care. She did wonder what they thought of her—why they seemed so fascinated. She didn't understand the language, but the tone was clear. It was the first time in years she'd felt so alive onstage. It was like being reborn.

Her finale was greeted by scores of tiny fans tossed onstage—the ultimate sign of Ephemeral admiration. She exited, breathless, holding her outfit against her naked body. Sesmon was there to greet her.

"They adore you," he said, "as I told you they would."

"Well, it's nice to be adored again," she replied. "It's been a long time."

---

The adoration didn't fade. Indeed, it swelled on a crest of acclaim Miranda could not fathom. She danced only three times a week, but each performance packed the house with an audience enthralled by her simplest steps. She was the star of every party, the headliner of every show. She found the homage exhilarating.

Everything was first-class. She had a luxurious home, the finest foods, even an exquisitely designed metamirror in her dressing room that shifted to a scenic Ephemeral landscape when she wasn't using it. She had them insert a holograph of Nick she'd brought with her into the metamirror's program then cried when she first saw his lifesize image there on the wall. She wished he was with her, to share all that was happening.

Between the parties and the performances she was alone. The Ephemerals were an introspective people, for the most part. They kept to themselves, never venturing to disturb the celebrated Miranda with more than a quick greeting or polite bit of praise. She, in turn, was wary of violating local customs, of appearing too gregarious. It wasn't long before she found herself isolated on a pedestal of prestige.

She thought learning the language of the Ephemerals might help, so Sesmon provided her with a tutor. She had demonstrated a knack for languages in school but found the phonetic clicks and tweets of the Ephemeral tongue difficult to master. During one such lesson, she asked her tutor what it was her audiences kept shouting.

"Their verbalization takes several forms, Madam Miranda." She had told her tutor the "madam" was unnecessary, but his own etiquette seemed to require it. "The most common accolades translate into your language as 'Beautiful ancient one' and 'Furrowed goddess.'"

"Furrowed goddess?"

"Yes. They refer to the lines that adorn the skin of your face and neck—the ripples of your flesh. We of Epheme pass from this plane of existence long before time can transform our appearance in such a way. It is rare for an Ephemeral to live long enough to show any signs of aging. Your body's maturation presents a glorious vision we relish and respect. Age is beauty, and beauty age."

"Yes, so I've heard," said Miranda, staring out the window at the Ephemeral sunset. Despite the warmth of colors spreading across the sky, she felt a chill. "They love my wrinkles, do they?"

"That seems to disturb you, Madam Miranda. I assure you that your performances are being exalted with the highest of praise."

"I'm sure they are," said Miranda with indifference.

She watched the billowing clouds. Something about their shape reminded her of Nick. She pictured him, full of life, leaning back in his wheelchair and laughing. Then again, maybe she was seeing what she wanted to see. She turned to her tutor with feigned exuberance and said, "Well, shit, if they love my wrinkles, they must be crazy about my cellulite."

—◦⧫◦—

Another sold-out performance, another triumph. Miranda swayed and gyrated and teased each night until the audience was poised on the precipice of a collective swoon. She couldn't have been a bigger sensation.

But the ovations didn't energize her the way they first had. Each one seemed less substantial than the last. She had gorged on success, and now it had become tasteless.

She had become known throughout Epheme's artistic community as "the venerable Miranda." She continued to be a prime attraction. Center ring in the circus, she mused, a dancing bear, a celebrated freak in an ET freak show.

Miranda gazed into her intricately designed metamirror with its edging of floral-inspired engravings and saw the same imperfect reflection she had seen in lesser looking-glasses.

"Mirror, mirror, on the wall—"

"Miranda," said Sesmon, poking his head into her dressing room. "I want to speak with you about a special performance I am planning." Seeing the look on her face, he asked with concern, "What is wrong, Miranda?"

"I'm not sure, exactly. I've never had better audiences than I have here, but it doesn't feel right. I go out on that stage, and I just don't feel it."

"Feel what?"

"*It.* On Earth, I could excite the men I danced for. Shit, I haven't had a single indecent proposal since I've been here. A girl needs that once in a while to make her feel wanted."

"You are wanted. The people love you. They worship you."

"Yes, but they don't *want* me. Not the way human men want me. Not the way I need to be wanted."

"You speak of a biological desire we do not share. But that does not mean we cannot see your beauty, Miranda. Can you not tell that everyone who watches you dance believes you are beautiful?"

"But you, your people, your idea of beauty is..." Frustration overcame her. She turned from Sesmon to compose herself. "I'm tired of being adored for my sagging tits and wrinkled butt. I don't want to be worshipped *because* of my flaws but in *spite* of them."

"I am sorry, Miranda," said the alien entrepreneur sincerely. "That is a desire I am unable to fulfill."

"I know. It must sound silly to you. It's just that I've been dependent on the way I look for so long..."

"Perhaps the time has come for you to depend on what is inside instead of what is outside."

She turned back to look at the alien. "I'm not sure what's there."

"You will never be sure until you look and see."

Miranda faced her metamirror, studied her reflection a moment then pressed the shift panel. Her image vanished, replaced by the holograph of Nick.

"Okay, that's better. Slooowly turn now—yes. Perfect. Remember that now. It's a beat, then the turn, slow as you can go." Miranda demonstrated the move as she described it. "If you do it right, you'll drop their tongues to the floor.

"Okay, everyone, that's a wrap for now. See you tonight."

A half-dozen girls scattered, and Miranda sauntered back to the bar to begin the inventory she'd put off. She loved working with her girls on their routines—the business end, she could take or leave. Usually she left it up to Nick. He kept the books and ran the karaoke nights, while she supervised the strippers. Business was good, and so were she and Nick.

She'd been lucky. She'd earned enough on Epheme for them to buy their own place. But she didn't want her girls to have to depend on luck. She was always mothering them, reminding them to save their money—reminding them they wouldn't be young forever.

She, however, felt younger than she had in years. On special occasions, she'd even get up on stage and dance. Their clientele seemed to appreciate it when she did. But mostly, she only danced at home now, for Nick.

Titty Kitty was pregnant with her second litter, Nick had become an entrepreneurial machine, energized with the purpose of making their nightclub a success, and Miranda—well, she couldn't remember ever being happier.

Fascinated by a documentary on older strippers, I latched onto the adage that beauty is in the eye of the beholder—especially if that eye sees through an alien lens—and wrote "Dance of the Furrowed Goddess." It was published as a mini e-book by Damnation Books.

# IN CASE OF DRAGON...

The foot soldiers gathered round ye olde notice board and stared at the announcement nailed in place by the sheriff's lackey. Of course, most of them couldn't read, so they waited for old Garon to limp forward and read it to them.

"What to do in the event of a dragon attack," he began, reading the bold words at the top of the document.

This immediately set the men to mumbling. As he continued to read, the grumbling was spiced with assorted curses and invocations.

When he was finished, opinions were neither tardy nor timid. The commentary ranged from indignant sarcasm to outright acrimony. Popular opinion was summed by one bold fellow.

"This plan be a crock of shit. It stinks to high heaven. The king's gone round the bend."

The pronouncement was greeted by a vociferous bellow of assent. The disgruntled assertions continued until Sir Sycophant, the brown-nose knight, rode up on his horse. The congregation quickly dispersed, leaving old Garon standing alone.

"Tell me, Master Garon," queried the knight, "what do the men think of the plan?"

Garon, doing what he could to gentrify the vox populi, replied, "Well, Sir Sycophant, I'm afraid the men believe the plan to be a trog of dung so foul-smelling it will offend the angels above. They hold that the king may be touched."

This troubled Sir Sycophant, so he went directly to the sheriff and told him, "The men believe the emergency dragon plan to be a full chamberpot of such powerful odor, heaven itself will take notice. They contend the king must be ill."

Such insubordination rankled the sheriff, but when the time came for his daily report to the Earl of Officialdom he stated simply, "The troops have been informed of the dragon plan, and they collectively agree it is a vessel of royal fertilizer with a heavenly scent."

The earl thought the metaphor a bit odd, but was too busy to conduct an impromptu session in semantics with the sheriff, who had a penchant for malapropisms.

Later, when he ran into Duke Doolittle in the castle foyer, the duke asked, "Has the garrison been informed of the contingencies in case of dragon attack?"

"Yes, Your Lordship," responded the earl. "Everyone agrees the plan is heaven-sent, and will enrich our defenses. There is growing support for the king."

"Good, good."

That evening, Duke Doolittle informed King Highness that a new plan concerning possible dragon attacks had been instituted. He laid the plan before the king, who scanned the document indifferently.

"Sire, the feeling among your men and officers is without dissent. They agree the plan is a potent one that will promote heightened security for the castle and your entire domain. There is strong sentiment that the plan is an inspiration born of your majesty's wisdom and sanctioned by God."

The king read with renewed interest and determined that the plan was good. Henceforth, the plan became policy throughout the land.

Bureaucracy is always funny—until it happens to you. While the concept of bullshit is universal, I stole this idea from an email joke that was being passed around. I put it away in a drawer and said "Someday I'll figure out how to turn this into a story." "In Case of Dragon..." was published by *OG's Speculative Fiction, Copper Wire*, and took 2nd place in the Whispering Dragons flash fiction contest.

# ACKNOWLEDGMENTS

The author would like to express his appreciation to those whose time and insights contributed to these tales. Thanks to Linda Bona and Carolyn Crow, long-time readers, editors, and friends for their feedback. I'm also grateful to professors Tom Huxford and Robert Metzger of San Diego State University for their scientific insight, to Darlene Santori for her inadvertent inspiration and to my editor/publisher Elizabeth Burton for her discerning belief in my work.

# ABOUT THE AUTHOR

Journalist, satirist, novelist...BRUCE GOLDEN's career as a professional writer spans three decades and more genres than you can shake a pen at. Born, raised, and lived most of his life in San Diego, Bruce has worked for magazines and small newspapers as an editor, art director, columnist, and freelance writer. In all, Bruce published more than 200 articles and columns before deciding, at the turn of the century, to walk away from journalism and concentrate on his first love—writing speculative fiction.

Since devoting himself to fiction, he's seen his short stories published more than 90 times in magazines or anthologies, translated into a couple of different languages, and read across eight countries. Along with numerous Honorable Mention awards for his short fiction from the Speculative Literature Foundation and L. Ron Hubbard's Writers of the Future, he won Speculative Fiction Readers's 2003 Firebrand Fiction prize, was one of the authors selected for the Top International Horror 2003 contest, and won the 2006 JJM prize for fiction. He's also written three novels—*Mortals All, Better Than Chocolate*, and *Evergreen*.

Learn more at http://goldentales.tripod.com/

# ABOUT THE ARTISTS

BRAD W. FOSTER is an illustrator, cartoonist, writer, publisher, and whatever other labels he can use to get him through the door! He's won the Fan Artist Hugo a few times, picked up a Chesley Award and turned a bit of self-publishing started more than twenty-five years ago into the Jabberwocky Graphix publishing empire. (Total number of employees: 2.)

He spends huge sections of the year with his lovely wife Cindy showing and selling his artwork at festivals and conventions around the country. Check out his website at www.jabberwockygraphix.com for the latest news!

CHRIS CARTWRIGHT is a computer artist who uses 3D programs and paint programs to create her works. Although she creates covers for any type of story, her favorites are fantasy, sci-fi and horror. She originally became interested in web design, which she went to school for, but after taking some art classes, found a new passion. Besides Zumaya, Chris has also created covers for *Apex Digest*, Outskirts Press, *Penwomanship, Whispers of Wickedness, Midnight Street, Insidious Reflections* and many other publishers and authors.

Her website is at www.digitelldesign.com